Seasons of Insanity

Julie Haines
Oct 2017

Seasons of Insanity

*Two Sisters' Struggle with Their
Eldest Sibling's Mental Illness*

Elaine Taylor
and
Julie Hanes

Library of Congress Control Number: 2017908508
ISBN: Hardcover   978-1-5434-2674-8
               Softcover   978-1-5434-2673-1
               eBook   978-1-5434-2672-4

Cover art by Lance Fletcher

Print information available on the last page.

Rev. date: 08/29/2017

To order additional copies of this book, contact:
Xlibris
1-888-795-4274
www.Xlibris.com
Orders@Xlibris.com
759602

Pacific Book Review Star

Awarded to Books of Excellent Merit

Seasons of Insanity is a harrowing true story of a family affected by mental illness. Elaine Taylor and Julie Hanes have written a book telling about how they tried to cope with their sister, Jane, and her bipolar schizophrenia. This book starts with Taylor and Hanes dealing with Jane's increasingly erratic behavior. As Jane gets older, she becomes more verbally abusive to her sisters and interferes with the care of their elderly mother. Taylor and Hanes become more troubled by Jane's behavior and have to decide whether to cut their ties to their troubled sister or to help her get the professional help she needs.

Seasons of Insanity is an insightful and very well-written book. Hanes and Taylor write in great detail about how Jane's manic episodes embarrassed them and drove the family apart. Readers will empathize with the sisters' attempts to curb Jane's destructive behavior. Jane is shown as a disturbed woman, but is also easy to sympathize with as well. The book shows that mental health is an ongoing issue that is complex and requires patience. Readers will see that Jane's antisocial behavior is beyond her control.

This memoir also delves into the problem of caregiving as the sister's battle over how to care for their ailing mother.

Seasons of Insanity not only deals with Jane's issues, but also deals with the dysfunctional relationship the siblings have with her. *Seasons of Insanity* would be best for readers who are dealing with family members who are living with mental illness. Fans of books like A Beautiful Mind or The Quiet Room will appreciate this account of people living with schizophrenia and the loved ones that are affected by their mental illness. Additionally, this would resonate with readers who liked Jeannette Walls' The Glass Castle about her eccentric and emotionally unstable family.

This book could be given to readers in support groups with people with mental illness and their family members. Taylor and Hanes have written a memoir that will resonate with readers. *Seasons of Insanity* sheds light on an issue that is hidden too often, and is an educational book about family ties.

"Julie sent Jane a care package...I sent lipstick...
it will have been a year since she got arrested..."

The title refers to Jane's episodes of severe mental breakdown as witnessed by her two younger sisters. Fifty pages in, readers will already be thinking, "Oh I have to show this to XYZ," because almost everyone has loved ones affected by a family member's mental illness. The authors feel the guilt, worry, and wear of abuse as they deal with their unpredictable, and sometimes violent, older sibling. The authors describe their difficulties, not just in dealing with Jane, but in coming to terms with their feelings about her. As Taylor tells Hanes, "She has taken us to hell and back and I can't seem to get past it."

The two most common dilemmas the sisters detail in this dual memoir are setting boundaries for self-preservation without guilt and understanding how best to help Jane. As Taylor puts it, "I was not informed of what behavior to expect or how to deal with Jane. I did not know Jane's hallucinations were real to her." Taylor and Hanes bravely tell readers what they have been through and how they felt about each incident with their sibling. Their candid style is invaluable as there is little professional help available for those who want to help without enabling or allowing abuse. "You need to be at peace. Cut off all communication with her...," one doctor advises Taylor. He explains that with Taylor's own heart issues to deal with, and considering everything, "You are not equipped to deal with her."

Taylor and Hanes are direct, detailed, and painstakingly honest—requirements for any interesting autobiography.

What is most obvious from the sisters' memoir is that there are no easy answers for dealing with mentally imbalanced loved ones. Still, this sometimes painful retelling of the family's struggles is a gift to society because it sheds light on a subject not often discussed.

—Toby Berry, Premium US Review of Books

CONTENTS

To everyone whose lives have been affected by a mentally ill family member, friend, or acquaintance.

ACKNOWLEDGMENTS

To all our friends and family, thank you for supporting our doubts that a book of this subject matter would be of interest to others.

A big thank-you goes to our high school friend, who spent many hours from her busy life to edit and offer valuable suggestions.

Most importantly, our husbands deserve multitudes of accolades for their suggestions, cooperation, and encouragement. They were always there with their support along the way.

INTRODUCTION

The mentally ill are among us everywhere whether we acknowledge them or are even aware of their prevalence. According to the National Institute of Mental Health, research shows mental disorders are common throughout the United States and affect tens of millions of people each year. This same reference goes on to state *the main burden of illness is concentrated among a much smaller proportion (about 6 percent) who suffer from a seriously debilitating mental illness.* Our story is about the more serious debilitating form of mental illness, which our eldest sister, Jane, displayed.

The following story describes circumstances involving a highly intelligent, extremely mentally ill sibling. From my earliest memories, Jane presented an upheaval in both my younger sister, Julie, and my childhoods. I received the brunt of Jane's physical abuse, which was hardly noticed by our parents, who were lost in their day-to-day routines.

Being the oldest, Jane assumed a role of dominance. She looked down on Julie and me as mere nuisances of little importance. Normal interactions with her were rare. Jane immersed herself in books when not stirring up trouble.

Jane craved our mother's attention and gravitated toward her instead of having friends. Julie and I were accustomed to Jane siphoning away our mother's time and attention. It was difficult for our mother to accept Jane's mental illness. She desperately looked for explanations and solutions. She had strong convictions, believing a cure lay in a healthy diet of fruits and vegetables.

Julie and I hid from our feelings of embarrassment and shame, which were too difficult to acknowledge. We were good at pretending things were normal; and in a way, they were normal, for us, at least. We were used to Jane's peculiar behavior ever since we could remember.

As adults, Julie and I moved away, which allowed us to continue coping by putting Jane's issues in the background. We were uncomfortable in her presence. Our solace was found in avoidance.

Jane's initial incarceration as a teenager was the beginning of a lifetime of bouncing in and out of mental health facilities. With each episode of being committed, once stabilized, Jane was released. After being home a short time, she stopped taking her medications. It was a matter of time before she got in trouble again. The vicious cycle kept repeating.

During the time, our mother suffered several heart attacks; and after her death, Jane went out of her way to complicate matters. Dealing with Jane was, at times, like dealing with a child having a temper tantrum. We strove to get through the worst times as best we could despite Jane's demented beliefs and opposition to traditional commonsense actions.

We invite you to join us in our journey through life, through growing up, happy times, sad times, and crazy times.

Perhaps you can relate to similar circumstances that have come your way not only through mental health issues but also in your own crisis with a family member who is addicted to drugs or alcohol, which has brought cruel discord to your life.

Elaine Taylor

REFLECTIONS

Elaine's Reflections

It is difficult to openly admit my inner most feelings that express negative thoughts toward my mentally ill sister. As far back as I can remember. I never liked Jane. In fact, by the same token, as far back as I can remember, I hated having her for a sister. It brings tears to my eyes as I recall discovering my baby book and reading my first words were "don't" and "stop it." Why would a baby's first words be verbs commanding to be left alone? It was evident Jane was mean from the beginning. She was continually trying to hit me, kick me, scratch me, or interfere with anything I was doing. There was no peace when she was around.

Even though we grew up in what was, for all practical purposes, a normally functioning family, my younger sister, Julie, and I knew other families were not like ours. Jane's weird personality and actions were as obvious to us as knowing the sky was blue, but our parents were blind to it.

Jane's cruelty and our overly strict parents, who spanked us for the mildest infraction, stole the joy from my younger years. I can still remember when the school photographer for my fifth-grade picture kept telling me to smile. I thought I was smiling, but I was not. I had nothing to smile about.

I found my big happy smile when I was twelve. It was not a smile of vengeance. It was an innocent smile of relief. That was the year Jane broke down mentally and was taken to a hospital and was gone the majority of the school year. There is no way to describe the peacefulness our home enjoyed in her absence. Life was simpler, and I was happy, turning into a silly seventh-grader who had found joy and freedom from Jane's menacing presence.

Upon her return, Jane did not dominate the years that followed. Julie and I had developed confidence and, for the most part, were rarely home. When we were not in school, we were enjoying the company of our friends or going to our jobs, making it easy to avoid and ignore Jane, for which we felt no guilt.

As Julie and I built our own lives, the unpleasant memories of growing up with Jane were locked away and seldom thought of; however, I was not aware that it was evident on my face.

During the years I worked at the college, I was fortunate to become acquainted with Harvey, my supervisor's husband, who was an extraordinarily intelligent psychiatrist. He would sit in a chair next to my desk while reading a magazine as he waited for his wife, Marion. After his death, Marion shared an observation he had made. He told her he could tell from the look in my eyes that I was a tender flower that did not receive water at a crucial time. It was amazing he could tell I lacked healthy nurturing.

After our mother's death, Jane and I spoke frequently over the telephone. She talked incessantly, babbling while I tried to decipher what point she was trying to make, if any. Attempting to reason with Jane was futile and exhausting. Her fabricated stories left me astounded. Insults and derogatory statements routinely flowed freely from her wild thoughts. As her sister-in-law said, "Jane has used up my *lithium crystals*." I related exactly to what she was expressing.

As kids, Julie nor I talked about Jane's mental illness, not even to each other or to any of our friends. The first time I ever brought up the subject was as an adult in my forties. I mentioned Jane to one of my friends, whom I had worked with a number of years. I was amazed to learn her first husband had extreme mental health issues and had been committed to a mental institution, where he remained until his death. No one would have ever guessed what she had been through, nor would anyone have any idea of the secret I had been harboring as well. At that point, I did not feel so stigmatized to talk about Jane and have finally reached a point in my life where I can comfortably talk about my sister's mental illness. Even though it is a guarded topic, as we open up our vulnerability, we realize we are not alone.

Julie's Reflections

I naturally looked up to my eldest sister, expecting her to be my role model. At some point, I noticed Jane acted weird.

Jane had no childhood friends. Our mother blamed Jane's failure to assimilate with her peers on them for ostracizing her from their clique, believing it was not Jane's fault. In place of having friends, Jane latched onto our mother and monopolized her, creating their special camaraderie, literally robbing me and my sister, Elaine, of our mother's attention. Elaine and I were left emotionally abandoned.

Our overbearing parents did not tolerate disobedience, turning Elaine and me into exceptionally well-behaved, submissive children with low self-esteem. I left home at the age of seventeen, two weeks after graduating from high school, to escape my parents and Jane's strange presence. I felt liberated and glad to be "free."

After marrying a military pilot at the age of twenty-five, I moved frequently, usually, long distances from my family home. My attention centered on my husband and personal goals with little thought of Jane and whatever trouble she was getting into. I felt sorry for her. I could not imagine the personal turmoil she was going through. At the same time, I wanted to stay away from her, and I did.

Jane dispensed havoc on all our lives. There were times she appeared relatively normal but peculiar. I learned through much frustration not to make the mistake of assuming I was communicating with a normal person who is capable of logical reasoning.

With further contemplation, I have come to the conclusion that Jane and our mother never came to grips in recognizing there was a major problem and acknowledging they could not cure Jane's mental illness using their methods.

I escaped the full impact of the multitude of Jane's mental health disorders until our mother had a heart attack. Jane consistently complicated the situation. Once we got through this critical time, I declared I would never ever speak to Jane again. Eventually, I learned to accept her on a clinical level, realizing her mental illness drove her aggressive and hurtful behavior.

Overall, the mental health system protocols were unable to provide the care Jane required. The system could only keep her stable for the periods she was in their custody and shortly thereafter. She defied court orders to remain on psychotic medications, which resulted in relapses into her insane behavioral pattern.

Her continual episodes of being committed or arrested by the police were difficult for Elaine and me to accept. Each incident brought us emotions of embarrassment, disgust, and hopelessness that the cycles of insanity would ever end.

Looking back as an adult in my sixties, I acknowledge growing up with Jane was a bizarre experience, which, along with lack of parental encouragement and support, thwarted my development to feel like an adult in my own right until later in my life.

Bringing this point to attention emphasizes the importance of recognizing the need that our mother completely missed regarding paying attention not only to Jane's mental health but also to her own and Elaine's and mine. Mama did not realize she was allowing Jane to dominate her life. Jane sapped every ounce of energy our mother had to offer.

Those dealing with mentally ill individuals need to be aware of their tendency to give too much of themselves as this puts a strain on themselves and takes away from paying attention to others for whom they are responsible through the *seasons of insanity.*

CHAPTER ONE

Days Gone By

Jane was annoyed with me from the moment I was born. Jane was no longer the focal point of our parents' attention.

In the late 1940s, Jane Graham lived with our parents, Milton and Marie, and me in the small mountain community of Wentwood. Jane christened the primitive stone house in which we lived, the Cricket House. There was no plumbing for a bathroom. Our mother cooked on an old coal cook stove. Occasionally, Jane talked about the time she dropped me on my head in the coal bucket when I was a tiny baby. Jane said that explained why I was the way I was.

Jane wanted to be held even when our mother was occupied nursing me. She tried to climb to our mother's lap, not heeding the warning to get down because there was not enough room for two. Jane slipped and went tumbling onto the hard wooden floor, resulting in a broken arm.

When I was five months old, Mama went deer hunting with Daddy. He was an accomplished hunter, and the game helped feed our family. Mama got excessively tired, causing her to lose her milk, resulting in me being fed from one glass baby bottle. I was frequently left unattended in the crib with the bottle that Jane consumed. It was not until Jane broke the bottle that our mother realized the reason I cried so much was because I was hungry.

In a conversation with Mama before she died, she talked about losing her milk and Jane breaking the only bottle.

"So did you go out and buy another bottle?" I asked.

"No," she replied.

"Well, how did you feed me?"

"From a cup," she answered.

From a cup! That was way too young to take a bottle away from a baby.

Daddy built a swing and attached it to a branch on one of the huge cottonwood trees in the large yard of the Cricket House. He took a picture of us swinging together. Jane made reference to that picture while talking to me after our mother's death.

"It hurt me when Daddy put you on me, so I pinched you, and you cried. Do you remember that?"

"I remember when Daddy took that picture. I have a copy of it in my picture album. But I don't remember crying," I answered. Getting hurt by Jane was a routine occurrence.

"Mama got mad at me and told me never to pinch you again, and I didn't, did I?"

Jane started talking about when she was little. "When I played outside, the older neighborhood kids came over and played with me. They had a wagon that they pushed me up and down the street in. I learned how to pinch from them. Mama didn't like me to play with them because she didn't know where I was. After that, Daddy rigged up a rope, and they tied me to the clothesline so that I could run back and forth and stay in the yard. Can you imagine that? I liked playing with older kids. I never did play well with younger kids."

One August day, Daddy took Jane and me to stay with the Cowans when Mama was in the hospital giving birth to Julie. We followed the teenage sons around as they did their chores. We particularly liked watching the cows chew their cud as they were being milked every evening in the barn.

Soon after Julie was born, our family moved into the partially finished two-story log house that Daddy built. Before contracting the mail route, he worked for the U.S. Forest Service. The house was built from large lodge pole pine trees that were cut down to clear campground areas.

Julie's crib was temporarily placed in the bathroom in the space of the future shower. A doorway with a curtain separated our parents' bedroom from the bathroom. Another door on the adjacent wall of the bathroom opened into a short hall that led past the other downstairs bedroom and opened into the "front room" as Mama called it. A door off the kitchen and garage led to the upstairs that would not be finished until ten years later.

I observed mornings beginning with Mama donning her dark-purplish chenille housecoat and nursing Julie as she sat on the edge of the bed. Visitors came by to see Julie. One asked if I was jealous; Mama answered yes. Afterward, I asked her what *jealous* meant. Upon learning the definition, I resented her response. I liked having a baby sister, even though she cried a lot. I liked hugging and kissing her and touching Julie's soft baby skin.

At the beginning of the following summer, Mama took Jane and me to Bible school. I loved to hear the Bible stories and was fascinated by the cutout characters as they were displayed on a felt board, illustrating the story of Joseph and his coat of many colors.

One morning after Bible school was over and the children were leaving, Mama appeared with a pair of panties, asking if I was wet. I was three and knew I was dry, but after a hasty check, Mama decided she needed to change my panties. Right there in the open, Mama took off my panties and put on a fresh pair. That was embarrassing, but later, it worked to my advantage.

One Sunday morning after another usual night of sleeping on the edge of the double bed I shared with Jane, I awakened to observe Jane still sleeping sprawled out. For no particular reason, I decided to sit on top of her. The idea of peeing on Jane entered my mind. After a moment of contemplation, I gave into temptation and let the floodwaters flow, wholeheartedly expecting to get spanked. It took Jane a little while to realize she had been presented a present.

All of a sudden, Jane yelled, "MAMA, ELAINE PEED ON ME!"

In an instant, our mother appeared. "What did you do that for?" she asked.

Immediately, Mama began stripping the bed, while I climbed off my drenched sister. To my glee and satisfaction, I did not get spanked. Mama surely must have thought I had a control problem. But oh, no, it was done on purpose. How sweet it was!

Jane started kindergarten that fall. Of course, I wanted to go too, but I was only three. Jane was actually too young also. Jane would not be five until November, but she was allowed to enroll early. Mama had spent a lot of time preparing Jane. She even knew how to tie her shoes.

Daddy left with Jane every morning, returning at noon. Julie was too young to play with me. I played alone with my dolls or went outside and waited for the train to go by. I waved at the train, and the engineer blew his whistle a couple of times and waved back.

Sometimes I picked wild flowers and brought them in to Mama; and sometimes I caught bugs, especially grasshoppers, and crushed them into the holes in the concrete. The following year, I taught that trick to Julie. There was always a plentiful supply.

Mama rarely insisted we wash our hands. At times, my hands were covered with grasshopper juice for an extended period. Mama gave us a bath every Saturday night in the large kitchen sink. Dial soap was used for both our bodies and hair. Mama made great devil horns, which we could see in our reflections in the big kitchen window above the sink.

When we outgrew the kitchen sink, all three of us were herded into the shower at the same time. We were not particularly well scrubbed as it was not always possible to get much of a turn under the shower before our mother announced it was time to get out. We could not run too much water because of the septic system.

One Sunday morning, when our parents were sleeping in, I noticed it was unusually quiet. I gathered up my clothes and dressed myself. I hunted down my favorite pair of shoes, taking notice of the absence of Julie's usual crying. The shoes were an ugly brown pair of high-topped baby shoes. I crunched my feet in them, even though they were too snug.

"Jane, will you tie my shoes?" I asked.

"No!" Jane said emphatically.

I begged Jane to tie my shoes to no avail.

"Tie your own shoes," Jane retorted.

I removed my old favorite shoes and instead put on a pair of hand-me-down buckle shoes, never to don my favorite brown shoes again.

Jane displayed more disfavor to me than she did to baby Julie. Jane and I were always bickering, and we both got spanked a lot for fighting. I got the worst end of the encounters and was always sporting scabs from Jane's clawing attacks.

Visits from grandparents were rare as Mama's parents lived in Oregon and came every few years. During the visits, they never carried on conversations with us kids. We never really knew them. For Christmas, Grandma sent fabric for Mama to make us dresses; however, most of the fabric was not designed for children.

Daddy's mother died when he was still in his teens. He had a stepmother, who had no affection for her stepchildren or step grandchildren. Daddy's father died in his nineties when Julie was three.

Jane and I attended church regularly and participated in church activities. One summer evening, we prepared to go to a gathering to roast weenies and marshmallows. Jane and I piled in the back seat of the Sunday schoolteacher's car with several other children.

As we traveled down the dirt street to pick up another child, the Sunday schoolteacher asked if we wanted to go faster. Everyone shouted, "YES!" except Jane, who said, "NO, it burns up more gas." I had no idea going fast would burn more gas and wondered how Jane knew that, but what was wrong with having fun?

Jane clashed with her first-grade teacher, Mrs. Barns. Mrs. Barns resembled the Wicked Witch of the East and was very stern and strict. It was not known exactly what the problem was, but I could not say I was disappointed later when Mama made sure neither Julie nor I got in Mrs. Barns' class.

Finally, it was my turn to go to kindergarten, where I got to play with other children. I was surprised that my friend and others could even read *Goldilocks and the Three Bears*. When talking to Mama about my classmates being able to read, Mama replied, "Jane was bored with kindergarten, so I didn't bother to teach you." I was nothing like Jane, and with Mama's assumption that I would be bored also, I felt cheated from learning and receiving rare one-on-one attention.

Jane had become mortal enemies with Carlotta Morin, who rode the same school bus. Carlotta was two years older and a lot bigger and heavier than Jane. They got into knockdown, drag-out fights and truly hated each other. I met Carlotta on the first day of school when starting the first grade. Carlotta approached Jane and me as we waited for the bus after school outside of the old yellow brick school building.

"This is my little sister," Jane volunteered.

Carlotta nodded to me. Before long, Jane and Carlotta were engaged in a quarrel about how much they did not like each other.

"Your sister doesn't even like you, do you?" stated Carlotta.

Being the naive little sister, who had no allegiance to my abusive big sister, I answered honestly, "No."

Carlotta reveled in my answer. "See? Even your sister doesn't like you."

Just then, the bus pulled up. When we got home, Jane told our mother about the incident.

"Why would you say such a thing?" Mama questioned, receiving no answer.

I thought about that many times. If given a second chance, would I have answered differently? Unless I was lying to myself, the answer would be "No."

Jane did very well in school. She did not socialize with her classmates but related more to her teachers and made excellent grades. Daddy bragged to everyone how smart Jane was and gave her a dollar for each A and more for straight A's.

I was another story. I had so much difficulty reading that my teacher told Mama I was retarded. Later when my second-grade class was given eye exams, it was discovered I could not see. I had the dubious honor of being the first one in what seemed like the entire elementary school to have glasses. I would never be a fast reader, and reading certainly was not my favorite activity as it was my straight A sister. Julie was not a straight A student either. That was Jane's claim to fame, which was not challenged by either Julie or me. We preferred not to study all the time.

Mama made her own clothes and most of us kids' clothes. She made each of us three new dresses every year to start school. By Mama's standards from growing up in the Depression, that was plenty. She always said what you put in your stomach was more important than what you put on your back.

Every year before school started and during the Christmas break, Mama cut our hair and gave us a home permanent. Julie and I hated looking like *Little Orphan Annie* and finally got freed from that look when we were older and told Mama we could take care of our own hair.

There was no television reception when we were little. Daddy spent his evenings reading, while Mama cleared the dinner dishes, and us kids played among ourselves in the one bedroom we all shared. One evening when Daddy was reading, my sisters and I were playing in our bedroom. As usual, Jane instigated squabbling. We got a little too noisy for Daddy's liking. He hollered at us and commanded we sit still on the couch and not let out a peep, or we would get paddled with the infamous board.

The board was over a foot in length with one end whittled down for a handle, flaring out and then narrowing down to a rounded point. When Mama said to do something *or else*, it was assumed getting paddled with the board was the *or else*. Beatings with the board were brutal, leaving us with lingering stinging pain on our posteriors and uncontrollably sobbing.

As I sat quietly on the couch, glancing at Daddy and then Julie and then Jane, I contemplated to myself. What will we be like when we are grown ladies? Will we be pretty and have nice things? Will Jane ever stop being so weird?

Jane broke her arm a second time when she was in the fourth grade. I was pushing Jane in a swing when she decided she was going too high and jumped out. According to Jane, both times she broke her arm were my fault, along with her buck teeth, which she blamed on me because she bumped her mouth on the ground when she bailed out of the swing. I ignored Jane's version and never said anything in my defense. It was obvious Jane's accidents were due to her own poor judgment. Jane's accusations were false, and they added to my dislike for my insufferable sister.

When Julie was five, our mother enrolled us in a beginning swimming class. The closest swimming pool that was open to the public was at a summer resort. Our mother was always deathly afraid of the water and wanted us to have the opportunity to learn how to swim. After having the lessons, Daddy took us on swimming jaunts throughout many summers.

Birthdays were celebrated after dinner with homemade cake and ice cream. Daddy got out his harmonica and played "Happy Birthday" to the honoree, while the others sang. After the candles were blown out and the cake and ice cream were served, Daddy entertained by playing old favorites, such as "Red River Valley" and "Home on the Range." It was a fun family celebration. We never had birthday parties with presents and friends. When we asked if we could get presents like our friends, we were told our present was being born.

We never went *trick-or-treating*. There was never an actual reason given. It seemed most of the time when we asked if we could go somewhere or do something, if the answer was not "No," it was, "We'll see," or "Maybe," or "I doubt it." One time I asked Mama why she did not ever say "Yes." She said she did not want to promise something and have to break it if something came up. If there was such a concern something would come up, why couldn't she say, "Yes, as long as nothing comes up." In my opinion, she did not want to be bothered. I made up my mind that when I had children, they would go trick-or-treating and have birthday parties with gifts and friends like other children.

Mama was obsessed with everything being equal, so much so that everything we received for Christmas was identical— identical dolls, identical sweaters, etc. When Jane declared she did not want any more dolls, all of us stopped getting dolls, even though Julie was only seven. Jane had never been a doll person. Her idea of playing with dolls was to twist off their arms, poke out their eyes, and squeeze their soft plastic faces into a permanent distortion.

One Christmas, Mama decided to ask each of us what we wanted. Julie was eight then and did not remember what she asked for. I wanted a little loom to weave pot holders on like my friend Denise had. And Jane wanted a chemistry set. Jane had decided she was going to be a scientist. She even made ammonia with her chemistry set.

Being the oldest, Jane naturally got to try things first. She joined the Girls Scouts, which was a disaster. She did not get along with any of the other girls. Most of them were from prominent families with money as opposed to our family, who was always scraping the bottom of the barrel. Because of Jane's experience with the clique, I was not allowed to join, even though I was invited by my friend Judy.

The highway department condemned our home when I was eight. The house was located in the path of the future service road that was going to be constructed next to the new highway. A hill was to be cut back by explosives to make room for the new highway. When our parents could not find a place they liked in town, it was decided to move the house to a different location. Daddy instated a house mover from Trenton, a town sixty-six miles away, and purchased two acres of land closer to town farther up on the Wentwood River. There was one major obstacle in that the house was too large to pass through the existing bridge and could not be moved until the new bridge was constructed. The house was moved over temporarily out of the path of rocks hurling through the air. It sat on stilts for one year, awaiting the completion of the bridge. Our family continued living there; however, the indoor bathroom facilities were replaced by an outhouse Daddy built.

During the year, while waiting for the bridge to be completed, Daddy prepared the foundation and cleared the new site. When the bridge was finished, the house made the journey across the river to its new location.

Daddy planted grass and a few trees and put in a hedge of honeysuckle along the irrigation ditch that emptied into the river from the front side of the property. Nearby, another irrigation ditch made its way through a swampy area. It was a special place full of new areas to explore. The irrigation ditches were full of wonders—minnows, snakes, frogs, spiders, and leeches. Julie and I waded several times near the honeysuckle, but the other ditch was the best as it had an island, and in the winter, it froze over to make an excellent place to go ice-skating.

Since we did not live in the city limits or close to other children, we spent the summers at home, playing among ourselves. Jane immersed herself in the *Encyclopedia Britannica* or books that were checked out weekly from the public library. On Saturdays, Daddy dropped us off at the theater to see the afternoon matinee.

We were never given an allowance. On Sunday afternoons, Daddy would take us on rides in the jeep. When a pop bottle was sighted alongside the road, he stopped for one of us to run and get it. When we had a tidy collection, we turned in the bottles for their deposits and shared the money.

I was ten when my new friend Denise moved to Wentwood from California. I was thrilled to be invited to Denise's house to play one Saturday afternoon. I was even more thrilled to be asked if I could spend the night. After that, I spent lots of nights with Denise until she moved back to California.

I continued to be Jane's punching bag until during one attack, I bent one of her fingers backward, which brought her to her knees in pain. From then on, she did not try to hit me anymore.

After Jane's experience with Girls Scouts, she was not into joining anything. I wanted to join 4-H when invited by a friend. Finally, Mama let us join when she was convinced there were sewing and cooking categories, and having a cow or an animal was not a requirement. By then, I was in junior high.

Julie and I knew we were dreaming when we asked for horses; however, we did get bicycles. Daddy located old, used bicycles that he painted and fixed up, one for each of us. They were bare-bones bikes with no gears. Julie and I spent many summer days packing lunches and riding our bikes to explore the countryside near our house. Jane was rarely interested in going with us.

Daddy talked a lot about taking a trip to Disneyland. The trip never materialized as from year to year, he was always busier than the previous year.

Jane was in the eighth grade when our family took our first trip to visit relatives. It was our first trip outside our state, and we were thrilled to go. It was December. We donned our matching red car coats with wooden buttons that Mama had purchased through the Army Surplus catalog. We visited relatives in Oklahoma, Arkansas, and Texas.

When Julie was nine, she met a new friend, Susan. Susan's father was part of a huge construction crew. Susan's family lived in a trailer park, which was a quick jaunt away on the bicycle. They became inseparable.

Later, Susan's family moved to a park twenty-four miles away, which was closer to her father's work. Julie and Susan went on adventures with Susan's brother, where they found arrowheads. Occasionally, in the isolated areas, they came across boulders that were three to four feet in diameter. They loosened some and sent them bouncing down the mountain like a rubber ball, watching the exhilarating scene until each boulder came to a resting place on the flats at the foot of the mountain. Julie remained friends with Susan into adulthood, although Susan's family moved away in their sophomore year of high school.

When Julie was ten, each of us bought a young rabbit from our cousin. She was the daughter of Daddy's sister, Betty, whose family had a large ranch. Julie chose a little white bunny with pink eyes, black ears, and a black wiggly nose. He was named Vanilla. I chose a little black bunny with a patch of white below her chin. Jane wanted me to name her Licorice, but she looked like a Sally to me. Jane had a pretty light brownish-orange rabbit, which was named after the flavor he resembled, Butterscotch. Julie and I played a lot with our bunnies. Jane did not pay much attention to Butterscotch. He got away and was never seen again. Julie and I took turns taking care of the rabbits. When Sally and/or Vanilla got out of their cages, Julie and I always caught them. In fact, we got so good we trapped a wild rabbit in a pipe and then let him go.

Sally had a litter of eight babies. Daddy built more cages to accommodate the additional bunnies. Vanilla had gotten out of his cage but stayed around the yard and was allowed to run loose. One day Vanilla was not to be seen. Around that time, Julie observed Mama had a lot of scratches on her arms. Absentmindedly, she mentioned she was surprised it was so hard to drown a rabbit and then caught herself. Julie did not make the connection until sometime later, it occurred to her why Vanilla had vanished.

One afternoon after school, I went out to feed the rabbits to find them all gone, along with their cages. In the house, I ran. "Where are the bunnies?" I asked.

"Your dad gave them to a family on his mail route. You weren't feeding them every morning, so we got rid of them,"

Mama said coldly. Julie and I felt betrayed. Our parents should have discussed giving the rabbits away first.

Sex was a big mystery. Perhaps our mother thought by not talking about it, we would remain pure as the driven snow. I asked innocently numerous times, "How do you get pregnant?"

Mama's response for the longest time was always "You climb a telephone pole." Of course, I knew that was another one of Mama's silly answers that lacked credibility. Our mother always kept us protected from any conversation or situation that would disclose the facts of life. I was twelve by the time our mother rounded us up for the "birds and bees" talk.

When we got older, we earned money working around the house. I ironed Daddy's clothes, and both Julie and I mowed and watered the huge grass areas. One summer I applied varnish to the outside of the log house. Julie and I also babysat routinely. Jane was not interested in doing those types of things. Apparently, she had enough money from her grades.

Jane and Mama researched a type of mushroom that was growing in the lawn. They harvested the mushrooms and fried them in butter and ate them. No one else was interested in partaking. Jane also did some kind of science experiment, letting mosquitoes bite her. What she was trying to prove was anybody's guess.

One day after school, a misfortunate garter snake crossed Jane's path. She picked it by the tail and whirled it around her head and then released it toward the river.

By the time Jane was fourteen, Daddy completed the upstairs of the house, providing each of us kids a bedroom of our own. There were no handrails on the staircase, but that was not an obstacle as Julie and I ran up the stairs usually two steps at a time.

One evening in the fall, shortly after Jane started her freshman year of high school, things began to significantly change for the worse. We were in bed, each in our own room upstairs. Jane would not settle down and go to sleep.

"Ouch! Ouch! Ouch!" she cried out periodically. Finally, she grabbed her pillow and blanket and went downstairs to sleep on the couch. Daddy told her to go back upstairs and go to bed, but she refused. The same thing happened the following night. Jane said spiders were biting her. In succeeding nights, she yelled out, "Bats in the belfry! Bats in the belfry!" She continued to have the perception of spiders biting her and insisted on sleeping on the couch. She also claimed there were people living in the unfinished part of the upstairs that was accessed through her room. Her behavior could not be ignored. Our mother conferred with the family doctor, and an appointment was made for our parents to meet with a psychiatrist at a hospital in Edmond.

My sisters and I were left at home, while our parents went to make arrangements for Jane to be admitted. That afternoon, Jane began pulling the living room drapes closed.

"Stop closing the drapes, and open them," I commanded. "It is daytime. We don't close the drapes during the day." I had grown to be stronger than Jane and was prepared to go to battle if need be.

To my surprise, Jane was insisting a wolf was looking in at her. Jane removed the lampshade from the floor lamp, put it on her head, and began dancing around. "If that wolf is going to look in here, I'm going to give him something to look at!" Jane exclaimed.

"There is no wolf out there. Take that lampshade off your head and put it back!" I exclaimed.

I was not informed of what behavior to expect or how to deal with Jane. I did not know Jane's hallucinations were real to her.

Our parents returned late that evening. Mama read Jane's diagnosis from a list of sophisticated psychiatric terms that were not familiar. Arrangements were complete for Jane to be admitted.

Dr. Weaver was Jane's psychiatrist. He requested to meet with Julie and me. Our parents brought us to speak with him. He was tall, thin, and very nice. After the interviews, he conferred with our parents, telling them Julie was the most likely to have mental problems later in life. Several years later, Dr. Weaver was killed by one of his patients.

Jane played mind games with her doctors. She thought it was funny to make up strange stories and laughed about how she had fooled them. The doctors surely saw through her nonsense.

There were lots of speculation as to what caused Jane to be mentally ill. One story was her mental illness resulted from spinal meningitis, which she caught from mosquitoes. Another excuse related to having a bad reaction from punch spiked with LSD at a church function. Mama even thought maybe she got *sick* from the mushrooms they had been eating from the yard.

Whatever the actual reason for Jane's full-blown psychosis, no one could say. The onset of some mental illness begins at puberty, and that was when Jane's schizophrenia became apparent.

With the essence of Jane's influence gone, for the first time, there was serenity and peacefulness in our home. The consistent tension from Jane's presence had vanished. There was tranquility.

Jane was released in May after missing the majority of her freshman year and began the next school year again as a freshman. Things were different now. I was a teenager, and Julie was not far behind. We had gone on with our lives normally and spent a lot of time with friends and activities.

Julie loved swimming and completed the more advanced classes. By the time she was thirteen, the local college had built a beautiful indoor swimming pool, where she swam frequently and joined a summer swim team. Julie got up early in the mornings to ride her bicycle two miles to arrive by seven o'clock for swimming practice. Our parents never attended any of Julie's swim meets.

Daddy's afternoon coffee-drinking friend was the manager of a clothing store. As a favor, Jane was hired to be a store clerk. She was not comfortable around people and switched to working in the stockroom. She did not like the stockroom either. That did not last long.

I wanted to get contact lenses. Daddy agreed with the stipulation I had to pay half the cost. I got a summer job cleaning cabins at the motel down the road. I began working every day throughout the summer until two weeks before beginning my junior year.

There were no optometrists in our town. Our family's optometrist was Dr. Allen, who had an office in Downtown

Edmond. I would need to see him periodically throughout a two-week period. Since neither parent could go, Jane accompanied me on the bus. An outgoing older girl sat in a seat near us. She was a singer, and before long, our section of the bus was singing joyfully. That set the tone for the entire trip. Jane was amazingly amicable, and we had a good time together. We stayed in a residential hotel that was down the street from the optometrist's office. For entertainment, we went on a sightseeing trip across Edmond by way of city buses and crossed the street daily to ride the escalator at a large department store.

The following spring, I had the opportunity to clerk at the clothing store where I worked summers and after school my junior and senior years. I sparingly purchased clothes using my discount and saved the majority of my earnings for college.

When Julie turned sixteen, she wanted contacts lenses. Dr. Allen invited Julie to stay at his home with his family during the two-week period that she would be staying in Edmond. She rode the bus and went by herself.

Jane had one friend, Kathy, who went to a country school until she entered high school. Kathy was the oldest of ten children. She did not dress like the other girls. Kathy did not fit in very well with most of the *city* girls in her class. Jane befriended her, and they remained friends throughout high school.

Jane continued to excel academically in high school; however, she had little interaction with others her age. According to one of her classmates, it was like Jane was invisible. She hardly talked to anyone. Jane loved to show up her classmates. Barry, a friend of mine, stopped me during class changes to tell me he was repulsed by her smug, gloating know-it-all air when she answered a question no one else had a clue about.

Jane definitely did not fit in. During a conversation I had with our mother about being different, she said, "We are different from other people." She made it sound like a good thing, but to Julie and me, it was more like being outcasts.

Jane joined the Candy Stripers her junior and senior years of high school. She performed volunteer work at the hospital, doing nonmedical tasks, such as delivering patients' meals. She received satisfaction from helping people.

Jane was not particularly interested in boys; however, in her senior year, she did have a date to go to the drive-in movie. When her date tried to kiss her, she yanked off his glasses and licked the lenses. She walked home, which was not far from the drive-in.

Julie and I both had numerous boyfriends in high school. Mama would not allow us to date anyone who was not in high school. She said college boys had *ideas*.

Many times, Julie and I asked if we could go skiing. Mama always said, "No, you'll break your neck, and it's too short to tie." We knew the true reason for not being allowed to go was that it cost money to rent equipment and buy lift tickets. Our parents guarded their money too closely for such frivolous activities. Julie was fortunate her junior year to have a boyfriend, Wally, who lived at a ski area. Wally worked in the ski rental shop, and his mother worked in the ticket office. He decked Julie out in skis, boots, and poles. His mother provided complimentary ski lift passes, and he taught her to ski.

I had spent so much time working at the clothing store, babysitting, and keeping up my grades there was not much time to spend with friends; however, I did go on a legal senior ditch day with my boyfriend, Ken Taylor, and some other classmates.

Even though I got my driver's license when I was sixteen, I never drove a vehicle to school. I either rode the school bus or relied on a boyfriend to give me rides.

Julie enjoyed high school and had a lot of friends. She was allowed to drive "the bomb," which was a 1948 Willys Jeep Station Wagon. She knew how to have a good time and had great fun taking her friends around.

The home high school football games were always on Friday afternoons. Before the games, Julie drove the bomb packed with her friends up and down Main Street, yelling cheers as was tradition with the high school kids. If our parents would have found out, she would have gotten in trouble.

Like me, Julie worked her last two years of high school in addition to babysitting. During the school year, Julie had a clerical job in the office of the superintendent of schools. She also had weekend jobs.

Prior to beginning her senior year, with some of her savings, Julie went on her first excursion to shop for school clothes with her friend Gail. Gail drove her car. They spent the night at a motel in Trenton, where they drank a beer and smoked cigarettes.

Julie and I had dreams of living fulfilling lives under our own terms. We were full of hope and high expectations.

CHAPTER TWO

Lives of Our Own

Upon graduating from high school, Jane received a full scholarship to a prestigious university. That fall, our mother took her to college. In departing, her farewell words to Jane were "Don't call home asking for money." Jane was in no way prepared to be dropped off where she had no friends or even knew a soul. Mama's parting words were very upsetting. She felt abandoned with no one to fall back on. Two weeks later, Mama received a call from a college official, informing her Jane had not attended classes and to come get her. Mama returned to the college to bring Jane home. Jane had a relapse and went back in the hospital, never to return.

Ken Taylor had moved to Wentwood his freshman year of high school when his father retired. Ken was born in Texas but lived in Germany as a toddler and all over the United States from then on. He asked me to the prom our junior year of high school, and we started going out.

We enrolled in the same required general classes our freshman year at the local college and became engaged in November shortly after Ken's father was killed in an automobile accident. We decided to get married before starting our sophomore year in college. Julie was in her senior year of high school, and Jane was living at home.

A simple wedding was held at the log house, followed by a reception. While Emma, Ken's mother, shed a few tears, Mama showed no sign of sentimentality or sadness. Someone mentioned something to her about missing me, to which she replied she would have more time to pursue her own interests. Overhearing this coldhearted response sent pangs through my heart. I had always longed for a more heartwarming, loving mother.

After honeymooning in Edmond, Ken and I returned home and lived with Ken's mother in a mobile home that was jointly owned by Ken and his mother. Several months into the fall semester, I discovered I was expecting. I was excited about the baby.

Daddy had put in three mobile home spaces in the open area in front of the log house. He proposed putting in another space behind the log house, where we could live rent-free if we paid for having the space added. The deal was made, and we planned to move the twelve by sixty foot mobile home soon after the baby was born.

During a visit with my parents, Ken joined Daddy in the garage, while I chatted with Mama in the living room. She informed me Emma was not allowed to live there. She did not give a reason but was very adamant about not allowing Emma to live on their property. I was caught off guard and totally speechless. I had always been intimidated by Mama. There was no arguing with the authority figure, whose demands were adhered to with the sanctity of the almighty. I was terribly upset and mortified of the thought of having to say anything to Emma.

Upon arriving home, I went into the bedroom and broke down in tears. Ken's mother owned half the trailer. There was no way I could tell my mother-in-law she had to move out. We had already invested in the construction of the mobile home space. By the grace of God, the following day, Emma announced she had made plans to take a government job in Alaska and leave soon after the baby was born.

Ken was working his night job cleaning the college student union when I went into labor. After a long night and through the following morning of back labor, I was rolled into the delivery room. I had a precious little son, whom we named Don. Ken got a quick glance of his new son through the nursery window and left to attend class, rest, and go to his evening job.

The second morning after little Don was born, the nurse brought him in for his early morning feeding, saying something about him being fussy. Minutes later, the nurse took him back to the nursery. That was the last I ever saw him.

Being a new mother and ignorant of hospital protocol, I was wondering why it had been so long since they had brought in little Don. Questioning authority was not something I had ever been allowed to do. That evening, Ken visited me. We were waiting for the nurse to bring our baby when Dr. Thomas entered. He announced our little baby had died. He did not know why.

Graveside services were held. Besides being devastated, I was a mess. I was recovering from the birth. My breasts were engorged with milk, which had come in the day little Don died. I had cried so much it hurt to breathe. My life was upside down. I felt empty but knew I could not wallow in grief. Ken was in class when I visited Dr. Thomas to learn the results of the autopsy. He reported the hospital staff was very surprised when our baby started having breathing problems. There was blood in the baby's stomach, which he could not explain, and there was amniotic fluid in his lungs that he explained resulted from the baby taking a breath too soon. I could not understand how little Don could live two days with enough fluid in his lungs to cause his death that was not detected. I had visions of him not being dead at all. Perhaps one day little Don would come back to find me.

I learned of an office job opening, which I started the day little Don would have been four weeks old. Since we needed the income, I continued to work and did not enroll in fall classes. I missed taking classes and being with people my age.

After graduating from high school, Julie wasted no time going out on her own. She was ready to get out from under the watchful, judgmental, and overbearing eyes of our parents. Within two weeks after graduation, at age seventeen, she was enrolled at a business college in Edmond. Daddy said Julie would be back in two weeks, but she was never to return, except to visit briefly.

Ken and I were friends with Clyde and Sandy Phillips. Ken knew Sandy through a business where she worked near the gas station where he worked. Clyde and I were in the same accounting classes. Clyde was the night clerk and bookkeeper for a restaurant and motel. One evening when we were having dinner together, Clyde told a story about someone coming to the lounge a few nights previously, causing trouble.

Clyde began relating the event as it was told to him. "Several evenings ago, a wild woman came in the lounge and approached the owner. She took his drink and poured it over his head. Then she approached the band. She grabbed the maracas and smashed them together, breaking them into thousands of pieces with beads scattering everywhere. She was shouting, calling everyone sinners and reprimanding them for drinking and smoking." As he was telling the story, he was laughing. It sounded very amusing. Clyde did not realize he was talking about Jane, and I did not tell him.

The night the incident took place, my parents received a call from someone who recognized Jane. Unbeknownst to them, Jane had slipped out, riding her bike to the restaurant, which was a mile down the highway. Jane was totally out of control when Daddy and Mama physically carried her out of the bar. Once they were home, Daddy began unloading the bike from the back of the Willys Station Wagon. Mama tried to keep Jane restrained as she climbed out from the back seat of the two-door vehicle. Jane fought, yelling and kicking and flailing her arms around. She bit Mama on the hand, which later developed into a serious infection.

That was the start of Jane making a nuisance of herself around the community. She went to the house of one of her favorite teachers. Jane must have scared her because she would not answer the door. Many years later when I learned of the teacher's death, I informed Jane. To my surprise, Jane responded, "Good. When I went to her for help, she turned me away."

Jane kept slipping away on her bike. On one occasion, she rode out to Kayton, a small ranching community twelve miles east of town. People were complaining about a strange person riding a bike through their yards. The sheriff arrested her for trespassing, and she was locked up. While in jail, she ripped up the sheets and stuffed them down the toilet, causing a big mess. She thought it was very amusing.

Jane bought a junker car for a couple of hundred dollars and registered it under Mama's and her name. To keep Jane from driving, Mama removed the distributor cap. Mama found a buyer and returned Jane's money to her. Jane was locked in the upstairs to keep her confined to the house. She tried to escape by climbing onto the roof and jumping off from the garage. She did not get away though. Another time, Jane decided to tie sheets together and lower herself down from what had been my bedroom. Her foot got caught in a sheet. She was hanging upside down out the window that faced the river. Someone in the house across the river saw Jane dangling from the window and called Mama.

"I know," Mama told them nonchalantly. "I'm going to get her down in a minute." Jane was admitted to the state hospital.

Julie completed the one-year course at a business college in eight months and got a good-paying job with a trucking company. She worked in Edmond for a couple of years and then moved to Preston.

While in Alaska, Ken's mother found a new husband, William Bennett. He had seven children, of which the three youngest were living with them. Emma and her new family stopped by to visit us on their move from Alaska to Texas, where William owned a home. During their visit, I miscarried at sixteen weeks. The miscarriage was traumatic but did not leave the void that I was still feeling from the loss of little Don.

Ken graduated from college with a double major in mathematics and accounting. He continued taking graduate courses. Meanwhile, I conceived, and Angelia was born in 1971. She was beautiful beyond compare as her face turned red, and she was crying healthfully—"Weh, weh, weh." Ken was jubilant as he left the hospital, singing at the top of his lungs while driving to one of his part-time jobs.

I was pleasantly surprised when Daddy appeared to see Angelia and me at the hospital. "Third time's a charm," he said.

I quit my job and stayed home to take care of Angelia. It was a very happy time for me as I followed Angelia's development. All was well, even when I discovered I was pregnant again. Angelia was only seven months old, but I felt ecstatic. Another little baby was a gift from heaven. Since we had no insurance, I got my old job back, which was opening up. Jane had stabilized and was doing well taking business correspondence courses. Jane babysat Angelia. Angelia gave her purpose, and she loved Angelia. Mama was close by.

We had hoped to stay in Wentwood. Ken was still pumping gas and had another part-time job while we were waiting for a teaching position to open. With our second baby on the way, Ken could not continue to pump gas indefinitely.

Job applications were sent out, and I started packing. He accepted the offer from Bingham, which came on the day

Justin was born. Justin was eight weeks old, and Angelia was eighteen months when we arrived in Bingham with all our worldly possessions.

Our budget was too tight to survive on a first-year teacher's salary. The lady next door agreed to babysit, while I went to work afternoons at the high school as a bookkeeper for the school's activity accounts. Later, I became secretary to an administrator and worked full time during the school year. During that time, I suffered three miscarriages; however, I successfully conceived again, and Jack was born in 1976.

My parents moved to Blackburn in 1975. Their new place consisted of two acres with a four-bedroom house. The property included a large garage, an outbuilding, a chicken house, a root cellar, and a barn. Mama was happy to have a place where she could keep chickens. Daddy had been talking about retiring to a warmer place to get away from the excruciatingly hard winters that aggravated his arthritis, which resulted from a war injury he acquired while fighting in World War II. Shortly after moving, Daddy had knee replacement surgery. Jane followed and got her own place to live, supporting herself with a job in a secretarial pool for a canning company.

Julie was living in Preston when she met Doug Hamilton. She first noticed him at a Bible study class in the fall of 1975. He was a second lieutenant and an instructor pilot. On their first date, they took a drive to picnic in the mountains and observe a protected buffalo herd. They enjoyed each other's company so much that after returning to their homes, they changed clothes and went out to a restaurant that evening.

From then on, they saw each other every day until they got married the following spring.

One of Doug's brothers, one sister, and a friend came to the wedding. Our parents and Jane attended also. Daddy walked Julie down the aisle with the assistance of his cane. I was unable to attend as I had recently given birth to Jack. Julie and Doug honeymooned in Hawaii. When they returned, the military packed Doug's house and Julie's apartment into a moving van. They were on their way to Texas.

Doug taught pilots to fly T-37s at the base. Julie was able to get a civil service secretarial job on the base. Her office supported flight simulators, which were controlled by computers. Although Julie did office work, she had the opportunity to climb in a simulator from time to time and "fly" the plane, usually crashing. Julie became interested in becoming a computer programmer and enrolled in classes.

Jane moved to Preston in 1977, where she worked in a secretarial pool at a hospital. She decided to pursue a career in nursing and enrolled at a community college. Jane was very opinionated regarding the care of patients. She did not approve of the routine use of prescription drugs. She did not complete nursing school; however, she did complete the certified nurse aide requirements and then worked as a nurse's aide.

Mama had an unquenchable thirst for knowledge. With her daughters gone, she began researching many topics, such as family linage, UFOs, numerology, and the lost continent of Atlantis. She talked about the San Andreas Fault and believed California was going to fall off into the ocean any day. She did research on Admiral Byrd's exploration to the North

Pole, where he discovered the earth is hollow, a fact that is not generally known per Mama. She believed in reincarnation and cited two lives she had lived previously. In one life, she was a man on Atlantis and was herding cattle onto a boat when she drowned. In another life, she told of being a girl around the age of seventeen, living in New England in the 1700s. She died from a spider bite. Mama claimed to be clairvoyant on limited occasions, such as envisioning Ken's father appearing before her with blood dripping from his fingers the evening he died. She also told of experiences she had knowing when her grandparents had died before she was notified.

Daddy, Mama, and Jane became absorbed in a church with which we were not familiar. They had become fanatical about the church. Mama talked about it constantly. They said prayers called decrees from a book, chanting quickly and loudly in unison to the ascended masters.

The church taught meditation and practiced astral projection or out-of-body experience, which according to Mama explained why she and Daddy could hear Jane making noise upstairs when she was in body, confined to a hospital during one of her breakdowns. Mama and Daddy went to many church conferences. Mama talked about church leaders, auras, karma, chakras, and the predictions of Edgar Cayce, St. Germaine, and Nostradamus. They purchased countless church tapes and books and hung a picture of a temple with an all-seeing eye on the wall in their living room. The religion incorporated teachings from Buddhism and other world religions. It was a conglomeration of everything. Doug called it the Baseball Religion because it covered all the bases of the major religions. Mama said it was the answer to what she had been seeking. They gradually drifted away from the church when the headquarters moved to another state.

Ken thought Mama was a bit dingy. Julie and I accepted our mother with an open mind, not judging her one way or another.

Ken and I bought our first house in 1977, and I began working at the local college. I enrolled in an evening class and was up every night until midnight studying. I received an A in the course; but it was evident I could not continue to be a good mother, work a demanding job, and have any sanity left with that kind of a schedule. Going back to school would not be in the cards.

Our children were fascinated with dinosaurs. Ken decided to take our family to Utah to see dinosaur exhibits and invited Daddy to join us while Mama was in California, taking a writing course. We had a carefree, enjoyable visit going through the exhibits of relics and the museum. Ken purchased a number of unique small realistic plastic dinosaurs for our children, while Daddy purchased a brontosaurus that cost $7. I was amazed. I had never seen that side of him. On the drive back, Daddy mentioned something to the effect of not wanting to live forever. That comment went over my head. I did not know then Daddy was hinting of not being around much longer, and this would be the last time I would see him alive.

Doug's next assignment was at RAF Woodbridge near Ipswich, England. Before leaving, Julie took a side trip to spend a few days with our parents before venturing abroad. A month later, Doug and Julie were living in temporary quarters when Doug went on a week-long assignment to Germany. Soon after Doug's departure, Julie received an early morning call from Mama, informing her of Daddy's death. Doug returned to England immediately. After fifty-two hours of travel, Julie and Doug arrived in Blackburn.

Mama, we three daughters, and our families viewed Daddy's body, which was laid out on a granite slab. We could hardly speak. He looked calm like he was sleeping. A small group of people were present at the memorial service. Mama did not show any signs of grief. It was like one big reunion. This was the first time we had been together since Julie left home over ten years previously.

A blood clot had lodged in Daddy's heart. The blood clot originated from his knee joint replacement, which caused blood clots to continually form. He knew it was a matter of time but did not tell anyone. Daddy died way too young at age sixty-two, cheating his grandchildren out of anticipated fishing outings and stories about when he was in the war.

When visiting with Mama about losing Daddy, Mama told me that several evenings prior to his death, they were sitting quietly in the living room, reading, when they heard the sound of a loud horn, which lasted several seconds. "They are coming to get me," Daddy said calmly. Daddy had been painting the barn from a faded-out brown to a sparkling green. On the afternoon of the day he died, he stroked in bold green lettering on a replacement section of plywood "Milton May 1980." Later that summer, it was painted over when Ken and I returned to finish painting the barn.

When Julie and Doug got back to England, they moved into a small house in Felixstowe on the coast of the English Channel. Anxiously, Julie watched as job openings were posted on base, but she was not eligible since the positions were reserved for British nationals. Not to be dissuaded, she found a job on the British economy as a data entry operator for a company that leased shipping containers and tracked them all over the world on ships and trains. The office was so close to her house Julie generally walked to work until the office moved ten miles away. She began taking the train, stowing her ten-speed bicycle in the bicycle car, and riding her bike the rest of the way to work in four-inch heels and a dress, just like the British women.

Julie worked in a large room alone with a dreadful English woman, who took pleasure in tormenting her. She mocked and bullied Julie continuously. Even though this woman's ridicule made Julie's life miserable, Julie was not comfortable initiating a confrontation. Julie was conditioned to be submissive after growing up on the receiving end of our mother. She was fearful she would lose her job if she brought attention to the conflict. After two years of abuse, Julie finally lost it. In no uncertain terms, she told this gal where to go and exactly how to get there. The English woman instantly ceased harassing her from that moment on. At age thirty-four, she finally allowed herself to set boundaries. Julie learned one very important lesson—some people will not respect you until you stand up to them.

Back in Bingham, Ken and David, a teaching colleague, decided to start a small janitorial service. The main client of the janitorial service was a large drugstore. Every other Sunday, Ken and David stripped the floors and put down a fresh coat of wax. Besides keeping the books, I went in an hour to wipe down the stainless steel counter bases.

At that time, besides teaching, Ken was driving school bus and working all night on Saturdays, cleaning floors for another large store. Ken was also working toward his master's degree, while I typed his critiques and projects.

CHAPTER THREE

Years Roll By

In 1982, Mama married Albert Archer. She met him at the used clothing store, where they both worked. He was sixteen years her senior, closer to her father's age than he was to hers. Albert was a retired railroad worker and kept milk cows. Albert had eight grown children. When Mama called to inform me she had decided to get married and asked what I thought, I replied, "We want you to be happy, and if that is what you want, then go ahead."

I was expecting to be invited to the wedding, but upon making reference to coming, Mama replied, "I got married the first time without you, and I can do it again without you." Her response was absurd but consistent with her personality.

Soon after Mama married Albert, they came for a visit. Albert was nothing like Daddy in any way. He was an old man of short stature with a growth on his nose. The remains of his jack-o'-lantern teeth were crooked and yellowing. His conversation focused around his cows or church.

Our family group went to a cafeteria for lunch. We all sat around a large round table with Mama and Albert. Albert announced he was going to say grace. Everyone held hands as Albert started to pray. He spoke in a low, monotone mumble. The cafeteria was very noisy with dishes clanging and conversations among the patrons, all speaking loudly to be heard above the noise. Several times, I looked up to see if Albert was still praying. Finally, after the longest meal prayer I had ever experienced, the hand holding ended, signifying the prayer was over.

The first time our family went to visit Mama after her marriage to Albert, I was horrified to see what Albert had done to Daddy's meticulous yard. Fruit trees had been planted in the front lawn with furrows dug to provide water to the trees from the nearby irrigation ditch. Further exploration behind the house revealed a rickety fence that had been jimmy rigged with bailing twine and wire to hold it together. There were milk cows grazing in the previously unused field.

* * *

The street where we lived opened up, turning it into a major thoroughfare. After living there for five years, it was time to move to a suitable place where our children could safely ride their bicycles. The house was put on the market and sold within several months. A new house was being built, which would take three more weeks to complete by the time we had to vacate our old house. Julie invited us to join her and Doug on their vacation to Germany. This was the perfect time to go. All our household belongings were stored in a moving van. While our good friends watched our children, we vacationed with Julie and Doug.

Julie and Doug planned to spend their vacation camping all over Europe, taking their English BMW with the steering wheel on the right-hand side of the car. We brought dome tents and spent most nights in campgrounds, mingling with the Europeans. A memorable stop was a concentration camp outside of Munich. It was a sobering experience to visit the camp, where millions of Jews perished during World War II. While in Berchtesgaden, it was eerie to walk the streets where Hitler had walked. Many castles and palaces were visited, each revealing elegant and spectacular displays of their own.

Suddenly, Doug was called back to his unit temporarily in Germany, leaving the rest of us to find our way back home. An express train out of Koln took us back to our parked car. Julie was not used to driving the autobahn, where speed limits generally did not exist. Road construction made it confusing. We decided to follow the signs to Umleitung and get our bearings from there. Upon finding our way back to the ferry, we learned *Umleitung* meant "detour" in German.

After three years in England, Doug was reassigned to Preston. Julie and Doug bought a new house. In 1984, Jane met Wes Hensley at the public library. Within five days, they decided to get married. Julie helped by making a bouquet of lace, pink ribbons, and flowers. Jane and Wes got married at the justice of the peace with Julie being their witness. They lived in a mobile home park on the outskirts of town. Wes was a truck driver. Jane continued to work as a nursing assistant.

She did not communicate with me about events happening in her life. It was assumed all was going well.

After two years in Preston, Doug was transferred to Germany. Julie got a civil service job in Bitburg, where she worked for the operations commander, who was the colonel that commanded all the fighter squadrons.

Our time was dedicated to our children, hardly having a spare moment for ourselves. Our children were kept busy participating in sports and various activities. We visited Jane in Preston, spending one night with her in her mobile home. Wes was gone driving truck. Jane got up at 5:30 A.M. to go to her job. Jane was functioning reasonably well. Wes had run up their charge card, buying Western shirts and other clothing for himself, which made Jane angry.

Julie and Doug were back in the States in 1988. Julie had been working on a degree in computers over the last twelve years and had finally graduated in 1989. They were assigned to a base in Florida and then moved back to Preston after Doug retired, returning to their old home, which had been leased. Julie found a job, this time as a computer programmer with a company that contracted software development. Doug was trying his hand at selling real estate while waiting to get a position as a commercial airline pilot.

Jane seemed to be functioning within normal limits. Her social awkwardness and inappropriate behavior was on display when she visited Julie at her home. During the visits, Julie noticed her staring at Doug. Jane routinely lashed out with ridiculing insults and telling Julie what she should do.

Julie mentioned Jane's behavior to a coworker, who had previously worked at a hospital with mentally ill patients. She explained Julie was trying to relate to Jane as if she was sane and not to expect Jane's behavior to make sense all the time.

Julie and Doug decided to visit Mama and Albert one Christmas and called about coming to visit. After spending one night, Mama told Julie undiplomatically she had to leave because they were going to the home of one of Albert's children for dinner. On Christmas Day, Julie and Doug left to go back home. Their Christmas dinner consisted of tacos, which they bought at a restaurant on the summit of a mountain pass.

Julie shared her experience with me. "Mama kicked us out on Christmas Day to spend time with Albert's family. I don't understand why we were not welcomed to the family Christmas dinner. Why couldn't she have asked if we could come to dinner with them?"

It appeared to me Albert's family, who visited frequently, had priority. "Our mother has been hijacked," I expressed in a joking manner. But it was true. That experience created ill feelings. Doug said if he ever visited again, they would stay in a motel.

Still in Preston, Julie changed jobs to take a position with a Fortune 500 company, and Doug was hired by an airline. It was becoming increasingly inconvenient for Doug to make his flight connections, resulting in a move to Georgia. Julie was able to transfer to another position within her company.

Jane wanted to move closer to Mama, but Wes did not. After five years of marriage, Jane divorced Wes. Years later, she regretted her hasty decision to dissolve their marriage. After divorcing Wes, Jane moved to Blackburn.

* * *

Jane got in the habit of calling us on our birthdays at 7:00 A.M. to tell us "Happy birthday." I received a birthday call from Jane early one morning. Breaking away from the usual chat, Jane spoke. "I was going to break you and Ken up, but I decided not to." I blew off Jane's absurdity. Jane was green with envy of my family. In another early morning birthday call, Jane did not get away with her belittling tactics. "You don't live in the real world," Jane remarked.

"What do you mean?" I asked. "You think raising children, going to work every day, and maintaining a household is not the real world?"

"You have never been out there on your own," responded Jane.

"So you think getting in trouble, being thrown in jail, and being hauled off to the state hospital is living in the real world?"

"I didn't mean that," Jane stammered.

I received a letter from Jane, saying, "You hurt my feelings." Jane never cared if she was hurting anyone's feelings; that seemed to be her goal.

* * *

Our children had grown up. Before we knew it, Angelia had graduated from high school and was off to college. The following year, Justin graduated and was off to college also. Jack was the only one left at home.

Justin married Phyllis, his high school sweetheart, in May after completing his first year of college. Angelia met Calvin at the university, and they married the following May. Ken and I had barely recuperated from Justin's wedding when it was time to plan for Angelia's. Mama did not attend any of her grandchildren's graduations or Justin and Phyllis' wedding. She had no plans for attending Angelia's wedding either until Julie *twisted* her arm. "What do they need me there for?" Mama asked.

I was getting worried when Mama and Albert had not arrived long after the expected time. Mama had been driving around for hours before stopping at a filling station to call for assistance. She had misread the map I drew and kept backtracking, going in circles. When she arrived, she obviously needed to have her hair washed. Angelia's wedding was a formal church affair, and her grandmother needed to look presentable. I volunteered to wash and curl her hair. She was not making the effort for her granddaughter's wedding that I expected. At least she was there.

The following year, Jack graduated from high school and chose to attend the local college. Jack rented a house with two of his friends and worked at an electronics store. It was a bittersweet change to have all our children out of the house.

We visited Mama and Albert once or twice a year. Jane rented her own apartment but never failed to be there upon our arrival. During one visit, Ken went with Albert to check on irrigation ditches. Mama suggested Jane and I go for a walk.

As we began our walk along the well-established graveled county road, Jane started talking. "When I can't sleep at night,

I like to take walks and sing. People sleep with their windows open and complain I'm waking them up. They call the police, and I get arrested. I'm not hurting anybody. If I had a lot of money and a lot of property, I could walk on my property and do what I wanted. They would just say I was eccentric."

Before I could respond to Jane's complaints of being treated unfairly, she changed topics. "I have a new boyfriend. His name is Jeff. He wants to get into my pants. He signed over an apartment to me. We want to get married, but Mama doesn't want me to. She said he is too old for me."

"Let's go back now," I choked out.

Jane continued talking as we turned around and strolled back toward the old farmhouse. "Believe it or not, but Mama is crazier than I am. You should be around her more, and you could see for yourself."

That thought had never occurred to me as I protested that idea. I had never considered Mama as having mental health issues, even though years later, that thought surfaced. For now, I interpreted Mama's behavior as *difficult to get along with*. I had always felt frustrated regarding her unconventional behavior. In hopes of achieving insight in dealing with Mama, I had attended a workshop on dealing with difficult people. According to the presenter, one has to adjust their own attitudes and accept there is nothing they can do to change someone else. I must have been delusional to think there was a solution. There was a choice between peace and conflict. I was consoled with my submissive choice of peace.

* * *

Jane did not marry Jeff. It was surmised Mama's objections resulted in their breakup; however, Jane maintained her residence in the apartment Jeff had signed over to her.

Our weekend visits to Mama entailed arriving Saturday afternoon, spending the night, and leaving Sunday morning. Since Mama left food out on the table with flies generally buzzing around the kitchen, Ken was leery of eating there, which started a tradition of Ken treating for pizza or other fast food. Jane monopolized the conversation, chatting about their church or people and places that were foreign to me, intentionally leaving me out of the conversations.

Mama had only met Justin's wife, Phyllis, briefly at Angelia's wedding and had never seen their baby son, Glen. For Mama to see her first great-grandchild, Justin's family joined us on one of our visits.

As had become customary, Ken treated our group to dinner. Upon entering, Albert staked out a table in the center of the seating area. While waiting for our group to place their orders, Albert handed out miniature booklets of Bible verses and engraved pencils to any children whose attention he could get. Mama and I were seated by Albert when Jane approached wearing a straw hat and sat down, offering to sing a song she wrote. As Jane sang, I looked around to find Ken hiding out with the kids at a distant table. I felt very conspicuous after being deserted by Ken. I put on the biggest smile I could muster and said to myself, "It's okay. No one knows you here."

* * *

Julie and I were surprised when in September 1994, we received announcements in the mail of Jane's marriage to Ben Jenson. Jane met Ben at a rehabilitation center while recuperating from her most recent relapse. Jane had made the announcements, which displayed individual pictures of each of them from the shoulders up. Ben had a balding head and a neatly groomed bushy white beard.

"Jane married Santa Claus," stated Julie.

"Yes, his beard sure makes him look like Santa Claus," I agreed with a chuckle.

Neither Julie nor I had ever heard of Ben before. Jane did not waste any time dragging him to the altar. Ben and Jane took up residence in the apartment Jeff had signed over to Jane.

Ken and I met Ben on one of our visits to see Mama and Albert. Ben's beard had grown bushy and unruly. He wore a hat that hid his balding head; his general appearance resembled an unmade bed. Ben had little to say until he got to know you. He had a great sense of humor and liked to tell jokes. Ben was a Vietnam veteran with an unexplained disability. From Jane's apartment, she took us for a walk to meet Ben's sister, Carrie, and her husband, Herman, who lived with their family in a house a short distance away.

It was too difficult for Mama and Albert to get away from the farm to come see us, so Ken and I embarked on a visit, bringing Justin and his family to Blackburn for a second time. This time there was also a little granddaughter named Stacy, who was two years younger than Glen. It was a delightful experience for Glen and Stacy. They had never been around farm animals and were fascinated by the three large wooly sheep that greeted them at the fence baaing.

The events of our visits had become routine. Being true to form, Jane would already be at the house when we arrived; she and Ben would always join us for dinner, and she would always make up an excuse to come back to Mama's house afterward. By the time Jane left, it was late and time to go to bed. This practice eliminated any time I would have to chat with Mama out of Jane's presence before we had to leave the next morning.

After another evening out during one of our visits, Jane returned to the house, saying she had left a book there. Albert had already retired to the bedroom. Moments after entering the house, Jane broke into a repertoire of obscenities. "Motherf— this and motherf— that." Perhaps the attention I was getting from Mama had ticked her off. The air turned blue with a gamut of profanities. Whatever point Jane was trying to make was lost to the cosmic void.

I was stunned to hear such expletives erupting from Jane. Generally, whenever Jane heard even the mildest swearing, she would gasp and remark, "You said a bad word."

Mama stared in silence, while Jane raged on in her profanity frenzy. "Let's go home," Ben repeated several times, but Jane was not willing to give up center stage easily. When Jane and Ben finally left, everyone went quietly to bed, drained of their energy.

* * *

Albert died in August 1999 at the age of ninety-two. His family had planned a Labor Day reunion before his death. Albert's body was preserved several weeks to combine his funeral with the reunion to accommodate distant relatives. Julie and Doug were planning to visit prior to Albert's death. Their plans were kept after first spending a few days with us. I rode with them to visit Mama, while Ken stayed home with his teaching obligation. The funeral took place the week before we arrived. Albert's family had returned to their homes.

Previously, I had asked Mama for a set of dishes she had been keeping for me. Mama was digging through a closet, looking for the dishes, when I appeared to help. "I don't need help," she told me. "Go join your sisters outside." I stepped outside, taking note of the beautiful, cool September day as I joined my sisters by the goat pen.

Earlier that day, Mama told us she had changed her will. The topic was fresh on Jane's mind. She glared at Julie and me through glasses that shielded her distrusting eyes. Out of nowhere, Jane blasted away. "You are only interested in Mama's money. You are trying to cheat me out of my share."

Julie and I were dumbfounded. We had no say in our mother's will. Jane was getting a good deal. The will made provisions for her to occupy the farm as long as she wanted. If she did not want to stay there or whenever she moved from the farm, the property was to be sold, and the proceeds were to be divided among us three. That was not fair by Jane's thinking; since Julie and I already had homes, the farm should be given to her outright. She was complaining that if she and Ben decided to move to Westbrook or somewhere, the house would not be there for them if they wanted to come back.

Jane finally calmed down when we assured her she would not be cheated.

Julie and I brought to Mama's attention our concern for what we would do with all her stuff when she was gone. "You three girls should be able to go through it in a weekend," she responded.

Julie and I looked at each other with *huh* expressions. Who was she trying to kid? We both knew that was impossible, even if Jane was not instigating problems, which was another impossibility. Our mother had no concept of how involved it would be to clear out the overwhelming abundance of things that had accumulated.

During this trip, Julie confided Doug was having a medical issue, but the cause of his discomfort had not been determined. When he returned home, Doug was scheduled to go for a scan of his gallbladder. Mama's research of her medical books indicated pancreatic issues. After a conversation with Mama, Julie requested to have the test include checking Doug's pancreas. The test was changed after Julie's insistence. The diagnosis revealed advanced stage IV pancreatic cancer. Doug was not expected to live past six months. The news was devastating.

Ken and I flew out to visit Julie and Doug in July of 2000. Doug continued talking about all the things they were going to do when he got well. He was very frustrated but refused to give up as his body kept withering away.

As Doug continued to get closer to death, he was admitted to the hospital. A friend paid him a quick visit but left and came back the following day. "I came by yesterday to see you, but you were sleeping," she told him.

"I was not sleeping," he replied. "I was watching you from behind that chair."

Doug was released from the hospital under hospice care. Being heavily sedated under morphine, Doug had strange hallucinations. "You have to get those cows out of the backyard," he told Julie in his semi comatose state. Doug died at home two days after being released in the presence of Julie, his mother, and a sister. It had only been a month since our visit when Ken and I returned with all three of our adult children to attend Doug's funeral.

Doug's death was very traumatic for Julie; she could not envision a happy future without him. She spent her days in a fog, going through the motions of living and working. It was very lonely with no family or friends around other than work colleagues. After several months, she realized Doug had died, not her; and she needed to get through her grief.

A year later, her company wanted Julie to move to Tennessee. Julie decided to move and bought a home. Her niece, Angelia, took off time from her job and helped Julie with the huge job of setting up her new house.

* * *

Our mother's siblings routinely communicated through e-mails and wanted her to join in. Julie decided to give her a computer that had belonged to Doug. It was sent to me for Ken to set up. Jack provided a printer, which he bought at cost through the store he managed. Julie and I went in together on a Christmas present to get our mother a chair with casters to use at the computer.

Ken and I squeaked in a quick Saturday trip. Ken assembled the chair, and the computer was set up. Remarkably, Jane was not there. Mama said Jane was not feeling well and suggested I call her.

I greeted Jane over the phone. She was cranky and rude. "You know I have Parkinson's disease?"

"No," I responded in surprise.

"Didn't Mama tell you?"

"No," I replied. "I'm so sorry."

Jane started screaming. "No, you are not sorry! You don't care about me! All you care about is yourself and your family! You don't care anything about me!" She slammed down the receiver.

I was in shock and extremely upset. "Jane said she has Parkinson's disease."

"It isn't for sure. I didn't think to tell you about it," Mama responded. As it turned out, Jane did not have Parkinson's.

With a snowstorm threatening over the pass back home, Ken and I left hastily. As we drove down the highway, I felt badly from Jane's verbal attack. Of course, I cared about Jane; but she certainly was not the focal point in my life, which Jane thought she should be.

* * *

Doug had been gone three years. During that time, Julie started dating but was disillusioned with the dating scene. She was still grieving and began attending a grief counseling group at a church. During her third visit, Julie met Gerald Hanes, a cattle rancher with three grown children. Gerald was a widower, who had recently lost his wife to cancer after a lengthy battle. Gerald was captivated with Julie. After a while, they became engaged.

After their engagement, Julie and Gerald traveled to meet our family, first stopping in Blackburn. They knew they would not be arriving until late afternoon and made arrangements to meet at a pizza shop for dinner. Julie and Gerald arrived early. They chose a table for six with Gerald seated at the end of one side. Mama arrived soon after, sitting across Gerald. Jane and Ben were the last ones to enter and took the remaining seats across from Gerald. Julie introduced Gerald to everyone before the group ordered. Mama chatted with Gerald in casual conversation with a few comments from Ben as they awaited the arrival of their pizzas.

Jane finally spoke as she addressed Gerald from her kitty-corner position. "You know why they didn't let me sit next to you? It's because I'm the crazy one." After Jane's proclamation, she nodded back and forth and smiled.

Throughout dinner, Jane refrained from speaking but constantly glared at Gerald, peeking under the brim of her straw hat that she customarily wore. Julie had forewarned him of what to expect, but anything she could have described could not have portrayed the uncomfortable feeling of strangeness that accompanied Jane's presence.

Later that summer, Jane decided to paint Mama's barn white. The job was barely started with a few strokes of white paint over the previous green when the chore was abandoned. Mama asked us to finish the job. We agreed to complete the task and had Jack join us. We arrived one Friday evening, ready to work, and began painting early the next morning.

All three of us worked briskly until lunchtime arrived on the hot August Saturday. Ken began rinsing the paint from the brushes with a garden hose as not to return from lunch to find ruined brushes with dried paint. Jane appeared out of nowhere, lumbering up to the barn with Ben following behind. Jane announced they had been in a parade. She was dressed like a clown, wearing a plaid blouse and striped slacks topped off with her straw hat. We were invited to go rafting with them. Jane was not happy when her invitation was turned down. The barn had to be finished that afternoon.

"Give me the hose," Jane demanded. "I'm thirsty. I need a drink of water."

"The water in the hose is hot from sitting in the sun. Go into the house where you can get a cool drink," Ken said as he continued rinsing the paintbrushes, while Jane jabbered. The calm conversation changed in the blink of an eye. "Give me the hose!" Jane rudely insisted. Ken repeated, "The water is not good to drink. Go to the house for cool water."

"Are you going to give me the hose or not?" Jane shouted. Ken handed her the hose. It had a metal nozzle, which controlled the flow of water by holding down a lever. Jane grabbed the hose from Ken's hand. Without removing the nozzle, she placed it up to her lips and pressed the lever. The water shot out with great pressure. It was rather hilarious as the water came spewing from her mouth, but no one laughed. Jane threw the hose to the ground with force, hitting my foot.

"Ouch!" I squealed in pain. Jane did not care she had hurt my foot. She marched off in a huff and drove off with Ben, not stopping for a drink of water at the house.

The following Monday, Jane began a writing class in which she had enrolled at a college in Westbrook. Jane had a disagreement with her instructor, quickly getting on his troublemakers list. When the class was over, Jane lay down on a bench to rest while waiting for Ben to pick her up. She had been there a lengthy time when the college security asked her to leave. Jane had a breakdown and withdrew from her class. She blamed her breakdown on becoming dehydrated because Ken would not give her water.

* * *

All our children were coming for Christmas of 2001. Ken thought it would be nice to have my mother join us. She had never seen Angelia and Calvin's two children. Clara was three, and Mathew was approaching his first birthday. Ken and I arranged to pick her up and afterward bring her back home. It was a great family Christmas. Mama was glad she had spent the time with her grandchildren and great-grandchildren.

* * *

Keeping up the farm was difficult for Mama. She decided to sell and find a place in town. She contacted a real estate agent and was trying to get organized. "How is the packing going?" I asked.

"Pretty good," she replied. "I'm making headway on sorting the mail."

I was mystified. Mama had been preparing for months, and all she was doing was sorting through old mail. "Why did you let so much accumulate?" I asked.

She replied, "A lot of it was Albert's. He didn't want to toss anything without looking at it. He said they wouldn't send it to him if it wasn't important. He was too tired to read it, so he kept it in a box."

"It is old. Why don't you just toss it rather than waste time going through it?" I suggested.

"It is a good thing I've been looking through it. I found some pictures of Albert's kids that would have gotten thrown out," Mama said to justify her project.

After a while, Mama's real estate agent contacted her with the prospects of purchasing a condo, which was exactly what she was looking for.

Mama was in a quandary wanting to buy the condo but needed help in organizing the move. Julie relieved the situation and bought the condo with funds she received from Doug's life insurance. Without Julie's assistance, she would never have been able to sell the farm and move out while also coordinating the purchase of the condo.

I mentioned to my high school friend Fran, who lived in Blackburn, of Mama's plans to move. Fran volunteered the services of herself and her husband, Charles, to help. On the appointed day to move Mama's things to the condo, Ken appeared with a rental truck. Our group got to work shortly after 7:00 A.M. Mama was unorganized and indecisive, by no means ready. Fran and I made a box run, while Ken and Charles started moving large pieces of furniture to the truck. Upon returning with an assortment of boxes, Fran began boxing a multitude of books from a wall of bookshelves, while I boxed miscellaneous items that were lined up on the floor against the living room wall.

One of the bedrooms was used for a food reserve, where Mama kept two freezers and a stockpile of canned goods. Ken and Charles wrestled the freezers through the narrow door and out to the truck. Ben appeared and joined me in packing canned goods. I noticed several cans had begun to expand; one of blueberries had burst with dried blueberry juice on the side. "These need to be tossed," I expressed.

"You think so?" Mama questioned.

"You could die from botulism if you eat these!" I exclaimed.

"Well, okay, go ahead and toss those," Mama said reluctantly.

A lot was accomplished that day. Fran and I made the beds at the condo, where Mama spent the night, along with Ken and me. The closets in the farmhouse were still full of clothes and items Mama had been hoarding for years. The bedroom that was used for storage had not been touched. It was still packed with all kinds of things, and the door would not open all the way.

Before her move to the condo, Mama had a series of garage sales; however, they hardly made a dent in her *stuff.* An auction company was contacted to sell items from the garage, outbuilding, barn, and miscellaneous things from the house. Ken and I returned to help with the auction.

During the auction, I stayed in the house, assisting Mama, and took on cleaning the refrigerator. Mama had neglected to clean a spill from years ago that had dried and was embedded on the lower section. I scrubbed the refrigerator over an hour before it was ready to be taken out to be auctioned. While the auction was taking place outside, Mama remained inside. The whole thing was too much. She was going in circles from one room to the next, confused as to what she should do next. After the auction, there was still a profusion of things lingering in the house.

The farm remained on the market for a year. Julie and Gerald visited while Mama was still in transition to help clear more of her things. Julie returned another time by herself and took several trips to a recycling center and the county dump. The farm finally sold.

* * *

Our youngest son, Jack, had remained a bachelor until he met Claudia in 2003. Claudia had moved recently from the East Coast when she got a reporter position with the newspaper. She met Jack at a soccer game after watching him play on an adult team.

Jack wanted both of his grandmothers at his wedding in June 2004. Ken and I retrieved Mama. Ken's mother, Emma, had flown in the week before. The outdoor evening wedding was held at a special wedding venue on the river. It was an exceptionally fun evening.

Unfortunately, Julie was unable to attend. She was still recuperating from surgery she had several weeks before. A small cancerous tumor had been found, and she opted to get it removed as soon as possible. During her recovery, Julie stayed at Gerald's home. He helped take care of her; and our daughter, Angelia, flew out to assist her during the most difficult part of her healing period.

Gerald was biding his time, waiting for Julie to decide when she was ready to marry him. Gerald was very supportive of Julie. His family was very fond of her as well.

I had retired from the college and, after a two-year stint with a credit union, was now working for the city.

Jane and Ben had their ups and downs. Jane found herself in conflict with anyone who rubbed her the wrong way. Julie and I evaded dealing with her as much as possible and had little knowledge of Jane's day-to-day activities. Jane had been able to stay out of jail and out of the state mental hospital for a number of years, even though her mental health issues were prevalent.

CHAPTER FOUR

The Phone Call That Changed Everything

The ringing phone broke the serenity of the peaceful Sunday evening in early November 2004. "Elaine, it's your sister, Julie," called out Ken as he went back to watching television in the living room. I was in my sewing room, finishing the inside edges on a fleece throw I was making as a Christmas gift for Ken's brother, Adam.

I picked up the extension. "Hi, Julie. How are you?"

Julie responded on a serious note, "I'm fine. I just received a call from Ben." That seemed strange. Why would Ben be calling?

Julie continued. "Mama may have had a heart attack. They took her to the hospital. They don't think it is very bad. Apparently, she got sick while at church."

A barrage of questions sprung from my mouth. "How is Mama? What happened? Why weren't we notified sooner?"

"Ben didn't say much. He was very vague, but he didn't sound concerned. Jane will call us when she gets a chance."

Did she have a heart attack or not? Maybe there was nothing serious to worry about. After the brief conversation, I went back to sewing. As I paused to stroke back a lock of light-brown hair, tears began to roll down my cheeks. After no word from Jane and numerous attempts to call her, Julie located the telephone number of the hospital and passed it on to me. On Monday morning from work, I called the hospital and spoke briefly to Mama's ICU day nurse, Jason.

"Your mother had a tough night. She was woken up periodically for vital signs. She suffered a massive heart attack and will be in ICU several days. She is stable and is resting comfortably," Jason reported. "Call back at eleven forty-five when she will be awakened for lunch. Meanwhile, you can talk to your sister to find out more. She was with her all night."

I was in stunned disbelief as I attempted to call Jane, only to be greeted by the answering machine. I was upset and furious. Jane should have notified us of the severity of Mama's condition as soon as it was earthly possible.

Simultaneously, Jane called my home. On purpose, I had never shared my work number with her. "Mama is in the hospital. I am taking care of everything," Jane told Ken confidently.

"How is she? What happened?" Ken questioned.

"I'm too tired to talk. I'll call back later," Jane responded.

Ken asked again, "How is she?"

"I'll call back later after I get some sleep," Jane repeated in her familiar demeaning tone and then hung up. She was now fifty-eight with graying hair but was still as mean and provoking as when she was growing up.

Just as I was preparing to call Ken, he phoned. "Jane just called, but she didn't tell me anything new."

"I just talked to Jason, the ICU day nurse. He said Mama had a massive heart attack and is sleeping. I will try to get in touch with her before lunch," I reported, still in disbelief.

As lunchtime approached, I phoned the hospital again. Mama was awake but sounded tired. "This was a big surprise. I had no idea anything like this would happen," she declared.

Mama was very talkative and rambled on about what the hospital was feeding her and all the medications she was on, including one for diabetes, which she did not know she had.

"I need to go home. Jane gave me some books the library was discarding, and I need to move them out of the way." Mama talked as if her heart attack was just a slight bump in the road.

I was happy Mama sounded so optimistic. "You need your rest. I'll call you tomorrow."

That afternoon, Jane called the house and spoke with Ken again. "I have arranged for Elaine to call Mama at three o'clock. You know she had a heart attack?"

"Yes, I know. I will call Elaine," Ken told her. Ken phoned once more, relaying Jane's message.

"I just talked to Mama. There is no reason to disturb her this afternoon. She needs lots of quiet and rest," I expressed.

I was perturbed with Jane. There was no need for her to set my agenda. At first, I was not going to call; but as the afternoon progressed, I reconsidered. Mama may have been waiting for the call orchestrated by Jane. Before leaving for home, another call was placed.

Jason picked up the phone. "Hello, Jason," I said as I identified myself and informed him I was calling to check on my mother. "Did my sister make arrangements for me to call at three?"

"No," replied Jason. I knew that question sounded strange. Jason gave a brief rundown on how Mama's day had gone.

Before speaking to my mother, I felt I had to say something about Jane's mental status. "Before you transfer me, I need to talk to you." Having not planned what to say, I blurted out, "Jane is a fruitcake. If she starts acting strange or you need to talk to someone else about our mother's condition, our younger sister, Julie, or I should be called."

Jason opened up. "We are having problems with your sister. Dr. Nelson was having a hard time talking to your mother with her there." Jason went on describing Jane's actions. "She was telling us what we should do and bullied the night nurse, who is a small Filipina lady. She tried the same on me too, but I don't intimidate. I'm over six feet tall and can hold my own."

Jason made note of my phone number before transferring the call. After a short conversation with Mama, I drove home to be greeted by Ken, who had just arrived home himself. "There is a message on the answering machine to call a Dr. Nelson," he mentioned.

"He is Mama's cardiologist. I told Mama's day nurse we should be called regarding her care. He said Jane is—"

Just then, the phone rang. Not bothering to complete my thought, I picked up the receiver.

"This is Dr. Nelson. Your mother is under my care." Choosing his words carefully, trying not to offend, he continued speaking. "I'm having problems communicating. Your sister wants your mother released, to go home, which would not be good. She needs to be transferred to Westbrook. We do not have the right type of equipment here in our small hospital. The hospital in Westbrook has an excellent CCU. I recommend she be transported as soon as possible. Your sister is standing in the way. We have lost valuable time. Every time I try to explain a procedure to your mother, your sister interferes and has become a big hindrance."

Dr. Nelson was upset. He proceeded speaking quickly in an excited voice. "She was trying to give orders for your mother's care, questioning the medications I prescribed, along with my judgments. She called me a quack."

Dr. Nelson proceeded to give his credentials. "I taught at a medical school for a number of years. If my mother had been in this situation, she would have been taken to Westbrook the first night and would have already had a procedure." Dr. Nelson went on talking briskly and started repeating himself. Jane's behavior had turned this doctor into a babbling, nervous wreck.

Jane's goal had been to be a nurse. Jane talked with authority, and therefore, our mother thought she knew what was best.

Perfectly understanding the circumstances, I interrupted, "You don't need to explain any further. I can relate exactly to what you are saying." Words could not describe the wrath of Jane when she was in a rage. She was very aggressive and could be extremely unreasonable.

"My sister Julie has our mother's medical and legal power of attorney," I volunteered. "You should talk to her about making decisions regarding our mother's health care." I gave him Julie's phone number.

Dr. Nelson called Julie immediately. For the most part, the conversation was a repeat of his discussion with me. By then, he had become more relaxed in expressing his feelings. "I don't have to put up with the *bullshit!*" he exclaimed in frustration. He went on to give Julie test results and explained our mother's dire condition further.

It was obvious she needed specialized care, which the cardiac care unit in Westbrook could provide. Julie reassured him she would talk to our mother right away about being transported.

Jane's behavior was not surprising. Julie and I were concerned our mother was allowing Jane to control the situation. It did not make sense to have lifesaving care withheld. Nevertheless, the decisions being made were not up to Jane. She had always thought being the oldest afforded her special privileges, which unequivocally included being the "boss."

Julie phoned our mother right away. "Mama, this is kid number 3. How are you feeling?"

"Weak," she replied. "I don't know what to do. Jane wants to take me home." She was not the forceful, strong-willed, decision-making machine Julie had known her to be.

Julie was no stranger to tough medical decisions. It had only been four years earlier since Doug had been stricken with pancreatic cancer. "Well, Mama," Julie proceeded, "the first thing we need to do is make sure you are well enough to be at home. I think we'd better get you to Westbrook."

Much to Julie's surprise, she readily agreed. To reinforce the decision to transfer to the better equipped hospital, I called Mama. "There is no doubt in my mind. You should follow Dr. Nelson's advice," I stated.

"Jane is against the transfer," Mama expressed.

"Your condition is serious, and you need to be where you can receive the best available care. Since Jane is complicating your transfer, it is best for you to be moved without her knowing," I suggested with trepidation. I could envision Jane appearing in an irate state, causing a horrible scene and trying to sabotage the transfer.

On Tuesday morning when Jane appeared at the ICU unit, she was enraged to find our mother was not there. Julie and I felt badly about the deception but knew it was necessary to keep Jane from interfering.

Julie was feeling peace of mind in the satisfaction of knowing our mother had been moved where state-of-the-art equipment was at the doctor's disposal. The calm was squelched when Jane called, yelling, "They'll kill her! You are stupid, stupid, STUPID! You don't know anything about medical things!"

Jane called Julie back that evening. "I have the phone number for the Westbrook Hospital, but I don't have time to give it to you. I'm late for choir practice." She hung up. Julie already had the number; she was not at Jane's mercy for locating information.

Dr. Conway, Mama's new cardiologist, talked to her about the possibility of having bypass surgery. Her brother, Andy, had a bypass several years previously. She had seen graphic pictures of his operation. "It looked like when you gut a deer," she told Julie. The thought of having to go through such invasive surgery scared her.

Dr. Conway kept in close contact with Julie. "Bypass surgery is continuing to be researched. It depends on if there are any healthy areas to which the bypass can be attached." Julie took notes as he explained details of our mother's condition.

Gerald Hanes's eldest son, Michael, was a physician. Julie wasted no time contacting him. She repeated everything Dr. Conway conveyed. "Your mother seems otherwise healthy for a woman her age," Michael stated. "It depends if further research shows a bypass to be beneficial."

Mama agreed to have the surgery. Later that day, Dr. Conway contacted Julie, revealing his findings. "Unfortunately, your mother is not a candidate for bypass surgery. The front part of her heart is not functioning, and there is nowhere to take the bypass. Your mother has less than a year to live."

The expectation of our mother's recovery was gone, and now there would be other difficult issues. Because Julie and I did not call Mama just to say "Hi," months passed without hearing from one another. Even though we did not take the subject lightly, we had previously joked about Jane keeping our mother's death a secret when she eventually died, maybe not notifying us until after she was buried. If that thought was shared with anyone else, it would have sounded absurd, but Jane was capable of such behavior. It was feasible for Jane to keep our mother's death a secret for a short time anyway, at least long enough for her to help herself to Mama's possessions. Jane believed that because she was the oldest, she was entitled to everything. At least now nothing close to that scenario would take place. Our biggest concern was how Jane would function without our mother's stabilizing presence.

Julie spoke to our mother's attorney, James King, over the phone. "You can invoke your power of attorney now to take care of your mother's affairs. Making arrangements now for her final expenses will make things easier later on," he told her.

After dinner, Julie checked her e-mails and came upon a horrible message from Jane, accusing her of all sorts of terrible things, such as wanting our mother to die and wanting her money, possibly projecting her own demented thoughts. The situation was difficult enough, and now it was compounded with Jane's ridiculous accusations.

That evening, I received a call from Dr. Conway, saying my mother was very ill; and if I wanted to see her, now was the time to come.

I was being bombarded with bad news. Just before Mama's heart attack, I had been diagnosed with arterial fibrillation and had been bouncing from doctor to doctor with my own ordeal. I had been admitted to the local hospital the previous week for constant monitoring to determine a safe medication dosage. The day before Dr. Conway's call, I had traveled to a large city for a consultation with an electro cardiologist. He recommended I remain on heart medications and be monitored by my cardiologist.

Dr. Conway gave the impression Mama could die anytime. There was a fresh heavy snowfall on the mountain passes, which influenced our decision to wait until the weekend before making the trip.

Ken and I left early Saturday morning, making our way steadily over the icy mountain pass into Trenton and then on to Blackburn and finally Westbrook, arriving at three thirty that afternoon.

Patients' rooms in the CCU occupied the circumference around the nurse's station. We could see Mama in a room to the left. She saw us in return and waved. A monitor displayed a constant heartbeat reading, along with her blood pressure and pulse. An IV was taped to her hand.

"It is good to see you, but you didn't need to come," she expressed.

Her remark caught me off guard. Did she realize the severity of her condition? She appreciated the soft blanket I brought and was pleased to receive the framed picture Claudia's mother had taken of her last summer at the wedding. She hardly resembled the healthy person, who just four months previously attended Jack and Claudia's wedding.

Mama related what had happened to her in detail. "After church services, I went to the car to bring in a cake I had baked for the potluck. I barely made it through the door. Someone rescued the cake as a tall man carried me to a chair, like one would carry a small child. Another church member who lives across the street ran home and brought back an aspirin. She saved my life. I told them not to call an ambulance and to take me home, but it was too late. Someone had already called 911, and an ambulance was on its way."

She had been feeling excruciating pains throughout the services but did not say anything. Her general philosophy was *ignore it, and it will go away.* She was an eighty-one-year-old independent widow, not taking any prescription medications, and did not even have a primary care doctor.

Mama desperately wanted to see her pastor. "Elaine, will you contact Pastor Bedford for me and let him know where I am? I would really like to see him."

A smiling nurse entered Mama's room, announcing, "Visiting hours are over. They ended at four o'clock." It was already four thirty.

"Oh," I said in embarrassment. I had not realized we had overstayed our visitors' privileges.

"You just got here, so we let you stay a few minutes longer. You will be allowed back in at six."

We checked into a nearby motel and then walked over to a dinner, returning to see Mama precisely at six o'clock. We visited briefly, but Mama was getting tired. We left to let her rest. On the way out, we met Pastor Bedford coming up the hall, looking for the CCU. "Do you know how Jane is handling this?" I asked.

"She is doing okay. Come to think about it," Pastor Bedford replied. "One thing seemed kind of strange to me. I called to let her know her mother had fallen ill and was on the way to the hospital in an ambulance. She said they had just sat down to have their lunch and would go to the hospital when they were finished eating. It seemed rather out of the ordinary that she took her time getting there."

On Sunday morning, we returned to Mama's hospital room. "Dr. Conway will be coming by soon to make his rounds, if you would like to wait and meet him. It shouldn't be too long," she said.

A short time later, a mature, robust man in a white lab coat entered. "Hello, I'm Dr. Conway," he said, introducing himself while shaking our hands. He went directly to Mama's status. "The blockage was extensive, much worse than originally thought. She had angioplasty, and three stents have been inserted. However, only one of the stents is functional. The myocardial infarction caused a lot of permanent damage to her heart. At this time, bypass surgery is too risky and probably wouldn't help."

Mama sat calmly in a bedside chair, appearing to be relieved she would not be facing surgery.

"You have less than a year to live. The medications will provide quality of life, not quantity. It is all in God's hands."

Matter-of-factly, Mama replied, "I am not afraid of dying. Whenever He wants me, I'm ready to go."

The room was silent after Dr. Conway's exit. Ken and I were uneasy, while Mama did not show signs of concern. Time was flying, and we needed to get on the road to make the long drive back. We said our goodbyes. "I will notify Uncle Andy, Aunt Lorie, and Aunt Rebecca," I stated.

"No, don't bother them," she replied.

She was the oldest of her brother and two surviving sisters, who lived on the West Coast. They kept in touch by e-mail and would be wondering why they had not heard from her lately.

As children, we learned to always obey without question. Contacting Mama's siblings was the right thing to do. After making that defying decision, Andy beat me to the punch. He had received an e-mail from Jane.

"As you know, Mama had a massive heart attack." There was silence.

He continued speaking in a solemn tone, slowly answering, "We got this e-mail from Jane, saying Marie was in the hospital but was doing okay."

I filled him in on the details as best I could.

"How are all of you *girls* doing?" Andy asked.

"Jane is not cooperating," I replied with frustration from fresh memories of the problems Jane was causing and the hateful things she was saying to Julie.

Andy took it lightly. "It's just sibling rivalry."

"Jane is interfering with life-and-death decisions," I expressed. Apparently, our mother's siblings had never been told the extent of Jane's problems.

* * *

Mama had stabilized and was ready to be released, provided someone could help her at home. Jane called me, complaining of the inconvenience it would cause her to bring Mama home. "Going to pick up Mama will interfere with my work hours! She will just have to stay there until I can get away!" Jane exclaimed.

Back home, Julie was spending an evening out with Gerald. As they were entering a restaurant, her cell phone went off. It was Jane.

"I'm going to quit my job," Jane announced.

Catching Julie off guard, her immediate response was "Don't quit your job." She knew Jane's financial resources were limited.

"You can't tell me what to do!" Jane screeched as she indignantly ended the conversation.

Jane only worked several hours a week, though Julie had assumed she worked considerably more. Her major source of income was received from Social Security disability benefits because of her mental illness.

CHAPTER FIVE

Julie Arrives

Believing our mother's time was near, Julie made arrangements to visit her prior to her discharge. Julie spent every possible moment with our mother. When she was up to it, Julie assisted her with short walks down the hall and back. Mama instructed Julie to contact Samuel Harrison with Golden Insurance, where she had a long-term care policy.

Julie's trip was heaven-sent; she would be there to drive our mother back to Blackburn, eliminating the burden on Jane. Mama was delighted to be home. It was time to take care of some loose ends she had postponed for ages. "Julie, will you do me a few favors? There is some old grain fertilizer in the back seat of my car. Will you clean it up where it has spilled and throw it out?"

Julie meticulously scooped up the spilled contents of the broken fertilizer bag from the floorboard of the back seat and tossed it in the dumpster for the condo complex.

Mama had another request. "The top box in that stack next to the dresser contains arsenic. It was left over from when your father did taxidermy work. It needs to be discarded."

Julie saw to the proper disposal of the arsenic but was curious as to why her mother had not gotten rid of it ages ago. "Why didn't you have Jane help you dispose of the arsenic before now?" Julie asked her.

"Jane might breathe it in and get sick," she replied.

That answer hit Julie over the head like a ton of bricks. Why was she concerned about Jane getting sick but not worried she could get sick? In truth, she probably did not trust what Jane might do with the toxin.

Julie had endured as much heartache as she could handle from the loss of Doug and had been in grief counseling from time to time. Because of the lack of childhood memories, her counselor thought she displayed characteristics of a person who had been abused and abandoned. Julie was confused from this observation. She considered her family to be stable with caring parents.

Julie's counselor thought perhaps this characteristic resulted from the many times Doug had been gone for extended periods throughout his career. Julie never felt abandoned by Doug and did not resent his absences. Even though they had no children, she was very busy keeping up with the obligations that went along with being the wife of an officer as well as her full-time job and working toward a college degree.

Something went off in Julie's head. The counselor's observation had nothing at all to do with Doug. Maybe she had been abandoned as a child, in a sense. Jane had demanded a lot of attention and got it. Maybe Julie did not consciously recognize she lacked attention. The focus was on Jane's needs, especially after her mental illness had been acknowledged. She began to think about her childhood. We were not encouraged to express ourselves. In fact, the opposite was true. Our parents' philosophy was *children are to be seen and not heard.*

Julie snapped out of her daze. Mama was taking this opportunity to tell her important things. "The original to my new will is hidden in a brown manila envelope in that cardboard box at the foot of my bed." Mama pointed to a box that was peeking out from under a towel and some sheets. She had been postponing updating her will, which had become obsolete when the farm was sold. Previously, I had been appointed the executor of her will and had told her I preferred Julie be assigned. The discovery of my heart condition must have motivated Mama to no longer delay the task, which couldn't have been timelier.

"Look over the will and the power of attorney documents," she directed. Mama shared information regarding where money had been stashed and other financial matters.

"May I make copies of your keys so we can get in your condo if we need to?" Julie asked, foreseeing future necessity.

"Yes, that is a good idea," she agreed.

Julie was relieved. With Mama's permission, she promptly had several sets of keys made.

That evening after going to bed, Mama started having difficulty breathing and was extremely clammy. "We need to call Dr. Nelson," Julie insisted.

"No, don't bother him. I'll be okay," Mama stated.

In spite of Mama's wishes, Julie called to speak to a nurse, who directed her to give Mama a nitroglycerin tablet from a supply she had received from the hospital. "Take this tablet. It should help," stated Julie as she handed Mama the nitroglycerin. She put the tablet under her tongue, but her irregular breathing did not subside.

"We need to call the doctor," Julie stated again.

"Give me another nitroglycerin tablet and let me rest. I don't want you to call the doctor."

There was no improvement, and Julie was getting anxious. She persisted in trying to persuade Mama to consult her doctor. "You can call the nurse," she reluctantly agreed.

It took an eternity for the nurse to return Julie's page. After describing Mama's symptoms, the nurse replied, "An ambulance is needed. Call 911 without delay. Your mother is having another heart attack."

A sea of boxes blocked the sliding glass door of Mama's bedroom that faced the street. Julie removed the boxes to open the quickest path through which the medics could enter. After unlocking the bars that protected the sliding glass door, the entry was accessible. The medics arrived, swiftly transferring Mama to a gurney, and rushed her to the hospital. As the ambulance disappeared, Julie stood in the cold, dark night, scrapping the heavy layer of frost from the windshield of the rental car. It was midnight as Julie made her way to the hospital.

If Julie had not been there, our mother would have never called for help and may have died that night. It was fortunate her first heart attack occurred while at church; otherwise, she would not have called for help then either.

Foreseeing the inevitable, the following morning, Julie set her emotions aside and began to make difficult arrangements to deal with our mother's affairs and prepare for the time when she would be gone. With the power of attorney document in hand, Julie proceeded to the bank. Julie had her name added to the account to permit her to pay Mama's bills. Unbeknownst to Mama, Julie opened a safe-deposit box to ensure safekeeping and accessibility of the new will and to prevent Jane from taking it or playing hide-and-go-seek with it. Mama believed banks could access safe-deposit boxes and did not believe in having one. Julie ventured to the post office to arrange for the mail to be forwarded to her home. Julie then went by the funeral home, where she talked to Mr. Logan, the director, and acquired information and appropriate forms.

Anticipating lack of cooperation from Jane, Julie took one garage door opener for herself and left the other opener on the dining room table for me to take on my next visit. Jane already had her own keys and possession of an opener. A box of checks arrived in the mail the previous day. Julie took our mother's checkbook and most of the checks, leaving a book at the condo.

Julie reluctantly returned to her obligations, while Mama remained in the Blackburn County Hospital. Before leaving, she paid Mama a farewell visit. She hugged Mama goodbye, telling her she needed to catch her flight home, and informed her she had arranged for her mail to be sent to her home. "I will take care of your affairs until you are feeling better," she explained.

Mama expected to go home from the hospital soon, however, was disappointed when her release date kept being moved back. She would be spending Thanksgiving in the hospital. The evening before Thanksgiving, Dr. Nelson spoke with Julie over the phone. "Your mother has less than two months to live. The angioplasty did no good, and congestive heart failure is resulting. Her EKG looks awful. I would not be surprised if she died within one month." He recommended in home care; however, he would not release her at this time because Mama could not take care of herself. It was time to send her to a long-term care facility. He suggested Chaparral.

Our three adult children, along with spouses and grandchildren, filled our home for Thanksgiving. "I want to see Grandma before it's too late," stated Angelia. Early Friday morning, Angelia and Calvin gathered Clara and Mathew, along with Stacy, to visit her grandmother.

Because of road conditions, it took longer to arrive in Blackburn than anticipated. Mama was delighted to see everyone; she especially enjoyed seeing her great-grandchildren. The group spent the night in a motel room. After bidding Mama a quick goodbye the following morning, they were on their way back to Bingham and would leave out early the next day to return home.

CHAPTER SIX

Chaparral Health Care Center

I notified Mama we were planning to visit her the coming weekend. "Justin and his children and Jack and Claudia are coming as well. Do you mind if we bring sleeping bags for the kids and stay at the condo?"

"All right, and while you are here, you can cut my hair. Jane has made arrangements to transfer me to a nursing home in Trenton. I will not be here when you come. Dr. Nelson doesn't practice in Trenton. I will have a new doctor. I prefer to keep Dr. Nelson. I really like him, but Jane thinks he is inexperienced and doesn't know what he is doing." Mama continued talking about how she did not know anyone at the Trenton home and stated she would rather not be moved there.

"Is there another place you would prefer to be?" I asked.

"Yes. I know of a nice rehabilitation center in Hasher. There is a couple who goes to my church. Her ninety-three-year-old mother lives there. I could keep my own doctor. Nobody asked me what I want!"

"Is it too late to change facilities?" I asked as I heard someone talking in the background.

"The discharge nurse is here," Mama responded.

The nurse came on the phone. "Your mother says she doesn't want to go to the home in Trenton. I would like to place her where she wishes."

"Is it possible to send her to Chaparral in Hasher?" I asked.

"She was scheduled to be moved this afternoon. There may not be an open room at Chaparral. I will call around to see what options are available."

"The arrangements should be coordinated though my sister, Julie," I commented.

Complying with our mother's wishes, Julie finalized the arrangements for the transfer to Chaparral after learning it held a five-star rating. It was confirmed to be a good choice by Gail, her old high school friend, whose husband was a caseworker for the area.

Jane was livid. She called Julie at work, yelling, "You aren't competent to make those decisions! The home in Trenton is better! I stayed there for a while when I was convalescing, and I know firsthand it is a good place! I know the doctors there, and they are very good. Mama should go to the home in Trenton!" Jane's attempt to intimidate Julie failed. She was overruled once more.

After our mother was transferred to Chaparral, I phoned to confirm our plans for coming. Mama loved being there and sounded very happy. "This is a new wing. In fact, I'm the first person to occupy this room. It has a beautiful view of the mountains, and I like my roommate."

The garage door opener needed to enter Mama's condo was in Jane's keeping. Jane was called to let her know we were coming and would be stopping by to borrow her opener that evening.

Upon arriving at Jane's ramble shack small apartment that evening, everyone got out of the vehicles and gathered in the alley around the door that Jane used. Ken tapped on the door. Jane appeared with curlers in her hair and was wearing a bathrobe. "You woke me up."

Ken spoke. "We need to get the garage door opener for the condo."

"Just a minute," Jane said as she vanished inside, leaving everyone standing in the cold alley. A few minutes later, she appeared with the opener.

"We will return it early in the morning," I said, unimpressed with Jane's hospitality.

Upon entering the condo, our family group was greeted by a familiar pungent, musty smell. I had hoped the odor would go away when our mother moved from the farm. The kitchen counter was covered with dishes and utensils. There were remnants of dried dill around the sink, counter, and floor, left over from one of Jane's visits. The dining room table was fairly neat. Julie had cleared most of the table and tossed a considerable amount of junk mail on her last visit. The garage door opener Julie left was not in sight. It was rather obvious Jane had taken it.

The condo resembled a warehouse with boxes taking a fair amount of space throughout. Mama had been there nearly two years and was still trying to sort and organize the remainder of her belongings.

Justin and his children rolled their sleeping bags out onto the living room floor, while Jack and Claudia occupied the once spacious guest room, which was overcome with stacks of boxes.

Ken and I stayed in Mama's master bedroom. Five large dressers hugged the walls. All of them were untidy with items scattered in disarray across the dresser tops. The boxes that had blocked the sliding glass entrance prior to the medic's visit were back against the door. A low row of boxes piled with indistinguishable items lined the foot of the bed. Behind the boxes stood a large closet with sliding mirrored doors that took up the entire north wall. How could Mama ever find anything?

Sunday morning revealed a new layer of freshly fallen snow. Everyone jumped out of bed and scrambled to get ready. After a quick fast-food breakfast, a stop at Jane's was in order.

Again, Jane met everyone at the door, leaving us standing outside. With the opener in hand, I spoke. "We brought back the door opener. Julie said there was an extra one on the dining room table. Do you know where it is?"

Jane hesitated, wanting to say no, but it would have been obvious she was lying. "Yes, I have it."

"Then do you mind if we keep this one so we don't have to bother you the next time we come?" I asked.

"No!" she snapped. "Mama doesn't want you to have it. She wants me to know when people are there." I did not want to have a confrontation in front of my children and grandchildren. Jane was handed the opener, and we left to seek the Chaparral Health Care Center.

Our upbeat group headed for Hasher on the snow-packed rural highway. Out in the middle of nowhere, we came upon a group of isolated buildings. It was the Chaparral Care Center complex. Everyone piled out of the vehicles and scampered for Mama's room. Our group inundated Mama at once. She was elated to see everyone.

I was shaken to see how frail Mama looked sitting in a wheelchair, receiving oxygen through plastic tubing. A portable oxygen unit was attached to the rear of her wheelchair. A wall divided the room down the center, allowing both occupants their own window view. Mama's half of the room was crowded with our entourage.

A passing nurse suggested we go to the dining area to spread out. Mama was too weak to wheel herself down the long corridor. Justin took charge, pushing her steadily to the distant room. Mama was presented with a conglomeration of items, including new slippers and a sweat suit. It was like an early Christmas. Pictures were taken as we visited. Eleven-year-old Glen eagerly told his great-grandmother his latest corny jokes.

The guys stayed in the dining room and brought out their laptop to play games, while the gals retreated back to Mama's room to give her a beauty treatment. I washed and cut her hair, while Claudia gave her a manicure.

Throughout the visit, we chatted continuously. Mama was in good spirits and displayed her sense of humor. Her brother, Andy, and sisters, Lorie and Rebecca, had been taking turns calling. Along with them, Albert's children and church members, she had plenty of company.

A nurse stopped briefly. "Your mother has improved greatly from when she first arrived. She should be well enough to go home soon."

The idea of Mama going home soon did not seem realistic. She could not even stand by herself, except with the help of a walker, and she needed assistance getting up. She would have to improve a great deal before I would feel at ease with that happening.

It was almost time for lunch and time for us to leave. Mama was happier than words could describe. She thoroughly enjoyed the invasion. "You can do this again," she said.

I lingered to say goodbye again. I told her of the conversation with Jane patrolling her condo. As I suspected, Mama had not assigned Jane authority over the garage door openers.

I did not feel comfortable leaving her there; but it was time to join the rest of my family, who were outside, engaged in a snowball fight.

CHAPTER SEVEN

Staying the Course

Jane e-mailed Julie about my family visit:

> Ken and Elaine were here. Mama said she does not
> want them having a garage door opener because it is
> needed here and she does not want to buy another one. I
> told Ken we want to have them check before coming in.
> Both may or may not be true. So you are not the only one
> getting the brunt of my terribleness.
>
> It has not been easy. I have loads of house work to
> do. When this all happened I had four or five bowls of
> fruit I was making into jam. I prepared 7 or 8 jars but
> the rest had to be dumped.
>
> I'm very glad Mama is ok. We wouldn't know how
> to act without her around to referee everything, would
> we? I'm the boss. No you're not. So who is to blame? No

one. Then why fight? It's the luck of the Irish, that's it. Hit um slug um.

I am doing my best for Mama. What were you going to do? Have her die on the operating table just because some zealous people wanted practice with the knife?

We can work together and not walk over each other. You think you need to have some kind of power position in the whole mess, maybe you can understand that even if you are making the final decisions if those decisions are bad, we all will have to suffer the consequences.

I didn't know if we could even budge her out of the hospital room, getting weaker and weaker. You can tell donkeys some things but you can't tell them much and since we belong to the best donkey family around I guess we should all put up or shut up.

Julie was making health decisions as responsibly as anyone could and discussing them with our mother every step of the way. Jane's behavior was wearing thin on Julie.

Julie noticed Mama's checkbook revealed $10 contributions to many nonprofit organizations, about five or so a month. These organizations covered things from "Save the Whales" to political contributions for out-of-state politicians. It was curious she gave to so many causes but did not send Christmas or birthday gifts or even cards to her own grandchildren or great-grandchildren.

The first week in December had passed. Mama was stronger and was hoping to be home before Christmas. Ellen, the administrator at Chaparral, suggested she be moved to assisted living. Mama was planning to go home and was not considering other options.

Four days before Christmas, our mother had improved enough to be moved to a room with a kitchenette. She was required to demonstrate she could cook for herself before being released.

"They are trying to teach me to cook pancakes. I never eat pancakes, and now I can't keep them down anyway," she told me.

January 2005 was here. Dr. Nelson planned to do an echocardiogram sometime in the coming week to give him a better idea of our mother's present prognosis. "She won't be released from the nursing home until I give the green light," he informed Julie. "Ten days ago, she looked great. Four days ago, she had declined a little. There is roughly a 30 percent chance of her dying in the New Year." Our mother's life was on a countdown, even though her doctors were not consistent with their guesses.

I called Mama, "We will be coming to see you this weekend. I would also like to meet Dr. Nelson."

"You can use the condo," she offered. "Chaparral is planning to discharge me January 18."

"The discharge nurse is pushing to have Mama go into assisted-living quarters," Julie informed. "Ellen, the discharge administrator, is surprised Mama wants to go home. Can you and Ken move Mama's belongings to assisted living?"

The thought of being alone with no one to take care of her was irrelevant as far as Mama was concerned. She would never go willingly into assisted living in a million years. In my mind, I envisioned Mama holding on to a bedpost for dear life, refusing to budge as her fingers were forcibly pried loose and being carried out, screaming—a scene that was portrayed to me by Marion, a previous supervisor, who was describing what had to be done when her frail Swedish grandmother was no longer capable of living alone.

"We don't have a choice," stated Julie. "Mama cannot manage by herself."

Ellen was called regarding the assisted-living facilities and apartments. From the description, I knew the limited space would be too confining. The idea of moving Mama into a tiny place against her wishes would be a horrendous undertaking. What about the condo and its contents that would not fit in the assisted-living quarters? The thought of it all made my head spin.

Mama had an episode of breathing difficulty and was transported by ambulance to the Blackburn Hospital during the night.

Ken and I left to see Mama early Friday morning. Julie had sent me an extra garage door opener that she had purchased. It was not programmed yet. We needed to deal with Jane again.

We arrived at Jane's apartment early afternoon. "Can I come along with you to the hospital?"

"Sure," I agreed.

"I need to get my coat." Again not inviting us in, she disappeared back into her apartment. She reappeared wearing a long old blue ragtag coat that went down to her ankles. On her head was a plaid scarf that had been folded in a triangle and tied under her chin like we used to wear when we were kids in the fifties.

Jane gave directions to the hospital and took the lead to our mother's room on the second floor. I began to chat with Mama, while Jane stood quietly, leaning against the wall, censoring the conversation. Mama was coughing a lot, which was very frustrating to her. "If I could just get this cleared out of my chest, I would be fine. They brought me here because they thought I was having another heart attack, but I knew I wasn't. Now that I am here, they are going to see what they can do about this cough."

Mama continued to speak. "I need to get home. I can't keep going back and forth from the hospital to Chaparral. Dr. Nelson was here a short time ago. He would like to talk to you kids while you are here. You can go over to his office later this afternoon. It is within walking distance from here."

"It is getting late. I have lots of things to do, and I don't want to talk to Dr. Nelson," Jane said sheepishly. "Ken, will you take me home? I'll call you in the morning," she said, giving me a glance. They left while I remained with Mama.

"Jane has been making things especially difficult for everyone," I mentioned. "Jason, the ICU nurse, told us she was giving orders to the nurses. She was very obnoxious the night of your heart attack."

"I didn't know Jane was giving them a hard time," she replied, shirking off any signs of being perturbed by Jane's inappropriate behavior.

"Julie and Jane are in a power struggle. Jane is acting mean, just like when we were kids," I revealed.

The opportunity came up to express my frustrations of growing up with Jane. I talked about how Jane hogged the double bed we shared as kids. "She would kick me to move over so she could sprawl out, allowing only a narrow strip on the edge of the mattress for me to lie on. I started kindergarten with scabs all over my hands from Jane's clawing with her long, sharp fingernails." This was evidenced by faint jagged scars that could still be seen on the backs of my hands. Reminiscing, I talked about fighting with Jane when we were children. "Jane was always starting fights, and when I tried to defend myself, I got spanked."

"Why didn't you tell me?" Mama asked genuinely.

I told on Jane all the time, but Mama never listened. Jane's excessive fighting and tormenting of Julie and me had been viewed as normal sibling spats. *How could you really not know?* I thought. *Weren't my scratch marks and scab-covered hands a clue?* Instead, all I could say as I remembered being intimidated by my domineering mother was "I was just a little kid."

Ken finally returned. A nurse came in to check on Mama and asked us to leave for a while. We walked down the hall and found the ICU, where we met Jason. We introduced ourselves and apologized for Jane's behavior. He was very gracious. "People get upset and act strangely in times of crisis," he said.

It was approaching 5:00 P.M. and time to meet Dr. Nelson. We left Mama to rest and walked over to a nearby complex of offices. As the last patient left and his staff bid him good evening, Dr. Nelson joined Ken and me in the waiting room. I could see where Jane thought Dr. Nelson was inexperienced as he had a young appearance. A closer look revealed him to be in his forties and short in stature. His lack of size gave Jane a sense of superiority and reason to try to dominate him.

"Your mother is a delightful lady," Dr. Nelson began, turning to a serious discussion. "Yesterday we did an electrocardiogram. It was a disaster. Her heart is functioning below the lowest level the machine can register."

He estimated her heart function to be around 20 percent. As he went on describing one bad thing after another, I asked, "If it is so bad, how could she still be alive?"

"That is the typical question of a first-year med student. Her heart has become much enlarged. It is a natural way for the body to compensate to pump enough blood."

Dr. Nelson then said, "I would not be surprised if she died tomorrow. She could last another six months. I spoke with Dr. Conway recently. He was surprised she is still alive."

"Can anything be done to stop her coughing?" I asked. "She said there is something in her chest she is trying to cough up."

"There is nothing to cough up. That is the sensation she has from the fluid collecting around her heart. Her heart is too weak to keep the lungs clear. It is developing into congestive heart failure. She has been given diuretics to help get rid of excess fluid, and that should relieve her coughing."

"If we are lucky, she will go just like that in an instant. If she lingers, she will die from the congestive heart failure. That is hardest, to watch them suffer," he said.

Oh my gosh, I thought. Mama kept saying she was getting better. The discussion then turned to getting Mama home. She definitely did not want to go in assisted living. "Is she a candidate for hospice?" Ken asked.

"Marie has been a candidate for some time, and that is a possibility. I am the head of the local hospice board and can arrange for assistance. Hospice nurses will monitor her vital signs and provide most of the medications. They come in two or three times a week to help bathe, care for hair, and check things in general. Your sister would have to agree to spend the nights and check on her periodically throughout the day."

I was confident Mama would agree to in-state hospice care. It would be an enormous relief not to face moving her to assisted living.

With Jane being a topic in the conversation, more of the events following Mama's admission to the hospital back in November were learned.

"Your sister was attempting to locate discharge papers. She insisted her mother be released. Security had to be called to remove her. It would have been fatal for your mother to leave at that time," Dr. Nelson stated.

Upon our arrival back in Mama's hospital room, she asked, "What did Dr. Nelson have to say?"

"The echocardiogram was not good." I made up something about the will to live. I certainly was not going to tell her she could die tomorrow for all the doctor knew.

"Dr. Nelson said you could be released to go home if you agreed to have hospice come in to monitor and help you. However, Jane also has to stay with you at night," I explained.

"Jane is against getting on hospice," she replied.

"They are there to help you, and Dr. Nelson will not release you to go home unless you are willing to accept hospice care. Jane will have to cooperate," I declared.

"I want to go home. I'll think about using hospice," she replied.

With that prospect, Ken and I left the hospital and went to dinner.

Julie called early Saturday morning. "We need to get Mama to agree to use hospice. She has been eligible for some time," I stated with high hopes.

Julie agreed to talk to her about it. They were very helpful with Doug before he died.

"Jane may be an obstacle though," I told Julie. "She will be calling soon. I'm not looking forward to talking to her about it."

It was a few minutes after 8:30 A.M. when the phone rang. I knew it would be Jane. I braced myself as I picked up the phone and began speaking. "Dr. Nelson has agreed to release Mama under the care of hospice. You will need to spend nights with her for a while."

Jane went ballistic. "I don't want Mama on hospice! They kill people! Everybody in hospice dies! This one hospice nurse was laughing, 'Ha, ha, ha' while she was bathing someone who was dying." Jane's high-pitched, mocking laugh was unsettling as she repeated herself again.

Jane continued going berserk. "Your husband's driving made me sick. He whipped the car around in the parking lot, and it made me dizzy. I'm glad he is your husband and not mine. You have to put up with him, but I don't!"

I broke in. "Jane, let me interrupt for a minute."

"You always do!" she snapped back.

"If Mama is going to come home, she has to be on hospice, and you have to agree to stay with her at night for a while. Don't you want Mama to come home?"

Jane would not settle down. I hung up.

Ken and I stopped by the hospital before leaving for home. Mama was finishing her breakfast as we entered. She had slept well and was feeling better. I mentioned Julie would be contacting her soon.

A nurse entered to clear the breakfast dishes. As she was leaving, Mama hollered at her, "Hey, bring back my applesauce!"

Ken chuckled. That was the most energy we had observed in Mama since the event of her heart attack.

"We need to get going," I announced. "We will be back again. Goodbye for now." We gave her hugs and were on our way.

Julie persuaded her to accept assistance from hospice, and arrangements were initiated for her care. Mama wanted to die at home, and Julie promised her request would be honored.

Ironically, Mama went home on the day that had been set for her release. Julie arranged to have Meals on Wheels bring by a noon meal Monday through Friday.

Jane was given a list of prescription drugs to have filled. The prescription for acid reflux particularly was not to her liking. The pharmacist gave her the name of a nonprescription drug that would work just as well, in her opinion. According to Jane, Dr. Nelson had prescribed a medication that would kill her.

Mama was getting along well with the current arrangements. Alternative plans needed to be found for when she needed around-the-clock care. Ken and I offered to have Mama live with us. We had plenty of room and could arrange for home health care during the day when neither one of us could be around. Mama was not open to moving from Blackburn. We would have to seek other options.

After a week of assisting our mother, Jane sent Julie an e-mail, saying she was tired and could use some help. Taking care of Mama was hard on Jane, but she was not alone. Julie had been spending many hours every week seeing to insurance matters, sorting and tossing junk mail, paying Mama's bills, and talking to nurses and Dr. Nelson.

Jane wanted Mama's mail to be redirected to the condo to receive magazines and newspapers, in pretense for our mother. Julie knew Mama was not up to reading. To satisfy Jane's request, Julie bundled up the magazines and personal mail and sent it to Jane. Jane was complaining about losing things "right and left." It would have been disastrous to depend on her to forward bills and important papers to Julie.

Jane was staying with Mama almost constantly. A lot of her time was spent on the computer and doing her own laundry as her washing machine had broken down. Jane said she had lots to do at home, but Mama needed someone to be with her.

"I need quiet," Mama told Julie. "Tell Jane to give me some space." It seemed strange that she did not tell Jane herself.

Julie complied with Mama's request. "Leave after breakfast to do your personal things. Stay only if you are asked."

"You can't tell me what to do," Jane said begrudgingly.

Jane needed a break, and Mama needed a break from her as well. Julie and I set up a preliminary schedule to relieve Jane. My daughter, Angelia, volunteered to take the first round, beginning January 30 and would leave Thursday, February 3.

One evening I called to talk to Mama, but she was tired. I ended up speaking to Jane. "It is much better having Mama here. The nursing home was not taking good care of my mother. They wouldn't do anything to stop her coughing. Dr. Nelson is not a good doctor. He doesn't know what he is doing. She would be much better off with someone else." Jane continued expounding how incompetent Dr. Nelson was. "Mama is vomiting. I need to go check on her."

* * *

The preliminary planning for our mother's memorial service had begun. Jane had already informed Julie she wanted to sing at the memorial service. As much as we dreaded honoring Jane's request, trying to discourage her would only cause further discord. Jane would choose the songs to be sung and pick out the cover for the program. I had the perfect poem: "Miss Me but Let Me Go." Angelia agreed to read it at the service.

Julie and I compiled information on our mother's life for the obituary. I would keep the ashes until we got our bearings and could plan for spreading them at a future date. The flowers would be selected when a date was known. Everything else for the service was under control.

We had been going through the motions, seeing to the worldly issues, but had not expressed our feelings about Mama dying. Julie will always grieve for Doug and talked about surviving the grief. I knew all about grief also, from losing my newborn son. "I'm okay with her passing," Julie shared with me.

"I have always felt it is harder on the ones left behind. Even though we know things are well for the one passing, it does not keep us from missing them and dealing with the void. Mama told me she had a good life. I'm glad she said that," I replied.

Julie and I discussed the management of our mother's belongings. We needed a plan of action to put in place once she dies. At this point, Julie was mentally exhausted. To anticipate one more thing was too great. Julie suggested Angelia be invited to help come up with a plan.

Angelia willingly agreed to develop a detailed plan of what was needed to be done and assign who would accomplish each chore.

CHAPTER EIGHT

Angelia's Stay with Her Grandmother

Angelia spent the night with us before heading over the mountains the next morning to be with her grandmother. Upon arriving at Mama's home, her aunt Jane greeted her at the door. While Jane loitered aimlessly, Angelia sat and began to visit with her grandmother, who was in the living room, sitting in her favorite brown upholstered chair.

A large mobile oxygen machine stood against the wall next to the television. Mama was receiving oxygen through a long plastic tube.

"I'm here now," Angelia announced to Jane. "You can go home and get some rest."

Jane remained reluctant to leave. She finally left briefly but returned moments later, complaining about the snow and road grime that had fallen from Angelia's truck onto the driveway. Jane decided to sweep the drive, exclaiming, "They are particular how things look around here!"

Jane returned. "It is okay to go now," Mama said. "I'm in good hands."

Jane finally left and phoned Julie.

"You all are just waiting for her to die. IT'S JUST A DEATHWATCH!" she yelled into the phone.

Julie tried to answer her back, "No! No! It's NOT a deathwatch. We just want to assist you in taking care of Mama."

Jane kept interrupting as Julie talked and did not hear a word Julie said. Now that help had arrived, she was envious she had to share Mama's attention.

Angelia helped her grandmother get through lunch and straightened the kitchen. While Mama took an afternoon nap, Angelia took the opportunity to bring in her luggage. Boxes lined one side of the hall leading back to the bedrooms. The boxes obstructed the path and made it difficult for Mama to maneuver her walker.

The next morning, Angelia cleared the long hallway, moving the boxes to the guest room closet. It was exasperating that her grandmother did not want to get rid of anything.

There were still boxes full of junk mail, which Mama never seemed to get around to going through. Angelia eliminated most of it.

Angelia brought her own food to keep things simple. She catered to her grandmother, learning how to fix oatmeal and other things just the way she liked. Mama's appetite was poor. Jane had been eating more of the Meals on Wheels lunches than Mama.

Angelia met the hospice staff Bridget, a young hospice nursing assistant, who came in twice a week to assist with bathing, and Jessica, a tall, pleasant, redheaded nurse. Jessica wore her hair very short in back, but as Angelia described, the front was wild with long curls that fell on her forehead.

Jane appeared periodically unannounced, which Angelia and Mama did not appreciate. Angelia asked Jane to call before she came over and invited her to leave.

Angelia and Jane tangled several times. Angelia responded with logical answers, which got her nowhere. When Jane was on the attack, throwing out insults concerning us, Angelia did not say anything. She smiled and ignored her. Jane ended the degrading, saying she loved us anyway.

During one of Jane's stays, she decided to sing. One song in particular that Jane said she wrote started out "Road kill, eating squirrels . . ." Jane hit some unnatural high, off-key notes. During the performance, Angelia observed her grandmother rolling her eyes and then massaging her temples.

Angelia left the condo briefly several times. During one of her outings, she brought back a cordless phone. When her grandmother received calls, it was an ordeal wheeling her to the phone in the kitchen and keeping her oxygen cord from getting tangled in the cluster of boxes stacked near the phone. The cordless phone was conveniently placed on the end table next to her favorite chair in the living room.

In preparation for Angelia's visit, Julie had sent her a set of keys. Angelia decided an alternate way to enter was needed, especially if a garage door opener was not handy. The back door opened from the living room onto the large shared grassy atrium. A key was safely tucked inside a fake rock Angelia had brought. It was set outside the garden door inconspicuously with a group of real rocks. Even though the combination was known, earlier attempts to access the atrium had failed. It still was not known how the combination worked to get through the tall wrought iron gate.

The afternoon before Angelia left was spent pampering her grandmother with a "spa treatment." Angelia gently applied lotion to her hands and arms. Angelia was troubled to see how her arms and legs had withered away to skin and bone.

Mama began talking about Jane having meningitis when she was a teenager. Meningitis was one excuse, along with several others Jane blamed for her mental illness. "The doctor said not to do anything that would traumatize her and to treat Jane with kid gloves as she was vulnerable while she recovered. I should have spanked her like the other two, and maybe she would have turned out more like them," Mama remarked. The treatment ended in one of Angelia's wonderful massages.

The last day of Angelia's visit arrived. She packed and was getting ready for her departure. Nine o'clock came, and then ten o'clock, and eleven o'clock. Mama was still sleeping. Angelia rubbed her grandmother's hands while tears rolled down her cheeks. The thought that she had died crossed her mind. Angelia kissed her on the forehead, but she still did not budge.

Within inches of her grandmother's face, Angelia said loudly, "Grandma, it's getting kind of late." Angelia was relieved when she woke up with a start. She was surprised it was so late, but she was not quite ready to get up and stayed in bed a little longer.

Mama ate a small lunch. Jane arrived, staying a few minutes, but had to leave for a dental appointment. It was twelve thirty, and Angelia needed to go. Bridget would be there any moment. Angelia gave her grandmother one last long hug. As she drove away, she knew in her heart this was the last time she would see her grandmother.

Angelia arrived at our home in Bingham that evening and reported the events of her stay. She also shared Mama's comments regarding Jane's mental illness being caused by meningitis. I shared my thoughts on the meningitis excuse. "When Jane was in the ninth grade, she started being more weird than usual. She was letting mosquitoes bite her for some kind of *experiment*. She claimed she caught meningitis from a mosquito, and the mental illness resulted. That explanation is rather far-fetched to me. I was aware of Jane being really sick back then but didn't know what it was. She was so caustic to be around Julie, and I stayed clear of her. She had mental issues long before the meningitis excuse."

Angelia left the next morning to rejoin her family. After Angelia had gone home, Jane told Julie she had seen Angelia trying to strangle Mama with the telephone cord.

CHAPTER NINE

A Challenging Visit

"I am changing my plans for staying with Mama," I explained to Julie over the phone. "Rather than going in March, I'm going this weekend. Jane will only have to stay two nights with Mama before I get there."

Ken and I left Bingham early Saturday morning, arriving in Blackburn at nine thirty. I entered the condo, expecting to see Jane, only to be greeted by the constant pumping sound of the oxygen machine instead. Mama was alone, asleep in bed. Jane was nowhere to be seen.

As Ken brought in the luggage, I spoke softly to Mama, receiving no response. An hour later, she finally woke up. Upon dressing, she tucked a folded crisp $50 bill in her pocket, to my amusement. She proceeded slowly down the hall with the assistance of her walker.

"It sure is a lot easier getting down the hall since Angelia removed the boxes," she said. "I'm really thankful she cleared the way."

I was hoping for a quiet afternoon when Jane appeared with Ben. Jane talked about a drive they took, gossiped about a lady's family from her church, and talked about other things that had no relevance to anything in particular.

Jane and Ben joined us for a dinner of roasted chicken that Ken picked up. When the food vanished, so did Jane and Ben. Their departure was Mama's cue to retire to the bedroom.

I assisted her as she struggled to get into her nightgown. "Jane does not help me," she expressed. "She says I need to do things for myself." That was silly. Mama needed help, and I was not going to sit there doing nothing.

After a very long day, it was time to retreat to the guest room. The room was covered in a mass of boxes piled in stacks of two or more. The floor was hardly visible. A path led from the door to the bed. Care had to be taken when an object was laid down; otherwise, it would disappear in the clutter.

A distant train whistle woke me. I had barely gotten up when the telephone rang. It was Jane. "I'll be over later."

"Okay," I answered, not looking forward to Jane's company.

I helped Mama dress and reach her wheelchair safely in the living room, while Ken ate a quick bowl of cereal. As usual, he was anxious to get on the road. On Thursday, Ken would return to bring me home.

I was rarely alone with Mama for any length of time; Jane made sure of that. The last time I could recall, before her heart attack, was shortly before Angelia was born thirty-three years ago. I remembered sitting in the wooden rocking chair at my parents' home while going on three weeks overdue. As I sat there rocking, we talked about the new baby and watched my stomach go in and out of contortions as feet, elbows, or whatever else could be seen protruding under the maternity smock. It was getting considerably uncomfortable as Angelia finally settled down from turning somersaults and intervened with the hiccups.

I remembered the story Mama related about her pregnancy with Jane. Jane had kicked her so much she was black and blue under her ribs. I knew Jane was a kicker from getting kicked every night when I had to sleep with her.

* * *

Mama ate breakfast slowly. While trying to eat my own bowl of cereal, I stopped continually to meet Mama's requests. After breakfast, Mama was seated in her favorite chair in the living room, where she fell asleep.

Jane arrived after lunch. We sat in the living room, talking over the music coming from a little teddy bear Jane kept winding up that played "Home on the Range."

"Will you take me shopping to buy a Walkman for Mama?" I asked. I had brought a meditation tape that Mama was enjoying but had no means for playing when I left.

We left our mother resting in her brown chair as we walked out to Jane's dilapidated, old, rusty brown car. We rode down the street, listening to a rattle that sounded like a bucket of loose bolts rolling around.

"It is shorter to stay on this street," I pointed out as Jane turned toward Main Street.

"I like going my way. Your talking while I'm driving is distracting me."

I took a deep breath, whispering, "Oh brother," to myself.

Even though there were many closer parking places, Jane parked an extraordinary distance from the store's entrance, which was isolated from other cars. "Why didn't you park closer to the entrance?" I questioned.

Laughing, Jane answered, "The way I drive, it is best to park way out here."

I picked up the pace. I wanted to buy the Walkman and get out of Jane's company as soon as possible.

"Slow down. You're making me sick. I can't walk that fast. It makes me dizzy," Jane complained. Jane looked frumpy as she limped along with a scarf on her head. Oblivious to people's stares, Jane trailed behind as we walked through the store, searching for the electronics department. This was not a fun little jaunt like it would have been with Julie.

Jane left shortly after returning to the condo. It was a good time to call my old high school friend Fran, who had helped move Mama to the condo.

After dinner, Mama was helped into bed. I would have liked to turn on the television or radio, but for Mama's consideration, it was kept quiet.

I lay in bed wide-eyed for what seemed all night. The sound of the obnoxious oxygen machine seemed louder now. Not being sure how it worked, I imagined the sounds it made being related to Mama's breathing. Julie's e-mail came to mind:

Remember if something happens and Mama passes when you are there, call Hospice (Push the button that is on a string around her neck). Try not to freak out. Hospice will come and pronounce the death and help from that point on.

Monday morning found Mama sleeping soundly. At nine thirty, she finally woke and dressed with assistance. As she reached for the walker to leave the bedroom, the doorbell rang.

I hurried to the door to find two men standing in the garage, asking for Mama. She slowly made her way down the hall and sat in the wheelchair. Once she was situated, the men were let in. Mama greeted them warmly. Two kitchen chairs that were in the living room were cleared of their contents for the guests to have a place to sit.

The two men were Samuel Harrison and his son, who owned Golden Insurance. They explained the benefits and insurance disbursements from Mama's policy for long-term care. There was a lot of small talk. They were old friends of Mama and Albert.

During their stay, the doorbell rang. It was a flower arrangement delivery of carnations from Fran. Soon after the Harrisons' departure, the Meals on Wheels lady made her delivery.

After lunch, Bridget and Jessica from hospice arrived. I knew who they were immediately from Angelia's descriptions. Bridget took Mama's blood pressure and asked if she wanted a bath, but she declined.

Soon after they left, the doorbell rang again. It was a handsome older couple from Mama's church. They visited for a while, said a prayer, and then left.

Moments later, Jane called. "We are bringing over pizza for dinner. We will be there in about five minutes."

"Okay," I responded, wondering if the steady stream of people would ever end. Soon after calling, Jane and Ben entered carrying two pizzas. Mama ate a small piece, while I helped myself, biting into the cardboard-tasting crust. Ben and Jane gobbled it down as if it was a gourmet meal. Ben watched television most of the time, while Jane and Mama talked about subjects foreign to me as usual. Finally, Jane retrieved what was left of the pizza, and they left.

I began on Tuesday suggesting the yellow dresser from behind Mama's bedroom door be removed to make her bedroom wheelchair accessible. I explained again that it was more practical to be wheeled down the hall when she needed to use the bathroom.

Reluctantly, Mama agreed to the dresser being moved to the living room. "If we empty the dresser, it will be easy to move," I suggested as I was praying Mama would choose to get rid of most of the dresser's contents.

Mama was seated in her brown chair in the living room while each drawer was sorted. Mostly old slips occupied two drawers. They were all past their prime and should have been tossed ages ago. Mama decided to give a number of them away and then decided to keep several, saying, "I might need them."

Old *Writers' Digest* magazines filled another drawer, which Mama said could be given away. A red-and-white crocheted afghan, which she had forgotten she had, occupied the bottom drawer. It was kept out for when she got cold. The dresser was moved to the living room in front of a closet containing the vacuum. The dresser could be scooted easily out of the way.

Mama's need to use the bathroom provided the opportunity to test how well the wheelchair would get through the door. The footrests were in the way as I attempted to wheel her around the corner. They were removed. Upon returning to the living room, I began placing the drawers back in the dresser. I jumped when Jane appeared out of nowhere, shouting and attempting to belittle me. "HOW WOULD YOU FEEL IF SOMEONE WAS GOING THROUGH YOUR PERSONAL THINGS?"

"Mama agreed we needed to make room for the wheelchair to access her bedroom. We had to empty the dresser to move it out of the way," I responded defensively while my heart was still pounding from the abrupt scare.

"Humph!" she grumbled. I was invading her domain.

"I forgot to put the footrests back," I said while walking over to get them.

"I'll do it," Jane said.

"That's okay. I will," I protested.

"I'll do it. I'm the oldest," Jane declared.

"What does being the oldest have to do with anything? You are here all the time to do things for Mama. Let me help for the limited time I am here," I said as I proceeded to attach the footrests.

Mama was amused at the bickering over who would help her. Jane's "I'm the oldest" attitude, which in her mind afforded her privilege over all others, was most annoying. Jane left, announcing she would be back later.

When washing dishes and gazing out the window onto the atrium over the last several days, I observed a neighbor taking her cat for a walk on a leash. "There is a lady out there with a cat," I said.

"Her name is Lotty," Mama informed. "They don't like to have pets running loose."

While Mama rested, I went out to meet Lotty and pet her cat. I enjoyed talking to Lotty about her cat and her daughter. "Do you know how to get the wrought iron gate to release?" I asked. "I know my mother's code, but we haven't been able to get it to open."

"Yes, I use it all the time," replied Lotty and then gave a demonstration.

Jane and Ben appeared at dinnertime, which was becoming a habit.

That evening as Mama was settling in her bed before going to sleep, she started to talk. "I have two normal daughters, and I have one who isn't normal, but she is getting there."

I was tired of Mama continually saying Jane was getting better. I blatantly spoke up. "Jane is not getting *normal*. She will never be *normal*." It surprised me when this came gushing out of my mouth. I hardly ever challenged anything Mama said.

Wednesday was going to be spent cleaning. I planned to clean the house as quickly as possible. Waiting on Mama was wearing me out, and I needed quiet time to rest.

"I'll be over later this morning," Jane announced over the phone.

"Don't come," I told Jane, the self-appointed watchdog, whose presence was not appreciated. "I am going to be busy changing the bedding, washing, and cleaning."

"Aren't you overdoing it?" Jane said in a snotty tone.

"I don't want to leave the house dirty," I responded.

"What about your so-called heart condition?" Jane chided.

It was time for some of her own medicine. "I lied" sprang out of my mouth.

"Well, this is the end of this conversation," Jane remarked.

I chuckled to myself.

On Wednesday morning, while the washer and dryer were running, Jessica and Bridget appeared. Mama still did not want to have a bath or have her hair washed. While Bridget was caring for Mama, I joined Jessica at the dining room table, where she was refilling the pill dispenser with Mama's prescriptions.

"Jane told me she had a pharmacist recommend a different medication for acid reflux because she thought the prescription was too strong," I disclosed.

"I noticed she had substituted the prescription," stated Jessica. "I changed the pills back to the prescription medication that was prescribed, and she has left them alone. She has been interfering with a lot of your mother's care. I was at the hospital the first evening your mother was brought in," Jessica revealed. "Jane was physically trying to remove your mother from her hospital bed. She was pulling on her arm and leg, trying to get her up."

I knew from the discussion with Dr. Nelson Jane had tried to get Mama discharged, but trying to drag her out of bed was news.

"Julie and I have talked. We are concerned about Mama being alone for any length of time," I stated.

"There is a grant that has become available recently for people in your mother's situation. She is a perfect candidate," Jessica explained.

The grant sounded like a godsend, but Mama had previously expressed she did not want people she did not know in her house. I could not see passing up the assistance. "You need help during the day when Jane can't be here. Would it be okay with you if we have home health people come stay with you?"

"Whatever you girls agree on will be fine with me," Mama responded as she sat back with her eyes closed.

"Julie and I know you need more help than hospice and Jane can provide," I insisted, purposely not mentioning Jane, knowing she would challenge the decision. "We are concerned you cannot be left by yourself."

"Okay then, if you think that is best," she replied.

From the list of home health agencies, only Loving Assistance could provide around-the-clock care. Jessica made arrangements for Rosemary, the owner of Loving Assistance, to meet with Mama after lunch. She tried to reach Sarah, the hospice social worker, who also coordinated grants; but Jessica was unable to contact her.

After lunch, Jessica explained how the grant worked, and Rosemary described Loving Assistance's payment policy. The necessary papers were signed to begin care the following morning. Jessica would contact Julie and straighten out the finances. The ladies left after the arrangements had been made.

I confronted Mama with Jessica's rendition of her first night in the ICU. "Jessica told me Jane tried to physically remove you from your hospital bed the night of your heart attack."

"Oh really?" Mama's voice sounded in genuine.

"Don't you remember?" I said, wondering if Mama was playing dumb.

"I don't remember that. I was very tired and goofy from the drugs."

Maybe she had been too drugged to be aware of the situation, but she shrugged off hearing of Jane's efforts to remove her from lifesaving care.

Mama snoozed in her brown chair while the beds were made, and the cleaning was completed. She was cold even though she was wearing a sweater and covered with two afghans. I was sweltering. I stuck my head out the garden door for a moment to get a breath of fresh air.

* * *

Jane was a certified nurse assistant and had been working part time as a home health aide before Mama's heart attack. The agency of Jane's employment provided service only between eight and five on weekdays. Having a different agency care for Mama would create another matter of contention. The dreaded call to Jane could not be postponed indefinitely.

"Hello, Jane," I said as optimistically sounding as possible. "Since I'm leaving tomorrow, we have arranged for a home health aide to stay with Mama to make things easier for you.

A home health person from Loving Assistance will be staying with Mama tomorrow beginning at nine."

I paused, expecting Jane to jump in yelling, but she was silent. "Ken will be here around nine in the morning to take me home. I would like for you to come over and meet the home health aide and say goodbye."

Mount Vesuvius still had not erupted. "Jessica told me about a grant that is available to help defray some of the home health assistance fees. She said Mama meets all the criteria, and all we have to do is apply for it."

"I'm checking into a grant also," Jane stated in a subdued tone. "Hold off on your grant. My grant pays more than yours, and it is a better grant. I have an appointment next Wednesday to learn more."

Shortly after the conversation with Jane, the phone rang. It was Jessica. "Sarah's schedule is full today. She has time next Wednesday. I can represent your mother."

"My sister, Jane, said she is checking into another grant," I expressed.

"I'm aware of only one such grant," Jessica responded.

A short time later, Jessica phoned again, "In talking with Sarah, I learned Jane has made an appointment with her. Routinely, Sarah goes to the client's home, but Jane insisted on meeting in another place, which is unusual."

Jane was conspiring to get home health care for our mother without conferring with Julie or me, besides not wanting Mama to know what she was up to.

"I just spoke with Jessica," I conveyed to Jane over the phone. "The grants are one in the same."

"Mama doesn't want just anybody in her house. I want to use my agency. I know the aides, and I want to handpick the ones to take care of Mama. I'm so angry we better end this conversation before I say something I shouldn't." Jane slammed down the receiver.

Meanwhile, Julie had spoken with Rosemary from Loving Assistance and set up a schedule for a home health aide to be with Mama.

Angrily, Jane called Julie, shouting, "You are so STUPID! I want people I know taking care of Mama during the day! Loving Assistance can come at night!"

"I already asked if that was an option. They said it would be too confusing to have two different agencies involved. Besides, there will be a smaller group of people taking care of Mama, which would be more to her liking," stated Julie.

Jane continued, yelling, "You are a self-appointed boss! You think everything has to be your way! Well, you don't know everything! You don't make good decisions! You—" Julie hung up.

Mama was finishing her dinner when her brother, Andy, called, asking how things were going. "Is Jane giving you a hard time?"

Mama was sitting at the dining room table within several feet. I did not dare express my frustrations. Mama would have gotten very angry if she knew Andy was aware of Jane's actions.

"Yes," I responded. "Would you like to talk to Mama? She is right here."

After their conversation, Mama was given a fresh cup of hot spice tea, while I took out the trash.

My mind was on going home in the morning. Being with Mama for days with a steady diet of Jane, no radio or TV, having little time to myself, exhausted from the constant flow of people and telephone calls, not to mention missing Ken, I was more than ready to get back to my life. It was good breathing in the fresh evening air. Relishing the idea of going home, I had forgotten after Jessica and Rosemary left the door to the garage had been set to lock.

Upon returning and finding the entrance locked, I was highly distressed. Mama was too weak to wheel herself to the door. Thanks to the conversation with Lotty, I entered the atrium. Through the kitchen window, I could see Mama sipping her tea. Angelia's hidden key in the artificial rock was located. I slipped in quietly through the garden door without Mama noticing.

Finally, it was Thursday. I was elated to know Ken would be there soon. Jack and Claudia were making the trip with him. Joy, the home health aide from Loving Assistance, arrived promptly at nine, followed by Ken, Jack, and Claudia. They stood around talking while waiting for Jane. I decided to familiarize Joy with a quick tour of the condo, pointing out Mama's bedroom and bathroom. Joy commented on the boxes stacked all over. "Your mother must like having her things around her. That is fine with me. It doesn't bother me," she stated.

After being out of Mama's eyesight a matter of seconds and returning to the living room, I heard Mama say, "What are they going back there for?"

I had forgotten how private Mama was and how she did not like people in her bedroom. I pointed out to Joy where

Mama's spice tea was, along with her strawberries, leftover corn soufflé, and the leftover Meals On Wheels lunch.

"CLOSE THAT REFRIGERATOR DOOR!" Mama hollered.

My heart jumped. Being startled in such a manner was not good for my condition. Between Mama's attitude and Jane's taunting, I was more than ready to go home.

It was ten o'clock, and Jane still had not arrived. I phoned Jane, receiving only a response from the answering machine. Surely she was there, choosing not to answer. A message was left. "Jane, we've been waiting for you to come by Mama's, but we have to go now."

We said our goodbyes to Mama and left her in Joy's care.

CHAPTER TEN

Management by Crisis

I had no sooner walked in the house with my suitcase and reached the bedroom when the phone rang. It was Julie calling from work in a panic. "Sarah called. Jane is not cooperating. She is refusing to stay with Mama."

Jane was not concerned our mother be left by herself. "After all, it isn't unusual for old people to be by themselves when they croak," she told Sarah, the grant coordinator and hospice social worker.

Julie was beside herself. "Mama should not be left unattended. They are talking about moving her back to Chaparral. I told Sarah it would be very hard on her to go back. They are trying to find someone to stay with her tonight. Sarah wants to know how soon I can get there. I need to change my plane reservations."

Julie had already purchased an emergency ticket to arrive Monday. Fortunately, the reservation could be exchanged for the next available flight, which Julie hastily arranged.

Julie was back on the phone, advising Sarah she would be arriving Friday afternoon on a two-thirty flight. To her relief, Loving Assistance had found someone to stay with Mama that night. Julie phoned to inform Mama of the new plan.

"Hi, Mama. I will arrive tomorrow afternoon instead of Monday," stated Julie.

Rather than tell Mama Jane had refused to stay with her, Julie made up an excuse. "Jane isn't feeling well. Arrangements have been made for a home health aide to stay the night."

"Jane just called and said she will be over at six o'clock," Mama replied.

Julie was horribly upset. Whatever deplorable game Jane was playing, Julie was not amused. In between the flurry of calls, periodically, Julie tried to reach Jane, but she was not answering. Julie persisted, and finally, Ben reluctantly answered, "Jane is not here."

Julie could hear Jane in the background barking out orders.

"You are lying. I can hear her telling you what to say."

Jane refused to come to the phone until Ben relayed the message that she did not have to relieve the home health aide.

Jane picked up the receiver as Julie was saying, "Arrangements have been made for an aide to stay the night since Jane has refused."

"Tell the home health people to go home! I don't want them over there!" Jane yelled belligerently.

"Arrangements have already been made. Don't interfere," Julie shot back.

Julie called Rosemary at Loving Assistance, not knowing if Jane would go by Mama's, and demand the home health aide leave.

"The health care aide will not get involved in a confrontation. In the event Jane tells her to leave, she will leave," Rosemary replied.

Julie had to assure Rosemary her aide would get paid for the hours they had arranged even if Jane ordered her to go. They were to notify Julie if Jane appeared. The evening passed with no calls.

The next morning, Gerald took Julie to the airport. Once on the plane, Julie's thoughts turned to the possibility of our mother dying anytime. Along with the dread of dealing with Jane, she was overwhelmed.

Upon landing, Julie rented a car and drove twenty-five miles to Blackburn. As she approached the condo, Jane's car was spotted parked along the street. *Oh great,* she thought as she pulled into the driveway and entered.

Jane greeted her with a hug and looked calm. "I didn't expect you to be here," Julie said with restraint. "You weren't going to take care of her."

"I was only joking," Jane said, laughing. Julie was livid. That was some joke. Jane was not confronted in Mama's presence. It was not the time or place to quarrel.

Jane took leave, and Mama started chatting. "I can't believe you kids are doing all this for me."

Isn't it natural to care for your mother and do everything earthly possible when she is very sick and dying? Our family had a huge void when it came to family togetherness and support. Mama did not generally go out of her way and did not expect anything in return.

Julie prepared dinner and helped Mama get ready for bed. I had informed Julie of the evening routine. Unfortunately, I left out one detail. After cleaning up the kitchen and settling in, Julie finally went to bed herself. Even though she was exhausted, the annoying sound of the oxygen machine delayed her ability to doze off to sleep. During the night, she was awakened by Mama calling out. She sounded mad. Julie leaped out of bed and ran into her bedroom.

"WHERE'S MY WALKER?" Mama demanded in a harsh, reprimanding tone.

Bewildered and half asleep, Julie made her way to the dark living room and retrieved the walker, placing it next to Mama's bed. She was satisfied and went off to sleep.

* * *

The previous week when Julie was making travel arrangements, she had the foresight to call James King, Mama's attorney, to set up an appointment for Tuesday afternoon. Julie made the mistake of mentioning the appointment to Jane. Jane attended the same church as the attorney and cornered him at the Sunday morning services. She told James to cancel his appointment with Julie. That afternoon when Jane informed Julie she had canceled her appointment, Julie became incensed. She called James at home and told him she did not want the appointment canceled. Julie was assured Jane was not taken seriously, and her appointment was still on.

Suspicious of everyone, Jane had assumed Julie was planning to conspire with him about her share of the inheritance. In reality, Julie wanted to talk about our mother's estate in general and her duties as the personal representative after our mother was gone.

In Jane's absence, Mama asked Julie to go through coffee cans that were filled with change. Julie was directed to check for valuable silver coins and old pennies. After the second night of sorting through thousands of coins, only a few collector coins were found. There were way too many coins to look at each one individually. Julie resorted to taking some of the cans to the bank and deposited them into our mother's checking account.

Julie wanted to get out of the house for a brief period each day. Rather than give Jane the power to decide if she would show up to relieve her, Julie arranged for home health aides to come in two hours every afternoon.

On Monday afternoon, Julie met with Sarah and Jessica in a conference room at the hospice complex. Julie was looking for help regarding how to deal with Jane. "Taking care of our mother's needs is comparably not as difficult as working around Jane to get things accomplished," Julie expressed.

Sarah could not believe Jane's disrespectful behavior and language. "Your family is one of the most dysfunctional families I have ever seen," Sarah declared. "It is a miracle you and Elaine function so well."

Later when Julie relayed that conversation to me, I was very surprised. I had never considered our family dysfunctional. Does one mentally ill person make the entire family dysfunctional? Perhaps but Julie and I did not operate on that premise.

"I am exceedingly tired of Jane's manipulation and interference. She is not a team player, and her reasoning is questionable. She goes off on her own, making decisions behind our backs. When I try to talk to her, she gets all hung up on who the *boss* is," Julie confided to Sarah and Jessica. "The issue is not who the boss is but rather what the best things are that I can do for our mother right now."

"I would suggest you ask your mother if she wishes to have twenty-four-hour care in Jane's presence," Sarah offered. "Since Jane respects your mother as an authority figure, it would be easier for her to hear it from your mother."

Julie returned to the condo after the meeting. As she had expected, Jane was there. Following Sarah's advice, Julie approached Mama. "Mama, would you like to have twenty-four-hour care now?"

"Yes, I think I need someone here," Mama replied to Julie's relief. Fortunately, this scheme did not backfire. Julie had already decided twenty-four-hour care was necessary and would be arranged in any case.

After Jane's exit, Mama started to talk. "If I could just get some energy back, I could do some things." Then she went into her "I have three daughters" speech. In Julie's version, Mama told her she had different relationships and ties to each of her daughters for different reasons. Later, Jane told me Mama had a similar conversation with her, only in Jane's version, she was our mother's favorite.

Upon occasion, our mother displayed strange behavior, which embarrassed Julie and me. She did not care what anyone thought. Such an occasion presented itself the following day.

On Tuesday morning, Jessica made her routine visit, appearing with an abundance of red curly hair intruding over her forehead. "I don't like your hairstyle. It's in your face. I'll cut it for you," Mama offered.

Jessica was a good sport. She reached in her pocket and handed Mama a pair of bandage scissors.

"Lean your head down so I can reach your hair," Mama directed.

Jessica bent down to accommodate the request. Mama took a piece of the red curly locks in her fingers and snipped some of Jessica's hair. Mama was not very strong and did not get a very large piece. The process was repeated. Jessica had a worried look on her face until she saw the small amount of hair Mama held in her hand.

"Are you finished?" Jessica questioned.

"Yes. It looks better now," Mama answered.

Julie was mortified but relieved the missing hair was hardly noticeable.

Jane stayed with Mama, while Julie went to lunch with her high school friend Gail, who lived in Blackburn. After lunch, Julie kept her appointment with James King, her mother's attorney. Besides getting to have lunch with an old friend, the lunch provided an alibi for Julie's whereabouts. Julie gained the needed information from the brief meeting and returned; Jane none the wiser.

Upon returning from her appointment, Julie decided to wash the bedding. One of the pillowcases on our mother's bed was very old and worn. It had a small tear when it was put in the washer. After being removed from the dryer, the tear was quite large, and the pillowcase was not usable.

Jane saw it and chided, "You better get the sewing machine out and fix the pillowcase that you tore, or Mama will be really mad!"

The fabric was so thin and worn there was no way it could be repaired properly. Julie replaced it with another pillowcase from the linen closet. At first, Julie was worried about Mama getting upset. Then she realized it was not a big deal. Julie tucked the pitiful pillowcase into a zippered pouch in her luggage to make sure Jane did not see it in the trash. She would take it home to throw away. Julie had learned from an early age to let sleeping dogs lie.

Jane had been accusing Julie of wanting Mama's money when in actuality, Jane was already making plans for her inheritance. She wanted to go on a trip to Oregon to visit Uncle Andy and Aunt Lorie and perhaps to California to see Aunt Rebecca. Jane totally disregarded the stipulation of our mother's will for her share to go to Julie or me to be under our control to pay for Jane's major expenses, repairs, and emergencies.

Jane told Julie she probably wouldn't help us clean up the condo as it would be too hard for her. We knew Jane would be there, but she did not want to do any of the physical work because it would make her *sick*.

Our parents had purchased a number of silver bars and valuable coins. Mama told Julie the silver bars were hidden in two old green metal ammunition boxes way back in the corner of her bedroom closet. Julie asked if she could locate the boxes for future reference. After getting past the barricade of waist-high boxes, the mirrored closet door was slid open. In a corner of the dark closet, countless old shoes were found piled high, camouflaging the ammunition boxes.

Without disclosing the hiding place, Julie suggested to Jane the silver should be inventoried. It was anticipated Jane would be helping herself to our mother's belongings at the first opportunity. Julie proceeded to document the contents of the boxes, carefully recording everything that was in each box. Afterward, out of Jane's presence, the boxes were returned to their hiding place. Photographs of the house and closets were taken. There was not a formal inventory, but Jane was lead to believe there was.

Later, after Julie had returned home, Jane phoned her, saying it was illegal for her to have gone through Mama's things and list them. Jane was full of hooey, and Julie told her so.

On Wednesday morning, Mama had just awakened and was getting dressed when the doorbell rang. Jane rushed to get the door to find Sarah from hospice, representing the grant assistance program. It was 10:00 A.M., the appointed time to make arrangements for getting the grant funds in place.

Upon Sarah being seated, Jane began grilling her with a series of peculiar questions. When Jane scurried off to the bedroom to check on Mama, who was having a bad coughing episode, Julie took advantage of her absence to apologize for Jane's bizarre conduct. Sarah assured Julie an explanation was not necessary. "Jane's behavior is well-known in this community," she responded.

Within minutes, Jane reappeared, pushing Mama in the wheelchair. She transitioned to her favorite chair and was ready to begin. The terms of the grant were straightforward. It should have been a simple meeting to explain what the grant entailed and how the vouchers would be distributed. Mama treated it suspiciously and examined the wording with methodical thoroughness before signing the form. At last, Sarah was on her way.

Jane must have told Mama something to make her suspicious of the way Julie was handling her affairs. Later that morning, with no warning or explanation, Mama came at Julie in a stern voice. "I WANT TO KNOW EVERYTHING, AND I WANT TO MEET EVERYBODY! I'm going to get to the bottom of this!" she exclaimed.

Julie was taken aback. Get to the bottom of what?

Julie was told not to pay Loving Assistance one cent before she met them. Mama had already met Rosemary, the owner of Loving Assistance, the previous Wednesday when Jessica had initiated the preliminary arrangements for home health care. During that visit, I signed papers acknowledging the expectations of home health aides and agreed to pay the costs. At that time, our mother had been agreeable to the arrangements.

Mama was being unreasonable, and Julie was not happy. Mama's finances had been discussed with her every step of the way. She knew Julie was paying her bills. Julie was a good advocate. She had discovered the bank was deducting fees for which she was exempt. The fees were in the process of being credited back.

As per Mama's demands, Julie arranged for Rosemary, Sarah, and the Harrisons from Golden Insurance to meet with her, each at a designated time. Mama interrogated them one after another all afternoon. She was finally satisfied all was well after a grueling day.

* * *

It was becoming increasingly difficult for the home health workers to get Mama out of her chair. Loving Assistance asked for a lift chair to be brought in. Julie complied, and hospice delivered one promptly. Having the chair would keep Mama from being confined to a bed.

Jane went into orbit upon learning Mama had the lift chair. "She doesn't need it, and it's too expensive!"

"Medicare is covering the $25 fee for the loaner chair," Julie explained to Jane, not that she heard one word, while lost in her tantrum. Even if it had cost something, Julie would have gladly paid.

Julie observed scenes of Mama eating breakfast or lunch, while Jane sat next to her at the table, staring at her. Perhaps she was trying to send her mental telepathy messages.

Julie took advantage of the final afternoon of her visit to hear our mother talk about her childhood and when she met Daddy. Mama also talked about when we were babies and young children. Julie took notes as Jane glared the entire time.

When it was time for Julie's departure, she was exhausted from Jane's interference and manipulative games.

CHAPTER ELEVEN

Entering Another Room

"I am going on a trip to Edmond. It is very hard on me seeing Mama declining. I need to get away," Jane informed Julie. She was bothered by Jane's announcement. One does not go far when their mother's death is imminent.

Jane had been talking to someone who told her Social Security could take claim of the condo to pay our mother's medical expenses. "Mama can't get thrown out because I own the condo," Julie replied.

"You are taking advantage of Mama! I know you are just out for yourself!" Jane exclaimed. Even though the condo belonged to Julie, our mother did not pay rent or any compensation for staying there.

"If I were out for myself, I would never have helped Mama to begin with," Julie told her.

The old diesel truck that Ben drove was evidence of Julie's generosity as she had given them $5,000 outright several years previously to buy a vehicle.

Mama was losing ground daily. Julie and I had to make plans regarding how much time we could stay in Blackburn when we came for her services. After careful consideration of time limitations and the horrendous cleaning task, it was decided to have an estate sale before leaving Blackburn. With the joint forces of Gerald and my family, the job could be accomplished. There was concern about appearances, having the memorial service one day and an estate sale the next. It could not be helped.

* * *

A hospice nurse answered my phone call to Mama. The receiver was handed to Mama. It took a lot of effort for her to speak. "There are a lot of people here," she said in a weak, hoarse voice.

"Who is there?" I asked, receiving no answer.

"When are you coming?" Mama forced out.

"Justin and his family are coming Saturday. I am riding with them. Are you up for us all to come then?"

She did not respond. The nurse came back on the phone. "Her breathing is irregular. She is not eating or drinking anything and is refusing medications. She probably will not be with us by the weekend."

I was in denial, not believing she would be gone that soon. Mama had a strong constitution. Surely she would hang on a few more days.

Julie received a call from Jane the morning of March 2. "I will be back in Blackburn on the bus tonight around eight thirty. I will go over to see Mama in the morning."

"Okay," Julie replied. "Yesterday, hospice brought in a hospital bed and set it up in the living room."

"Well, humph. You didn't do what I told you, did you? I have to go. Goodbye," Jane responded rudely.

Earlier, Jane had agreed the hospital bed was a good idea, but she wanted it in the bedroom; however, there was too much stuff in the bedroom.

Julie tried to ask what her plans were for moving our mother's car. It had already been established Jane would get the blue Plymouth Belvedere that our parents had bought new in 1965. Her name was already on the title jointly with Mama's.

When Julie called, the caregiver could not rouse Mama. She had gone into a coma and would be gone soon. Our mother had always said dying was like going from one room to another. She took the journey into the next room late that night at eleven thirty.

The caregiver who was present notified hospice. Carmen, the nurse on call, arrived and confirmed our mother's death. The official cause was advanced congestive heart failure and coronary artery disease. She was six weeks short of reaching her eighty-second birthday.

Julie phoned us early the morning of March 3. Ken answered the phone. "Mama died just before midnight," stated Julie.

Jane had already called Julie. "Where are the keys to the Plymouth?" Jane demanded.

"I have no idea," Julie told her.

"I need to move the car for Mama's body to be carried out through the garage!" Jane bellowed.

Julie started to suggest she open the sliding glass doors in the master bedroom, but Jane would not listen and hung up.

After locating a set of car keys, Jane called Julie back. "I can't get the car to start!" Jane declared angrily. She was nasty to Julie and acted like it was Julie's fault. The car had not been driven since November when Mama had her heart attack. It was no surprise it did not start.

The next morning, hospice came by the condo to pick up the lift chair, hospital bed, oxygen machine, and other items. Julie was notified the items were being removed. "Jane was at your mother's this morning while we were there. She was frantically going through things in the house and made a mess," relayed Sarah.

With the knowledge Jane was rummaging through our mother's things, Julie tried to reach James King, but he was out of town. Foreseeing this situation could happen, Julie had previously discussed her thoughts with James. He promised he would *take care of everything* if Jane got out of control.

"Should I call the police?" Julie asked me. "She is trespassing, and I'm sure she is taking things."

"If we call the police, it could get pretty wild. Maybe we are overreacting," I suggested. It was decided not to call the police; it would cause more trouble for Jane, and she had been in enough trouble.

Nine months after our mother passed, I contacted Carmen, the nurse who pronounced our mother's death. Some of the events of that night were learned.

"Jane was not present when your mother died but arrived shortly after I notified her," explained Carmen.

"Was Jane upset?"

"She wasn't crying. She was okay. She acted a little different. She didn't seem to be terribly upset. I called the funeral home, but Jane did not want them to pick up the body until later. She said it would bother the neighbors.

"Jane did not want to leave," Carmen continued. "I called the coroner to see if they minded waiting until morning to pick up her body. They agreed that would be okay."

When Daddy died, Mama anointed his chakras with frankincense. Jane had told me we should do the same for our mother. With that in mind, I asked if Jane had anointed our mother's body with oil.

"She put oil on her forehead and feet. There was a sheet covering the body. I couldn't see where all she was putting the oil," Carmen said. "She helped wash and groom the body and put in the dentures."

"Was she going through our mother's things?" I asked.

"I was busy and did not notice. I was gathering up all the medications and flushing them down the toilet. She objected to wasting the medications."

Upon completing the established protocol, Carmen left Jane alone with our mother's body. Julie and I wondered what Jane was doing all night. One thing we were sure of was that Jane had taken our mother's wedding ring that Daddy had given her. Julie knew Mama was wearing it when she was there the previous week.

Jane wasted no time e-mailing Uncle Andy and the others about our mother's death. Her e-mail stated she was there mopping up after Mama's passing.

Last-minute arrangements were being made. The memorial service was set for Thursday morning.

Through a phone number Julie provided, I contacted Marcus, who lived in Missouri. He was one of three of Mama's stepsons, who was a minister. Marcus would get in touch with Pastor Bedford and assist with organizing the service.

CHAPTER TWELVE

Mama's Belongings

Mama had a tremendous amount of possessions that she had hoarded over her lifetime. A large part of her belongings was only of value to her. Knowing there would be an abundance of things to toss, Julie arranged to have four small dipsy dumpsters placed on the street in front of the condo.

The details for the estate sale were finalized. Angelia contacted the *Blackburn County Independent* in time to meet the deadline to have an ad placed in Wednesday's edition, the only day the weekly paper was published.

Meanwhile, Jane had an agenda of her own. She visited the Comrade National Bank and closed the POD account, retrieving the full balance. She also proceeded to claim her third of a CD.

Jane informed Julie she was going to take funds from our mother's checking account, which was kept at a different bank. Julie was not going to wait around for another one of

Jane's *jokes.* Julie contacted the bank, requesting the account be frozen.

Since Jane had limited space in her apartment, she was asked to reserve a storage unit to hold items she was getting. It was her responsibility to move her things to the storage area. Julie needed to have everything out of the condo by the time she left Blackburn for it to be put on the market.

Jane reported she had our mother's car but had not removed the items from the trunk because she was a little "addled" right now. The trunk was full of tools that were part of the estate. "You both can fight over Mama's beautiful set of china. We need to be concentrating on God and the funeral more than who gets what." In her next statement, she elaborated on items she wanted.

It had already been determined who would get the big items before our mother died. With all due respect to Mama, Julie and I made it known we wanted to have some of the countless smaller items. We did not consider the dividing process as being a fight. "I feel like saying grabby, grabby, grabby," Jane expressed. She did not like the idea of Julie selling the condo.

"Give Julie credit for handling a horrendous responsibility," I told Jane. "Julie is not greedy. She is one of the fairest and bighearted people you will ever know. Keep in mind you are getting most of our mother's possessions."

Jane did not want Mama's obituary to appear in the Blackburn newspaper. She did not want the mental health agency staff to know her mother had died as they *might come get her.* Julie was in a quandary. It would be inappropriate not to acknowledge our mother's life. Julie decided not to let Jane's distorted motives dictate actions. Mr. Logan, the funeral director, was instructed to have the obituary printed in the Blackburn paper; but to satisfy Jane's fears, her name would be omitted.

* * *

Upon Julie and Gerald's arrival in Blackburn, they checked into a motel. Early Wednesday morning, they arrived at the condo and began sorting items in Mama's bedroom, where the biggest challenge lay.

Ken and I arrived with Angelia and her family shortly before noon. The first of the four small dipsy dumpsters was almost full from Julie and Gerald's morning work.

In accordance with Angelia's carefully planned cleanup agenda, Ken began working in the kitchen, emptying the cupboards and tossing and packing items in an orderly fashion. Calvin began removing Mama's collection of books from the shelves that covered an entire wall in the living room. Five-year-old Mathew was assigned the job of sorting the remaining coffee cans of change. He was doing a good job and having fun separating the pennies, nickels, dimes, quarters, and occasional fifty-cent pieces into piles.

Angelia began going through the multitude of boxes that were stacked up in the guest bedroom. Clara and Stacy were busily taking clothes off the hangers from the guest room closet, checking the pockets and neatly folding and placing the clothes in garbage bags for Jane. Jane had requested to have Mama's clothes to give to charity.

I joined Julie in sorting through dressers in the master bedroom, while Gerald was buried in items from the master bedroom closet. Among the items Gerald found was a front-page newspaper clipping declaring World War II over. There were ration books for sugar, flour, and gasoline. All these items would be kept, of course.

I kept getting distracted from the interesting things Gerald was finding, such as my baby book. I did not even know I had one. Stopping to take a quick glance, I noted my first words: "daddy," "don't," and "stop it."

Why would "don't" and "stop it" be among a baby's first words? Sadly, I knew why.

It was back to the dresser. Our mother's collection of old jewelry and odds and ends was discovered. Julie had been told there was money intermingled with the contents of envelopes in the dresser I was going through. The money was well hidden. At first glance, one would not realize there were all denominations of bills inconspicuously stashed inside envelopes with old bank statements, insurance coverage notices, and the like.

The blue Plymouth had been moved from the garage, but the tools that were not intended to go with the car were not in sight. According to Jane, they had been stolen from the trunk. That story was not believed, but she was not confronted.

Jane appeared after lunch to nose around. She had spent the previous week gathering a collection of things from the house that were boxed up and placed in the garage. We had no idea of the boxes' contents.

Jane wanted some of the items Julie had claimed. Besides the old chiming clock that had belonged to our paternal grandfather, Jane wanted an antique end table. Apparently, Jane had taken the key that wound up the clock as it was nowhere to be found. She may have thought without the key, Julie would have considered the clock useless and let her have it. If that was her plan, it was spoiled by the discovery of several other clock keys that were found among the jewelry.

Jane arranged to have special services for the family to be held at five o'clock that evening at the church *to save Julie's soul* and socialize with Albert's family, the Archers. Julie and I had an overwhelming amount of work to do. There was no time for socializing.

"Ben will be over later to load my things. He is taking a nap on the couch. He has negative energy," Jane announced and then walked back over to her apartment to wait for Ben to get off his *couch.*

The condo was humming like a beehive with every one fastidiously attending to our assigned chore. A nearby neighbor was enjoying the entertainment as he sat leisurely outside the front of his condo on a portable lawn chair. It surely must have been a spectacle to witness the parade of trips to the dumpsters.

Jane returned with Ben. She had not gotten a storage unit yet. She was not sure how to go about it. I reluctantly volunteered to go with her and Ben. Ken joined us.

Ben and Jane were already in their old diesel truck as I approached with Ken. Ken motioned them to go ahead, while we followed in our vehicle to the location of a storage company's office. I arranged for a unit and paid cash for three months from money we had found in the house. Having that accomplished, we went back to the condo. While Ken put garbage bags of clothes in our SUV, I carried Jane's collection of boxes to Ben as he organized them in the back of the truck. "Give me a hand," I called out to Jane.

"I can't. I have to save my energy for tonight," Jane declared as she looked on.

I was highly discussed with Jane's lack of assistance. This was her stuff!

Once loaded, we were on our way to the storage area. Ken and I carried items from the SUV to the storage unit but did not stay to remove Jane's boxes from the truck as we needed to get back to excavating the condo. Jane was furious when she and Ben were left to unload the truck themselves.

Upon returning to the condo, Julie asked me to accompany her. We needed to go by the mortuary to pick up our mother's ashes and also go by the bank to claim our shares of the CD.

We waited in the reception area of the funeral home while our mother's ashes were being retrieved. Julie asked if they had Mama's wedding ring. We were assured she was not wearing a ring when her body was picked up.

A young woman appeared with a gift bag-type container. "I put the snaps from the coin purse your sister insisted being held in her hand at the bottom of the container beneath the ashes." Jane wanted the coin purse to be incinerated with our mother's remains to prove they did not replace her ashes with someone else's.

"All metal is removed before cremation takes place," said the lady. "However, in this case, we made an exception."

Julie and I looked at each other with blank expressions. Then we thanked her and were on our way to the bank. It was almost five as our business was completed, and we left the bank. There was no way we could make Jane's family prayer service, which we never agreed to attend in the first place.

Ken picked up a bucket of chicken for the working crew to share. After dinner, Julie and Gerald took reprieve to their motel, and everyone else settled into their beds at the condo. As exhausted as we were, Ken and I were restless and got up to sort through more items in yet another dresser. It was after midnight when we finally gave in and went back to bed.

CHAPTER THIRTEEN

Memorial Services and Aftermath

The Lord provided a gorgeous spring day for our mother's memorial service. Several of us set off to pick up the flowers that Angelia had arranged through a phone number she located on the Internet.

A short time later, we arrived at the church. The flowers were placed on each side of the altar, along with an enlarged picture of our mother in her pink dress. Already sitting on the altar was Jane's contribution, a poster drawing of flowers. Sloppily printed at the bottom were the words "Flowers for Mother."

Mr. Logan directed us to join family members in the basement as others attending the services began to take their seats in the auditorium.

While I had been in the auditorium attending to the flowers, Pastor Bedford aggressively confronted Julie in the basement. "Why was Jane's name omitted from the obituary?"

Jane walked up at that moment. Julie suspected Jane had brought the omission of her name to his attention. While looking Jane straight in the eye, she replied, "Jane ordered me NOT to put her name in the paper, but I was not going to let our mother's death go unnoticed."

Without saying a word, Jane walked off, realizing she had been caught in her own web. As we were entering the basement, Jane, with Ben alongside, was escaping up the stairs.

"Aren't you going to stay down here with the family members?" I asked.

"No, I'm a free spirit," she said as she exited the basement area.

I met Marcus and the other Archer family members for the first time. Everyone visited congenially until Mr. Logan announced it was time to join the congregation for the service to begin.

Pastor Bedford opened the services followed by short sermons from Jasper, the oldest of Mama's stepchildren, and Marcus. Julie and I were relieved to see the vocalists on the program were listed as Bernard and The Archer Family Singers. Jane and Ben joined The Archer Family Singers for their pieces.

Angelia delivered the poem "Miss Me but Let Me Go" without a flaw. She began by saying her grandmother was a very spunky lady, to everyone's amusement.

After the eulogy, Pastor Bedford spoke again, acknowledging Angelia's observation that Mama was a very spunky lady. On those lines, he told a story of a previously portly gentleman who attended their church.

"After services one Sunday, Marie went up to a portly gentleman in the congregation and tapped on his stomach, telling him he needed to lose that. Stating she had some books that could help him and if he would like to call her, she would tell him what he needed to do. At first, he was offended but thought about it for a while and then decided to take her up on her offer. A little over a year later, the gentleman had lost a significant amount of weight and was grateful to Marie. He was now off his prescription medications and felt wonderful."

Mama did the same thing to Claudia's father. Claudia and Jack had arranged a pre-wedding activity for the families to enjoy the festivities at an outdoor chuck wagon. Claudia had just introduced me to her father moments before Mama was introduced. We were standing outside the ticket building. After the formalities of the introduction, I just about died of embarrassment when Mama tapped on the stomach of Claudia's father and said, "You need to lose that."

Fortunately, he took it in stride. Later, Claudia told me her father knew he needed to lose weight, and he should learn from the wisdom of someone who had been around as long as she had.

After the services, our family and the Archers visited while indulging in a buffet of chicken, baked beans, rolls, salad, and desserts provided by ladies of the church.

"Jane is planning to take the flowers to a nursing home," Pastor Bedford informed me.

"She can take the flower arrangement our cousin furnished. I was planning for the church to have the flowers we brought for the Sunday services. But I would like to keep the vases, in memory of our mother," I stated.

"I'll remove the flowers and bring them by later," Pastor Bedford volunteered.

Back at the condo, everyone changed into their jeans and went back to work. Justin's wife, Phyllis, was sorting through old files.

"Do you want to keep these files on Jane?" Phyllis asked.

"What does it say?" I asked.

Phyllis began reading an excerpt. "Jane was kept in a drug-induced coma for three days . . ."

I assumed it was referring to a time when Jane was taken to the state hospital after she had been picked up by the sheriff. She had been walking out to our mother's farm down the middle of the county road with her dog, Ginger, while yelling obscenities at cars that were dodging and barely missing her.

"Shred them," I said without hesitation. This was sensitive information, and I did not want to be reminded of it or hear anymore.

Phyllis found another piece of paper among Mama's personal files. It was an old evaluation of job performance. Phyllis read the evaluation. "Secretarial skills are excellent. Needs to work on interpersonal skills."

"Shred that too," I announced.

The garage was filling up quickly with things for tomorrow's sale. Angelia and Calvin had brought several folding tables. Items were piling up on top of the tables as well as underneath. A grouping of other miscellaneous things was starting to line the opposite wall of the small garage.

Great headway was being made when members of the Archer family appeared. They asked if they could look at the garage sale items. I had just set out some knitting needles and fabric, which one of the ladies asked if she could buy. There were other items they wanted also. Julie and I let them have what they wanted. It would not have felt right to charge them.

The sliding glass door in the master bedroom had been left open for a shortcut to the garage. The guests were gathering in the bedroom. The quilt Thelma, Jasper's wife, had made was still on the bed under copious boxes. The quilt was made especially for Mama in payment for a piano Thelma wanted. The old upright piano had been a gift from Albert. Not that she could play, but Mama had been trying to learn at one time. In exchange for the piano, Thelma agreed to make Mama a quilt.

Thelma had died the year before. Her grown daughter recognized the quilt and asked if she could have it. Thelma's daughter sobbed with sentimental tears as the quilt was removed from the bed for her to take.

Sometime during their visit, Calvin and Bernard moved the two freezers over to Jane's apartment. The Archers finally left. Our family resumed sorting and discarding.

While taking another load of sale items to the garage, I glanced up. In the distance, a frumpy-looking person wearing a coat and big hat was seen walking with a limp coming down the sidewalk. At second glance, I realized it was Jane. I went back into the bedroom and continued working.

Julie was in the living room, taking a moment to look around, pondering what to do next, when Jane entered through the garage. Smiling, Jane approached Julie. "Well, I'd say we made a pretty good team taking care of Mama."

Through the entire ordeal, Jane was yelling at her, telling her how stupid she was. They were in constant conflict. Julie stood there, assimilating Jane's words. *Team,* she thought. It was a BAD team if it could be called a *team* at all.

Jane caught Julie off guard, grabbing her and giving her a big hug, and kissed her on the mouth. Julie was repulsed and pushed her away. Laughing, Jane ambled off, calling Julie a lesbian. Julie was speechless and so furious her face turned red.

There were probably thousands of dollars' worth of church cassette tapes in the boxes remaining in the guest room, which Jane claimed.

"I want the cedar chest also," Jane stated. "It contains books and tapes and writings by prophets."

I objected, "You can have the chest's contents, but I am claiming the chest. It is the only other big item I am getting besides Mama's old sewing machine."

I proceeded to empty the contents of the chest into several boxes, while Jane watched from our mother's brown chair. "Would you help me with these?" I asked.

"I can't. It will make me sick," Jane excused. This behavior was typical, but as much as it did not set well, I said nothing. "I would like the answering machine," Jane stated.

The answering machine had not been disconnected yet. Since I was engaged in emptying the trunk, I hollered, "Ken, Ken!" But he did not answer. He was working in the guest room, where the answering machine was. I thought he could get it for Jane.

Jane got up slowly and started to walk out, while I was bent over the chest with my arms full. There was a sudden thud against the back of my head. Jane had taken the palm of her hand and shoved me. It hurt, but I let it go, even though Jane deserved to be smacked back. Getting into a brawl would accomplish nothing.

I had foreseen the possibility of clashing with Jane and had discussed it with Julie. We decided neither one of us should be alone with her in case she claimed we hurt her, but with everyone working in different areas, this plan slipped away. It had already been decided we would not touch her under any circumstances for fear Jane would interpret any aggression shown toward her as an attack on a *defenseless* person. The occurrence passed without notice. Jane lumbered off without saying a word.

"You can't put Mama's nice dishes in the garage sale for strangers to use!" Jane shouted at Julie. That was how she felt about everything headed for the garage sale, for that matter.

"Then you can take them!" Julie exclaimed to console her.

Jane was checking out the garage sale items and gave Jack $20 for things she had collected. Ben had driven his truck over and was selecting things he wanted. Jane came back inside and was milling around. It was getting late, and the children were hungry. Giving up on waiting for Jane to sense it was time to leave, Ken spoke. "You need to leave now so we can go eat."

Jane was highly insulted and became furious. Meanwhile, Jack had given me the $20 bill. Jack wanted me to return her money, saying, "Jane gave this to me for things in the garage sale. Would you give it back to her?"

Unaware moments earlier Ken had asked Jane to leave, I followed her as she tromped angrily out to the truck.

"Wait, Jane. Here is your $20. You can keep it."

Jane turned, looking back, and shouted, "How would you like to get thrown out of your own place?"

She got in the passenger side of the truck, locked the door, and turned her back on me. I knocked on the window and repeated, "Here, take your $20 back."

Jane halfway turned around and stuck her tongue out. With that childish gesture, I returned to the garage, where Ben had been checking out our mother's old tape player stereo system and gave me some money for it. After carrying it off to the truck, they left. I went back inside. "Ken, what is going on? Why is Jane saying she is being thrown out of *her own place*?"

"She perceives the condo as hers. I asked her to leave so we can go eat." It did not occur to Ken or any of us that we should have invited Jane and Ben to join us. We pretty much had all her company we could stomach. After calling Julie a lesbian, bopping me in the head, and being an all-around nuisance, we did not care to have her glaring at us through dinner.

It had been an extraordinarily emotional day. Things were somewhat under control, and it was time to call it quits. We would be getting up early for the garage sale.

At 6:30 A.M., I dragged myself out of bed. I had just started to put hot rollers in my hair and was attempting to look presentable when the first of the bargain hunters appeared. Ken jumped in his clothes. As I stood at the master bathroom mirror, brushing out my hair, Ken let the first person in.

The whole plan was shot from the beginning. People were not going to be allowed in the condo. The items for sale were going to be carried outside. Considering the first person was Trudy Gray, who had been an old neighbor in Bingham, Ken made an exception. We had not known Trudy had gotten married and moved to a nearby town. As Ken led her into the living room, Claudia and Jack were scrambling to get dressed. Trudy was into antiques and got the pick from what was being sold. She probably got a steal, but we were not concerned about haggling.

In spite of how early it was, the place was already swarming with people. Breakfast was hit or miss with whoever could steal a minute to consume a bowl of cereal.

Gerald's calving season was beginning, and he had to return back to his cattle. Julie drove him to Trenton to catch a plane and would join the garage sale circus as soon as she returned.

Justin appeared at seven o'clock to help. I caught a glimpse of Justin and Jack carrying a mattress out to the lawn that was probably still warm. Pillows were sold still in their cases. As the garage sale progressed, Ken removed the bookshelves from the long wall in the living room and took the shelving out to the front lawn to be sold. People were carrying things off right and left. Many items that were thought doubtful to sell went like hotcakes.

I was checking on some items that remained in the small storage area at the front of the garage when Pastor Bedford appeared with the glass vases from the memorial service. Stepping over some buckets that were blocking the door into the condo, I invited Pastor Bedford in to get away from the madhouse in the garage.

"Thank you for making a special trip to bring the vases by. I really appreciate it," I expressed. "We've been through a lot lately. It might seem premature to be having a garage sale so soon after our mother's services, but under the circumstances, we have to take care of things when we have the chance."

We stood in the kitchen talking. "This has sure been taxing, especially dealing with Jane. She bopped me in the head when I asked her to help." Pastor Bedford said a prayer for Jane and our situation before going on his way.

Word was out the condo would be sold. A lady, who said her name was Edith, appeared, looking for a place for her mother. Julie showed her through the rooms, while I showed the condo to one of the neighbors, who was looking for a place for her aunt.

As the garage sale rambled on, Julie stole me away for a late lunch to regroup and slow down from the whirlwind of the past few days. "This would be a good time to close the safe-deposit box," I mentioned.

"Oh, that's right. I forgot about that," said Julie.

The garage sale was winding down when we returned. The entire town must have stopped by. It was the first garage sale of the season, and the weather could not have been more perfect. Calvin and Angelia took the rest of Jane's items to her storage unit, while Julie and I dropped off the receipts from the garage sale to James King as he had directed Julie to do. He would deposit the funds into the bank account when the frozen status was released.

Our exhausted group was ecstatic that it would not be necessary to stick around to continue the garage sale into Saturday. Ken loaded Julie's share of items into our SUV, along with my share. Julie's things would be held until she could come get them or have the items shipped.

That evening, Julie, Ken, Angelia, Calvin, and I took Jane a large box of detergent and the second key to her storage unit. We entered her apartment from the alley in through the dark kitchen. A freezer took up the majority of the kitchen floor, forcing everyone to turn sideways as we passed, groping in the dark. Jane led us to the opposite end of her small apartment, passing through a narrow room, which housed the bed in which she slept.

We stopped in the last dimly lit room, where we stood the entire time. I recognized the couch that at one time had belonged to our mother and now was where Ben slept.

Jane was very cordial and acted normal. She talked for quite a while, speaking about our mother being gone and saying she wanted to be friends. She spoke of how happy she was when my children were born. Julie was shocked at how normal she presented herself and her friendly mood. This was the face she presented to my children, who had trouble believing Jane had been as abusive as I described. As we left the crowded apartment on amiable terms, I thought Jane should be nominated for an Oscar.

Since Gerald had gone back home, Julie invited Ken and me to stay with her in her motel room using the spare queen-size bed. Everyone else had also gotten a motel room.

The next morning was a mass exodus with everyone on their way back home.

CHAPTER FOURTEEN

Perplexity

In the week that followed, Jane contacted the Blackburn newspaper, demanding a correction be printed with her name listed in our mother's obituary. She would remain on *bereavement leave* indefinitely. Julie and I went back to work the following Monday with confused feelings of being relieved the inevitable was over but wishing it had all never happened.

As executor of our mother's estate, Julie was now busy probating the will and getting our mother's affairs finalized. It was depressing for us to think we would never see our mother again. There was a big void in our lives.

Julie received an offer from Edith for the asking price to purchase the condo. James King took care of the legal technicalities of the sale and drew up a contract. Julie agreed to have the garage wall repaired, where a previous owner had cramped their wheel and left a big dent on the right side, and the vinyl floor would be replaced in the washer/dryer area, where it had been torn by a previous owner. The condo would also be painted and the carpet professionally cleaned. Ken and I would take care of those matters.

The worst of the ordeal was over, but for Ken and me, it was time to visit Ken's mother, who lived in a tiny town near the northern state line. Since Jack and Claudia were planning to move to Kentucky and didn't know if they would see Emma again, they went along and were present to celebrate Emma's eighty-sixth birthday. An evening was spent with Ken's brother, Adam, a divorcee of five years. It was good for us to get away. The upcoming weekend would be spent fixing up the condo.

Ken and I arrived in Blackburn early Friday morning of the last week in March and started working immediately. At lunchtime, Jane appeared, inviting us to go out to lunch. Ken was wearing his old, torn, paint-splattered jeans and was engrossed in painting. We did not want to take time to get cleaned up. Besides, there was food in the cooler we brought.

Jane was unhappy and started to leave when I remembered I had a picture for her of our mother. "Wait, Jane, I have something for you." Emma had taken a picture of her the night of Jack and Claudia's wedding. It was not a very good picture; her blue eyes looked brown. She had a stern look on her face and was not smiling.

I held the picture out for Jane to take, but after one glance, Jane did not reach for it in return. "That's not my mother," Jane said in an angry tone.

"Take it. Ken's mom had copies made especially for each of us."

"No. I don't want your rejects. You may have to put up with Ken's mother, but I don't." With those words, she marched out in a huff.

On Saturday, the professional carpet cleaner completed that chore, while Ken continued to paint, and I cleaned.

Bright and early Sunday morning, the remnants of painting and cleaning supplies were gathered. On the way out of town, Ben was observed sweeping the sidewalk around a big white church. It was an odds and ends job he had.

Our mother had been gone a little over a month. Her ashes would be disbursed in the same place as our father. Julie wanted to take care of the ashes the end of July when Gerald could get away from his cattle, and she had accrued more vacation time. Jane was contacted to see if she could join us at that time and afterward have a picnic in the park. Jane responded that July was not a good time for her as it might interfere with her travel plans. When asked when would be a good time, Jane did not reply.

* * *

"I wish we did not have to go through Mama's things so quickly. Things were tossed that we might have wanted to keep," I suggested to Julie now that it was all over and done.

"That is true," Julie responded with a fresh memory of the enormous amount of our mother's things to go through and with a bit of resentment for our mother putting us through the ordeal. "It was her own fault. She should have never let that much stuff accumulate." Mama saved the strangest things. As Julie explained it, "She kept all the seeds from every apple she ever ate."

The end of April was approaching. Julie and I were reminiscing over Jane's behavior in dealing with our mother's heart attack. "I think Jane was against so many things because of the cost. We were raised to do without things and cut corners to the extreme. Jane still lives that way. She never buys new clothes. She gets them from used clothing stores," I said.

Julie and I discussed visions of what could have happened to our parents' farm had Jane taken it over. She did not have the resources to pay the taxes, insurance, or upkeep. It also would have been too much work for her.

"I shudder to think of what might have happened if Mama had not sold the farm," Julie expressed.

"Yes," I agreed. "Jane would have moved in lock, stock, and barrel and assumed ownership of everything. And then she would expect us to pay the taxes or end up losing it. I don't even want to think about it. Thank God things did not work out that way!"

* * *

Julie wanted to finalize her plans for flying out the end of July. Since Jane did not give Julie an answer, I sent Jane an e-mail, informing her Julie could get away the end of July to take care of Mama's ashes, and asked Jane if that would work for her.

Jane had no obligations that would interfere with the proposed plans. The drive to Wentwood would only take an hour and a half; however, she was reluctant to agree. Julie and I were left dangling.

Plans were being made for the event, even though Jane had not agreed to the date. The ashes would be divided into three bud vases. Each of us would take part in disbursing our third. A verse from the Bible would be selected and read.

The end of May was approaching when Jane finally responded to Julie's earlier e-mail. "Elaine and I are supposed to spread Mama's ashes. If you had made different decisions, maybe Mama would still be around." She accused Julie of keeping her share of the estate below a certain level. "You are quite a rascal, but you always were." She also accused Julie of not telling the truth.

Fireworks were set off when Jane accused Julie of lying. She was not going to let the last set of insults roll off. Jane's cynical attitude toward Julie's judgment regarding our mother's care was unwarranted.

Julie responded in an e-mail. "Just because you lie doesn't mean I do. No matter how nice I am to you, you always say bad things and yell." Jane was not going to be allowed to call the shots. She was informed plans were made to spread our mother's ashes. "Are you going to be there or not? Yes or no?"

Julie placed another call to Jane regarding our mother's ashes.

"Well, we might be able to make it," Jane replied. "I'd have to make sure Ken doesn't throw me into the river. In fact, I don't want him there."

"Gerald is coming with me, and Ken will be there," Julie stated firmly. Julie could not resist jokingly adding, "I know Ken won't throw you into the river, but Gerald might."

Jane went into a slow rant, yelling, "IT'S SUPPOSED TO BE JUST US KIDS! I WAS EATING BEFORE YOU INTERFERED WITH MY DINNER!"

"You didn't have to answer the phone! Bye," Julie said as she hung up.

Julie called me to discuss the situation. "I told Jane where we will be that day. If she refuses to show up, we could send her third of the ashes to take care of as she wishes. We both want our men there. If she doesn't want Ben there, it's her choice," Julie expounded.

"Jane can't really think Ken would throw her in the river, but it is a thought," I replied lightheartedly. "She has not given any reason why she can't be there. If we wait another year or ten years, we will still have to deal with Jane sabotaging the plans."

CHAPTER FIFTEEN

Oregon or Bust

Per Jane's request, Julie released $1,000 from the estate for her to visit our uncle and aunts on the West Coast.

On June 7, Uncle Andy called regarding a card he received from Jane. "She says she is leaving for Oregon June 13 to come for a visit and something about having seven days. Does that include the two days she will take to get here by bus and return?" Andy inquired.

"I don't know," I answered. "She didn't even tell me she was going."

"Ben is coming with her. How stable is Ben?"

I was afraid to answer that question as I did not know Ben's history. "I don't know him that well. I think most of his problem is that he is lazy," I responded.

"Jane says she wants to see the ocean and her cousin Karen. Karen lives in Southern California, which is 1,500 miles from us. I'm wondering how she is going to get to all these places. Is she going to take the bus or expect us to take her?" Andy asked calmly but confused. Here again, I had no idea.

"Jane has a bus ticket to Sloan and has asked Lorie to pick her up. Who does she know in Sloan?" Andy asked. He was confused as to why Jane did not purchase a ticket to Fleming, where Lorie lived, in the first place.

"She is bringing her dog. We don't want the dog in our house. She has Lorie worried about whether she should go out and buy groceries and how she is going to entertain them and how long she is going to be there. Lorie has been having problems with her health and is on oxygen at night. She is not used to driving very far."

Aunt Lorie was a widow in her early seventies. She had contracted polio at the age of twenty-three, which had left her with weak lungs, limited movement in a crippled left arm, and other problems associated with the disease.

"Does Jane expect me to pick her up at Lorie's and drive her and Ben the 150 miles to stay with us?" Andy wondered. "And when she is ready to go home, am I expected to take her back?"

Jane's plans were so vague that Uncle Andy and Aunt Lorie were in a quandary as to what to expect.

"I am worried about Jane traveling so far on the bus. Traveling is exhausting, and when Jane gets overly tired, she gets *sick*," I told Uncle Andy.

"Will she do something that might cause her to get put in jail?" Andy questioned.

"It is a possibility. She has been in jail before. With Jane, you never know. As long as she stays on her medications, she should be okay." I promised to see what I could find out and get back with him.

Aunt Rebecca called moments after Uncle Andy. "We are trying to figure Jane out," Rebecca started.

"Well, when you succeed, let me know," I answered lightheartedly.

Rebecca was trying to determine whether Jane was going to visit her daughter, Karen. It did not seem logical that Jane would go that far by bus, but I could not answer that question either. Jane's thinking was so far out it was impossible to second-guess her.

I called Jane to simply ask about her plans.

"Hello, Jane. How are your trip plans going?" I asked.

"We are getting our things gathered up and plan to leave Monday morning. We are going to camp out, and we are taking Ginger, our dog, with us."

"Oh," I responded. "So you decided to drive rather than take the bus?"

"No, we are taking the bus."

"How can you take the bus with Ginger?"

"Ginger is a special care dog, and we can take her anywhere like a Seeing Eye dog," Jane explained.

I did not understand why she needed a special care dog but did not dwell on the point. Later, it was learned the *special care* status of their dog was given because of Ben's condition, not that it made any sense either.

"Did you know it is against the law to make fun of people with disabilities?" Jane offered.

"No, I didn't know that," I answered.

"Well, it is so people can't make fun of me."

"You aren't disabled," I said in turn.

"Yes, I am because of my illness. I'm thinking about letting my hair grow and going incognito."

"How can you take all your camping things on the bus? Isn't there a limit to how much you can take with you?" I asked.

"We checked, and we can take what we need," Jane replied.

"How long are you going to be gone?"

"That's none of your business," Jane answered brashly.

"Why is it a big deal to tell me?" I asked after feeling like I had been slapped in the face.

"You heard that click on the line a few minutes ago?"

"Yes," I admitted. I had heard an unexplained break during the call.

"That was the Bass Club. They monitor my line, and I have to be careful what I say."

"Why would they be interested in anything you are doing?"

"Because I know things," Jane responded in her know-it-all frame of mind.

As soon as the call ended, I phoned Julie with major concerns about Jane's plans. "Jane is planning to take their dog, Ginger, with them, and they are going to take all their camping gear on the bus. Can you imagine trying to haul their tent, sleeping bags, and I don't know what all besides the dog? She wouldn't answer my questions about her trip because she said the Bass were listening. What if she does something outlandish and ends up in jail in another state? I'm afraid she is going to get in major trouble. Can we do anything to stop her from making this trip? I'm worried about what might happen," I declared.

"I'll call the mental health people and see if they can stop her," Julie said, agreeing this trip sounded like a major fiasco. Julie was told as inappropriate as Jane was, she could not be stopped unless she was a danger to herself or others.

Andy called Jane to learn details. She was not nice to him, stating she was not going to visit any of them, except Aunt Lorie, because she was mad at them all. She told Andy they all helped hasten Mama's death.

Jane left for Oregon as planned, arriving in Sloan Tuesday evening. She called Aunt Lorie, announcing their arrival. They were spending the night in Sloan and would catch a bus to Fleming the following day. Jane did not know when the bus was scheduled to arrive but would call when they got there. Aunt Lorie learned a bus from Sloan would arrive at one thirty and another that evening around six o'clock. Jane and Ben were on the one-thirty bus but could not locate Lorie's phone number and did not call until late that evening. Jane explained that someone finally helped them find the number.

When Lorie drove to the depot, she did not see anyone and drove around the block. Not knowing what to look for, as she came around the block, she caught sight of them across the street from the bus station on the courthouse lawn, sitting on some of their things. At first, she did not recognize them as they resembled homeless people. They were both wearing big hats. Jane was also wearing an old, stained, tan-colored raincoat.

Lorie's station wagon was packed with their things. They would have to come back in the morning to pick up the rest of the camping gear that was locked inside the closed bus station. Lorie got the impression they were prepared to set up camp anywhere along the way if they saw a desirable spot. She was mystified as to how they would ever have gotten back on a bus to continue their trip. Jane had also told me if they saw a nice place to camp, they were going to get off the bus. I shared the same thoughts.

Before reaching Lorie's home, a stop was made to pick up hamburgers and some items for a salad for their dinner. As Jane entered Aunt Lorie's home, she caught sight of an old radio. "That is my dad's radio. He left it here years ago," Jane announced.

Lorie was not sure what Jane was implying but was now on guard for whatever other strange things Jane might be thinking. Jane and Ben spent the night in the guest room, while the dog slept in the garage. Ginger was not allowed in the house. She smelled putrid because of a very bad infection on her side. Lorie felt for the unfortunate people on the bus who had to tolerate the horrific stench.

On Thursday morning, the remaining camping gear was retrieved from the locker at the bus station, and a side trip was made for Jane to buy dog food. Mark, Lorie's only son, and his wife and children came for dinner. His wife brought food, and everyone enjoyed a delicious dinner. After the group finished the satisfying meal, Mark expressed his pleasure, saying, "I'm full."

"You are full of satin," Jane blurted. Mark ignored Jane, letting what she said go by unacknowledged.

Jane and Ben insisted they wanted to go camping. After dinner, they decided to set up camp near the creek at the end of Lorie's property. Ginger was left in the yard while they set up their tent for the night.

Lorie was concerned for Ginger, who was whining and barking while they were gone. Ginger was part poodle and badly matted from neglect of proper grooming. Jane placed a cardboard contraption around Ginger's head to keep her from chewing her infected side. The lesion was awful, and the poor dog was attracting flies.

After the campsite was ready, Ginger joined Jane and Ben inside their tent. Jane was happy and insisted on singing and talking, keeping Ben awake. Ben went to the house to get away from her. Lorie refused to let him in, telling him, "NO! Either you both sleep inside or both outside." Ben did not like it, but Lorie did not really care what either thought. They both remained outside.

During their visit, Jane chatted incessantly, telling Lorie all kinds of things, some of which she doubted was truthful. According to Jane, Lorie should have her lungs collapsed and reinflated to solve her breathing problems. Jane could not understand why it had not been done. Lorie did not share Jane's enthusiasm for having that procedure.

Jane talked about a correspondence course she was taking in law. She thought with the course and her writing, she should be able to make enough to live. She was planning to go off the antipsychotic medication.

Lorie wanted to take a picture of Jane, but she refused. Once her hair had been washed, she changed her mind. She started acting silly and donned three hats at the same time. She then told Lorie she could take her picture. Lorie wanted a more sensible picture so did not take any.

There were times when Lorie said something disagreeable to Jane. Jane would react by placing her hands on her chest, saying Lorie was causing her to have a heart attack. When Lorie asked her if she had seen a doctor, Jane responded by saying she was taking care of it herself. Lorie could see through Jane's childish behavior and pitied Julie and me since we were constantly being bombarded by Jane's bizarre behavior.

Lorie skipped church to take Jane and Ben to the bus station. They would spend the night in Sloan and begin the long trip home Monday morning. Lorie sent a short e-mail to Jane, asking if they got home okay. The following day, there was still no word. Jane finally called Lorie. She had not responded sooner because the public library from where Jane sent her e-mails was closed for renovations.

Jane reported the dog got home safely; however, twice someone tried to take the dog from them. Jane was going to complain to the bus company.

Jane left one of her pillows at Lorie's and wanted it sent back. Lorie suggested she get a new one and offered to send money to cover the cost, but Jane insisted she wanted the pillow she left as it was theirs. She had no regard for imposing or the inconvenience she was causing our fragile aunt.

During the time Jane was in Oregon, Julie and I discussed the matter of Jane's diagnosis. The mental health worker whom Julie had spoken to regarding Jane's trip to Oregon had revealed Jane had multiple personality disorder. She gave a brief description of different mental illnesses and disorders. Specifically where Jane stood in the mix was not said.

We did research on the Mayo Clinic website for more clarity.

Jane displayed dysfunctional thinking from all the personality disorder categories. Noted behaviors included distrust and suspicion of others, hostility, constantly seeking attention, unstable mood, disregard for others, desire to be in control, lying or stealing, recurring difficulties with the law, and aggressive behavior.

I knew Jane was schizophrenic. It was a term our mother had used. Schizophrenics are out of touch with reality. They have bizarre delusions and can have difficulty organizing their thoughts or connecting them logically. The disorder needs constant management. It cannot be cured but can be controlled with medication.

Jane had told me she was bipolar (manic-depressive), which causes shifts in a person's mood, energy, and ability to function. The mood changes from severe highs to lows of depression.

Both schizophrenia and bipolar disorder are genetic but are not likely a result of genetics alone. There are environmental influences. Even though there were lots of references to genetic vulnerability, Jane was the only one from both sides of our family known to be mentally ill.

Julie and I were satisfied we at least had a better understanding of classifications and behaviors Jane displayed. But it would not make getting along with her any easier.

CHAPTER SIXTEEN

Ashes, Ashes, We All Fall Down

Jane was back from her trip, and so were her problems.

Julie eagerly listened to a voicemail at work from Jane, expecting to receive an answer regarding whether she had decided to participate in disbursing our mother's ashes. The message started out. "I really need to talk to you. I keep losing your phone numbers. Ben has been playing a game of push and shove. I don't know what my plans are for August. But I think during July, we are going camping. By August, we have a special needs camping trip, WHICH YOU ARE NOT INVITED TO. It is going to take one weekend. When you pick this up, my little dearest sister, maybe you'll realize that I've been your big sister for a long time. So get back to work and call me when you have a chance."

Julie called Jane after work. She shared the content of the conversation with me.

"Jane said a couple of days ago Ben said he was going to kill her. She is going to the Veteran's Administration to get him straightened out. Ben is out of the house now, but she has planned a couple of camping trips with him this summer. She said she and Ben are staying together no matter what.

"She said she loves her little sister, but I could have learned from her when I was little instead of being so 'smarty.' She should have been the first one to marry because the Bible says so. She said Mama and Daddy didn't give you and Ken permission to marry until she said it was okay and that you and Ken sat down with her to decide who Ken should marry."

Julie continued. "She said when Mama cut my bangs too short when I was a kid and I cried, that was just what needed to be done, that I should have been learning from her, blah, blah, blah . . .

"I laughed at her and told her all this was just stories. She said, 'NO, THEY AREN'T.' I told her she was making up lies, and she started yelling. I yelled at her to stop yelling. She quieted down but kept moving from one pile of hooey to the next. I listened for about fifteen minutes and didn't say a word. Some of what she said was how bad I treated Mama after she had the heart attack, and I better not ever do that to her!

"Finally, she was silent. I said, 'Oh, do I get to talk now?' I had some comments earlier, but she didn't let me speak, and I forgot what they were."

We discussed managing Jane's share of the estate. Julie was tired of dealing with Jane's nonsense. I reluctantly agreed to take it on.

* * *

Aunt Lorie informed me of a conversation she had when Jane called her. Jane was preparing to go camping. Lorie asked how her dog was doing. Jane told her Ginger was biting herself all the time and not getting any better. The veterinary could intervene, but Jane did not want to spend $300. Jane reported she had decided not to go back to work at the same home care agency where she was employed as they were crooked.

During Jane's conversation with Aunt Lorie, Jane sang "I'm Forever Blowing Bubbles," which she also sang continuously during her visit. Several years previously, Jane assisted our aunt in finding the words. Since then, every time they talked, Jane sang it to her. Once the library's renovation was completed, Lorie was hoping Jane would go back to writing her e-mails rather than calling so often.

Toward the end of July, James King, who had been our mother's attorney, phoned me regarding Jane. "She is dressing quite shabbily. I suggested she get some new clothes," stated James. "She said new clothes are too expensive, and she has plenty of her own clothes."

He revealed an incident that happened at church. "Jane was acting inappropriately in the choir, being loud and obnoxious, and was asked to leave. She sat in a pew temporarily and then wandered down to the children's church in the basement and sat down with the children, where she talked baby talk.

"In another incident, the police were called to the supermarket where she was causing a disturbance and almost got arrested. They let her go when she agreed to leave peacefully," reported James. It was learned later she had been banned from going there.

"I contribute her behavior to her medications. They need to be readjusted," James stated. I doubted she was on medications.

* * *

The time had come to take care of our mother's ashes. Julie and Gerald arrived in Wentwood on Friday. Ken and I arrived the following morning. It was decided to enjoy the afternoon by retracing Daddy's old mail route. The mail route was a contracted route where Daddy or Mama delivered mail six mornings every week for twenty-five years.

It had been decades since we had been that way. The road had been rerouted and bypassed the deadly curve where Ken's high school friend had been killed in a car accident when he was nineteen.

Memories returned of the pleasant summer days when my sisters and I would take turns going on the mail route with Mama and assisted putting mail in the boxes. Mama delivered the mail to free Daddy to take tourists down the river in a rubber raft on morning fishing trips. He was generally booked both mornings and afternoons beginning from May into the fall.

When Mama had finished sorting the mail, she would stop by the corner supermarket before beginning the mail route. The sister whose turn it was to go with her was given a nickel to spend on a candy bar.

The two of us who stayed home took turns washing and drying and putting away the dishes. There was always quite a stack! Mama routinely cooked full-fledged dinners, which generally included the pressure cooker and other heavy, greasy pans.

Jane did not like doing dishes, not that Julie or I relished the chore either. Her approach was to tackle the task head-on and get out of the kitchen. There was no diddle-dallying on her part. She wanted to go read.

Julie was another story. It would take her forever to decide to begin, and then she would play with the bubbles and spend hours pouring the water back and forth between the cups and other containers. The water was stone cold by the time she finished, which was minutes before Mama returned.

The mail route ended at an old mining town, where there was a water trough. Sometimes we would stop to get a drink from a pipe that fed the trough with fresh mountain spring water. It was the best-tasting water anyone could ever find and well worth sidestepping mud that had formed from the excess water tumbling over the edge of the trough.

Upon returning, Julie and I wanted to locate the residence that was listed on our birth certificates. Julie was only three weeks old when we moved from the Cricket House to the log house our father had built in 1950.

A For Rent sign listing a phone number was posted in a window of the Cricket House. Our group circled the empty old house, looking in the windows, yearning to experience the inside.

"Let's call the number and see if it is possible to go through the house," Julie suggested. From her cell phone,

Julie reached the realtor, Mrs. Atwood, who agreed to meet us at the house after church the next day.

The day was getting away. Four boxes of our mother's papers that I had brought were waiting to be sorted. Many love letters Daddy had written to Mama while he was a marine in World War II were found. Julie wanted to keep them and stowed them away in the corner of an empty suitcase she had brought for this purpose.

Picture albums full of people we did not recognize were given to Julie for the keeping. Countless miscellaneous items and souvenirs were found that had been kept in remembrance of a time long past.

Dinnertime was approaching when we decided to take a break. We walked along Main Street, which now had an entirely different demeanor than when we were growing up. The clothing store where I had worked while attending high school was gone. The old brick school building, reminiscent of most of our schooling, was now a government services building. There were numerous other changes that had gradually taken place. It hardly resembled our hometown. Whoever said you can never go home was so right.

After enjoying a relaxing dinner, it was time to return to the motel to finish sorting the remainder of the contents from the boxes.

A beautiful Sunday morning was emerging for the long-planned event. Our mother's ashes were divided among three bud vases, which included one for Jane in case she decided to appear. The snaps from the incinerated coin purse were found at the bottom of the ashes, where the lady from the mortuary had said they would be. The snaps were removed to give Jane as proof we had received our mother's ashes.

Our group arrived at the designated spot early, maneuvering the steep drop-off from the highway to an open area by the river. The rented SUV was parked in the shade offered by a grouping of willows. Close by, a blue pickup truck was parked on the small sandy area. Ripples of the clear blue water lapped against the bank.

It was 10:45 A.M. with no sign of Jane and Ben. Julie and I shared mixed emotions about Jane's absence. Even though it made things simpler and pleasanter, she should have been there to participate.

Standing by the SUV, Gerald took the Bible out from under his arm and read a carefully selected verse, followed by the release of the ashes from our respective bud vases. I handed Julie the vase that was intended for Jane, and the remaining third followed. There was an unsaid mutual feeling of sanctity in letting all the ashes go at once.

Our goal had been accomplished. Our solemn group did not linger. An early lunch was to follow with browsing through shops before meeting Mrs. Atwood at the Cricket House.

Mrs. Atwood graciously unlocked the front door and waited patiently as we inspected each room with delight. The house had been well kept. There was a unique cupboard that opened both from the kitchen side and the dining room side. The dining room harbored a cute built-in bookcase. A bay window was the highlight of the living room. A small isolated room inconspicuously came off the living room. I could picture the space with a baby crib and envisioned it being where I had slept.

An addition had been built to the back of the house, which included a large master bedroom and a bathroom. "Where was the original bathroom?" I asked.

"It didn't have one," replied Mrs. Atwood. "They used an outhouse. The house was built around 1880 when most people did not have indoor plumbing."

I never had quite understood why Mama said when she went to the bathroom, the whole neighborhood knew. I followed her and stood outside the door, crying, "Mama, Mama." She failed to mention the important detail that she was referring to an outdoor privy.

Julie and I were mesmerized by the old stone house and were curious as to who owned it. With Mrs. Atwood's assistance, Julie later contacted the owners and learned the house was built in 1879. It had been inherited by a man who had inherited it from his mother, who had inherited it from her mother, who was a midwife. The ranchers would come in town to have their babies there. After Mary passed away, it was estimated she delivered over one thousand babies there. Julie and I were fascinated to learn we had lived in a house that had served an important role in the history of our hometown.

After the tour of the Cricket House, the events of the gathering came to a close. Julie and Gerald spent the afternoon fishing, while Ken and I embarked on our five-hour drive home.

CHAPTER SEVENTEEN

Going Haywire

Upon returning home, Julie found a birthday letter from Jane. Jane drew a picture that depicted Julie and me releasing our mother's ashes. One figure in the drawing said, "We are finally rid of the old hag." The other figure said, "Too bad the old biddy didn't kick the bucket sooner!"

The letter accused Julie of being a social climber and stated all Julie was interested in was money. Jane had drawn a picture of a head with teeth eating money. "Chop, chop, yum, yum." The letter ended, saying, "Our dog, Ginger, died of maggots, same as Ben's mother. Lovely way to go! Sorry for the sarcasm. Learn from it."

There was a message on Julie's answering machine from Jane. She tried unsuccessfully to return the call. Julie resorted to sending an e-mail:

I have tried to call you several times and your phone just rings and rings. In your voicemail you said Elaine and I are after your money and that I was mean to Mama.

First off, I followed Mama's wishes to the letter. I don't want your money. I know you are mentally ill, but do you have to be so mean? If you want to call and talk, leave out the lies and insults. Either be civil or stay away.

Mid-August, Jane responded to Julie's e-mail.

One reason I can tell you these things, is because, in my opinion, you follow the money. The answering machine is not plugged in.

I hope you received your birthday card. Sorry it was late. You do not understand me, and am not certain I ever will you, either.

I am taking some people camping soon and am working toward that goal—have been for the past few weeks.

There is a lot to do. The goal is to get people well, did you hear that? I am a nurse's aide with that milieu. I always was here or in heaven and I am happy that I never had to figure some things out, even though there are a lot of things I really need to learn more about.

It is a zany world, and I don't believe much I see and certainly not a lot of what I hear.

* * *

"We buried Ginger," Jane announced in a call to me.

"What did she die from?" I asked.

"The kids in the apartment next door go by the porch and tease her, which makes her bark and jump around. Ben left the saw blade uncovered," said Jane, leaving the rest to my imagination.

Ginger was very excitable, and that hint of an explanation sounded logical with the information Aunt Lorie had supplied regarding the open lesion.

* * *

Aunt Lori had expressed to Jane she had not been able to accomplish much lately. Lori was dumbfounded with Jane's reply that made no sense whatsoever. She forwarded it to me to see if I could understand it:

> *Not getting anything done is part of the grief we feel right now. Ride it through because it is a dear and tender time to reflect on how much she meant to us all. Remember the Old Oaken Bucket? And Silver Cords among the Golden Ribbons? I like Clementine and Old Dan Tucker. The Ship of Fools seems like the good ship Lollipop compared to today on the Spaceship Beagle (which by the way is the name of a book first written in the 1960's).*
>
> *Anyway, I hope you know that my time is come, like the old time song, Our Time Will Come. We pursue happiness all our lives. Mama and I had a very difficult time. We now live in the age of the Water Barer. We were*

in the Age of the Fish. What exactly does that mean? I do not know, but I do know that the change has been very gradual and we are simply in the decennium of Jesus, or maybe it is time for a new leader such as He.

These are some thoughts in profoundness that came to me when I could not see when I lost my glasses.

Jane sounded like she was headed for the state hospital in Baldwin to me.

Upon returning from an extended weekend out of town, I was greeted by e-mails from Jane:

It has been a long time since I have heard from you. Does Ken still have the hiccups? I love you both, but I will not let you take me out of circulation by your proving what is not true. Did you catch that? I understand you are trying still. Gemini? Love you Elaine. Are you there? Calling from outer space . . . this is Jane . . . No reply . . . Trying again.

I responded to Jane's e-mail:

We have been gone for a reunion with Ken's family. I have not been ignoring you. We just got home late yesterday afternoon.

Jane e-mailed the following response:

I am pretty worried about Julie right now. Did the storm fly by? And there's more to come so they say.

What are you all doing these days besides being swift and coy?

Do you want the next hurricane (Katrina) *to be named after you?*

So more of what you handed me. Toss it up in the air, catch it, and smile for the camera. Love you much.

Jane e-mailed me again:

I plan to have the business "The Rosebud Design" as the basis for a future LLC.

In going forward today I am hoping to work on another project: Assisting the American Red Cross over the internet in routing relief efforts to the disaster areas. (Hurricane Katrina) *Julie could have died. Are you guys in some kind of selfishness fog or something?*

Have you ever read James Bond pocket novels or followed the line of such authors as Katherine Anne Porter or Willa Cather? The Maltese Falcon, *I read shortly before leaving Preston. So, think about life, not just you. And please tell Emma, Jane is very glad Mama and she had some quality time together in spite of the rest of you;* (referring to when they spent time together when coming for Jack and Claudia's wedding). *Julie sent me the remains* (snaps from our mother's coin purse) *due me and it made me ill.*

May the force be with you is out of Star Trek?

I answered Jane's e-mail, telling her Julie was okay; I had talked to her last night.

It was already September. Jane was requesting funds from Julie:

> *Julie, I am working with the Red Cross relief effort*
> *for the Blackburn area as chief communicator something,*
> *so can you send me $300. Fast, no strings attached and I*
> *will use the paid qualifiable bills as fast as I can. When*
> *I can I will send receipts by US Postal Service mail. The*
> *less electrical stuff, the better . . . don't you think . . .*
> *sorry for the delay.*
> *With much love for a really sweet slick little sister.*

On September 2 at six thirty in the morning, Julie received a phone call from the Trenton Mental Health facility. Jane had been *caught* by the Blackburn police and taken to the hospital in Westbrook, where she would be held for seventy-two hours until she *leveled out*. The lady who called Julie said Jane had not been taking her medications. Jane was quoting English literature and had been singing to them for the past half hour. They were trying to locate Ben.

The following day after playing telephone tag, Dr. Clayman from the psychiatric unit reached Julie. "Jane is not cooperating. I need her history. She won't tell me which medications she had been on or anything else."

"The Trenton Mental Health facility has a file on Jane. There are records at the state hospital in Baldwin also." Julie proceeded to give him Jane's maiden name and her two married names. He was surprised Jane was married.

"Jane has been in and out of mental health facilities most of her life. She is bipolar and has other issues," Julie offered.

"That goes along with my observations. She is displaying manic tendencies," the doctor stated.

"Why has she been picked up?" Julie asked.

"She was out in the middle of the highway, yelling at people as they drove by. The speed limit is sixty-five, and she was in danger of being hit," replied Dr. Clayman.

"What will happen to her at the end of the seventy-two hours?" Julie questioned.

"Depending on how things go, she may end up in Baldwin," he replied.

Julie called me to see if I knew how to locate Ben since he was not staying at the apartment. I knew Ben had a sister named Carrie and where she might work. She would know where Ben was. The following day, Julie spoke with Carrie and learned Ben had received the message left with her husband, Herman, and that Ben had gone to Westbrook to check on Jane.

Carrie began speaking, freely divulging information that was new to Julie. "Jane started going off the deep end when her mother died. She almost got in trouble recently at Blackburn Super. She was threatening the customers because she thinks everyone is out to get her. She will pound on people's doors at night. A couple of months ago in July, Jane had set up camp at a dinner in Trenton. I went down and got her. She had been out in traffic, yelling at cars."

Carrie acknowledged she had helped Ben "rescue" Jane on numerous occasions. Carrie kept spewing more information. "When Jane kicks Ben out, he sneaks back in and sleeps on the porch to watch that she does not go out. When she cannot sleep, she takes walks and sings songs. Once she was arrested for being out in the middle of the night, disturbing people.

"Ben will do everything he can to keep her out of the state hospital. The last time, he did research and found that she had spinal meningitis when she was a teenager. He got this information from her records. Ben found they had her on the wrong medications, which caused her to be really violent. When she gets this way, she especially hates men. Ben had to really fight to get her out."

Ben's family was aware of Jane's history before he married her. "I sat down with Ben and asked him if he really wanted to take it on. He really does love her. Ben is exactly like his father, very kind and loving." Carrie continued. "Jane is very intelligent, and Ben has the IQ of a genius in science and math, and that is why he understands Jane. Ben had a heart problem and epilepsy. They said he would not live to be two years old. When he was a teenager, he was healed at a Billy Graham Crusade. Ben went back to his doctor, and the healing was confirmed. He went into the navy after that.

"Every so often, Jane stops taking her medications because she feels she is fine and doesn't need them any longer. Her mother didn't help as she believed in healing through vitamins and nutrition."

Carrie talked about the problems they had getting Jane to take her medications. Sometimes Jane would hide them. One time when Carrie was trying to get Jane to take her pills, she bit Carrie's finger. "She bit down very hard and would not let go. When she finally did let go, the tip of my finger was hanging on by a piece of skin. I had to go to the emergency room to have it sewn back on. It took a long time to get the feeling back," Carrie reported.

Another time when Jane did not want to take her meds, she scratched Carrie's granddaughter on the back with deep scratches. There was such a commotion the neighbors called the police. Carrie talked the police into dismissing the call.

Carrie made reference to Jane removing Mama and Daddy's clothing from the storage unit. She had not yet given the clothes to charities as she had claimed were her intentions; instead, she was wearing them, coming up with some very strange outfits.

During the conversation, Carrie confided that Jane resented us coming to help care for our mother.

CHAPTER EIGHTEEN

Trust Who?

I called Carrie to inquire if Jane had been released yet. "She is still at Westbrook," reported Carrie. "They were going to transfer her to Baldwin, but yesterday Ben talked her into cooperating. They are going to keep her there for now. She is on a new medication. The medication isn't bringing her back as soon as Ben thought it should.

"It has been five or six years since she was in Baldwin. Since Ben and Jane have been married, she has had three major events, which led to her being institutionalized, and numerous minor times," Carrie volunteered.

"It has been a hotter summer than usual, which contributes to Jane having an episode. Heat and crisis could cause Jane's medications not to work as well," Carrie told me.

Whenever Jane went outside, she wore a hat. According to Mama, too much exposure to the sun contributed to Jane getting *sick*. Whether the sun was a legitimate excuse, it was already known Jane had not been taking her medications.

"Between your mother and me, we were pretty much able to keep her somewhat under control," Carrie stated.

"Ben and Jane haven't been getting along very well," I related.

"Ben would not hear of divorcing Jane. He loves her so much. He took her camping throughout the summer to help her get over her mother's death."

Carrie's version was sugarcoated and inconsistent to what I already knew. According to Jane, she was going camping, and Ben would probably go along as he liked her cooking. And why was he punching Jane if he loves her so much?

I relayed the news to Julie. Julie reacted. "Just an interesting thought—if Ben can talk her into cooperating, doesn't that mean she DOES have control over her actions?"

"That is EXACTLY what I was thinking," I replied. "That means she does have some control and chooses to be a pain in the butt. It is rare that I've seen her when she doesn't get mad. We must be a catalyst for her anger to surface."

Julie informed me about the call she received from Jane at 6:30 A.M. at her home. Julie was in the process of transferring Jane's share of the estate for me to manage. "Jane said she didn't know what I'm doing with her money, but whatever it is, she said, 'I don't like it ONE BIT!' I told her I didn't care whether she liked it. I am following the law.

"Then she said she had been in the hospital. I told her I knew. They called me. She was surprised. I said if they hadn't gotten in touch with me and I wouldn't have found Ben, they would have taken her to Baldwin. She started yelling, something about when we were kids. Then she told me I needed to get married because people in the South didn't like women of ill repute. I told her I had to go to work and hung up. Sometimes I feel guilty for hanging up on her, but what am I really supposed to do? Just keep taking her abuse?" Julie related.

"I'm in a quandary about dealing with Jane also," I replied. "Since we have always been out there, being batted around in the wind with no direction, it is difficult to know how we should respond to her. Just as I'm beginning to think things aren't that bad and wonder if we are being too sensitive, we get freshly raked over the coals again."

Julie received an e-mail from Jane:

> *Thanks Julie, for your take charge attitude. It does me wonders of nothingness . . . My glasses are not ready and I don't know how much the settlement was for.*
>
> *It really hurts that Mama did not trust you two to make sure I received my share and that is why she and I kinda decided this would be the best way to go.*

Julie responded to Jane:

> *Your portion has been set up according to Mama's will. It would make me very happy if you could take control of your share, then you wouldn't call me names. I'm sorry you were in the hospital. They said you were in danger of getting run over. That is why they picked you up.*

Julie was Jane's favorite scapegoat for now.

Ken and I were sleeping in as usually on a Sunday morning when the phone rang at seven o'clock on the dot. Ken answered; it was Jane. "Your driving in circles made me dizzy. It's against the law." Jane was referring to the time we took her to see Mama when she was in the Blackburn Hospital, and he turned around in the supermarket's parking lot.

The phone was turned over to me. "Mama would still be here if we had lived in a bigger city, where she would have gotten better care. My optometrist told me not to go there again." Jane went on talking about losing her bills, her glasses, and her keys.

"Clear off a spot and always put those things in that place," I suggested.

"I do, but Ben plays tricks on me and hides them. He is staying at the shed now. I am working on a newsletter."

Jane was referring to the *Rosebud Design*, which she named the newsletter publication she prepared and sent out to a few subscribers every other month or so. Her publication consisted of several pages created on a computer. She wrote derogative statements about the mental health care system, making reference to being forced to take medications against one's will and being kidnapped by the system and how the system exploits unfortunate people. She made little drawings, quotes, and jokes and even included a "Questions to the Editor" section, where she answered the questions. It was obvious she made up the questions herself. For the most part, it was a bunch of malarkey, but it gave her purpose.

Jane brought up her recent hospital stay. "I got put in the hospital because Mama wasn't there to tell me not to go out and stop cars."

"You are mature enough you should not need Mama to tell you that sort of thing," I stated.

"Yeah, in years but not mentally. I need Mama to talk to me about those things. The medication they have me on is making me lose my sight. The doctor is going to cut back on the medication. I want you to invest in a stable stock in copper. It has been around for years."

"I am not going to invest in a stock. It is too volatile," I told her.

"Put it in bonds like Daddy and Mama had during World War II. You can get a lot of interest from bonds. Why don't you just take the money and put it in bonds and send them to me?"

She went on and on, not pausing to give me a chance to speak. I began talking at the same time. "There is no way I am going to buy bonds and send them to you." I had to get my point across then; otherwise, by the time Jane came up for air, I would have been led through Wonderland and back and lost track of what I wanted to say.

Jane was on the attack again. "Mama didn't trust Julie or you to handle her money. Blah, blah, blah."

I jumped right in again, knowing Jane would not stop talking. "Mama trusted Julie and me, or she would not have specifically stated in her will for us to be in charge of her estate."

Jane responded with a deflated "Oh."

Jane started talking about the truck needing repaired and other things that needed fixed. I tried to reel her in, but she was way down the road and started talking about a lady who came over and helped her wash dishes. Jane failed to mention she paid the lady.

CHAPTER NINETEEN

Never-Ending Conflict

It was the first few days into November when Jane called my home. "Call back this evening when Elaine will be here," Ken told her, but she insisted on talking to him.

"I found a new will, and I'm contesting the one used. Have investments been made with any of my money?" Jane asked.

"I don't have anything to do with it," Ken answered.

"If Elaine has, she is breaking the law." Jane knew the funds had been invested. She had been sent a bank statement copy, which included a note listing the investments.

"Stop your breathing thing," Jane spouted. Jane claimed Ken used hyperventilation and repetition techniques over the phone that could set up an irregular heart rate, which made her quite ill. "Have Elaine call me back this evening."

"You can call her," Ken said in return.

Ken notified me at work that Jane was claiming to have found a new will. I e-mailed James King, Mama's attorney, who set up her new will only days prior to her heart attack.

James e-mailed back immediately:

> *There is no other will; Jane sometimes does not have the same reality you and I have. You <u>should be</u> investing the funds. I have seen Jane twice recently. She is not tracking very well.*

That evening, Jane phoned, throwing out insults, calling me stupid and a weasel, and then went on with a multitude of topics. "I've read books on family dynamics. The middle child causes trouble. You played me and Julie against each other, just like the book said. While Julie and you were playing, I read books and watched Mama cook. I'm better off for you shutting me out."

"You would not play with me," I responded back.

"We played paper dolls. Mama didn't like the names you gave your children. She wanted you to name them after family members rather than popular names." Jane quickly changed topics. "The preacher should not have called the ambulance because Mama told them not to, and they should have done as she said."

I broke in. "They had already called for an ambulance before Mama said not to."

"They shouldn't have taken her without asking her," Jane claimed.

"If they had not taken her to the hospital, she would have died," I chimed back.

"That is okay. That is what Mama wanted. They were overstepping their bounds. They should have taken her home like she asked!"

There were times Jane totally defied common sense. Julie would comment, saying, "You have to remember she is nuts." Not that I had forgotten, by any means, but I was making a mistake in thinking Jane could be reasoned with.

The conversation continued. "I have a tooth that fell out," Jane reported.

"The estate will pay for your dental work," I stated.

Jane suddenly got very angry. "I don't want you handling my money! I don't want you to know my business. The bill for my hospital stay was $40,000. They are billing me for $900. I am paying a small portion of it."

"The estate can pay the $900," I mentioned.

Jane flew into a rage, yelling, "ONLY DENTAL CARE CAN BE PAID FROM THE ESTATE!"

While my ears were still recovering, the topic took an abrupt change. "You should have moved closer to Mama so she could see your kids and the grandkids."

As far as I was concerned, we lived close enough. If Mama wanted to see her grandchildren and great-grandchildren more, she could have made an effort to come see them.

I received a Christmas card from Jane with a scribbled letter, saying, "We have a communication gap." She claimed I kept interrupting her every time she had something important to say. She made accusations of Julie and me playing dirty tricks on her. She claimed I would not release information regarding her money, even though she had been sent bank statements every month and been told over the phone besides written documentation of the particulars of the investments.

I answered Jane's letter, saying, "You are right, we have a major communication gap. Since you dominate the conversations, you cannot blame me for not having a chance to say what you want. Julie and I are not playing tricks on you. We have never done anything to make things difficult for you." I ended by saying, "Here is wishing you a much happier New Year in 2006 than 2005 was."

* * *

Julie's responsibilities for settling our mother's estate had finally been completed. Issues between Jane and Julie had simmered down tremendously.

Julie spoke to me over the phone. "Jane told me she is going to take you to the Sixth District Court if she has to. She said she is going to get her birthright back as being the oldest."

As I was sitting down to eat dinner, Jane phoned. "The will says the money is for my personal enjoyment."

"My copy does not say that," I stated.

"There are three different wills. Each of ours is different," replied Jane.

Jane went on about needing dental work and would have to go to Edmond for an evaluation. She talked about "potholes" in her kitchen floor and needing new linoleum, besides the truck needing repairs.

"Do you remember when we were kids, and you were playing with blocks, and I knocked them all down, and you didn't know what to do?" Jane touted, trying to get her point across that she was in charge, and I could not do anything about it.

"No," I replied. Later, I recalled when I was little, it was rare when I would play with the wooden blocks, or anything else for that manner, when Jane did not take great pleasure in messing up whatever I was doing.

"You are knocking me off my throne!" bellowed Jane.

"You were never on a throne!" I retorted back. "You are not better than Julie or me!"

"I don't mean to imply I'm better," said Jane. "Being the oldest has more clout. The pecking order is all messed up now. I stayed around to take care of Mama. If you and Julie had stayed around, you would have turned out differently. I don't even know you or Julie.

"You are a crook," Jane announced out of nowhere.

Angrily, I quickly replied, "I am not a crook, and you have no business calling me that!"

Evading the situation entirely, Jane said, "We need to make a trip to Wentwood to spread Mama's ashes." Jane still had not realized Julie had not sent ashes. She had possession of the snaps from the incinerated coin purse.

"I can't talk anymore. My head is going to fall off," Jane stated, not literally meaning her head was going to fall off; it was a term Mama used to say when she was tired and had a headache. With that remark, she hung up as I resumed eating my now-cold dinner.

* * *

When Ken and I returned home from work one day in February, there was a series of seventeen voice messages from Jane on our answering machine. When the machine clicked off, she pushed redial and kept going, not skipping a beat. Her stammering message began:

"What a pain in the neck am I? I paid $39 of the ambulance bill. I kind of think what I want to do instead of having you take care of my finances. I'm going to pay it on credit."

"I've studied a lot of English literature and stuff, and I love you, guys. We are getting ready to go to the VA today. I've been working on the computer quite a bit, and I've been under quite a bit of stress, but that doesn't mean I'm going to fold. It just means that the way life is outside of things, and to tell the truth, I held out just about as long as I thought I was going to."

"It's the bills from the incarceration that makes my life miserable. I love you, folks, but as long as I'm staying away from you, folks, that makes me happy too. I've been on the wrong end of the stick, and I don't want to stay there! So if you think I'm proud, if you think I'm haughty, if you think I am wrong, that's okay. That's your attitude, but I've got my pride, and I'm also taking a criminal justice course, and so far, my grades have shot up to an A."

"I think I know what I'm talking about. It's a government of the people, by the people, for the people, and I'm one of the people too."

She talked about a spaghetti dinner she put on every year to raise funds to take people camping who had been in the mental health system. The funds were also used for taking clothing and books to Baldwin. Jane complained about how things from our mother's estate were divided up.

"I'm sorry, Elaine, but that's not the way life is. YOU'RE NOT MY BIG SISTER! As far as you are concerned, I don't even exist. You showed that when you helped with the obituary.

"You guys live the wannabe, gonna be lives, while we live the rank and poverty mess. I will tell you one thing. I bet we are a whole lot happier.

"In the process of you guys having your fun, you are hurting my feelings. Also, I might mention the monies from your trip to Disneyland were supposed to be deducted from the amount that everybody got from the will.

"I don't have very much time. I'm busy paying bills, and when I'm not paying bills, I'm busy working on the newsletter, and when I'm not doing that, I'm doing something else.

"I'm signing off. Too bad I just love to talk so much. Do you want to pay my phone bill? Thank you. Goodbye."

Two days later, Jane called again. She was chatting about when she was little and said she started walking when she was eight months old. She talked about when we lived at the Cricket House before Julie was born. But mostly, she talked about Ben's relatives, his nieces and nephews, and how cute they were and Ben's aunts and uncles and who had divorced. She mentioned she wanted to buy the apartment next door.

In the days that followed, calls routinely came from Jane. One morning at six fifteen, while I was rushing around, getting ready for work, Jane phoned. I was later than usual, getting up with a headache and discovering a crop of cold sores on my lips. Jane was complaining about letters she was receiving for the ambulance bill, threatening to take her to court. "Every time I get one of those letters, it makes me sick, same as when I get a bank statement from you."

Jane wanted to buy the apartment next door using estate funds. "The estate money is for emergencies and supplemental expenses," I replied.

Jane got mad. "I never have emergencies! Can you remember all this?"

"I need to leave soon. Write it down," I told her as a diversion to pacify her for the moment.

"I don't have a pencil, and it is dark. If I write it down, it could become a contract, and I might change my mind," she said, reinforcing her irrational thinking.

I repeated, "I have to go. Goodbye." I then hung up.

* * *

The first anniversary of our mother's death was upon us. Her death was most devastating to Jane. Our mother was the only one Jane could always rely on to be there for her. She was a part of Jane's everyday existence, and she had been Jane's stabilizing force. The chaos caused by Jane's actions had not allowed Julie and me the peace and serenity that we were entitled to in coming to terms with the loss of our mother.

* * *

Jane phoned one evening. "I want you to invest some of the funds in a stock I like. YOU BETTER DO WHAT I'M TELLING YOU!"

I had no intentions of changing the investments.

"You are giving me a heart attack, and that is okay if I die. I'll go to heaven, and I won't need the money. And you will be in the *other* place," Jane said angrily.

I refrained from saying "If I died and you were there, I would know I was in hell."

CHAPTER TWENTY

Potentially Toothless

Jane had not been heard from in several weeks. Suddenly, she popped up like a hydrogen bomb blast, flaring with fires from hell, demanding I give her money to go to the dentist.

Jane was hysterical, yelling, making accusations, and saying I was taking away her citizenship. She would not stop yelling. I hung up. I was concerned Jane may end up back in a psychiatric unit.

When I got home from work the following day, there was a message on the answering machine to call Megan Spice, explaining she was Jane's sister-in-law and needed to talk to me about getting Jane's teeth fixed. I returned her call.

Megan began, "Jane has talked to me about needing to get a tooth fixed because she is in pain, and she wanted to know if you could help. Can you see that a dentist gets paid?"

"Yes, of course," I responded. "Jane was yelling so much she didn't make sense. I couldn't talk to her. Jane never mentioned being in pain."

"I am a dental hygienist for Neil Mitchell. Since Jane is family, he has done dental work for her at little or no charge. I am no longer working for him. Eldon and I are preparing to move soon. I don't feel Dr. Mitchell should be asked to cover Jane's dental needs. Could you possibly bring Jane to Bingham to take her to a dentist there?"

NO, NO, NO! I was screaming in my head. That was totally out of the question. I would rather be shot at dawn than have to deal with Jane going into one of her inevitable stark raving mad episodes at a dentist's office. Besides, it would be a major thankless imposition to transport Jane back and forth. I replied calmly, "I would have to miss work, and it would not be practical for us to go that far to get her to appointments and back home."

"There are two low-income clinics in Westbrook, but I do not know if they would be willing to work with Jane because she is so difficult. Jane gets mad easily and goes into temper tantrums," stated Megan. "She has a high pain threshold. She doesn't want to put Novocain in her system. She also does not want any X-rays or partials."

"Jane is very bad about keeping appointments. Because of that, it may not work to have a treatment plan. I will see if Dr. Mitchell will work on one tooth at a time."

Megan made several references to Jane getting out of the hospital. I assumed she was referring to when Jane was at Westbrook in September until I realized Megan was making reference to Jane getting out several days ago. Megan began talking about strange things Jane had been doing.

"Last summer, just before she went off the deep end, she disappeared for three days in the Dodge truck. By chance, I recognized their truck parked alongside the road. The police were there talking to Jane. I stopped to see what was going on.

"Jane was wearing a pair of your dad's long johns and was in the back of the truck, making a tent. She got in the truck and drove off, saying, 'You can't catch me.' She stuck her tongue out at the police and drove off. She had not done anything wrong, so they could not take her in.

"Another time she was out in front of a restaurant in the back of the truck, wearing your father's long johns, and waving at people. The police were there. While trying to contain her, she somehow slipped away and got in the truck. She locked the doors and rolled up the windows. She yelled at them, 'You will have to catch me first!' She stuck her tongue out at them and drove off with a smirk on her face."

I was mortified to listen as Megan kept on going.

"Around Easter, she was making some spooky comments, threatening Ben. She said, 'I don't know what I will do to you. You better go stay with your sister.' Ben sleeps with one eye open. She got worse when your mother died. She said to me, 'Some day they will take me away, and I won't be coming back. Then who will take care of Ben?' It is probably a matter of time before she gets committed. Her episodes are getting more frequent than usual."

"What did she do this last time?" I asked.

"I don't know specifically. She had been threatening the neighbors. They are really afraid of her. Jane is welcome at our family events like birthday parties. She gets tired, and we take her home. When she says off-the-wall things, we just smile. She licks the sugar spoon and puts it back in. We tell her, 'No, you can't do that here.' She does bizarre things to get attention.

"From the clothes she has of your mom and dad, she dresses up in these weird outfits, and she always wears a hat. She looks like a character out of *Hee Haw*. She was wearing a bicycle safety helmet and carrying around a lunch box. She is very entertaining."

Ben's family was used to Jane's strange behavior and did not seem to get upset with her outlandish actions.

"Jane is planning to build a wall by the alley and wants me to go with her to get blocks. I talked my way out of it." Megan talked about several other situations before the hour-long conversation culminated.

The following day, Jane called me, going into her bashing routine. "By the way, my phone might be tapped. They think I am a danger." In her next breath, Jane lit into me. "You are a weasel. Have you heard that before? Thank you for working with the dentist to get my teeth fixed. A couple of children said I threatened to kill them, but I DID NOT! Now we have that hanging over our heads." Changing the subject, Jane abruptly said, "Megan finally got through to you."

"I was able to talk to Megan in a civilized matter. She did not yell. You should have told me you were in pain, and I would have arranged to pay the dentist," I stated. The attorney had told me not to give her cash.

"I was trying to, but I was too upset. You are a shithead," Jane blurted. "You are trying to get me committed."

"I am not—"

Jane broke in. "You are in trouble with God."

"I'm not in trouble with God."

"Yes, you are," Jane retorted back. "You said you were going to take care of me. I don't want you controlling me."

"I have no intentions of controlling you," I replied, doubting if it was possible for anyone to *control* her.

"I have to hang up. I am waiting for a call regarding my blood test."

"Wait a minute. I need to tell you something—"

"I already know what you are going to say. Goodbye," Jane said as she hung up.

I called Julie to let her know Jane had been in the Westbrook psychiatric unit again. Julie had missed a call from the Trenton Mental Health, where no message was left. Julie phoned to find out why they had called. She spoke with a member of the emergency team for Blackburn Mental Health. Jane had actually called to receive treatment.

They were working hard to coordinate Jane's medication, and she wanted to let Julie know. "Jane is very paranoid and very, very sick," the lady revealed. "She has severe bipolar. I have been doing mental health for a long time, and Jane is THE MOST severely mentally ill person I have ever seen. She suffers with mania a lot and mostly cycles in the manic side. Jane is difficult to examine. She will get up and walk out in the middle of her appointment. When she receives a bill for as much as $5, she goes into a manic mode, and it ends up finally being written off."

The dental office called me to remind Jane of her teeth cleaning appointment. In turn, I left a phone message for Jane.

Indignantly, Jane returned the call. "I already knew about the appointment, and I don't need you to remind me. Stop talking down to me."

"I'm not talking down to you," I said. "The dental office asked me to remind you of your appointment, so I did."

Then from nowhere, Jane spewed, "Your teachers passed you because you were cute."

What is she talking about? I thought as I digested the remark. I was not cute; in fact, I felt ugly until I got contact lenses and refused to let Mama give me any more home permanents. Besides, I WAS a good student.

"All you wanted was to get boys, while I got straight A's," Jane said with her superior attitude.

"I did not chase boys. They chased me." I threw back in her face. "People don't care what grades you made in school. You don't go through life with your transcript tattooed on your forehead."

"If you won't buy the apartment next door, Frank, Ben's brother, is going to help me buy it," Jane informed.

"I will not pay money out of the estate for the apartment," I said adamantly. There were not enough funds.

"So you won't give me the money to buy it?"

"No," I said firmly.

"We need funds available to care for your teeth like now to resolve your pain!" I replied.

"I'm not in pain," Jane claimed.

"Megan told me you were," I said back.

"Well, I'm not. I'm putting Numbs-It on it, and I'm NOT IN PAIN! The dentist is NOT GENTLE. He is rough, and I don't like that guy. It is his fault that I lost one of my caps!" Jane exclaimed.

"How could it be his fault?" I asked.

"I paid him $100 to get it fixed. When Ben hit me in the jaw, it came apart. The dentist charges too much. Dentures would cost less."

"Dental work is expensive," I explained.

"Well, I'm not going to have the dental work done," Jane ranted.

"That is not a good decision. Your teeth will start bothering you, and you will lose them," I expressed.

"I don't care. I'll just pull them out myself," Jane raved.

After pausing for a second, Jane said, "I will go to the dentist if you will let me buy the apartment."

If Jane thought she was manipulating me into letting her buy the apartment, she could not have been more wrong.

* * *

I received a lengthy call from Jane one evening in June. "I sent a letter to the attorney general. You will get a copy. The neighbors next door are smoking marijuana. I can smell it in my apartment, along with the fumes from the traffic. The neighbors have a grandmother and two kids living with them, all in a tiny apartment the size of mine.

"The dentist is a crook. I've known that for a long time. I've heard people in his office screaming bloody murder. I got two root canals before, but I can't take any more dental work. I prefer to have my teeth rot in my head before I will go to the dentist. I don't care to look cosmetically pure," Jane expressed.

"I gave Mama a chance to be a person at the end. I am still suffering from losing Mama. When Mama died, I helped prepare her body with oils. I closed her eyes, adjusted her jaw, and put her arms across her chest. I was there when they came in with the body bag. Hospice was doing all kinds of things to speed up Mama's death as was Angelia. I was the only one with professional experience, so I could see these things," Jane explained from her point of view.

"I made good grades to please Mama and Daddy. I don't know why the oldest always picks on the next child, but it is natural." Jane went on, "I'm known as Jane the Clown. I love life sometimes. I'm happy sometimes, and I'm sad sometimes. I'm going to live until I die. If I have a heart attack, I don't want to be hooked up to all this stuff like Mama. I would rather die. We are scrimping a lot. We don't have enough money for food."

"Doesn't Ben contribute anything?" I asked.

"He gets paid $50 a month for sweeping around the church and feeding the minister's goldfish. He spends his money on cigarettes. He does not contribute anything. I am planting radishes, and they are coming up."

The copy of the letter Jane sent to the attorney general arrived the following day. It was a big misrepresentation of circumstances. She kept referring to herself as being handicapped and stated she was having legal difficulties in freeing her share of her mother's estate.

After wading through the mixed-up rhetoric, my interpretation of the letter boiled down to Jane requesting to have the money from the estate so she could buy the mortgage to the "condominium-type home" occupied by her "burdensome neighbors." Along with a number of irrelevant statements and criticizing me, the letter also stated Jane was fighting a rights issue that she hoped would be taken to the Federal Supreme Court if necessary.

If whoever screened the attorney general's mail had not figured out right away the letter was written by a mentally unstable person, it was clear to see toward the end when she stated she was becoming vexed.

CHAPTER TWENTY-ONE

Hodgepodge

Jane phoned, talking about the place our parents had lived in Wentwood. "Our old log house is in receivership. You should buy it. I can run a guide service out of it, and it could be used as a place where the family can go to get away. My brown car needs repairs. It keeps stalling. It is having the same problem that we paid to have fixed before, and I took it back."

"Why don't you get rid of it?" I suggested. "Now that you have Mama's car, you don't need the expense of three cars to keep up."

"NO! The car has sentimental value, and it is one that Ben can work on. Besides, it is made of metal, and people avoid hitting me because it is so sturdy it would damage their cars a lot if they run into me. It is an excellent antique."

"I need it to take homeless people to a shelter. Sometimes I meet people hanging out in the alley by the supermarket, and they need help. That is what I do—I help people." Jane felt it was her duty to assist misfortunate rejects of society with whom she related.

"Why don't you use the blue Plymouth?" I advised.

"Sometimes they have accidents in the back seat, and it gets dirty."

The people at State Mental Health did not like Jane picking up indigents and were unhappy with her for presenting herself as their advocate. She was treading into territory for which she had no business.

The following day, Jane left a series of messages on my answering machine. "I am schizophrenic because I refuse to divulge information about my clients. I wouldn't give their Medicaid numbers."

The answering machine continued with Jane's messages. "The maximum dosage by law takes three or four weeks to get out of your system. It makes your muscles jerk. It is making me go blind, and my senses are going down. I got a dog three days ago. He is a big hound dog I call Topper."

Later, by phone, she talked about other puzzling issues, which I discussed with Julie. "They are going over her medical files and will make changes under authorized circumstances, whatever that means. She is on the docket for a hearing. According to her, State Mental Health wants to incarcerate her. She said something about them filing for the police to do surveillance on her. Jane would be committed to Baldwin now, except they don't have enough beds. She wanted me to talk to Judge Green."

Julie spoke to Ben's sister, Carrie. "Other than what we had already figured out, it was learned Jane had been taken to the psychiatric unit in May because she had attacked the grandchildren of her neighbor." Attacked?

In short, the DA was petitioning to review Jane's case. She was in trouble for not staying on her medications and, as a result, was facing being committed. Marvin Olsen, Jane's attorney, contacted me. He was representing Jane pro bono in a civil case. "Jane has missed her appointment for medication with State Mental Health and refused to come in. She said her husband gives her the medication. She feels harassed. Does the family feel she should be committed?" asked Mr. Olsen.

I was caught totally off guard. I was not prepared to answer that question. The state hospital had turned into a revolving door for Jane. If she was committed, when she got out, Jane would revert back to her old behaviors. I should have said, "Yes, and keep her there, or it won't accomplish anything." I was afraid to answer in that manner; it would come back to bite me. Jane would never trust me again.

"We want what would be best for her," I responded, assuming the system would get her the help she needed.

* * *

I had been dealing with atrial fibrillation by staying on heart medications. Occasionally, I found myself slipping into fibrillation. The frequent blood tests to monitor blood coagulation were annoying. I decided to have the ablation procedure on my heart to hopefully remedy the condition. Julie was informed of my plans to have the procedure, and I relayed the most recent conversation with Jane. "Jane said the attorney was very promising. She thought they will stop bothering her. She sounds relatively normal and then pops up telling me when she was in Baldwin they were doing experiments on her ovaries. They put her in an MRI machine and were banging on it to torture her."

* * *

A lady from Trenton Mental Health phoned Julie. She did not know what was going on with Jane because Jane had been very quiet lately. Jane had not been going there for her medications. The lady thought Jane was getting them from a private doctor or possibly through Westbrook. Julie was satisfied with the lady's assumption that Jane was taking lithium, and Ben was seeing she kept on it. They were fooled into thinking she was on her medications.

I took off a week from work to recuperate from the ablation procedure in mid-August. I was not feeling too great when Jane called.

"I've been cleared," Jane stated.

"Cleared of what?" I asked.

"Of what you talked to the attorney about."

Why couldn't Jane ever come out and give a straight answer? I was not in the mood to play guessing games.

"So you don't have to worry about being sent to Baldwin. So you are taking your medications?" I asked.

"Yes, but it is none of your business. I can't talk to you about it because you and King are plaintiffs."

"Why are we plaintiffs?" I asked.

"Because you won't give me any money," Jane answered.

Wouldn't Jane be the plaintiff?

Jane continued. "You are as crazy as me. Ken and Justin keep you out of trouble."

"Ken doesn't follow me around, keeping me out of trouble!" I exclaimed angrily.

"I didn't mean he follows you around . . . ," Jane said, trying to redeem herself. I was so angry it was a wonder smoke was not rolling from my ears.

"Can you hear the guitar in the background? Ben is playing," said Jane.

I did not answer.

"Maybe we should end this conversation."

"That is a good idea. Goodbye," I said.

Jane was still talking as I hung up the receiver.

* * *

Aunt Doris, Uncle Andy's wife, notified us of the death of our cousin Teddy Winters, the oldest son of Abigail, our mother's deceased sister. Teddy was overweight with diabetes and had a heart attack.

* * *

It had been an unusually long period since Julie or I had heard anything from Jane. I decided to call. No one answered; however, Jane had left the strangest greeting on the answering machine, which included in the greeting, "If you are not a friend, don't call back." I wondered if Jane was in trouble again and contacted Carrie, Ben's sister, who informed me Jane was not taking her medications.

"She is not ready to be hauled off yet, but she is about to go off the deep end," Carrie reported. "We've been keeping her inside and away from people to keep her out of trouble."

"Should we contact the mental health people about her not taking her meds?" I asked.

"No," replied Carrie. "It only makes it worse as they send her to Baldwin, where they keep her about six months. If she gets in trouble on her own, they take her to Westbrook, and she gets out in about three weeks. Sometimes she snaps out of it and decides to start taking her pills on her own."

Carrie went on, "Jane calls me every other day and accuses me of something, such as stealing her writings that she creates for her newsletter or accuses my son of stealing her grocery money. Recently, she would not let Ben out of the house."

"How could she keep Ben from leaving if he wants?" I asked.

"When she is in her manic state, she is very strong, and she picks up knives and things," Carrie explained. "He had been at my house. He was going over to the apartment for something and said he would be right back. When he did not appear after a while, I went over to check on him. Jane would not let him leave. I held up my cell phone and threatened to push the button to call 911. Jane is afraid of the police, so she let him out. She can be really scary."

* * *

The second anniversary of Mama's death was here already. The date was noted with reverence while Julie was recuperating from a horrible virus, and I was back at the cardiologist for another follow-up on the ablation procedure.

"I have not heard a word from Jane," I told Julie. "Carrie is supposed to notify us if Jane gets 'hauled off,' her words. The last time I left a message for Jane to call, she did not get back with me."

"I called Jane on my way home from work. She sounded pretty nutty," Julie explained. "Michael, Gerald's son, who is a doctor, told me there are monthly shots that can be given to alleviate people like Jane from having to take their meds every day."

* * *

Ben called me to report Jane was being sued by a collection agency on behalf of the Westbrook Hospital. There never seemed to be a break from Jane's issues.

I sent an e-mail to James King, explaining a credit agency was after Jane. He phoned, saying, "When Jane gets released from Westbrook, I will try to talk to her."

"I wasn't aware she was in Westbrook again!" I exclaimed. I was getting dizzy keeping up with Jane's frequent admissions.

"The police need to be reeducated about Jane," stated James. "Apparently, there are a lot of new policemen who don't know the routine in dealing with her. When Jane is downtown doing weird things, people call the police. The police usually talk to her and take her home."

That evening, I called Ben. "I just learned from James King Jane had been taken to Westbrook again. What happened?" I inquired.

"She was involved in confrontations at the library and with the neighbors," Ben replied.

I could picture in my mind's eye Jane flying off the handle with people for some perceived injustice. "Jane needs to stay on her medications. Julie told me there is an injection Jane could have instead of taking pills."

"We are aware of an injection that is available. She would have to go to the mental health clinic or the hospital for it, and she is not good at keeping appointments. The idea is to find a solution that will work for her," explained Ben.

"If there is a solution that would work, they should have found it by now. Getting committed is no one's fault but her own!" I exclaimed.

"Jane thought if she did not pay the hospital, they would not admit her as long as she owed them money," Ben shared.

"That sounds like Jane's reasoning," I said. "But it backfired!"

* * *

Julie called the mental health facility to learn details about Jane's incarceration. She only learned that Westbrook no longer had a psychiatric unit but rather what they called a stabilization center.

Jane had been released five days before calling me at 7:00 A.M. The medications made Jane's speech slurred. "I'm going to take a bus trip to Edmond to see Aunt Hazel. I am taking my hound dog, Topper, with me. I have rights. You are trying to take away my rights," Jane slurred. "I got calls saying I was surrounded by the police. Carrie and Ben were playing tricks on me. I was in a trauma center for about a month."

Then she started quoting her version of scriptures from Isaiah about taking care of other people. "Look it up," she commanded.

Jane was speaking rapidly, jumping from topic to topic, and stopped abruptly. "I don't trust you. You are helping yourself to my money. I'm supposed to be number 1, and you are number 2. It isn't fair that you made yourself number 1. You are trying to take away my rights, and you can't do that!" Jane went back to talking about her trip to Edmond. "I'm going to see a dentist."

I knew she was referring to Ben's uncle. "Ben's uncle is not a dentist. He is an orthodontist," I said.

"I'M GOING TO SEE HIM ANYWAY!" Jane bellowed. "My gums are hurting, and it is hard for me to eat. I have arranged for Topper to ride on the bus with me and stay in the motel with me. While I'm there, I'm going to the library."

I got the impression she was going to research her rights for being the oldest.

Jane quickly calmed down. "The windshield on the truck needs replaced. I need dental work done. The glasses I got two years ago have scratches on them."

I wanted to talk about getting dental work scheduled and new glasses, but that went to the wayside. "We need eggs and cereal. While I was gone, Ben ate all my food. I have a broken foot that causes me to limp. I haven't gotten it fixed because the doctor would not do it the way I wanted." Jane was getting hoarse and ended the call.

* * *

I informed Julie of recent events concerning Jane. "She wants to take a trip back East, something about visiting a company that will publish some of her poems. She said we could go to Disneyland, so she thought she should be able to travel also. The trip we took to Disneyland was thirteen years ago. Her entire point has nothing to do with anything."

I continued. "Jane has been complaining her mouth hurts, and she has a boil. She has a semiretired dentist, Dr. Rice. He agreed to take Jane back. She said the receptionist in his office keeps throwing her out because she says things that offend people. I told her when she goes to wait for her appointments to not say anything to anyone and get a magazine."

CHAPTER TWENTY-TWO

Moving On

The day after my birthday in June, Ken and I decided to put our house on the market to alleviate caring for such a large yard. We contacted our friend Gary, who was a real estate agent, and a sign was posted in the front yard on a Monday. We were shocked when a serious offer was received with no negotiations on Wednesday.

"You better start packing," Gary announced. "The buyers have cash and want to move in as soon as possible."

I began preparing for a garage sale and packing while dealing with more of Jane's concerns.

Jane left a series of phone messages on the answering machine.

"I've been accepted into a poet's society!" Jane exclaimed. "I have written some poems they like." She proceeded to sing one of them.

She went on to say, "A year before Mama died, she told me she did not want me to lack for anything. Aunt Hazel is going to come out sometime around the middle of July. I need to get motel reservations for her. I've joined her church now. I want to forget all the bad things I've done."

Jane called me again the following day. She wanted me to pay the utility company to move a telephone utility box. She explained the utility box was in the way of the wall she was building. "I need the wall to keep the neighbors from treading on my garden," she explained.

I arranged for funds from her account to pay the expense.

Jane wrote a letter to thank me for "helping with some things that are going to make our life more pleasant." In the same letter, she wrote, "What would have happened if I had trusted that I would receive the parents' property? You two would have come in and demanded your share, just as you did." She was still angry about not taking over Mama's condo. The four-page letter included a lot of other thoughts from Jane's disturbed mind, including reminding me that I was born second in line.

Julie and Gerald were discussing a wedding date. Julie was very busy preparing for the sale of her home, along with a lot of furniture and household items.

She had been working for some time cleaning things from the upstairs/attic area of Gerald's substantial brick home that had been built by his grandfather in 1934. The collection of things that should have been discarded ages ago had not been touched in decades. It was comparable to cleaning out our mother's things.

Julie was given free rein to remodel Gerald's family home as she liked. She had plans for completely changing the kitchen and renovating the master bedroom to include a roomy walk-in closet.

Things were happening very quickly for us as we had to be out of our home soon with no idea of where we were going to go. Along with packing, evenings and weekends were spent house hunting. We were considering finding a temporary place until we made an offer on an existing new home.

During the spring, Julie and I had planned a vacation to Oregon to visit our aging aunts and uncles. The time of our departure was approaching quickly.

Julie called, "Well, we leave on Friday for Oregon! I got a contract on my house this past weekend. I will close August 30. Gerald has been moving some of my stuff to his home."

"Isn't it funny that we have both sold our houses about the same time and are moving? The trip to Oregon isn't happening at the best time. We hadn't planned on the house selling so quickly," I replied.

Ken and I just moved in the day before. With boxes remaining to be unpacked, we were preparing to leave that evening to drive to a larger airport over two hundred miles away. We would spend the night to catch an early morning flight to Oregon. It was the end of the summer session. Ken was giving his last final for an evening class. As soon as he got home, we were leaving.

Jane called at the worst time ever. "I'm looking at buying a travel trailer. I want to live in it when I work in Edmond," she announced.

"We are getting ready to leave. We can talk about it next week when I get back from vacation," I told her.

After our flight, Ken and I met Julie at the airport and rented a car. The first evening was spent with our cousin Anita and her husband, Evan. Anita's younger sister, Faith, was there also. It was great getting reacquainted with our cousins whom we had not seen in ages.

I was in college, and Jane was living at home when our parents decided it was time to take us to see our grandparents and other relatives who lived in Oregon. Julie was a junior in high school at the time. That was the last time she had seen any of them.

The next morning, our group left to visit Uncle Andy and Aunt Doris. Aunt Rebecca and Uncle Ralph, who had taken the train all the way from Southern California, were already there, along with Aunt Lorie, who had ridden with them from Fleming. We were delighted to see everyone.

Mark, Aunt Lorie's son, and his wife came later as did Victor, Aunt Abigail's youngest son, and his wife.

Everyone reminisced around the dining room table. I asked what our mother, the oldest of her siblings, was like as a kid. There was silence. Uncle Andy, who was three years younger, was not around that much as he was always off working with their father. Aunt Abigail, the next sibling, had died in an automobile accident. Aunt Lorie came after Aunt Abigail and was nine years younger than Mama, followed by Aunt Rebecca, the baby of the family, who was eleven years younger.

Aunt Lorie and Aunt Rebecca were so much younger they did not remember much about Mama when they were children. After completing her elementary education at the one-room country schoolhouse, Mama had spent her high school years away from the younger children, living in town and working for her room and board. After graduating from high school, Mama went to Edmond to attend a business college and work.

"Marie would always bring candy when she came back from Edmond every three or four months," Rebecca recalled. "I got to know Marie more after we had children when we had more in common."

"Marie was very independent," Andy stated. "She always felt she was right, overall. I do remember something else," he added. "We were poor, you know. This neighbor kid used to tease Marie. Once he told her he didn't like her ugly dress. She told him when he started buying her clothes, he could have a say in what she wore."

Yes, that sounded like the feisty mother we knew. It was getting late. Julie, Ken, and I retreated to our motel and returned the following morning.

Sunday was spent with more visiting, along with venturing out to the beach. It was a cold, windy, dreary day. Faith, Julie, and I removed our sandals and walked out into the Pacific waters, just enough to get our toes wet. We took a group picture of our feet. Aunt Lorie, Aunt Rebecca, and Uncle Ralph did not go down to the water. Ken climbed all over the rusted-out hull of an old shipwreck, while Uncle Andy and Aunt Doris strolled in the sand.

Our group got back into our respective cars and drove to a solemn cemetery to see the graves of our grandparents. As

Julie and I gazed upon their shared headstone, we felt regrets of not being around them while growing up.

Our clan stopped at a cozy restaurant for lunch, and then it was time for parting. Julie and I left with fond memories of our aunts and uncles, who were, above all, warmhearted, loving people. We vowed we would return, and it would not take so long the next time.

Upon returning home and getting back into her routine, Julie phoned me. "I talked to Jane on my cell phone while driving to work this morning. She got funds by writing a check on her credit card to buy a camper trailer that she could live in when she works in Randolph. She said you wouldn't give her the money."

"She called the evening we left for our vacation, saying something about wanting to buy a camper. I told her we were getting ready to go on vacation, and I had to finish packing before Ken got home. I told her we would discuss it when I got back," I explained.

"Doesn't Jane realize how much interest she will be paying?" Julie said in disgust. "She is really being taken."

"I guess Jane is serious about getting a job in Edmond or Randolph or somewhere," I added. "Whether that materializes is yet to be seen." Jane was asked to send me the next statement, which I paid.

Jane called during my lunch hour to report the phone company had moved the utility box, and she was continuing to work on the wall. She was happy about both.

I informed Julie of Jane's call. "They are taking the trailer camping this weekend. I thought she bought it to stay in when she went to Edmond to work."

"Personally, I don't care what she uses it for, just as long as she doesn't come see us!" Julie exclaimed.

"It is parked on the street. I told her there were ordinances against keeping a trailer on the street for very long. They are going to take some people camping. When I asked her about it, she said they take handicapped people around. That is what the *Rosebud Design* does. She is planning to have a bake sale to raise money.

"She mentioned she will have Dr. Rice, her dentist, contact me when they are ready to start working on her teeth. She is working or, rather, volunteering, doing something with the library board. She works an hour a day and keeps her mouth shut, and it is working out. Jane had to go to work at one o'clock. She told me I am not the only one who is busy and important."

Jane called a week later, informing me of her latest plans. "Now that the trailer is paid off, I am thinking about publishing my poetry book and building an inner stairway to the roof!" Jane exclaimed. "I am going to take a trip back East for publishing research," Jane declared. "I will buy bus tickets and charge motel, food, and incidentals. Ben and my dog, Topper, will go along."

Jane had already sent the manuscript of her poems to Redcow Publishing and got it copyrighted. "I need help with your *enthusiasm*," she informed me. In other words, she wanted the publishing costs to be paid through her estate funds.

"I need a check written to Redcow Publishing Company to take with me."

"I'm not going to write a check to a publishing company," I said emphatically.

"Well then, I will mortgage my house if I have to to get the money."

* * *

Jane sent Ken a birthday card with a shark on it that when opened played the music from the movie *Jaws*. He called her to thank her for the card.

"I'm having problems mortgaging the apartment because it doesn't have a thermostat, which means I can't get it insured," Jane told Ken.

Later, Jane called me, "I had a bake sale yesterday to raise money for the *Rosebud Design*. It netted $23. I had the bake sale and didn't keep the dental appointment."

"You should have kept the dental appointment and scheduled your bake sale for another day!" I exclaimed.

"I asked the dental office what would happen if I decided not to keep my appointment. The receptionist said, 'I don't want to go there.' I told her, 'Well, I don't want to go there either.' I am dressing nicer."

I was glad to hear she was making an effort to dress more sensibly and hoping Jane was donating the excess clothing to make more room in her tiny apartment.

Julie and I talked about the estate paying the publication costs for Jane's book of poems. "I don't think it is a reasonable expenditure," I expressed.

"I think it will be okay. Writing poetry is Jane's passion," shared Julie.

Jane had turned into a loose cannonball with jet fuel. It would be easier to harness a snake. I told her Julie thought the publishing fee could be paid from the estate, and so I would pay it, even though it was against my better judgment, and it was a lot of money. Then she went into how this was a lifelong goal of hers. She talked about how everyone thought her poetry was so great, and she gets these awards. She thanked me "from the bottom of her heart." I told her not to thank me, to thank Julie.

The payments were to be made in three installments. Jane was getting ready to travel to meet with the people at Redcow Publishing before she signed a contract. I asked her if she was taking her dog with her on the bus. She decided to leave him with a friend. I agreed that was a good idea. She said when traveling with Ginger, it took a lot of time seeing after the dog, but it was good though too as people would talk to them.

While we were on the subject of Ginger, once again, I asked her what happened to her. I thought Jane would tell me Ginger died from an infection. Before, when we talked about it, she did not really give an answer. Jane said, "She died." When I asked her how, she gave me the story that she had glass cuts on her stomach. Earlier, she had told me Ben had left a saw blade out with the blade exposed. People told her she should put the dog to sleep, but she did not want to do it that way. She said watching the dog go through the dying process actually helped her deal with Mama dying. It took two and a half months for Ginger to die. She admitted that sounded strange. That sounded sick to me. I'm sure the poor dog suffered a lot.

* * *

Our fortieth wedding anniversary was coming up. We had made plans to have a quiet anniversary by going hiking in the Mason area and spending the night at a motel when we received a call from Angelia. "How would you like to have some company this weekend?" It was agreed Angelia would bring Clara and Mathew, and we would all go hiking together. Calvin was scheduled for a National Guard drill weekend; however, his schedule had been changed at the last minute when he learned days earlier he was being deployed to Afghanistan, which meant he would be coming also.

I was very surprised when Jack and Claudia appeared at my office. I was so happy to see them; tears streamed from my eyes. Justin and his family joined in, which rounded off the celebration. It was a joyous occasion to remember with all our children and their spouses and grandchildren.

Sunday morning was too quiet. The excitement had faded, and everyone was going home. I was now in the middle of Jane's publishing escapade. Jane had given me the name of a person to contact and a schedule of payments with the amounts due. I wrote a detailed e-mail to Redcow Publishing with Jane's information, asking for confirmation. After jumping through some hoops with the publishing company, the accurate figures were provided, which were different from Jane's.

Jane made the trip by bus accompanied by Ben. Upon arriving, she called me, "We got here and are fine. We just checked in a motel."

Upon returning home, Jane called. It was a thirty-hour bus ride, and they slept on the bus. Jane was very happy and kept thanking me. Jane talked about promoting her book and traveling to do book signings. She had all kinds of grandiose ideas. At the end of the conversation, she sang a song she wrote titled "Sing a Happy Song."

Jane talked about the cover of her book. She decided to draw some pictures of children swinging.

I expressed to Julie, "As long as things are going her way, she is very amiable. However, she has taken us to hell and back, and I can't seem to get past it."

CHAPTER TWENTY-THREE

This and That

"I received a notice from the city to move the trailer, or it will be hauled off for being abandoned," Jane told me. "We got permission to keep it at our church parking lot for now. I'm thinking about selling it. I put an ad in the newspaper. Three men came to look at it to use when they go hunting. When they came, I had been working outside, and my clothes were all raggedy. One look at me, and they scrambled for their car without even looking at the trailer. I might have you pay for a crane to put it on the roof of our apartment."

I almost broke out laughing. Where did she ever get such a cockamamie idea as that? The roof of the white-washed apartment was flat, so it made perfect sense to Jane. Her apartment faced the highway. Anyone going through town could not miss seeing it.

"I don't think putting the trailer on the roof is a good idea," I expressed.

"Oh, it will be okay. I'm not going to hook it up to the water or use the toilet. I am going to use it for an office. A city inspector is going to come out and talk to me about it in a few days."

She could not possibly be serious about such an absurd scheme. Surely the city had regulations prohibiting such things. With that in mind, I refrained from getting into an argument.

During a subsequent call, I asked Jane if she had talked to the inspector yet about the camper. She responded, saying he talked about an ordinance that said it has to be parked a number of feet from the street, but they don't have enough property. I asked her what he said about putting it on the roof. As I expected, there is an ordinance against putting an existing structure on a roof.

The reason she wanted to build the wall by the alley was to have a protected place to grow vegetables. And now she was telling me it is to keep people from encroaching on their right-of-way. Then she talked about when Mama had her heart attack. "Julie panicked, and that caused Mama to go back to the hospital, where the treatment hastened her death." Actually, the opposite was true.

I called Julie to chat. "I wanted to wish you and Gerald a very Happy Thanksgiving. We are spending Christmas with Angelia. Calvin will be in Afghanistan by then," I informed Julie.

* * *

The new year of 2008 slipped in quietly for me, while Julie was busy finalizing wedding plans. The wedding had been moved up from March to January. Ken and I could not get away because of Ken's teaching responsibilities and the expectation of hazardous traveling weather.

Meanwhile, Ken's brother, Adam, learned he had early stages of bladder cancer. He had an operation in early January and expected to be released to go home after a week's time.

Routine calls from Jane continued. "I popped the boil in my mouth, and it has gone away. The tooth in front is growing back," Jane reported.

"Teeth don't grow back!" I exclaimed.

"Yes, they do," she said, fully believing that they do.

"No, they don't," I asserted.

"According to my church, they will if you believe they will, and I can't talk about it not happening. I can see where my tooth is growing," insisted Jane.

"There is no way your tooth is going to grow back, no matter what you think," I reinforced.

"Yes, it will," Jane insisted. "If not in this lifetime, it will in the next."

"Julie was trying to take away my rights."

"What rights did she try to take?" I asked.

"I won't go into that now," Jane answered, evading her lie.

"Are you going to Julie's wedding in March?" asked Jane.

"The wedding has been moved up to January and will be in about a week. We cannot go then because Ken has classes to teach."

"I would like to go if I had a way of getting there," Jane hinted. Enabling her to go was not even a remote consideration. Julie and Gerald had a simple wedding with thirty guests. Jack and Claudia were present with Jack giving Julie away.

Ken and I were worried about Ken's brother. Because of complications from the first surgery, he remained in the hospital and had four more surgeries. Everything that could go wrong did go wrong. He died in early March.

The third anniversary of Mama's passing came shortly before Adam died. Memories of events and struggles prior to her death and afterward were still fresh on our minds.

Ken was concerned how his mother would manage without Adam, who helped her buy groceries and with many things in general. Ken and I discussed asking Emma to live with us. "No, I'll be fine here," Emma answered. "I've got lots of friends, along with Jake's kids and the people from my church. I'll get along fine."

Ken and I attended Adam's memorial service. Upon arriving at Emma's house, she started talking about boxing up her things. "I need to figure out what to do with my cat."

"Where are you going?" I inquired.

"To live with you," Emma answered, catching me by surprise.

The move would be in May to give Emma time to get organized. The house Emma lived in belonged to the family farm, which her deceased husband, Jake's, son maintained. There was nothing tying her down.

"I was surprised to hear from Jane this morning," I told Julie over the phone. "She has canceled all her dental appointments. The dentist wanted to build a partial. She claimed it would interfere with her chewing. She did not get the e-mail I sent regarding Uncle Ralph having a stroke. I was going to tell her about Ken's brother, but she hung up. We are preparing for Ken's mom to come live with us. Ken is leaving here around noon on Friday to go get her. He will be coming back with her and her cat Sunday."

"I hope you get along with Emma. It will be nice for the kids to get to know their great-grandmother," stated Julie.

"I get along well with Emma, whereas I know I would have had issues with our mother," I professed.

"Oh, by the way!" I exclaimed as I changed topics. "I haven't told you Jack's wife, Claudia, is expecting." I was looking forward to welcoming another grandbaby into our family.

CHAPTER TWENTY-FOUR

Happy Times/Challenging Times

For a summer vacation, Ken and I had plans to meet Jack and Claudia in Philadelphia and then go on to the beach house of Claudia's parents. Angelia and her children were joining us for a family vacation.

I was sewing away happily, making a set of placemats with matching napkins to give Monica, Claudia's mother, as a thank-you for her hospitality. Jane called and kept talking using up my valuable sewing time.

Jane claimed Fran, my high school friend, had hit her and pushed her around. She went on with more outrageous accusations.

"Fran tries to get me in trouble," expounded Jane.

"What does Fran do to get you in trouble?" I asked.

"I won't tell you because you will try to do the same," Jane stated.

Jane talked about things that needed fixed on the blue Plymouth. "The plastic cover to the clutch is gone. Someone stole it. I don't really need to drive anyway. That is why I live where I do so I can walk everywhere. If Ben messes up the truck again, it can just sit. I don't want to spend any more on the truck. Don't tell your kids not to talk to me," Jane spouted next.

"My kids can talk to whomever they want. I certainly don't tell them not to talk to you," I replied back.

I kept telling Jane I had things to do, but she kept on talking and talking. Finally, the conversation ended.

The time came for our family to go on vacation to the East Coast. Every morning our group walked just under two miles from the beach house to the beach. Jack spent time in the ocean with Claudia, who looked cute as she sported her maternity swimwear, bearing her obviously pregnant tummy.

Clara and Kerry, Claudia's fourteen-year-old sister, enjoyed floundering around in the ocean on their floating devices. Ken made sand castles with Mathew, while Monica looked out on the horizon, watching for a school of porpoises to come by.

Angelia and I spent most of the time enjoying the beach from underneath a large umbrella. I ventured out in the ocean several times, reveling in the idea that the previous summer, my feet were in the Pacific Ocean, and this summer, I was in the Atlantic.

Mathew was complaining about his leg hurting. Angelia thought perhaps it was from growing pains. She would have it checked when they got home.

* * *

Upon arriving home, X-rays revealed a mass above Mathew's knee, which was diagnosed as osteosarcoma, bone cancer. The news was devastating. Angelia was trying to reach Calvin by e-mail in Afghanistan. Finally, Calvin was contacted.

It was decided to take Mathew to a special children's hospital near Julie. Hastily, Angelia made arrangements for Clara to stay with a friend. By noon the next day, she arrived at the hospital, where she was met by the welcome face of her Aunt Julie.

Angelia contacted Calvin's commander, requesting an early release. Julie met Calvin at the airport and took him directly to the hospital. Calvin was at Mathew's side when he woke up from being sedated for his first MRI.

"Jane called this morning and was going on and on. She asked if you had told me about Mathew," shared Julie. "I said yes, but I didn't offer any information. She said Mathew should be taken out of the medical system."

"We talked to Angelia last night. It is hard to explain because we knew in our hearts Mathew had cancer, but Angelia had a lump in her throat when she told us the biopsy was positive," I relayed to Julie. "Then we were blessed with Jane's call. She started rambling. I interrupted her to tell her about Mathew, which was a mistake. I think she said an insincere 'I'm sorry.' She said, 'Some children aren't meant to live. All the medical system wants is your money, and he should not be in the system.' That made me very angry! I said, 'Sure we're supposed to just sit back and let him die.' She said she has been in contact with Aunt Hazel, and our beliefs are very different. I said, 'They sure are!'

"I asked why she called. It was about her property tax listing. On the website, her apartment was listed under the name of some people who live in another county.

"We had a disjointed conversation. She needs to make more money and is going to rent out the trailer. She is eating weeds. She cooks them, not to get high but for vegetables. The neighbors keep pulling up her lilac bush and cutting back the rosebush that has been there for twenty years. They also spray her with the garden hose. She got their dog, Topper, back yesterday. He doesn't have rabies. He was in quarantine for rabies since the neighbors said he bit them. The neighbor kids make her mad by calling her by her first name. She said, 'We were taught to respect people older than us. It is disrespectful to call me by my first name.'

"Ben has stopped slugging her so much since he is on the medication. She said something about the Old Testament, saying it was okay to beat your wife. I think she was talking about where the Bible says the woman should be submissive to her husband. We got into a big argument about that.

"Jane wants to travel to pick up her books in May. She wants me to help her sell them. When I wasn't very receptive, she said in her high, mocking voice, 'I don't like poetry.' When I told her I never said that, she started singing a poem in the book. 'God, God, God, you are my friend, friend, friend.'"

"I got about the same conversation but not as long," replied Julie. "Her poetry book came. I haven't had a chance to read it."

* * *

Angelia's family was assigned accommodations. Calvin had ninety days' readjustment time after his deployment before he was required to return to his teaching position. He would be spending those ninety days caring for Mathew, while Angelia returned home to keep the home fires burning.

* * *

Julie had been through a crisis of her own. She was on her way home after shopping for a dress to wear at an upcoming wedding when out of nowhere, she felt a piercing pain on her left side. The pain gradually became more intense. After arriving home and fixing a quick dinner, Julie continued to feel strange. She took a steaming hot shower to relieve a cold chill, to no avail. She stepped out of the shower, quickly drying off, and then slipped into her warm nightgown to join Gerald in the living room. She lay down on the couch, covering herself with two warm throws. She was still freezing cold.

Gerald gently touched her forehead to find her burning up. Gerald called his son, Michael. His daughter-in-law answered. With Gerald's description of fever and chills, she suspected Julie had a staph infection. Michael would come over as soon as he got home. It was comforting to have Michael, who was a doctor, nearby. His family occupied the smaller brick house, where Gerald had grown up.

Julie went to bed with a temperature of 103. When Michael arrived, he took one look at Julie and announced, "You need to go to the hospital now! Don't let it get worse, or you could be delirious by morning."

With that being said, Michael placed a phone call, arranging for Julie's arrival at the nearest hospital, which was a half hour away. Julie was placed in a curtained room and given an IV of antibiotics. Her fever came down, and she was released to go home at 3:00 A.M. after receiving a vaccination of another antibiotic.

Julie described her experience to me. "I could have died from the staph infection."

I was grateful Julie was okay. Losing Julie would have been earth shattering to me.

* * *

Jane phoned, speaking in at a slow rate, leaving an unnatural amount of time between each word.

"Don't talk to me like that," I protested.

"I've been under a lot of pressure," Jane excused. "I'm mad at the guy who was supposed to fix the car. I'm going to stop driving. I've almost gotten run over twice. There are hunters out there, and farmers' crops are coming in, and they are all in a hurry. We had to go to court over the dog and pay a $250 fine. The neighbor kids were harassing him. He was tied to a sharp spike, and a kid got cut on it and blamed it on the dog. The police came and got Topper and kept him in quarantine for two weeks because his rabies tags had expired. The judge told Ben he could be sentenced to a year in jail. We are looking for someone to give Topper to."

Jane sent me a copy of her poetry book. The paperback cover was yellow, with a drawing of three happy children swinging. At first glance, one would get the impression it was a children's book.

I did not care for most of the poems. Two of them looked familiar. I could not swear to it, but I thought they were poems Mama had let me see many years ago. They had Mama's spirit, not Jane's. It could have been possible for Jane to include some of our mother's poems; she had been given Mama's writings.

* * *

On September 26, Jack called me at work. Claudia was in labor, and they were taking her to the hospital. That afternoon, Jack and Claudia welcomed sweet baby Andrew into the world. It was quite a coincidence that Justin was there. His job had required him to conduct a training session in the area.

Ken and I put our heads together with Julie to plan a trip to see Mathew and Andrew. Julie picked up Ken and me from the hospital and drove us to the farm. We admired the changes Julie had made to the home.

We were introduced to one of Gerald's prize young breeding bulls, which resided in a protected pasture area behind the house. The bull was used to Julie hand-feeding him tall grasses that she plucked from her side of the fence. When Julie appeared, the two-thousand-pound bull bounded toward her for his fresh hand-picked grass and to have the hide scratched behind his huge ears. Julie treated the bull like a dog.

The next morning, Julie drove Ken and me to see Jack and Claudia and to meet the newest member of the family. We were delighted to see the new little bundle of joy. He definitely would have Claudia's blond hair.

* * *

I received a call at work from Emma. Jane wanted to speak with me right away. Jane was filling out some kind of form, which I later concluded was a questionnaire typically sent to perspective jurors. The form asked if she had been involved in a civil suit.

"Should I refer them to you?" asked Jane.

"What is this form?" I asked. After a jumbled-up explanation, I told her that was not necessary.

"I have to be careful how I fill this out so they won't drag me through the judicial system. The system will kidnap me if they get a chance," Jane claimed.

"That would not happen," I replied to Jane's objections.

"I would like to serve on a jury. It would be very interesting, and I could learn from it."

I could only imagine what kind of a free-for-all it would be if Jane ever got selected to be on a jury. Surely she would never squeak through the screening.

"The court could channel me through the judicial system!" Jane exclaimed.

"What do you mean by channeling you through the judicial system?" I asked.

"If you are that stupid . . ." Jane said in a condescending tone.

I was getting very peeved at Jane for assuming I should know what she was thinking in her cement-mixer mind.

Jane changed the subject. "The kids next door think it is time for the yearly ritual to send me to the nuthouse. I'm trying to give away Topper, the big dog. People who are interested in taking him expect him to have all his shots and the amenities.

"I HAVE TO GET OFF THE PHONE! I HAVE TO GET OFF THE PHONE!" repeated Jane suddenly, yelling loudly.

"What is happening?" I asked.

"I HAVE TO GET OFF THE PHONE."

"Okay. Goodbye," I said.

* * *

Mathew had a successful surgery on December 1 to remove a large portion of the bone in his left leg. Angelia's family brought in the 2009 New Year together at the hospital. Angelia traded places with Calvin in caring for Mathew, while Calvin went back home with Clara.

* * *

"I didn't go in to work today," Julie informed me. "I was attacked by a cow. I was helping Gerald with a normally very docile cow that had recently given birth. Cows are very protective of their young. Gerald's three-year-old grandson was next to me in the pasture. We were standing to the rear of the cow chute near her calf. The cow came out of the chute with her head down, ready to charge. I threw Gerald's grandson aside and tried to fend off the cow by kicking her nose with my foot. I missed. She threw me about ten feet, and I landed on my back, partially on the side of a cattle scale. The good news is there was no fresh manure close by. Gerald shooed her off. His grandson didn't have a scratch on him, but I could hardly move. I rolled over on my stomach somehow and got up. I hobbled with Gerald to the truck. When we got to the house, Michael gave me some painkillers. When I called in sick, my boss said she had never had someone call in because they had been attacked by a cow."

* * *

It was early April. "Jane called me yesterday and left a message on my work phone," Julie reported. "She wanted me to talk you into letting her have money to get T-shirts for her book signing. She went on and on about how money isn't everything and how I threw cold water on everything when we were taking care of Mama's affairs. She never did get back to the T-shirts."

"I called Jane and reached the strangest message on her answering machine," I expressed to Julie. "She sang "Happy Days Are Here Again" in a high-pitched voice. If you ever want to be entertained, call her number to see what she has recorded. She changes the message just about every day. When I started to leave a message, she answered, and before I could say anything, she started talking saying, 'What is happening here, etc.'"

"She talked about leaving her apartment to the Forest Service. She said Ben can live there until he dies. After that, he can't. I said to her, 'You mean he can't live there after he dies?' We both laughed.

"I told her I was going to retire. All she said was GOOD like she didn't approve of me working in the first place. Then she went on talking about her things. Did you know they had another dog?"

"No," Julie replied. "She should not have gotten a dog. She can hardly take care of herself."

"She had a hound dog named Topper, and now she has another," I said. "The second dog's name is Strike, but I never heard her talk about the second dog again until she mentioned both of them died from something they ate. She said at least now she didn't have to worry about taking care of them."

I formally retired on May 15, 2009, but continued to go into work just about every day for several hours and sometimes almost the entire day. My replacement would not be starting until July.

I had not heard from Jane in a while and decided to call her. The answering machine took the call as usual, which was Jane's screening device. The first part of the message was in a low mumble followed by Jane abruptly shouting, "ONE, TWO, THREE!" I was startled and jumped. I left a message, requesting my call be returned.

I called the number again to see if I could understand the first part of the greeting. It was undistinguishable. Perhaps she was saying, "Leave a message on the count of three."

* * *

Mathew's progress was significant. The long haul for Mathew was drawing to an end. Angelia and Calvin were grateful, more than words could ever express, to be going home with Mathew. There was a time when we did not know how his struggle with cancer would end.

CHAPTER TWENTY-FIVE

Do Not Pass Go

It was July of 2009. I received an e-mail from Redcow Publishing, reporting there were no earnings from Jane's poetry book. Rather than printing out the e-mail and sending it to Jane, I decided to call. Ben answered the phone.

"May I speak to Jane?" I asked.

"She is not here," responded Ben. He paused for a moment. "She's in jail. They are waiting to do a psychiatric evaluation."

I was taken aback and was not sure what to say. "I was calling to let her know Redcow Publishing sent an e-mail, stating there were no earnings from her book sales for the last period. I haven't heard from Jane for a while. I thought you had gone camping."

"We haven't been able to go. The truck needs new rings. It would cost between $5,000 and $7,000 to have it fixed," Ben explained.

"The truck isn't worth that much," I stated.

Ben talked about possibly selling the engine and other parts to get more money for it than trying to sell it in one piece. The truck had over two hundred thousand miles.

The conversation went back to Jane. "How long has Jane been in jail?"

"Since June," Ben replied.

"What was Jane doing?" I asked.

"She was trespassing in one of the vacant apartments in our row. She was in there fixing it up."

"For herself?" I questioned.

"I don't know. She never tells me what she is up to," Ben said.

"Do you know how long she will be there?" I questioned.

"She has a hearing the middle of August," Ben replied. "They have had some delays getting the psychiatric evaluation scheduled."

"Doesn't she know what she is doing?" I asked.

"She doesn't know what is real and what isn't. She is out of touch with reality and is not in control of her actions," Ben explained.

"Isn't she taking her medications?" I asked.

"No, she hasn't been taking her meds for two to four years. She is going to this church and is relying on that," Ben stated.

I kept grilling Ben. "Wasn't there a hearing that required Jane to stay on her medications?"

He responded, "Yes, there was a court order, but they don't know how to enforce it if she doesn't come in to get her medications. The last time when she was in the stabilization center, we learned of a new shot she could take instead of taking pills. I went to get it filled, and it cost $1,000."

"Well, when you see Jane, tell her 'Hi' for me, and I hope everything works out okay." I hesitated. "Once when I was talking to your sister, Carrie, I asked her to let us know when Jane gets in trouble. She told me Jane gets in trouble with little things all the time, and it wasn't practical to let us know every time. So Julie and I never know what all she is up to. I guess she is always doing something strange."

"Did you hear about her getting arrested on Moth's Day?" Ben asked.

"Mother's Day?" I asked, wondering if I heard Ben correctly.

"It was Mother's Day back several years before your mother moved to the condo. Jane was having delusions of moth people and computers taking over the world. She dressed up funny and took the dog with her into the church." The police were called, and they chased her all over town. Now we call Mother's Day Moth's Day."

I was very surprised to learn Jane had gone off in such a manner and wondered what other strange things Jane had done that Ben's family took in stride. For now, I was distracted from Jane's escapades as I prepared for a second trip to Oregon with Julie.

* * *

Ken and I flew into Portland as planned and met Julie at the baggage terminal. We picked up a rental car and were on our way to Uncle Andy and Aunt Doris's house. Uncle Andy wasn't as peppy as when we visited two years ago, but that was to be expected with his heart problems.

We had a wonderful visit, which included a stop with them at the historical Fort Clatsop the following morning. Upon bidding Uncle Andy and Aunt Doris goodbye, we were on our way, stopping to see the Devil's Punch Bowl and a charming lighthouse. After spending the night at a motel, visiting Aunt Lorie was on the agenda. An aquarium visit was on the way, along with an unplanned tour of a cheese factory.

Aunt Lorie welcomed us to her home. She was relying a lot on a walker now. The effects from contracting polio when she was a young adult were causing her increased difficulty now as she was getting older. She moved slowly as we made our way to the entrance of a popular seafood restaurant for a late lunch. After lunch, we were on the road, traveling to Cousin Anita's, where we stayed the night before continuing on to spending another day visiting other sites.

The next day was dedicated to getting back home for Ken and me, while Julie and Anita spent the day at the zoo. Another memorable Oregon vacation concluded with disturbing thoughts of Jane spending her summer locked up in jail.

A letter to Ken from Jane was among the collection of mail awaiting our return. "UNCENSORED Inmate Mail, Blackburn County Jail" was stamped in bright red on the front side of the legal-size envelope.

On the backside of the envelope, "Sign of Disapproval" was written in the center of a wavy circle, encircled by another wavy circle. Among other markings was a heart surrounded by loops. "John 3:16" was written inside the heart.

With a scrap piece of notepad paper and a pencil, Jane created her own birthday card. The front had a good drawing of a cake with candles. A note stated, "Hearing is August 14, be there please." "Call sheriff and get me out of here!" was written at the bottom.

The date of Jane's psychiatric exam passed. In an attempt to call Jane, I was amazed to find Ben's voice was still on the answering machine. That was unusual since Jane dominated the answering machine messages. This meant Jane had not been released.

A social worker from Human Services contacted me, asking if I knew Jane was in jail. The lady stated Jane was being sent to the state hospital for stabilization. "Jane asked me to contact you to pay her utilities and taxes while she is at the hospital."

"She has plenty of money in her checking account. She should arrange to have her husband, Ben, pay them," I informed.

The social worker mentioned Jane was not on medications right now. I told her I had talked to Ben about Jane taking her medications, but he said they could not enforce it.

"It is up to a guardian to see that a court order is in place to mandate she takes her medications. A court order is only good for two years at a time," stated the social worker. The social worker seemed to think having a guardian to keep a court order in place was the solution. But Jane did not comply with court orders. "We need a long-term solution. Jane needs a guardian. We prefer to have a family member involved," stated the social worker.

"Neither I nor Julie, our other sister, can control her. We don't feel we could be responsible for her," I explained. "Ben would be the logical person to be her guardian, or perhaps his sister, Carrie. She needs someone who lives in Blackburn who knows what she is doing. Neither Julie nor I could be her guardian as she would be too disruptive to our lives. It is a matter of self-preservation."

"I understand," replied the social worker.

I called Ben's sister, Carrie, to ask if she knew details regarding Jane's arrest.

"Jane took an axe and broke into an apartment," reported Carrie. "We had all the papers ready to get Jane bailed out, but she refused to sign them. We wanted to get her out and back on medications before the trial. Jane insisted the apartment was hers, and she didn't do anything wrong. She was personally going to file a habeas corpus. She had Ben bring her information on what to do. At the hearing on August 14, Jane was declared incompetent to stand trial and was ordered to be sent to Baldwin. Once Jane gets stabilized, she will have to face the charges."

Carrie considered Jane to be dangerous. She talked about the time Jane scratched her granddaughter on the back and the time Jane bit off the tip of her finger. They routinely got Jane off and protected her from getting into trouble. Carrie said it may have been a disservice to her; Jane had gotten away with an abundance of weird stuff.

Carrie told me some strange things. Ben had been really sick for a period. They suspected Jane was trying to poison him. He ate with them and got better. Once, Jane baked cookies with glass in them and brought them over. They won't eat anything Jane brings them.

Carrie explained, "When Ben doesn't stay at the apartment, he goes over to the shop. It has a bathroom, but there is no bed, so he sleeps in a sleeping bag on the floor. It is hard for him as his health isn't the greatest. He has high blood pressure and heart problems contributed to by Jane. When Jane is at our house and starts getting weird, we tell her to go home and take a nap. Sometimes we tell her, 'Get out of here, or we'll have to call the cops.' That is how we deal with her when she is out of control in a manic state."

Carrie talked in length about encouraging Jane to take her medications. "She takes them as long as she is being monitored. Then as soon as the monitoring stops, she stops taking them. When Jane was doing okay, your mother said she was well and didn't need to take her meds anymore. Of course, when Jane got off the drugs, she would go back into not being sane. I argued with your mother about keeping Jane on her medications, but she would not listen and hung up on me."

I had a conversation with Ben regarding paying the utilities. "Jane wants me to pay the utilities, but I have a problem with that because it is not like Jane doesn't have the money. I don't want to leave Jane in a bind, but I expect her to cooperate," I stated.

"That is just it," said Ben. "She won't cooperate."

"We might want to talk to an attorney to see if you can get access to her checking account to pay her bills," I suggested.

* * *

"Jane called me about looking up her property tax back when she was using the library computers," Julie informed me "She was listed as owning another apartment. I accessed the records and found, indeed, there had been an error. It was obviously a mistake, but that may have been the reason Jane thought she was entitled to be there."

"When I have time, I will review the tax rolls to see if the records have been corrected," I replied. In the meantime, I wanted to see if Marvin Olsen, Jane's legal advocate, knows of a way to pay Jane's utilities from her checking account.

While waiting for Mr. Olsen to return my call, I began a quest to explore the Internet in search of the county tax rolls. The records showed Jane owned the apartment that she was occupying and none of the others. The site led to an image of the quitclaim deed that was initiated to give ownership of the apartment to Jane. It was dated September 11, 1992, and showed transfer of the property from Jeff Ramsey to Jane for the consideration of LOVE AND AFFECTION.

I had been curious about who Jeff was when Jane occasionally brought up his name. Jane had told me they wanted to get married, but Mama would not let them. Jane would have been in her forties. It was not as if she was underage. I found records saying he died in January of 2000.

While I was researching, Marvin Olsen returned my call. "Are you still Jane Jenson's advocate?" I asked.

"I'm not sure. I have not received anything from the courts for a period. I received a call from Human Services about trying to get a family member to be her guardian to see that her bills got paid. I am aware Jane has been apprehended," he informed.

"Jane is a difficult case," he began. "She is always getting into confrontations with people, who should just ignore her, but she gets into spats with strangers who overreact to her antisocial behavior, and they call the cops."

I had heard that dialogue before. He continued talking about Jane doing annoying things and explaining her behavior was not a crime.

"I acted as her advocate in court some time back. I was able to persuade the judge that Jane was harmless, and her intentions were not criminal. Jane said she was all right, and she didn't want to take the medication. Jane told both the judge and me just how the cow ate the cabbage. The judge let it go and did not force her into a compulsory treatment program. Jane does just about anything she wants, and sometimes her actions are treated as a crime. She is always going to get herself diagnosed as being someone who needs to be on stabilizing medication."

It was clear to me he had no idea why she had been arrested. "With this last incident, I could see why they have her in jail," I remarked.

"What was she accused of?" asked Mr. Olsen.

"Jane has the idea she is the manager or owns another one of those apartments in that row of apartments. She broke into it with an axe."

"That is a serious offense. Maybe she is not capable of knowing right from wrong, or she was hallucinating," Mr. Olsen suggested. "Jane is very self-righteous about things. She thinks she can tell anybody how things should be and then blames the judge, me, and the whole world. She thinks everybody is wrong in their judgment, and she is perfectly right, but she is very wrong."

"The reason I contacted you was to see if the court could allow for Jane's bills to be paid from her checking account," I stated.

"It isn't that simple. It has to happen through due process, and a guardian or conservator has to be assigned for that purpose, but no one seems to want to do that because it would create tense relations. Since Jane won't stay on her medications, she needs to be committed. A guardian or conservator could have her committed," he explained.

At least the court had her committed this time, but Julie and I had our doubts she would ever stay on her medications and stay out of trouble.

I was quite surprised to receive a collect call from Jane, who was still at the Blackburn County Jail. Jane had just talked to Ben, who had given her my phone number.

"I was fixing up the apartment. I am the apartment manager under Sunny Side something, something. I told Uncle Andy I was fixing up apartments. Have you talked to him lately?" Jane expounded.

"Yes," I answered. "I don't think he said anything about you fixing up apartments."

"Uncle Andy is more out for himself. Did you know Aunt Rebecca has an infection in her knee from the replacement?" Jane asked.

"Yes, I knew that," I answered. Andy had mentioned it during our visit.

Our Uncle Ralph had had a serious stroke around Christmas. He was in a wheelchair. Jane began to talk about him.

"Uncle Ralph could get better and manage a Baskin Robbins like this guy I used to know who had a stroke. I helped him get his job," Jane bragged.

"Uncle Ralph could never manage a Baskin Robbins, not that he would want to," I replied. Jane obviously did not realize he could not speak and had to have people lift him.

Jane got angry. "You shouldn't say he couldn't do anything because that sends out negative thoughts."

"Are you on medications yet?" I asked.

"Yes, I'm on speed and marijuana. I'm swifter than you are. I am the hare. You are the tortoise," Jane announced.

Bringing our conversation back in line, I remarked, "A lady from Human Services called and said you are being transferred to Baldwin to get stabilized."

"I can get stabilized faster at home. They won't take me because I don't have enough money. The social worker had me sign for Ben to get $300. They put me in manacles when I am let out of my cell to go to the sunroom. I need to get out of here. Call the sheriff and put bail up for me to be released so I can go to church," Jane commanded.

"Carrie and Ben have already made arrangements for your bail, but—"

The instant I mentioned Carrie's name, Jane burst out, shouting, "CARRIE IS A LIAR, AND SO IS BEN! She has been trying to get me confined! YOU BETTER STAND UP FOR YOUR SISTER FOR A CHANGE!" Jane yelled hatefully.

I hung up. My heart was pounding as if I was being chased by an eight-hundred-pound gorilla. Jane tried calling back. I let it go to the answering machine. After several minutes, my heart was still pounding. Jane's startling roar had caused my heart and blood pressure to go wild. I wrote a letter to let Jane know her actions were not acceptable:

> *As you can see I have enclosed some paper and envelopes. I will not accept any more collect calls from you, so stop calling. If you want to tell me something, send a letter.*
>
> *Whenever I do talk to you, you are not allowed to yell. If you do yell, that is the end of the conversation; period.*
>
> *I wanted to tell you when we talked previously that I spoke to the lady from Human Services. She said you wanted me to pay your utility bills and taxes. There is no need for me to pay those expenses. You have enough of your own money. Make the same arrangements you have in the past for paying your bills for when you have been incarcerated.*

Several days later, I received Jane's response, which was written on the back side of my letter:

> *I can hardly believe you, Elaine. If I had acted, and by chance did, toward you in the manner you have in this letter, let alone every conversation we have, when Mama was around, I would have been severely verbally reprimanded.*

*Please allow me, via you to reach Julie. Does she
know? How did you learn? I have been here doing hard
labor.*

*Send care package, including street clothes so I may
stand trial. By law it is required. Do you believe me or
misinformed liars?*

*Tell Ken and all your progeny I'd like to hear from
them despite wedges placed by Mama. Are we going to
lose the unsold Redcow books while you "play games?"*

Jane's response was typical. She could do no wrong, and I
was the bad guy. It was unheard of for me to set boundaries.

"Jane wants us to send a 'care package.' Do you have any
clothes in good condition you aren't wearing that might fit
her?" I asked Julie.

"I don't know what size she wears," replied Julie. Neither
of us knew.

I contacted Ben. "Jane needs some clothes to wear at her
trial. Could you take her some?"

"I'm working on gathering up some clothes," said Ben.
"There are piles of clothes stacked everywhere. It is a matter
of figuring out what will go together. As far as the trial goes,
people do stand trial in their orange overalls."

I had not envisioned Jane wearing orange prison uniforms
and manacles. The image was disturbing.

"Doesn't she have to get stabilized at Baldwin before she
faces trial?" I asked Ben.

"Jane is mixed up. She is preparing her case for a jury
trial," he replied. Jane could not possibly be serious about
representing herself. It would be a disaster.

"What is going on with the truck?" I asked.

"It is just sitting at the repair shop, and they are waiting for me to tell them what to do."

"Are you receiving VA benefits?" I asked. I knew he had little money of his own.

"I have not applied for them yet," he responded.

I was treading in an area that was none of my business, but I told Ben he needed to apply as he was entitled to them.

"Is Jane still in the Blackburn jail?" I asked.

"I haven't heard," he replied.

Julie spoke to the jailer, asking why Jane had not yet been transferred to Baldwin, where she could start getting help. They were waiting for a space to open up. The charges were trespassing and criminal mischief.

I called Ben to inform him Jane was still in the Blackburn jail. I mentioned Jane wanted me to bail her out. Of course, I had no intentions of doing so.

"It is a consideration of what kind of trouble she would be in if she was out wandering around on the streets," replied Ben. "She is always getting into confrontations with people. Sometimes they keep her in a separate area of the jail in a protective area, away from the general population. It depends on how she is behaving."

Many months later in a conversation with Jane, I was told about her jail experience.

"The jailers have some commodities they sell, and so I bought some colored pencils and paper, and I was doing a lot of drawing to stay occupied. I was waking up about three o'clock in the morning, yelling and screaming and usually singing. It made a lot of sense to me, but other people didn't like that because they could hear me, and they kept complaining. Then I stopped doing that. I was considered getting better.

"They started me out in an isolation cell. Then they put me in a cell that had room for more people, only they didn't have anyone in with me for a while. I had a television set and a shower. I was on good behavior. They had me in with two hardened criminals at the last, and we played Monopoly together.

"You had to clean your cell completely in the morning before they would let you do anything else. They come in with mops, and we scrubbed the floors, and then we scrubbed the walls, and we made sure the bed was clean and all sorts of things like that. They would come in with changes of clothes. I was wetting my pants.

"I found out my bail was only $100, but Ben wouldn't bring up the bail. Ben won't stand behind me. He lets me get in trouble and just watches. He can't give me good advice because he is stupid. He got D's in school."

Julie contacted an official at the Trenton Mental Health Emergency Services. Julie told her she was concerned about Jane being in jail so long, and she was contemplating seeing an attorney.

Jane's file was located. "We are aware of recent events. You are right. She has been in jail a long time. I am going to contact the jailer and try to get some medications to her."

In mid-September, I received a letter from Jane. It was mailed from Baldwin. I talked to Julie regarding what had been written. "In her letter, she wrote, 'I am to be evaluated for things that have already been proven. Please stop thinking

I am crazy. I am not and have not been for a long time, and I think you all know that.' Well, I don't know that."

Julie replied, "I finally talked to Bea at the Blackburn jail. She took Jane to Baldwin September 16. The mental health people went by to see Jane. She refused to take her medications when she was in jail."

CHAPTER TWENTY-SIX

Certified Nuts

It was the third week of October. Julie was concerned that it had been especially rainy. Gerald had not been able to get the last cutting of hay out of the fields, and frost was expected soon, which would ruin the grass for hay.

"Ben called last night," I informed Julie. "He said the police turned over the axe to him. He thought the DA was dropping charges since they were not keeping the evidence. Jane had been going in the apartment before when it had been left unlocked. This last time it was locked, and that is why she used the axe. The neighbors called the police."

All my children and grandchildren spent Thanksgiving with us. Christmas was quickly approaching. I spoke to Julie regarding the latest encounters with Jane. "Jane has called me about three times recently. She sounded drunk. She is sensitive to the medications, and the doctor has her on a new one. She is still planning to be her own counselor and is going to claim habeas corpus, which means she is claiming to be innocent."

"I'm getting together some clothes for Jane," Julie replied. "The sweater is roomy, and the pants are stretchy. I'm pretty sure the shoes will fit."

Christmas was only three days away when I phoned Julie. "Jane called this afternoon. She is still pretty mixed up. She has a hearing in February to discuss her medications. She said she is incompetent to stand trial because she gets upset when they say bad things about her. They could keep her five to eighteen years. She knows that because she has been arrested for trespassing before. She has to eat with these big spoons because she is on a unit for the criminally insane."

"I had no idea Jane was in these circumstances," Julie expressed.

With the arrival of the 2010 New Year, Jane ceased to be heard from. I felt a need to contact Jane to make sure she was okay. After some detective work, it was learned Jane had been moved to a geriatric ward in a different building. Jane sounded drugged, and her speech was difficult to understand.

"How are you doing?" I asked.

"I'm doing okay. I've got new glasses now. They are thinking about operating on my foot," Jane answered. "They are taking a portion of my money out for my medicine each time. I'm going to have to take it."

"That will help you stay more stable. I was wondering how the clothes are fitting that Julie sent," I stated.

"They are fitting okay," Jane answered. "They are just a little bit big, but I like to wear my clothes loose, so that is no big deal. I tried them on once. I want to wear them February 10 to a meeting. I do not want to get them dirty before that."

"What is the meeting for?" I asked.

"February 10, for drug reclaiming. That is what they are keeping me here on is the fact that I'm not making sense when they talk to me."

Drug reclaiming, I pondered. Is that Jane's terminology? "The last time I talked to you, you said something about the Five Times Rule. What is that?" I asked.

"Oh, they have a rule here that's part of old state law. If you've been in here over five times, you're considered incorrigible. People in my category can be on the streets, or their places would be too full. It is called certification. Have you heard of certified nuts? That's what I call it, certified nuts. That is what I am. So when they have the trial, I'll try to behave as best I can," declared Jane. "When I get out, will you come help me box up extra clothes?"

I indicated I would try to help.

"If they say I'm up for trial, I will be sent back to Blackburn. The trial lawyer said it isn't going to be nearly as bad as I think."

It was a big relief to hear Jane mention an attorney. Her mental health advocates insisted she have legal representation by a lawyer.

Jane started talking about the apartments in Blackburn. "There are two units at the end of that row that are under social services. I would like to find a way to start placing people from mental health there and me receive their rent. They are not owned by anybody. I can use the rent money to fix up their places.

"I'm trying to figure out a way to make a living. I could have one of those houses to rent and watch over. That house needs to be fixed up. Would you and Ken help me if I can get enough money gathered up to do it?"

"I don't know. I couldn't say right now. We are really busy taking care of Ken's mother," I said, evading Jane's request. The entire idea sounded farfetched.

Jane was declared competent to stand trial. She wanted me to contact Dr. Rice, the last dentist who had agreed to work on her teeth, and see if he would take her back.

Ben phoned on February 19. "Jane arrived in Blackburn last evening. She is being detained at the county jail for now until she sees the judge next week. I'll let you know what happens," Ben affirmed.

The evening of Thursday, February 25, I received a call from Jane. "I have the pants on that Julie sent. It is the only decent thing I have to wear right now. I'm planning on going to church Sunday."

"Tell me what happened yesterday," I commanded.

"They put me home on my own recognizance. Today Ben and I went downtown, and I went to the bank, and nothing bad happened. I didn't expect it to, and I will be taking pills for the rest of my life, probably. I am on Zyprexa. It is bad for people with heart disease, so I don't know how this is going to work out for me. It may shorten my life."

"You don't have heart problems though, do you?" I asked.

"Yes, I do, a little bit."

"I didn't know that. What kind of heart problems do you have?"

"Angina," answered Jane. Her response was vague.

"Oh," I responded.

"You don't believe me, do you?"

"Sure I do. You hadn't said anything."

"I didn't want you to know. Well, I had an, ah, ever since, ah, I was at . . . I don't want to go over it now. It is nobody's business but mine. I found out about it. I just wanted you to know. Okay?

"I'm having to sign up for Medicare B and C, and so then they can have somebody come in my home and help me clean up the mess for free. I need to get off the phone. I'm expecting a call," Jane announced.

"First, tell me. Was it a jury trial?"

"No, it was just before a judge, and I was in a separate room completely. I was dressed in prison fatigues. I had to sign that I wouldn't drink, and I wouldn't use firearms for the next three months."

Later, I learned Jane's case was a hearing to set a date for the trial.

I called Julie to let her know Jane was home. "Apparently, Jane has resigned herself to staying on her medications," I stated.

"But she is going back to that church!" Julie exclaimed. "They may get her off her meds."

I called Jane to discuss loose ends. "Hi, Jane. I tried to call Dr. Rice's dental office, but it was a Friday, and he wasn't there. And then I decided to wait to see what was going on with you. I will—"

"I'm getting ready to go to the post office. Just get in touch with Dr. Rice. Tell him to call me if I don't call him."

"I won't tell him that. It is your responsibility to call him," I replied.

A pleasant-sounding lady's voice answered the phone at Dr. Rice's office. There was an instant coolness upon informing the lady I was calling on behalf of Jane Jenson.

"Jane wasn't happy with us and hasn't been here for a while. She is an inactive patient. I will ask if he will take her and call you back."

Moments later, the receptionist phoned. "Dr. Rice is not accepting new patients," she said curtly. The rejection was not a surprise.

I phoned Jane after allowing time for her to return from errands. "Dr. Rice isn't accepting new patients," I stated.

* * *

Another year had passed since Mama's death. It was hard to believe it had been five years. We always knew it would be tough managing Jane when Mama was gone, but it was worse than Julie and I had ever imagined. Soon after the anniversary of Mama's death, we lost Ken's mom. Emma died the evening of March 8, ten days short of her ninety-first birthday.

* * *

Jane decided to confer with Dr. Mitchell, another dentist to whom she had previously visited, and was able to schedule an appointment that week. I spoke with Trisha, the dentist's wife and receptionist. Options and costs were discussed. Jane would have one implant, a root canal, several fillings, and some extractions.

* * *

She phoned on April 21 to inform us her trial had gone well. She had been acquitted of the trespassing charges. "They told me I had better never ever do anything like that again," Jane stated.

Jane's calls were coming every third day with nothing in particular to talk about other than the progress on her teeth.

Our son, Justin, was working in Edmond. He came back to Bingham some weekends, which took him through Blackburn. Knowing this, I asked him to drop off a red suitcase for Jane the next time he went that way. The suitcase had belonged to Emma and was packed full of her clothes that it was hoped would fit Jane.

When Justin stopped by Jane's apartment to leave the clothes, she was not home. The suitcase was left inside the screen door of the porch. He was aghast to see the condition in which Jane was living. "Jane's place is a dump," he expressed.

Ken and I discussed going to Blackburn toward the end of May to help Jane box up her things after we returned from attending Jack's graduation, where he was receiving his accounting degree. Ken suggested he and Ben could explore car lots for a used truck, while Jane and I worked organizing the apartment. Ben had been hauling wood in the trunk of Mama's old blue Plymouth, which was currently in the shop. The suspension on the Plymouth had been compromised, and it drove like a boat. Jane explained it needed a tune up, and the radiator needed flushed, plus other things. They did not have any transportation.

I left a message on Jane's answering machine to tell her of our plans to visit. When she returned the call, she was panting like she had just run a marathon.

"Why are you out of breath?" I asked as Jane gasped into the receiver, sounding like a creature from a horror movie.

"We just got back from buying groceries." Jane had walked to the adjacent supermarket. I informed her of our idea to help her clean up the apartment and find a truck if she wanted us to come.

"Ben is going to get a storage unit to move his things into from the shop. There should be room there to put some of my things."

"Are you going to keep it all?" I asked.

"Yes. I have a license to sell things. My apartment is like a warehouse," Jane explained. "I sell things now and then for a quarter and collect two cents tax that I send in."

Jane would never cease to amaze me with her wackiness.

"Sometimes I sleep in the camper, where there is more room. It is parked nearby. Tell Justin thanks for dropping off the clothes. I want him to know I really appreciate it," Jane expressed.

As usual, Jane was not staying on topic. The offer was made. I would wait for her response.

CHAPTER TWENTY-SEVEN

To Jane's House We Go

Upon returning from Jack's graduation, Jane informed me she did not want me to come and take over turning her apartment upside down. "I don't want you going through my things!" Jane yelled.

"That is perfectly okay with me," I replied calmly. I was dreading the trip anyway and had decided to go only because I felt obligated. "I was only coming because you asked me."

"I did? I forgot," she said.

"If you don't want me to come, I guess that means you don't want to get a truck," I replied.

"You can get us a truck if you want to," said Jane.

"It doesn't matter one way or another to me. Do you want to get a truck or not?" I asked.

"Yes, Ben needs a truck to haul wood. While you are here, will you bring your sewing machine tools? My sewing machine is jammed up with threads."

Several weeks prior to the expected excursion to Blackburn, Ken had contacted a car dealership in hopes of finding something to suit the budget. Buck, a salesman, described a truck that sounded promising.

Upon arriving in Blackburn the afternoon of the specified day, Ken's eye caught sight of the dealership. He stopped briefly to see if the truck in consideration was still available, which it was. We would return upon checking into a motel and collecting Jane and Ben. I called Jane from my cell phone to inform her we would be there shortly.

Ben and Jane were waiting outside by their alley entrance when we arrived. Jane was wearing a purple flowered muumuu and had a straw hat on her head that resembled a flowerpot. A strap made from twine caressed her chin.

"How do you like my hat?" Jane questioned. "I made it."

"Oh," I responded while smiling my accepting weirdness as perfectly normal smile.

Jane's new glasses with lenses the thickness of pop bottle bottoms had slid down on her nose, causing her to look like Mother Goose.

The facial hair she had neglected to shave for a while was visible under her jaw and extended onto her double chin. She made chewing contortions with her mouth and clicked her teeth. Maybe her dental work was bothering her.

Her head bobbed, and she had slight uncontrollable movements as one might have with Parkinson's disease. These were side effects caused by her psychiatric medication. Her eyes were exceedingly squinty, and her face looked puffy. Perhaps this was caused by the medication also.

Ben looked as usual with his scrounge white beard and tobacco-stained teeth. His plaid shirt needed to be tucked in. His dirty jeans had a big tear on the upper right leg where the fabric was unraveling, and he smelled badly.

A truck was noticed across the highway from her apartment at a financial institution where repossessed vehicles were on display. We decided to inquire about it before returning to the Chevy dealership.

Jane took me by the hand as she wobbled along with her limp. We walked hand in hand across the grocery store parking lot to reach the street corner and crossed at the light. After getting information on the truck, we began walking back to Ken's truck, which was parked by Jane's apartment.

At the dealership, Buck pointed out several used trucks to consider. As Ken and Ben drove off to test-drive a well-maintained white 2500, 4 X 4 long bed with a locked toolbox, Jane started to sing. "Way down upon the Suwanee River—"

"Don't sing here," I commanded.

"It is a Stephen Foster song," Jane expressed.

"I know. Let's go inside where we can sit in the shade," I suggested.

A lady offered us drinks and popcorn while we waited at a table adjacent to the showroom.

Jane asked for water and popcorn. I asked for water but was also brought popcorn, which I later gave to Ben when he complained about Jane eating all of hers. We sat chatting as Jane crammed popcorn in her mouth. I pointed out the popcorn stuck to Jane's lip, not that removing it made her any less conspicuous.

The men returned from the test-drive. The truck was very much to Ben's liking. Ken negotiated for two new front tires and a half tank of gas.

After gulping down the last of her popcorn, Jane belched several times. Fortunately, Buck's attention had been diverted by a couple purchasing a brand-new bright lime green Camaro. Buck returned, sitting directly across Jane. Jane started coughing without covering her mouth. Buck gave her a quick glance, forgiving her uncouthness as he began collecting information for the truck title.

The necessary papers were signed, and I wrote a check for the truck. Ken and Ben would return at 11:00 A.M. the next day to take possession. Meanwhile, we all went to dinner.

Ben selected a small café on Main Street. We all ordered hamburgers, except Jane, who ordered a bacon, lettuce, and tomato sandwich. I glanced up occasionally to observe Jane taking large bites with food hanging on her lips. She took another mouthful before swallowing all the previous bite. Food fell out of her mouth onto her plate as she chewed with her mouth gapping open.

After completing half of her sandwich, Jane complained to the waitress her sandwich hurt her mouth to chew. Jane asked if she could trade the uneaten half of the BLT for half of a hamburger. The waitress obliged her, taking away the uneaten half and bringing a hamburger, which had been cut in half, at no charge.

At the end of the meal, Jane yawned a number of times without showing us the courtesy of covering her widely opened mouth. Somewhere along the way, Jane had lost any manners she ever had.

After eating, Ken and I escaped to our motel.

The next morning, Ken and I joined Jane and Ben at the apartment. Jane was wearing a blouse from among the clothes Justin had dropped off. It fit very well and looked nice.

As I entered the apartment through the alley door into the kitchen, I was stunned to see the squalor in which Jane and Ben were living. Only one chair in the kitchen was free from being occupied with sundry items until Ken placed some boxes on it containing more of his mother's clothing that we had brought for Jane.

The white steel sink unit was stained and dirty. Spills from dried food remained where they had run down the sides of the sink as well as the refrigerator. The duct-taped linoleum kitchen floor desperately needed to be swept and mopped to be free from small wood chips and other debris. Absolutely no uncluttered counter space existed in the cramped kitchen.

First thing, Jane approached Ken, asking him to help Ben install a portable air conditioner in the kitchen window. Ben was in no mood to start the morning with a chore. He cursed as he went out the door, saying he was going for coffee.

"Have you already eaten?" asked Jane.

"Yes," Ken replied. There was no way we were going to eat anything at Jane's apartment.

"Good. I'm eating the other half of my hamburger for breakfast!" Jane exclaimed.

Ken had the air conditioner set up in no time, completing the task long before Ben returned.

Jane kept bumping into me in the confined space, almost knocking me off balance several times. When I stood by the kitchen sink, Jane nudged me to get out of her way. "There is no place for me to go," I protested. "If you want me to move, you will have to back up and let me out!"

After making way for me to exit the trapped area and completed her task at the sink, Jane led me to the nearby vacant lot to see the camper. It was in ram-shackled condition, same as the apartment. Jane pointed out how she had rigged the broken ceiling vent to open and close with a bent wire hanger.

Back at the apartment, we passed through the kitchen to the center room, where a floor-to-ceiling mountain of miscellaneous stuff inundated one side of the room.

"This is normal for people in my condition," Jane stated. "Mama's place was like this too." She had taken on our mother's penchant for hoarding; however, she was much worse than our mother.

Jane wanted to get the rake to pull things down from the tall pile. "There is no need for a rake," I told her. "There is plenty to work with on our level."

I took the lead attacking the grueling chore by first assembling some boxes I had brought. Finding no space to set them, the vacuum cleaner and two of Ben's guitars that were encroaching onto the narrow path were placed in the back room. Now there was room for the boxes to sit on the floor in the limited pathway. I folded two large quilts and a blanket from the pile and then placed them on the unmade mattress of the top bunk of the bed that was not being used in the back room.

Staring me in the face was an enormous pile consisting of clothes that had been tossed amid tangled sheets, towels, and boxes with heaven only knew what all.

A box was set aside for clothes Jane wore. Other boxes were designated for other categories. Jane was losing interest as I persisted diligently going through items one by one, asking Jane what she wanted to do with them. Jane disappeared once, returning with a bag of potato chips, and another time, eating an ice cream bar.

Jane was distracted by the newly delivered boxes of Emma's clothes. She opened the box to find a pair of light-blue linen slacks. She decided to try them on. Clearing a kitchen chair of its contents and after removing her skirt, she sat and attempted to put the slacks on.

"You should take your shoes off first," I suggested. Jane had not intended to go to the effort at first and would have gotten her foot stuck.

Jane could not get her leg high enough and asked for help.

I gathered the legs of the slacks and slid them on one at a time. Then I assisted Jane with her shoes. The slacks fit well.

Jane joined me briefly back at the pile before being sidetracked again to do a load of laundry, leaving me in the midst of boxes, waiting for her return. When the washer was finished, Jane took leave again to drape some of the larger items over the railing around the back door landing. She also had a line hooked up across the kitchen, where she placed socks and small items to dry. I turned around to see Jane standing under the line, gazing at me with a sock riding on her forehead.

Headway was being made slowly. Lots of papers that needed to be thrown out were put in a box by the woodstove in the back room to burn for heat when the weather got cold.

Jane wanted to keep part of a church announcement that had the words to a song she liked. "Glory to God . . . glory, glory, glory," Jane sang from the announcement in her high-pitched, off-key voice.

I was getting frustrated. Jane could not bring herself to throw hardly anything away. She was saving old calendar pictures because she liked them. An unused 1981 calendar had been kept because it would be accurate again if it was kept long enough. Begrudgingly, Jane tossed it in the trash.

Jane did not like being told she should discard a lot of the useless items. "How would you like your sister coming in your house and sorting through your . . ." Jane stopped in mid-sentence.

I was distracted, trying to decipher what the next item taken from the pile was.

"I fell," said Jane. "Help me get up."

I turned around to find Jane stuck in the box containing fabric remnants. At least she had a cushioned fall. I chuckled to myself.

"If you don't want my help, I will gladly stop and go home right now," I proclaimed as I pulled Jane out of the box.

"No, I need your help," said Jane.

Ken and Ben returned from picking up the truck. Ben was thrilled and had already moved his tools to the tool chest. It was time for a lunch break. The four of us went out to another nondescript café on Main Street.

Upon returning to the apartment, Jane set up her sewing machine table in a space she cleared by the kitchen window. After presenting the sewing machine for me to fix, she retreated to the camper for a nap. Since it had gotten warmer, Jane was sleeping in the camper, which was under some shade trees. Ben slept in a chair next to the bunk bed in the back room.

The bobbin area of the sewing machine was impacted with a knot of threads, which was a simple matter to clear. Ken helped unscrew the outside case, which was necessary in this model to access the places that needed oil. To have reference to locate the places requiring oil, the instruction booklet was needed. The pages of the manual were stuck together with dried jelly or some sticky substance. I peeled the pages apart carefully to reveal enough information to complete the task. Grunge was wiped from the outside of the machine, and then I sewed on a sample piece of fabric I had brought. The test piece was not sewn to my liking, but the machine was working when Jane lumbered in.

Ken had already checked out of the motel and was ready to leave. We had not gotten as much accomplished as I had intended. I insisted we stay long enough to reach a section of the floor to have a level place to stack the boxes that blocked the pathway.

Jane wanted me to come back, but I had already told her this was a one-time deal. More could have been accomplished if Jane would have stayed on task. As it was, she had done little to help, and I was not going to take ownership of organizing the overwhelming mess.

Ken and I left Blackburn with plans to spend the night in a tourist town along the way. As we began the drive, I collected my thoughts, gazing at the peaceful country side, taking note of horses and cattle grazing in the pastures. Contending with Jane had taken an emotional toll on me.

The motel room was a welcome sight. I retreated to a warm bath, putting another whacky experience behind me.

CHAPTER TWENTY-EIGHT

Ibee Weebee

Jane kept calling, thanking me for getting the truck for them. She complained Ben would not let her drive it. She said the refrigerator was sounding funny and blamed it on the devil for giving her problems.

Julie and I received an e-mail from Aunt Doris with the news of Uncle Andy's declining condition. It was difficult news to accept.

* * *

Julie and Gerald planned a fishing vacation, which involved a boating trip. Ken and I joined them after the fishing trip that afternoon.

The following day, our group went on a road trip, retracing Daddy's mail route again, only this time, we went further into the mountains. We hiked to an old beaver dam and then continued down the well-maintained graveled road until a place was found to share a picnic lunch of roasted chicken. Not a cloud was in view in the vast blue sky. The air had a familiar summer chill common to the high altitude. Nearby was an old abandoned graveyard located on a peaceful hillside covered in wildflowers. One grave of a teenage girl surrounded by a wrought iron fence stood out. Engraved on the large granite headstone was a message that demanded reverence. "As you are now, I once was. As I am now, you must be. Be prepared to follow me."

That evening ended at the rodeo, complete with bucking horses and a clown riding a motor cycle. The evening was followed by a gorgeous Saturday morning, perfect for viewing the parade of majestic horses and old pioneer wagons, which were occupied by ranch families wearing pioneer clothing and being pulled by teams of horses. The parade brought back memories of past parades that we had enjoyed as wide-eyed children.

Upon returning home, three messages from Jane were waiting on the answering machine. Jane was worried she had not received anything from Redcow Publishing regarding arranging to have her unsold books sent to her. She wanted me to check on it since she "did not have time." I spoke to a Redcow Publishing representative and learned Jane's contract was still in effect, and they would keep her poetry books for now unless she told them otherwise.

I gave Julie a belated birthday call. During our conversation, I learned Jane had stopped taking her medications. The next call from Jane confirmed Julie's information. "I can think more clearly when I'm not on medications," stated Jane.

"You need to stay on them, or you could end up back in Baldwin!" I exclaimed.

"I'll be okay because I go to church, and I'm doing okay," proclaimed Jane, pooh-poohing me.

"That is a big mistake. You are opening yourself up for getting into trouble again," I expressed, recalling the mayhem of the past five years.

"I'm not an animal, and I have the right to decide if I want to take them," Jane said arrogantly. "I'm just about finished with my dental work. They said I'm their best patient." *Sure they like you for all the dental work is costing*, I thought.

Hardly a day passed that I did not receive a call from Jane.

"You are my full guardian," Jane announced, catching me totally off guard. "I met with a Social Security representative yesterday to notify them I had been receiving Social Security payments while I was in jail. Social Security checks are supposed to stop when you are incarcerated. I was unable to contact them to stop the checks because the jailer would not give me a telephone book to look up the number. They said the guardian usually calls."

"I gave the lady your address, and they will be sending you my checks. So now you have control of my finances. They may want you to pay my bills."

"Wait a minute. They cannot make me your guardian without my consent!" I exclaimed.

"Well, anyway, you are going to be assigned that now. You are responsible for me."

"I cannot be responsible for you. Since I don't live there, I have no control over what you do," I declared.

"You are selfish and don't care about me!"

"You are not going to put me on a guilt trip!" I exclaimed. "We made the trip to Blackburn to help clean your apartment and find a truck for you. Plus, I've been giving you nice clothes that belonged to Emma. How can you say I don't care?"

I didn't feel I could put myself in a position to deal with Jane any more than I already was.

"If you won't do it, then I will probably be in big trouble. There will probably be court proceedings, and I could very easily be declared incompetent," Jane proclaimed.

A lull of several weeks passed with no word from Jane. I was hoping things had been cleared with Social Security. My refusal to be Jane's guardian could not be as catastrophic as Jane portrayed. In any case, Jane was a worry. I placed a call to Jane.

Jane started talking immediately. "I went and saw a social worker, and they signed me up for food stamps, but they don't have all the paperwork done yet. I've been going out to the mental health empowerment thing in a building on Eighteenth Street, and well, I had a good time today. We worked with each other, trying to improve ourselves, and can I be silent for a second and ask what you want?"

"I was wondering how things are going with the Social Security Administration," I replied.

"I will be on Medicaid from now on."

Jane talked about the insurance company that covered her medications and her "shrink" who changed her medications and then began talking about unrelated topics. "So were you going to say anything?"

"You told me you stopped taking your medications," I replied.

"Well, my insurance wouldn't cover it anymore. They said it was too expensive. So I waited a month, and then I got back into their program. They have ordered me not to work ever again in my life."

"How come?" I asked.

"Because they have the power to do so. What they are going to do is make sure we don't have any money. I have been sleeping out in the trailer, and I finally got a good night's sleep. I've been getting along well with neighbors and everything else. I can even smile once in a while. My church says phooey on all that stuff, depend on God, and He will come through, and so that is basically what I am doing. Thank you for Emma's radio."

"I'm glad you are able to use it," I acknowledged.

"I don't know how to put the CDs in it, but I've been listening to the PBS station quite a bit, and it is relaxing. It helps me when I go about my work in the house. Basically, Elaine, I'm doing okay.

"I've been going to my church, and so I haven't been paying attention to the dogma of Mama and Daddy's old church.

"For a long time, I wasn't on medications, and I was doing just fine. One time when they brought me in for trial not too long ago, I claimed kidnapping and collusion. I had been working in the apartment complex, helping by sealing up the nail holes and stuff like that, but I didn't get permission from the sheriff or from these people. They had a SWAT team man take me away. That is what I was in jail for, Elaine. As far as it was concerned in my mind, I thought I was helping them out.

And it does look better in that apartment after I got through." Jane paused for a brief second.

"If I get in there one more time, they will keep me in Baldwin the rest of my life. We were planning a trip to New York when the bottom broke out of everything. I wanted to go to New York to see the people of the Academy of American Poets, which I am part of. It just ain't gonna happen."

After some more of Jane's long-winded conversation, I announced, "I need to go, and I'm sure you do too."

"Goodbye," Jane said abruptly.

* * *

I was focused on finishing Glen's quilt that was to be his high school graduation present. The days were starting to cool as the end of September approached. Things were generally calm. Jane called occasionally just to talk.

"Thanks for sending some more of Emma's clothes. Those clothes are distinctive. I love them. I really do!" Jane exclaimed.

"Ken's mom really liked the bright colors and a lot of splashy prints, which looked great on her, and I think they will look good on you too if—"

Jane interrupted me, "The tops work fine. It's the bottoms that are a little big. Oh, do you know what Social Security did to me? They simply don't want me working anymore at all." Jane kept on jabbering about her finances, not giving me an opportunity to speak. "As I send them a little bit each month, I think they are fairly well satisfied. I'm growing a beard. Did you know that?"

I laughed. "I could see where you had some hairs growing when we were there," I responded.

"I'm going out to the Vo-Tech school and let them use wax on my beard. I let it grow long, and I really look awful. Once I get rid of all the excess whiskers on my face, then I will look a lot more presentable. It hasn't been fun," Jane said, laughing.

"Thank you so much for that box." Jane had just received more of Emma's clothes that I thought would suit her. "Sometimes I get the feeling people don't love me. Most of the time, people are wrapped up in themselves, and they don't worry about anybody else unless they come barging into their life, and I guess I have a habit of barging in. Do I? I don't know if I want you to answer that or not."

I laughed. "That is the last of her clothes. We gave a lot of them to Goodwill. I didn't think they would fit you, and I knew you didn't have room for more."

Jane started talking about the Goodwill Store and the senior citizens' center and a lot of nothing in particular and then was back on the topic of Social Security. "I called up Social Security and found out I will always be on it because of the fact that I was sick in high school. And Social Security said that I am not to work."

"Why are they saying you are not allowed to work? How can they tell you that?" I asked.

"Well, they did. They sent a mimeographed sheet out to me. So the reason they don't want me working is because . . . I don't know why. I think I didn't do a satisfactory job, but that wasn't true. I think it has to do with the fact that I remind people of things they don't want to be reminded of and stuff like that. I haven't been sewing. I had a handbook with instructions for where settings were to be on. I really enjoy sewing when it doesn't have snags in it because of the tension. It needs some kind of adjustment."

"Take it to a professional sewing machine repair shop and get it adjusted," I suggested.

"I'm always afraid when I take something like that to get fixed they will say it isn't worth beans, and they will want to sell me a new one and so . . . By the way, we really like the pickup. Ben has a new kiddy car. Oh, he loves it. We went down to the Veterans Administration last week, and they did some tests, and he is normal and everything. He has a good blood count and everything like that. They have him on some kind of stuff so that he doesn't bother me like he was there for a while. And I was there when we saw the psychiatrist. She was asking questions about craziness, and most of them didn't fit the bill. It looks like Ben has got a lot of moral support since he was in the service. And I'm really glad I married him. He works in the evening from about eight to ten, guarding a church, and he does the landscaping outside. Well, sometimes if you marry a sailor, what kind of a mouth do you expect it to have?"

"I was wondering if he is going to be able to salvage some of the parts from the old Dodge truck, or what is he going to do with that?" I asked.

"The neighbor next door said they want it for the chassis. They have a perfectly good engine on this one they have.

"Do you know that I am part of the Academy of Poets, and they send me materials, and I had one book signing of my book at the library? And you say Redcow is willing to keep my books?"

"The man I talked to was supposed to send you a letter? Did he ever send you one?" I responded.

"Yeah, he sent me a letter, and it said, "Do you want this person taken off your list?" and I certainly do not. They have around four hundred books of mine in their possession. I'm wondering if they like them enough that they want to keep them," Jane stated.

"He told me the contract doesn't abruptly end. If you want to end the contract, you need to send them a letter and tell them," I replied.

"I'm a different kettle of fish . . ." Jane continued talking about her experience in getting her poetry book copyrighted and lots of mumbo jumbo. "Redcow is a vanity publisher. They sure know how to make a lot of money. Before I got sick, I was going to go over to the high school. They wanted me to pick out some poems and share them with the high school students. I'm waiting until I feel good enough to get in touch with them again," Jane stated.

"I need to go, Jane. I'm glad you liked the clothes," I said.

When Jane phoned me again two weeks later, she was very depressed. Her voice was shaky, and she stammered a lot. "Did you know I got my beard worked on, and they did it out at the Vo-Tech school a couple of times, and I don't know when my appointment is at the beautician, but I tried clipping off some of my hair, and it stands out in all directions at once. There's a woman who is a caregiver there at the mental health thing, and if we are not doing anything else, we can go there and work on psychiatric stuff. They also take us bowling and things like that."

"I'm going to a place downtown, and I don't know what time it is, so I think I'm supposed to be there at nine, I think it was, but I keep getting everything all mixed up right now.

"Oh, the man next door died about three or four days ago. His wife has claimed cancer ever since 1977. To tell the truth, most cancers have to do with self. Any that I have run across have to do with self-mutilation, and so once I found that out . . . ," Jane did not finish. "Well, we are getting along better, and that little trailer is too cold now, but for quite a long time, I would go over there and just sleep and rest."

"What did your neighbor die from?" I asked.

"Congestive heart failure," replied Jane.

"He wasn't that old, was he?" I questioned.

"No, he wasn't, but he was real obese. What I do when I want to help the rest of the people who live here is I buy a bag of oranges and put an orange on their doorknobs. That is what I have been doing for years. The only trouble is last year, I was gone most of the year. The judge apparently is running all the convicts through the mental health process, and lastly, what I am really grateful for is . . . Did I tell you how it happened that I got home?"

"How you got home from where?" I asked.

"From Baldwin. This lady, the one who determines the sanity of people who are put in the hospital, all I had to do was tell them I wanted to see her, and two days later, she came in and gave me a simple intelligence test. She sent back the report that I was okay to stand trial, and that is how come I am out of there now. The last ward they had me on, the geriatric ward, they were much kinder there than on the one where they deposited me at first. The geriatric ward is brand new.

It has great, big, high-vaulted ceilings, and they have them watch TV so they know what the news is and stuff like that.

"The man who was going to do the surgery on my foot was told, 'No.' They didn't have enough money for it, and so really, it is doing pretty good right now. It is from some bones that were broken or misplaced over the years. So I left it alone. They put me over with the elderly on the geriatric floor, and I got along a lot better over there.

"And so some of the same feelings of depression that I would get there while I was in the hospital, my church seems to be the only thing that can pull me out of it at times."

Jane was in one of her talkative moods and kept on and on until I got a chance to get in a few words. "Jane, I need to go."

"Thank you for letting me talk. I have really been run through the mill. They expunged the charges against me, and so my record doesn't show that I'm a convict or anything. I have an appointment with Dr. Fulton. He is a psychiatrist. He laughs at us a lot. He thinks we are funny. We run around crazily I guess. I started to tell you about him."

"Okay, Jane, I need to go. We are getting ready to leave. I need to go."

"Did you hear what I said though? I really need to talk about it. Can you pray for me?"

"Yes, Jane, I do all the time," I expressed.

"Oh great. Thanks for telling me. I'm better after hearing your voice. Bye-bye."

* * *

Julie and I received word our Uncle Ralph had passed away. "The news about Uncle Ralph is upsetting, but I know things will get easier for Aunt Rebecca once she gets through the funeral," I told Julie over the phone. "Jane called last night to wish us Merry Christmas. She was stammering all over the place, which makes it very difficult to listen to her. She said when she first got to Baldwin, she grabbed someone's arm and was put in seclusion because if they don't like you grabbing them, they can charge you with assault."

* * *

Ken and I had gone to visit our son Jack and grandson, Andrew, for Christmas. A number of phone messages from Jane were left in our absence. "Thank you very much for the picture page. I showed it to the people who are my friends. MERRY CHRISTMAS. HAPPEE NEW YEAR!"

Jane lacked the ability to state anything in a straightforward manner. The gist of one of her messages was that she wanted me to locate a manual for her sewing machine on the Internet. "There are some really nice ladies who are working for me," Jane informed. "One of them worked with Mama at the last and the other one . . . They are helping a lot, AND YOU DON'T HAVE TO PAY FOR IT.

"I went in and had my face waxed at the college because I have a lot of facial hair where I tried to imitate papa. It is a side effect from a drug I HAD TO TAKE FOR A NUMBER OF YEARS. I'm sorry, I'm getting really angry, and I don't mean to do that.

"I hope you are listening to me when you come home. Please realize that what you did for our Cousin Teddy was no favor. I tried to keep up with Teddy for years, and every time I turned around, it looked like someone in our family was giving him a hard time. No wonder he died. Don't hate people when they are trying to do the best they can."

As usual, I had to read between the lines, but with her last comment about our cousin, I had no idea what she was talking about. I had only seen him once many years ago and didn't know him.

* * *

On the first week of January 2011, I phoned Jane. "I called to tell you some information I found on your sewing machine. I couldn't find the specific manual for your machine, but I found some that are close. That brand is basically the same," I informed.

"All I need to know is where the tension should be set at the stretch stitch. I have two girls coming in at three o'clock every weekday unless I cancel them, and it would be ideal if you could call up then, and that would get me away from them a little bit because we are running one another ragged. I have a friend, and we were talking about atriums. Do you know what atriums are, Elaine?"

"They are little areas where there are plants like a small yard," I answered.

"You have caught up with me and then some. Okay, to get back to what we were saying, we've been okayed for full disability by the U.S. government. Is Uncle Andy still alive? Do you know?"

"Yes, he is," I stated.

Jane kept talking. "I talk to Aunt Lorie on the phone every so often. My heart is fine. We are probably in better shape physically than everybody else I see because I had a year of relaxation, you know."

"Oh," I said, laughing. "I'm sure that was very relaxing."

Jane took over, monopolizing the conversation, talking about Ben's family and other subjects.

"And so I worry about you guys an awful lot. I guess that worry is kind of a prayer from what I study. A moan is a prayer. A sigh is a prayer. A thought is a prayer. But that is what I believe. You don't have to believe a thing if you don't want to. I don't care it is my life, just like it is your life." Jane interrupted herself. "Let's get back to brass tacks. Over three minutes from here, cars equipped with listening devices can pick us up, but I don't think that is happening all the time. Angelia sent an insignia a few years ago that was put on the same picture frame that I'm using for something else. I recognized the insignia of the Marine Corps, and I put it on a helmet. I wear those downtown every so often just for the fun of it, and everybody thinks I'm crazy. Well, I don't care."

After Mama died, Angelia prepared shadowboxes for my sisters and me, which consisted of Daddy and Mama's wedding picture. To the right of the picture was a poem. Below the poem, Angelia had glued an insignia of the Marine Corps as a tribute to her grandfather and a small wooden spool of thread that had belonged to Mama. Angelia went to a lot of work making the shadowboxes. I was appalled to hear Jane dismantled the tribute to our parents.

"What is it that you are wearing?" I asked.

"Oh brother, Elaine, I shouldn't have told you, the Marine Corps hat. I've got three. I've got all his safari hats. I'm getting off track again."

Jane started babbling about Ben. "He likes to dwink, and so we had a whisky rebellion here a couple of days ago, and I shared it with a neighbor, and I started talking in my sleep."

I kept listening as Jane chattered incessantly about our grandfather on our father's side and his second wife, whom he married after our grandmother died many years ago.

"So we paid the bill off at my doctor's. We are in fine shape financially now, but we have got to get our marbles together because we have never been in a situation like this before. We are more prosperous now than I've ever been in my life since before Mama passed away."

I finally got another chance to speak. "Back at the beginning of our conversation, you were saying there are a couple of girls who come in to help you."

"Yeah, and I was trying to tell you their names. You don't need to monkey monk with that. We are cleaning in the kitchen right now, and it is up to me what they do. In the meantime, they are revving me up.

"I am in the process of trying to figure out a way to give a talk at the high school, but I have a lead bird around my neck, kind of like the albatross, but it is not for real. Do you want to talk to Ben?"

"No, I don't. Did Redcow Publishing contact you?" I asked.

"I called them like they said in the letter."

"So everything is straight with them?" I asked.

"Pretty much so. I invested in an advertisement just before I went to the hospital, and it cost me 125 buckaroos of my savings. They are the biggest and the best in the whole world. Talking about that, Carrie across the way is mad at me because I have not dotted my 'i's' and crossed my t's.' I said it right that time. Do you think we should say good night?"

"Yes," I agreed, wondering how I could have let the conversation go on as long it had.

Jane started up again, "LEEP is going to help us with the heat we have in the front room, and they are going to pay us. It is a state program that will help subsidize poor families. Arizona didn't become part of the union. I'm not sure it must have been forty-fourth, but anyway, it was one of the very last to join the confederacy."

"Confederacy? Don't you mean the United States?" I challenged.

"Yeah, I was wrong. You see, it comes out backward. I've got so much knowledge. I've probably forgotten more than you ever learned." Jane was laughing. "So I must be the smartest thing on two wheels, but that doesn't mean a thing in God's eyes."

"Well, I think you are—" I was laughing and was going to say "full of yourself" before being interrupted.

"Because you are normal. When somebody is smart and somebody doesn't understand them, they say they are crazy," Jane stated.

"And I'm sure that is your problem. You are just such a genius nobody can figure you out," I declared.

"Ibee weebee," Jane said in a high-pitched sound. "Well, now did I prove it?"

"I need to get going," I said.

"I'm on medication." Jane kept going. "It doesn't make any difference whether I'm on or off. The only reason they have me over there is because I am socially undesirable because I'm so smart."

"Jane, you have delusions of grandeur," I expressed.

"Oh yeah, phooey on that," Jane blurted.

"I have got to go," I repeated. Our conversation finally ended.

* * *

On January 28, 2011, Julie and I received an e-mail from Aunt Doris, informing us of Uncle Andy's death the previous evening. Losing another relative was a sad blow.

Jane had not called for a while. I decided to notify her of the recent events with our Uncle Andy and Aunt Lorie, who had fallen just before Uncle Andy died. I also needed to speak to Jane about a call received from Dr. Mitchell's dental office.

"Hi, Jane," I started.

Jane was in a grumpy mood. "Why don't we call it a day, and then we can write? That would be better," she muttered in a low tone.

"Jane, wait a second." She had already hung up. I placed another call.

"This is Jane," she answered.

"You didn't let me finish telling you about Uncle Andy and Aunt Lorie, and also, I got a call from your dentist that I need to talk to you about."

Without responding, Jane slammed the receiver down. I was ticked off. I learned Dr. Mitchell had a serious heart attack when I was speaking with a lady from the dental office. She told me Jane needed to make another appointment. I told her Jane may have decided to stop her dental work, and she would not talk to me about it.

To my surprise, Jane phoned the following evening, saying, "I called Aunt Lorie's house. She wasn't there, but I talked to Mark. He told me about her accident and Uncle Andy dying. Well, I'm glad I know now," Jane proclaimed.

"That is what I wanted to tell you," I expressed.

"I had a feeling you did, and that's why I didn't want to know it then. I worked really hard. I just sat to rest now. We have our lives to live too. You and Ken aren't the only ones who are important. Ben works around here an awfully lot. He cuts all the wood and stuff like that just like your husband, you know. There is no difference. We're not super people, and you guys aren't either. And so just because we have different ways of going about earning our livelihood doesn't mean we are any better or any worse off than you guys are. Did you know that?" Jane blasted.

Where did that outburst come from? I did not react to Jane's derogatory statements. There was no need to have a battle over nothing.

"There are some bugging devices on the computer, and I am wondering if you all have tuned in to that," Jane expressed.

"We get a lot of nonsense over the radio, and apparently, they are doing the Jane thing right now."

"What is the Jane thing?" I asked.

"Well, I wrote a lot of music, and Daddy did too. I think Mama did too. But anyway, a lot of the songs they sing–I was actually in the third grade, writing the poetry for some of the songs that they sing. Did you know that?"

I was caught way off guard. Jane certainly did not write songs as a third-grader, and neither did Daddy nor Mama. We were not a musical family. I answered, saying, "No, I didn't know that. What songs were they?"

"Western songs like "Back in the Saddle Again." Well, the kids were beating on me at school. Mama was always trying to get my poetry. I was so happy to be writing it I didn't think it was worth anything, and so what they did was they used it without my copyright, and it apparently went on some fundraisers and stuff," Jane stated.

She continued, saying, "It has really been an interesting life now that I'm beginning to understand a little bit more, but the reason why you and Ken are the way you are is because you have different lots in life. Just like I said before, I mean, a professor is a lot different from someone who went into the navy. And Ben's family comes from an ordinary family. Have you ever seen what they look like when they go down the road? They are dirty, they smoke, they drink, and they do all the things that common people do. And every time I turn around, I find myself doing something more and more common, and yet I've been getting a lot of fulfillment in that respect."

"You guys came in like a whirlwind when Mama was sick, and I was sure glad you got a chance to see her. I wouldn't have called you guys in if I hadn't needed you. She didn't want you guys to know. One of the funny things about this whole mess is that Mama was feeding some of the neighbor kids eggshells because they weren't behaving, so I mentioned that over the public broadcasting that we have down here. If you stand too close to the radio, they will hear you on public TV. This stuff is confidential. So anyway, what happened, you see, I've been working all day long . . . I lost my train of thought there. Could you remind me?"

"You were talking about Mama feeding kids eggshells," I replied.

"Yeah. They were trying to get these kids to mind, and so what they did was—she did this at my suggestion—was she told them to crumble up the eggshells and put it on top of cereal. Everyone around here doesn't get enough calcium, and so what you do is mix it up with your food and chew it up. It is just like taking a vitamin capsule.

"Well, Elaine, we all have our ups and our downs, and I'm really sorry Uncle Andy passed away."

"I need to talk to you about something," I said, hoping to stay on topic.

"No, you can't! So thank you. You have a good night. God bless you."

"Don't cut me off," I squeezed in. There was silence. Jane had hung up on me again.

I poured out my frustrations to Julie. "Jane really sounds cuckoo, thinking she wrote lyrics to Western songs she hears on the radio. I wanted to talk to her about going to the dentist, but she hung up on me."

"She called me last night also," Julie shared. "She went from one thing to another and also said something about a publishing company finally publishing all her poems in a new book."

* * *

By Mid-February, I phoned Julie. "I've been thinking about Jane a lot lately, and am wondering if we might want to contact Dr. Fulton. I'm afraid she is about to get into trouble. I don't think she is on her medications. Do you?"

"No, I don't think she is on her medications," Julie agreed. "But she is a little different, not quite so combative."

"She is not behaving normally for sure. She won't talk to me about her dental appointments. Right now, I'm feeling like she can just go do her own flipping thing," I expressed. "She keeps saying Ken and I think we are more important than she is. Then she got mad about buying the truck. She said they didn't need it. She was screaming at me for getting the truck for them when she didn't want it. I told her Ben needed a truck to haul wood. Then she totally shut up on that point. The next burr she had up her butt was that she didn't want me to control her funds. That was most of the conversation. Talking to her is like being in a sparring match."

CHAPTER TWENTY-NINE

Here We Go Again

"I called to ask you if, well, I can't remember, Dr. Daramandara, or whatever his name is, well, he put a rivet in my mouth, you know, and attached it to my jaw," Jane began.

"Are you talking about the oral surgeon?" I asked.

"Uh-huh. It is a direct line to the rest of my system, and there is a little hole in the middle of it. I do, of course, need to get in and get it finished. In the meantime, I'm working on our income taxes. I've been having a lot of foot problems, and that is basically why I've been having to be in a place where I get more rest than I do at home. It's not nutty nuts. It's life. Okay?"

"Where are you going?" I asked.

"On a bus ride to Edmond, just a day drive up, as soon as I can figure out how to budget in the ticket on my own. We've worked it so that every once in a while when I'm about ready to blow my stack and my mind is rambling, when it does that, we find a way just to walk down the street, and there are motels close by."

"You go stay in a motel?" I questioned.

"For a night, anything to get it so that we are doing better. Ben is on a pension right now. We found a cheaper source for wood, and so he boogies down there on weekdays and gets some pine slats. I worked in a lumberyard once or twice. I think at least once when I lived in Westbrook."

"Okay. My question is has the dentist contacted you about my teeth?" Jane changed topics again.

"Only to tell me they were ready to proceed," I answered.

"Probably next month, I will find the time to go into the dentist office," Jane announced. "I just thought I would fill you in on some of the things so you know what kind of a spectacular life I have," Jane proclaimed.

"Yes, you are leading a really spectacular life," I said, laughing.

"Okay," Jane said, laughing. "Goodbye."

* * *

Julie phoned to inform me she was back from vacation.

"I'm glad you are back. By the way, Jane called again Sunday. She was in a good mood and was laughing. I'm sure you noted March 2 was another anniversary of Mama's death. She has been gone six years now.

* * *

Jane phoned the following Friday morning. "I talked to Aunt Lorie last evening," Jane announced. "We are working on this and that. The names of Ben's relatives are Tate and Eve, and their mother got remarried, and she has another little baby. It is really fun trying to get through to them. Wuacka, wuacka. I just lost my plate in the woodstove. It is filthy dirty it has dog fur all over it. We lost our dogs, you know," stated Jane.

"What happened to them?" I asked.

"He froze to death basically out of lack of love and a worried wife. We lost Strike first. He was a little border collie. We got him up in the forest. We lost Ginger, and then we got Topper. Topper lasted two years. He looked like a German hound. He died about three days after Strike."

"What happened to him?" I asked.

"Froze to death."

"Outside?" I asked, puzzled.

"He stiffened up and wouldn't get up," Jane explained.

"Did he have some kind of disease?" I questioned.

"A man threw a rock with hamburger on the outside of it and a rock on the inside of it," Jane answered. "All three of them had that happen over at the property of Ben's brother."

"You lost me," I said, trying to follow Jane's reasoning for the dogs dying since I knew Ginger had died from an infection.

"I said the grieving process is supposed to be something that some people never get over," Jane declared.

"Are you grieving for your dogs?" I asked. Jane was giggling wildly in a high-pitched, weird voice. "What's so funny?" I asked.

"We had someone who was dying next door to us. I told you that they died," Jane stated and then quickly changed her train of thought. You know what? I don't trust ya," Jane said, laughing.

"You don't trust anybody," I responded.

"Yeah, I know. It says in the Bible not to. You know what?" Jane chimed in. "You are a very good sister because you trust everybody. And I like your bigoted attitude."

"Bigoted?" I said in anger.

"Uh-huh. I think you're proud and haughty and have never learned humility."

"Well, you are totally—" I began, but Jane cut me off.

"Ben went out about three o'clock this morning to get a smoke. Your husband doesn't smoke. He couldn't be smoking because nobody smokes that's a teacher. We had a temperature of 71 degrees yesterday. Oh, it was beautiful. I was out working my fanny off and ran across some local yokels, if you want to call them that."

"What were you doing?" I asked.

"Cleaning things, moving wood around, trying not to hit myself with a ten-pound hammer!" Jane exclaimed.

"Were you fixing something?" I asked.

"My life," she replied. "We buy used cars that are about twenty years old from individuals not from agencies because we get a better deal. It also means more upkeep. The fender on the right side of the Plymouth AND DO NOT TRY TO FIX IT! It is still under warranty for miles, but it's not for years. We have an insurance agent who will repair it for a reasonable amount. Ben pays the insurance taxes."

Jane went on talking, "I'm tired of being put in the clink because I get upset about things I didn't understand. By the time I start making two and two out of things, Ben does…" I could not follow what Jane was saying as I moved a load of laundry to the dryer. "I'm really pretty happy, aren't you?"

"Yes, things are going pretty well," I answered.

"Our place is so full of stuff. Is your place that way too?" Jane questioned.

I blatantly answered, "No way. I need to get going. I have things to do," I stated.

"Okay. Good-bye," Jane said.

It was now well into March when I phoned Jane to see where she was with completing her dental work. I began the conversation, commenting about some typed pages Jane sent, which was part of a story Mama had written. "I noticed it was some of Mama's writings."

"Yeah, it was something she had written when she took a journalism course through a writers group at my suggestion, and she worked at it until she got it finished. She got all her assignments in on time and had good rapport with the instructor," Jane stated.

"You sent only pages 2 and 3. If you are going to send me something, why do you just send part of it?" I questioned.

"All my stuff is in such a mess I thought you would enjoy what little I had together. I wrote one short manuscript. It turned out pretty good, just before I left high school. I wrote it under Mama's name. It took me a while to figure out that is what happened," Jane explained from her mixed-up thinking.

"How is your dental work progressing?" I questioned Jane.

"They want to charge way too much for what they are doing," she answered.

"We've got the screw drive in or whatever you want to call it. I want to pay for it myself on a payment plan. I was listening to some of the stuff you and Julie were doing with the cassette recorder. I got batteries in that now. We have batteries coming out of our ears, and so why use electricity? I was absolutely astounded at how melodic and how original you two became while I was working on my scholarship."

"Jane, we need to complete your dental work soon," I stated getting back on track.

"I might end up with some baby teeth coming in if I give them long enough," declared Jane. "The liquids that go through that rivet hole actually is giving me a main line of nutrients into my body. And as far as I'm concerned, I probably would have to eat a lot less. I don't believe in the germ theory. We are going to have to slow this down. So you tell me I'm not on a fast track because of some youngsters pushing me around. You tell me. Tell me."

"I don't think—" I was trying to express my opinion, but Jane did not let me finish.

"COME ON, TELL ME! TELL ME! And I'm not angry! I'm just telling you!" Jane yelled.

"Jane, I talked to Dr. Mitchell—" I said in frustration.

"You can talk to him as much as you want." Jane broke in. "He has a lot of other clients besides me, and they take rich vacations every time they get through with me after they have drugged me up and make me as dizzy as they can possibly do because that is part of the professional ethic. Then Trisha comes over to me and gives me A GREAT, BIG, HUGE HUG, and I walk out of there feeling like I've been smooched by a gorilla. Okay. DOES THAT HELP? DOES THAT HELP? Huh, Elaine?"

"No, it doesn't help. It's your mouth, Jane," I said, to no avail.

"I do library work, and I might start working with them on a more regional level," Jane went on. "I have lots of fun in life while you pretend you are a worry wart with me. I need to hang up now. I'm really, really tired.

* * *

I phoned Dr. Mitchell's office to inform Trish that Jane was not cooperating. "I don't think Jane is on her medications," I told Trish. "I'm thinking about contacting Dr. Fulton when I find his number."

"I can give it to you," Trisha volunteered.

During our conversation, Trish brought up she was a good friend of Megan's, Jane's sister-in-law, who had worked in their office as a dental hygienist. Trish provided Megan's phone number, along with Dr. Fulton's.

Several days later, I spoke with Megan.

"Do you know what is going on with Jane?" I inquired.

"I haven't seen Jane since December," Megan replied. "She comes to our family activities. We don't dare leave her alone with any of the younger children because she has strange ideas on disciplining them. I make sure I am never alone with her either. There was one time when I was afraid of Jane. It was right after their dog, Ginger, died. Jane wanted me to go into the bathroom to point out the spot where Ginger died.

I told her I could see it from the door. I was afraid she was going to corner me in there."

"I'm afraid Jane is headed for trouble again," I stated. "She is missing her dental appointments and keeps hanging up on me."

"She has used up all my lithium crystals," Megan said jokingly. That was a good way to express the way I felt also. My energy had been drained to my core.

"Ben is being treated for depression through the VA. Not too long ago, I helped him fill out the forms for his disability. He has post-traumatic stress disorder," Megan explained.

I called the number Trish had given me for Dr. Fulton and reached his private practice. The receptionist provided the number to the State Mental Health office, which I called, leaving a message. A lady with a husky voice returned my call several days later, apologizing for not calling sooner.

"I don't know who to talk to about my sister Jane Jenson," I started. "She is acting very strange in her conversations, and I wanted to make sure she is taking her medications before she gets in trouble."

"You know I cannot tell you anything," stated the lady.

I asked her some general questions. Then phoned Julie, who had taken off the day and was on the road, returning from a bull auction with Gerald.

"Gerald purchased a five-year-old prize bull named Starbucks," Julie informed. "We will name the bull's first offspring Latte."

"You could name others Brown Roasted, Hazelnut, and other coffee-related names," I suggested. We laughed about potential names for Starbucks's calves.

"I just finished speaking to a lady from State Mental Health. They cannot force people to take their medications. If there is a court order and they feel there is a problem, they can notify the authorities, and the law decides what to do," I explained. "I'm guessing there is a court order for Jane to be on her meds. The most they can do is place her under police surveillance."

"Whatever happens, I'm washing my hands of it. I'm done. The purpose of my call was to alert Dr. Fulton to talk to her about taking her medications. Maybe he has. The ball is in Jane's court," I stated in frustration.

Several weeks later, I placed a phone call to Julie. "Jane has started calling again. Every peculiar call is followed by another one. She told me she is a technocite, which is a title she made up since she works with technology. I asked her if she was on the Internet now. She said, "Yes, no, yes, no, yes, no" and started laughing.

"She is smart, but all of it has gone to waste," replied Julie. "Too bad she isn't normal."

"She isn't smart anymore," I replied. "She gets confused easily, and if she was smart, she would realize her condition requires her to be on medications. She has proven that enough times." I continued. "She called Monday morning. Mostly all she talked about was a bunch of hooey she has imagined. All of a sudden, she got mad and yelled, saying I killed our cousin Teddy Winters, which she has told me before. I asked her where she got that idea. She said I hated him, and that killed him. I didn't even know him. It is very irritating listening to the rubbish she dishes out. We have to chalk it up to her mental illness. Just the same, I wish she would shut up," I expounded.

Jane generally called weekends when Ken and I escaped to the mountains. She left insulting messages on the answering machine, telling me such things as Noah would not let me on the ark.

In other phone calls, Jane claimed she had written *The Mouse That Roared, The Revenge of the Nerds, Part I and II,* and also that she assisted in bringing The Beatles to America. Another trip to the state hospital was inevitable; it was just a matter of time.

CHAPTER THIRTY

Chaos Breaks Out

Just before Halloween, Jane started to pour paint in the wood-burning stove of her apartment. Ben told her to get away from the stove. She started hitting him, pulling his hair, scratching his face, and biting him. She even hit him with a stick. Ben tried to call 911, but Jane yanked the phone cord from the wall before he could speak to anyone. The phone rang twice before the connection was broken, which was plenty of time for the emergency center to get a fix on where the call was originating.

Ben went outside after the incident. Shortly thereafter, the police appeared. As the police began to enter the apartment, Jane threatened them, saying she had a gun. Ben told them she did not. When the police got inside, Jane began throwing things at them. She was Tasered on her hip to get her under control and seated in the police car. She was charged with domestic violence and resisting arrest. Jane remained in jail several weeks until she was transported to the state hospital in Baldwin in mid-November.

I first learned of the situation when Jane called collect from the county Jail. I refused her calls but contacted Ben to see why she was in jail. I notified Julie Jane was in trouble again.

Julie called the jail to learn more. Jane was arrested in her nightgown. She was taken without her glasses. She was livid. She told Julie she was going to sue the police for $11 million.

* * *

In January of 2012, I finally decided to check on Jane. Rather than speaking with Jane directly, I phoned Ben, who revealed she was recently *jumped* by five staff members, who held her down to give her a shot. Obviously, she was still not cooperating.

I was extremely angry with Jane in general for yet another incarceration. I could not bring myself to call her until March. Upon reaching Jane, I was surprised she did not want to talk. Jane's exaggerated slurred speech was evidence of her heavily medicated state. She was not feeling well.

During the call that followed, Jane was more talkative. "There is a court order for me to take medications. I've decided I had better follow it. They should not have brought me here. I did not do anything wrong. The police beat me up," Jane complained. "They should not have taken me away for a simple domestic spat."

"When do you think you will be released?" I asked.

"Never," Jane stated with flat effect.

In another call, I asked Jane once again, "When do you think you might be released?"

"I could be released anytime, but they do not know where to put me. I think I'm better off here in Baldwin. It is too hard to be on the outside. It is dangerous out there.

"I need some underwear, lipstick, and talcum powder to put in my shoes," Jane requested in a conversation with Julie. "I have a review on September 26, and they will let me know if I can go home."

Julie sent Jane a *care package* with hand lotion and other personal items, while I sent lipstick. I spoke to Julie over the phone. "By the time she has her review, it will be close to a year since she got arrested. She has burned me out. When they release her, she had better not be calling me like she was," I expressed to Julie. I did not feel I could stand any more of Jane's lengthy, chatty calls that were full of gibberish and insults.

Jane sent letters every now and then. In one scribbled handwritten letter, Jane wrote, "I bumped my head, and finally, today it doesn't hurt as much. I have a new doctor. He has a ponytail and is in 'harmony.' I like him as a person. He lowered my medication. I felt better today than I have in a long time. I walk like a zombie. I lose my balance often, so I am working on that." Partially colored pictures from a coloring book were enclosed.

"From the last letter, I would say she is not functional," I expressed to Julie. "Why is she sending half-colored pages? She has problems spelling, and she is still signing her letters Aunt Jane."

* * *

September 26 came and went with no word from Jane. The second week into October, I decided to check on her.

"I'll be here in Baldwin a while longer," Jane replied when asked if she had any news on her status. "Would you like to talk to the nurse?"

A moment later, I found myself speaking with another person. "Do you know how much longer Jane will be there?" I asked.

"No, but I can have Jane's social worker call you."

"Okay," I agreed.

I was surprised to receive a call the following week. "Hello. This is Cecilia, Jane's social worker. Jane is here with me now. She is a very sweet lady. She is one of our special patients."

I was surprised by Cecilia's enthusiasm toward Jane. *Could we be talking about the same person?* I wondered. "How is Jane progressing?" I inquired.

"Jane is evaluated every ninety days. The last one was September 26. It was to determine if she was ready to be returned to Blackburn to face the charges against her. Her psychiatrist felt she is not."

"Are they working with her to help her improve?" I questioned.

"Her psychiatrist is working with her, and she has a public defender, who is working with her also. Before she can be released, she has to complete the *competency restoration process* successfully. It is a complicated process. She understands what she must do," Cecilia explained.

"What I'm concerned about," I went on, "is when she is released from Baldwin, that she will fall back into her pattern of getting off her medications and getting back into trouble again like she has done more times than I know."

"When she is released, there will be something in place to keep her out of trouble. The system has failed her. If there was something in place, she probably would not have gotten into trouble this time," stated Cecilia.

A lot was learned from the conversation; however, I wished I had asked more questions regarding what the system could do. All *the system* had accomplished was to get her stabilized and then release her back into society to go amok again. Where was this allusive system Cecilia spoke of, which was supposed to keep Jane out of trouble?

The third week into January 2013, I phoned Jane. She was in a talkative mood and rambled, speaking in her familiar drug-induced, slow, slurred voice.

"I'm going to be here a while. I'm legally tendered here."

"What do you mean by that?" I questioned.

"That means I'm crazy. If you're in here over a year, you lose your rights. I'm schizoaffective, which is a mixture of disorders. I don't know when they will let me out."

"What have you been doing?" I asked, wondering how Jane spent her days.

"Nothing. I try to stay out of trouble by sleeping a lot."

"How can you get into trouble?" I questioned.

"There is this girl whom I try to help, but she tells me to leave her alone. There is a nurse I don't like. There is nothing worse than to be treated like a child when you are an adult.

I've been trying to keep my head on straight. I'm not helpless, just hopeless," Jane said, laughing. "How is your family?"

"Everyone is fine," I answered. "Stacy will be graduating from high school in May and is applying to colleges. I told you Glen went into the military. He is engaged now and will be getting married in March. Mathew is the president of his seventh-grade class. Clara does well in school, is on the volleyball team, and was the freshman attendant for the basketball home coming. Andrew is growing like a little weed and is the terror of his preschool class," I stated jokingly.

"They bring in this little char-colored dog sometimes. I really like him. I pet him, and he wags his tail. They let me go outside in a protected area. The workers here are very cheerful and treat us well. I'm glad you called. I'm very lonely."

It was sad talking to Jane. There was nothing we could have done to prevent her from getting into this situation. Jane felt she had a right to do whatever she wanted, and she did, no matter how unorthodox it was. For the time being, Julie and I were saved from worrying about Jane getting into serious trouble.

CHAPTER THIRTY-ONE

Are We There Yet?

Late afternoon of February 28, 2013, a surprise call was received from Jane and Cecilia, Jane's social worker. Cecilia informed me of a meeting on March 7 to see if the court felt Jane could be released from Baldwin.

"If it were not for the charges, Jane would have been released before this. I'm checking into getting Jane in assisted living," Cecilia informed. "They won't release Jane to go home to her apartment until it is cleaned up. The police saw what a mess it was and reported Jane was living in squalor. It was declared unsafe."

Jane broke into the conversation. "Carrie died. Elaine is very upset over her death."

"Who is upset?" I asked.

"Elaine is, I mean, Ben is very upset," stated Jane. She was obviously confused.

The news of Carrie's death was upsetting to me as well. Carrie was a stabilizing force in Ben's family, and his sister would be greatly missed. She had helped keep Jane out of trouble and tried to keep Jane on her medications.

Jane kept asking me, "Do you think I'm ready to go home?"

I had my doubts but certainly was not going to ruin it for Jane by answering, "No." "How should I know?" I answered. "Things need to be in order."

Jane was hyperventilating. Cecilia directed her to take slow, deep breaths and relax. Cecilia asked about Jane's assets and Medicare, information needed to qualify for assisted living.

March 7 arrived with no word from Jane or Cecilia. The following day, I called Jane to learn the results of the meeting.

Jane spoke in her drugged, slow, shaky voice and sounded depressed. "I'm tired. I'm losing my citizenship."

I took that response to mean Jane was not going home yet. "When is your next evaluation?" I asked.

"Sixty to ninety days," responded Jane, talking more to herself than to me. "Talk to Cecilia, my lawyer."

"Cecilia is your social worker," I corrected.

Cecilia came on the phone. "I was going to call you next week." Cecilia assumed Jane had mentioned she was being released the following week. "The sheriff is going to drive her to Blackburn for the bond hearing."

"Jane didn't tell me that. I thought she was going to be there another ninety days," I said, confused.

"I thought Jane understood. After the bond hearing, she will be released to go to her apartment," Cecilia revealed.

"Ben is cleaning it up. Adult Protective Services will come in to check the apartment to make sure it is safe and sanitary."

I phoned Cecilia on Monday morning. I wanted to learn more about Jane being monitored.

"The Blackburn sheriff picked Jane up at 3:00 A.M. and took her back already," Cecilia informed. "Jane was in bed asleep when the sheriff arrived. He was dropping off another person so took her back while he was here. She is in the Blackburn jail now, waiting for her bond hearing on Wednesday. Adult Protective Services has checked out the apartment. I assume it is livable. That does not necessarily mean it is neat. Between State Mental Health and other services, she will be monitored."

"Is the monitoring only for a limited time?" I questioned.

"It will be for as long as they think it is necessary," responded Cecilia.

"With Jane, it needs to go on forever, or most likely, she will decide to stop taking her medications like she has done before," I interjected.

"The hearing is scheduled at three," Cecilia stated. "The charges may be dropped, and then Jane will be released to go to her apartment. I checked into getting Jane in an assisted care facility. There are not many around. Jane had been in one before, and they did not want to take her. They said she didn't fit in. Her only option is to go to her apartment."

I took notice of Cecilia's comment that Jane did not fit in. Everywhere Jane went, she burned her bridges. She had been barred from the grocery store, the library, senior citizens' center, the church kitchen, and choir and was always feuding with her neighbors and asked not to return by her optometrist and a dentist's office.

"At some point, you might want to move her closer to you," stated Cecilia.

"That would not work for us. She would cause too much turmoil for our family," I stated.

"A lot of families have told me it is too hard for them," Cecilia replied. "I can understand that after a lifetime of dealing with the situation."

"Is there anyone in Blackburn we can talk to when we are concerned Jane may be having issues?" I asked.

Cecilia gave me the name and number of a lady with State Mental Health. "Jane will have to sign a release with HIPPA for people to talk about her. I will make a note to encourage her to sign. Right now, Jane isn't very cognitive."

"Jane sounded confused the last time I talked to her. I was wondering if she is ready to be released," I confided.

"It will not accomplish anything to keep her here. Jane has met her maximum gain. Basically, all she was doing is serving time," Cecilia replied.

Four days after the bond hearing, I phoned Jane. Ben answered, saying Jane was lying down. A long moment later, Jane spoke. Both Jane and Ben sounded happy and upbeat during the lengthy conversation. Jane stammered while asking if I could come see her.

"I don't know," I responded, not welcoming the thought. "But I will keep in contact with you."

"The judge said the next time she sees us, she wants to see us happy together," Jane stated. I surmised they must have been ordered to report back to court as a follow-through regarding the domestic violence episode. "Ben has been a lot of help. I told Cecilia I would keep the apartment clean without help from the aids from Loving Assistance. There are papers all over that I'm sorting through. Ben wants to talk to you."

Ben talked about his sister dying. "Carrie had bone cancer. Then she got a tumor in her brain. She was in a nursing home and had seizures. When they decided there was nothing more they could do, her treatment was stopped, except for pain medication. She died two days later."

"I'm very sorry you lost Carrie," I conveyed with sincere sympathy. "I know she will be greatly missed, and what a major loss this is to your family. She was a very special person."

Jane came back on the phone. "Ben is still smoking, but that won't keep him out of heaven."

"No, it won't, but it could get him there sooner," I responded jokingly.

Ben and Jane laughed and sounded happy, to my delight. I had high hopes they would settle down into a compatible relationship.

* * *

Julie sent Jane cleaning supplies when Jane informed her they were eating their meals out because the kitchen was too dirty. *How can they possibly afford to eat out?* Julie wondered.

Jane was always lying down when Julie and I phoned. She had lost her vigor and did not sound happy. The medications were suspected for making her groggy, causing her to sleep a lot. Julie and I had great compassion for what Jane was going through.

"What kind of life is that?" I remarked to Julie over the phone. "Maybe they can adjust the medications that zap her energy."

Julie always was concerned what it must be like to be Jane. "I understand more about her illness. However, I still think she can control it more than she lets on. I understand she really is in a horrible place," Julie conveyed.

"Understanding Jane is complicated," I told Julie. "Jane's distorted thinking is beyond my comprehension."

I had become acquainted with Randy Carpenter, who worked part time at the shop where I frequently spent time taking sewing classes. Randy was a pleasant, intelligent man who had retired from operating his very successful Mexican food restaurant.

In mentioning Jane to Randy, I was astounded when he revealed he had ADHD and severe bipolar, which were controlled by lots of drugs. He explained he had caused his family lots of grief. Randy expressed that he understood from both Jane's point of view and mine. I was in awe how such a successful, amiable guy could have serious mental health issues.

"You said you understand things from Jane's point of view," I mentioned to Randy. "When you were causing trouble, could you control what you were doing, or did you even care?"

"I could control it, but I did not care," Randy expounded.

What a revelation! Our thoughts had been confirmed. Maybe Jane actually could control her actions to some degree but chose to go off in her tantrums.

Randy spoke of his two sons who shared the same disorder. "One is in jail right now. He refuses to take his medications. The other is doing fine. He is taking the medications."

"Are you still taking medications?" I asked.

"Yes. I have to take them the rest of my life to stay in balance, or I will revert back. It is just like being an alcoholic. I'll never be cured."

I shared my interactions with Randy to Julie. "He even writes cookbooks!" I exclaimed. "I'm very impressed with Randy and how he has turned his life around. I know there are mentally ill people who maintain their careers and function in society. I've been thinking about it and wonder why with all Jane's promise, she was not able to amount to much."

After contemplating how Jane differed from Randy, besides refusing to take the medication, it came to mind that drugs are not the only answer. Medications cannot change one's personality or change the basic core of who a person is.

"I have been thinking about where we are now, and I honestly don't think that if we *understood* Jane any better, we would react much differently," I expressed to Julie. "We act on instinct. She is always verbally attacking us. She constantly tries to put us down, calling us stupid and calling me a weasel. She said I am in trouble with God and that I'm going to hell, not to mention keeping on saying I killed our cousin. We cannot just sit back and say, 'It's okay. She can't help it.' We have learned to ignore some things she has said as it would only put us in a no-win conflict. She does not respond to logic. When we challenge her, she gets mad. It is demeaning to us to let her get away with it all the time."

"When she is stabilized, she is still weird," replied Julie. "She needs our support, and we will be there for her as much as possible, not to our detriment."

* * *

It had been weeks since I had spoken to Jane when I decided to phone her. Jane answered, sounding much more energetic than usual. "I've been going over to Herman's, my brother-in-law, to take baths. He is very affectionate. He keeps kissing me." Jane was back in her pattern of rambling. "They want to operate on my eyes for cataracts. They could cause me to go blind. I could have holes in my eyes."

"The operation won't make you go blind. You will see much better afterward. Remember how much better Mama saw after the cataract operation," I reminded her.

It was strange that Jane was going to Herman's to take baths and what was stranger was his advances toward her. I surmised it must have been his way of coping with the loss of Carrie.

I phoned Jane every few weeks as promised. Something was strange about the call placed toward the end of June 24. Jane was talking quickly. "Ben expects me to wait on him. He calls me you fuck'n Jane bitch, and he keeps telling me to shut up. Herman keeps kissing me. I told him he can kiss me when he first sees me and then at the end."

Without skipping a beat, she began singing, "I love you, I love Ben, Ben loves me, and all is good. They have changed me over to private care. I have an appointment with a regular doctor. I have a cleaning lady who is paid for by Medicare. I have to go give Ben some loving. Will you call me back?"

"I will call you back another time," I said, bewildered from the bizarre conversation. The call wasn't at all what I had expected. Jane was not focused, changing topics so quickly she hardly made sense like she had done previously. Jane appeared to be in a manic state.

It was time to phone the person Cecilia had said would be a possible contact in Blackburn regarding Jane's welfare. A message was left. A return call finally came several days later. The woman coldly stated at the beginning of the conversation she could not tell me anything.

"Cecilia, Jane's social worker when she was in Baldwin, gave me your name and number. She said you would be Jane's social worker or would know who is," I stated.

"I can't tell you anything," the woman repeated.

"Cecilia said she would try to get Jane to sign the HIPPA form so that you could talk to me," I said, feeling very frustrated.

"I'll check on it and call you back if she signed." The lady never returned my call.

A few days later, I received a call from Herman. He was confirming he had reached the right person and then passed the phone to Jane.

I greeted Jane cheerfully. "Hi, Jane."

"You said that like you love me." I did not reply. "Herman had your number. He has free long distance and said I could use his phone."

Jane talked about her upcoming cataract surgery and chattered about having floaters that bothered her. "Medicaid is paying for the surgery. People look down their noses at you when you are on Medicaid. I could go blind. You don't get as good of care when you are on Medicaid."

"You won't go blind," I stated. "Many people have that operation all the time. Julie said she sent you some cleaning supplies. Have you cleaned up your kitchen yet?"

"The cleaning lady is allowed only in the kitchen and bathroom," replied Jane. "I would thank Julie, but I lost her address." Jane jabbered on and suddenly got mad about me not meeting her in Westbrook a number of years ago when Ben's family was having a get-together.

"There was this girl whose family turned their backs on her. No one would go camping with her. The girl went camping in a tent by herself, and they found her dead. She committed suicide by letting the elements kill her."

Jane changed topics. "Ben keeps telling me to shut up. He says it so much that I made up a song." Jane started singing, "Shut up, shut up, shut up, shut up, shut up . . .

"You've lost sight of God!" she screamed at me. "I'm not crazy!" she yelled as she verbally bashed me up one side and down the other. "You need to see a psychiatrist!" she shouted. "My eyes are going to be poked out!" she exclaimed. "Ben's sister died last week."

"No, she didn't." I challenged. "She died the end of February."

"You have social issues with me. We think very differently."

"You are right on that one," I agreed.

"It is because I am so much smarter than you. You only call me to find out my business," Jane taunted, shoveling out more demeaning remarks that she was so good at.

"My phone is dying. I have to go," I announced.

I was very upset as I hung up the phone. My heart was pounding out of my chest. "Why does she upset me so much?" I asked myself. I was used to Jane's unpredictable explosive temperament, but it was not healthy for me to tolerate.

I informed Julie of Jane's tirade. "I can't remember all the garbage she was throwing, but I cannot take it. Since Jane accused me of only calling to find out her business, I'm not going to call anymore."

My wishes of sustaining a compatible association with Jane were dashed. It was clear underneath it all Jane harbored unjustified feelings of anger and hatefulness that would never go away and would never diminish.

The summer of 2013 passed with no contact with Jane until I received a call on September 13. Jane stammered around.

"Today is Thursday, isn't it?" questioned Jane.

"No, it is Friday," I responded.

"Oh. Well, I lose track of things."

"How are your eyes since you had the cataract operation?" I asked.

"I didn't have the operation. I kept missing my appointments. After you miss the third one, they won't take you anymore. I don't see very well. I'm almost blind without my glasses," stated Jane.

"I want you to call me," Jane expressed next.

I responded, saying, "Why, so you can yell at me, saying the only reason I call is to find out your business? The last time I spoke with you, you were very nasty to me."

"I don't remember that," Jane responded. I sure remembered how hateful Jane was. "It is because of my illness. "You should know I didn't mean it. When I get some bills paid, I would like to get together and go on a picnic."

I did not give an answer. I truly did not want to deal with Jane in person; over the phone was bad enough. The call ended.

* * *

It was November, and Jane's sixty-seventh birthday was tomorrow. I was compelled to wish Jane a happy birthday, even though I had promised myself I would never call again.

The conversation began as usual by me saying, "Hi, Jane. I am calling to wish you happy birthday."

"Oh, I had forgotten about that. I'm busy right now. They are delivering a new refrigerator, and there is a woman in the other room. Would you call me back?"

An hour later, I phoned again. Jane answered in an annoyed tone, "Joe's Bar and Grill."

"Hi, Jane," I responded, recognizing Jane's grumpiness.

"You are calling to check on me. The cleaning lady just left, and I'm getting ready to lie down. Call back when I'm in a good mood. Do you want me to hang up now or later?"

"NOW would be good." I heard a click, and the call was over.

I was consoled by my attempt to be a good sister but was disturbed by the rudeness that resulted. Any contact with Jane was subjecting myself to potential offensive treatment.

Over a span of time, some things are destined to remain the same. A consistent compatible relationship was not attainable.

CHAPTER THIRTY-TWO

The Last Time

On Friday evening, several days after New Year's Day of 2014, Jane phoned. Jane was congenial at first but then announced she was going into a diatribe.

Jane lit into me giving no mercy. "You don't care anything about me. You think you are so much better than me. I should have married first. The Bible says so. You didn't take good care of Mama. You should have moved closer to Mama so she could see your kids more often. You shouldn't have bought the truck. All the diesel needs is a new battery, and it will run perfectly fine. You hated Teddy Winters, and you killed him with your thoughts. You never listen to me. You never do what I say . . ."

The phone was put on speaker and was sat on the kitchen bar. Jane ranted on and on without pausing for an extended period. I held my forehead from the headache that had developed. Jane was unleashing all her built-up anger, plus spewing some X-rated information I had never heard before. Several times I almost hung up and should have. When Jane slowed down, Ken picked up the phone. After talking to Ken briefly, her anger vanished. She calmly said, "Goodbye."

A week after the call, while I was in a sewing class, Dr. John Bancroft brought in a vacuum for servicing.

Dr. Bancroft came over to say "Hi." He was a psychologist, whom I had known many years. I asked him if I could talk to him sometime about an upsetting telephone call I had received from my mentally ill sister. "Call me, and we can set up a time for you to come to my office."

On Monday morning, January 27, I met with Dr. Bancroft. In answering some of my questions, he stated Jane did not develop schizophrenia from spinal meningitis as she claimed. "It is in her genes. It was determined upon conception. The gene could not show up for six or more generations, which could explain why no one on either side of the family had known of its presence. Her condition cannot be controlled by diet. Eating fruits and vegetables does not make a difference. Her medication isn't working. Her counselor or whomever is determining her medication level should be able to pick up on that. She will only get worse with age."

I showed him a scribbled note from Jane that had been received a few days earlier.

"Her hand writing is like a child's, and she jumps all over the place," stated Dr. Bancroft.

I relayed the story Jane had told me about a girl who went camping by herself because her family would not go with her. As a result, she died, committing suicide by way of the elements.

"Do you believe that?" he asked.

"No, of course not," I replied. "She was trying to make me feel guilty for not paying more attention to her."

"She is a great manipulator," responded Dr. Bancroft. I already knew that.

Dr. Bancroft was aware I had a cardiologist appointment the following week. He gave me the names of two psychologists whom he thought could help deal with the stress Jane was causing. "Whether you are aware of it, she is causing you stress, and that can affect your heart. Make sure your cardiologist is aware of her," he emphasized.

"I really don't think I need to see a psychologist. I know the best solution is to avoid Jane, and I've been doing that as much as I can." I shared.

"You need to be at peace. Cut off all communication with her. Totally cut it off," Dr. Bancroft repeated. "You are not equipped to deal with her."

* * *

"I went to the cardiologist this morning," I mentioned to Julie." My blood pressure was the highest I've ever seen it. That may have been a result of Jane's 7:00 A.M. call. Ken told her I was still asleep. I thought she would call back again, but she hasn't. I'm trying to take Dr. Bancroft's advice and not talk to her."

"Maybe I should step in," Julie suggested. "Then you wouldn't have to talk to her at all." Julie was worried about my health. She had recently retired and felt that she related to Jane.

After three months of dealing with Jane, Julie was totally fed up. "Jane is separated from Ben," Julie informed me. "He is living with Herman, his brother-in-law. There are restraining orders against both Jane and Ben. Jane wants to sell the truck. Ben was arrested for drunk driving after running into a fence and lost his driver's license."

Julie wanted to be freed from talking to Jane.

"If you lose communication with her, we won't know what is happening with her," I expressed.

"I don't care," Julie replied. "Mama told us we were not responsible for her."

Jane continued calling Julie, leaving continuous marathon phone messages, the same as she had been leaving for me. She was told to leave only one message at a time. Any more would be deleted without listening to them. Julie was hanging in there, coping with Jane's harassing calls.

Instead of dreading anticipated calls, Julie chose to try something new. She would turn the table and call Jane once or twice a week. Jane's ranting stopped, and Julie was more in control.

It was now October. "Jane's calls have slowed down," Julie told me. "She talks about when we were kids, we would go up to Aunt Betty's and write songs with Gene Autry. Of course, I don't remember because I was too little. When Jane says things like that, it reinforces how nuts she is.

"Jane has a homeless woman living in her basement," Julie reported. "It is filthy down there."

* * *

Ken answered a call from Jane. "We have two satellites going around Mars. Martians live underground. They don't like us sending satellites around their planet, so they are shooting rays at us, which is causing me to lose my balance." He hung up. She did not call back.

* * *

In mid-October, Jane called, leaving several messages throughout the day on my answering machine. She wanted me to call her. During one message, she stated she was going to check on a poet's scholarship. "I still have enough years left to do that."

The final message was left that evening. "I haven't seen the lady living in my basement for a while. There is nobody here but me and the door knocker. I'm having a ball. I'm registered with the federal government as Jane the Clown."

Jane was supposedly being monitored and complying, but the question remained. How come is she acting like such a fruitcake? My suspicions were correct Jane had not been on her medications for months. She had gone to court to remove the mandate that required her to take them. It was a civil rights thing. As long as she was staying out of trouble, it was not enforceable. Jane got away with so much.

In mid-November, Jane was taken to the psychiatric unit in Westbrook. Jane told Julie she got in trouble at the courthouse for heckling at a political event. But that was not a crime. Later, I heard Jane got in trouble for yelling at a judge when checking on getting a divorce. Could that lead to grounds for sending her to Westbrook?

The psychiatric unit could only keep clients ninety days. She was released on January 8, 2015, but that was too soon.

CHAPTER THIRTY-THREE

A Place for Jane

Walter, a social worker from Adult Protection Services, contacted me. Jane had provided them with my phone number previously when she was being sent to Baldwin. Since Julie was riding reins on Jane, he was referred to her.

"I have a good rapport with Walter," Julie told me. "Walter checked on Jane's apartment while she was in Westbrook. When she got released, they wanted to put her in a halfway house, but no one would take her. She is back in her apartment."

Jane was still getting in trouble. She was going to the Catholic Church. She went in for a while and then decided to lie down on the floor. They were going to call 911, but she talked them out of it. Herman came and got her. She was in conflict with a catalog outlet. She ordered a pair of earrings but lost one. She refused to pay for it. Julie told her she should pay the $20, but Jane didn't see it that way. A collection agency was also after her for $400 for something else.

Jane had put something on the stove and then left to go to church without turning the burner off. She was not permitted to stay at the apartment for fear she would cause a fire. Herman called Julie, saying they had put her up in a motel for a week. She had stayed at his house the night before.

On March 10, Walter spoke with Julie, saying Jane had dementia and did not have the capacity to take care of herself. Jane was declared incompetent by the state. She would not be allowed to return to her apartment. Jane entered a behavioral facility in Preston that day. Walter was trying to convince Julie to be Jane's guardian.

That week, Julie found herself talking with the Blackburn City building inspector. The city was planning to put a lien on Jane's property for putting some mattresses and trash out in front of her apartment. A notification letter was being prepared, telling her to clear it out. "She won't receive the letter," Julie informed him. "She is in Preston."

On the last day of April, Walter informed Julie the behavioral facility was ready to release Jane. "If they are going to release her, at least they need to bring her back to Blackburn," Julie demanded.

Walter continued to pressure Julie to become Jane's guardian. Under duress, she agreed, but after an agonizing sleepless night, she recognized she could not put herself in that position. James King had advised against it, however, suggested Julie could be assigned conservator, which would give her authority over Jane's finances. Julie had already been receiving Jane's mail and paying the utilities from her own funds.

In early May, an emergency court order appointed Renee, with a local senior care company, to be Jane's temporary guardian. She worked with clients in the Trenton/Blackburn area and would represent Jane until a new guardian could be assigned.

Walter was overwhelmed with frustration in seeking a facility that would accept Jane. In an attempt to let Jane go back to her apartment, city inspectors checked out the condition of the apartment. It was declared uninhabitable. The wood-burning stove was a major fire hazard. Julie was informed the electricity was being shut off because of electrical violations. Renee, the temporary guardian, cleared the food from the refrigerator.

Jane would never be allowed to live on her own again. The time had come for Julie and me to step in to look after the apartment. Julie chose to pursue the conservatorship for overseeing Jane's finances. Julie and I began discussing the logistics for cleaning the apartment.

The allotted time for Jane to remain at the behavioral facility had long passed when she was finally sent to an assisted-living facility in Preston, where she would remain. The assisted-living facility closely monitored its residents. If Jane was cleared to leave the building, she would be accompanied. She was mandated to stay on medications. If she got out of line, she would be sent back to the behavioral facility for a "tune up."

Tony, the director of the assisted-living facility, spoke with Julie regarding providing clothes and personal items for Jane.

They would not accept clothes, bedding, or other belongings from her apartment that could harbor roaches, bedbugs, or rodents. Julie bought clothes and other items, which were mailed to Jane.

A hearing date was set for June 15 to assign a permanent guardian for Jane from her new county. Jane failed to call in. She had an "episode" declining to receive her injection and was taken to the behavior facility for a "tune up." To proceed, Jane needed to be included on the conference call. A new hearing date was set to June 30.

A hearing date to assign Julie as Jane's conservator was set for June 25. Meanwhile, Julie conferred with James King to receive answers to her many questions. Julie learned Ben had been living in a tent in Herman's back yard, where he had spent the winter. James had seen Ben around town using a walker. The hearing date to assign Julie the conservatorship was postponed because of a court oversight.

Meanwhile, the guardianship hearing went well, with little comments from Jane, other than her citizenship was being taken away. Julie spoke several times with Rachel, the new guardian. Rachel thought Jane was sweet, and they would get along fine.

Finally, in July 2015, Julie was assigned conservatorship with no difficulties. There was one complication. Jane stipulated the apartment could not be sold without her approval. There were financial limitations that would prohibit Julie from correcting the code violations. Selling the apartment was the logical solution. It was learned Jane's opposition to the sale would be overridden by the court since the court had declared her incompetent. That required another hearing.

CHAPTER THIRTY-FOUR

Farewell

"I hope we aren't getting in over our heads," I said to Ken as we approached the Mason airport to pick up Julie on July 21, Tuesday. From there, the three of us drove to Blackburn to tackle the overwhelming task of cleaning out Jane's apartment.

Fortunately, Julie's plane was on time. We were on our way to an unforgettable experience.

Julie was on top of things. "I have done as much as I could to save time once we get there," Julie announced. "Herman gave me the name of some men who can haul the mattresses to the dump. James King has word out we are looking for help. He gave me the name of a car dealer who may be interested in buying Jane's vehicles. The city is going to deliver dumpsters, which should be there now. I've talked to the lady at the utility department about temporarily turning on the electricity. Since we cannot send any of Jane's belongings to the assisted-living facility, we have to dispose of everything!" Julie exclaimed.

Upon arriving in Blackburn, our group checked into a motel with joining rooms. Renee dropped off the keys to the apartment and talked about Jane's situation. "Jane has lost a lot of ground," Renee explained. "Every time a person stops taking their meds, they do not obtain the level they were at previously. She has only gotten worse."

After having dinner at a café on Main Street, we decided to survey the condition of Jane's place. We saw the mattresses that had been propped up against the side of the building among the tall overgrowth of weeds. Boxes and other items pressed against the windows inside the small enclosed porch area. A condemned notice stating the apartment was not safe and not inhabitable was posted on the door to the porch. Upon opening the door, which was not locked, a scene of junk greeted us. Sticks and weeds had been tossed on top of the debris. It was surmised they were to be used for fuel in the wood-burning stove. The door to the apartment was barricaded behind the squalor, forcing us to go around to the back door, passing the graffiti Jane had painted on the outside wall.

A condemned notice was posted at the back door as well. The key did not work, but with a slight push, the door opened to reveal the biggest mess imaginable. The apartment was filthy. Using some empty boxes that were handy, Julie and Ken started filling them with trash from the kitchen that I emptied into one of the dumpsters, returning the boxes for more loads. Two hours later, one could not tell a dent had been made.

On Wednesday morning, our cleaning brigade returned at eight o'clock. I began carrying out more boxes to dump and decided to pick up large pieces of broken glass by the dumpsters. The last thing we needed was a flat tire. I was greeted by a tall well-groomed man, who introduced himself as Frank Johnson. He occupied the adjacent apartment. After a brief explanation of the situation, Frank asked, "Do you mind if I look inside?"

"Go ahead," I replied.

He entered and looked around, surveying the overwhelming disorder. "Where is Jane?" he asked.

"She is in assisted living in Preston," Julie replied. "She is not coming back."

Continuing to look around, getting the full impact of the clutter, he asked, "What are you going to do with this place?"

"We haven't gotten that far," Julie answered. He left to go to his office.

Roger, one of the neighbors, stopped by and offered to help. His wife asked if she could have a set of bookends with small globes that she admired. They were covered in decades of dust when Julie handed them to her.

I spoke with her briefly in the kitchen. "Jane was my friend," she shared. "She would come over, and we had conversations. We watched TV and ate ice cream. Sometimes she would get upset and yell at me for no reason. I told her she was in my house, just calm down. I will miss her."

An electrician Julie had contacted arrived to check what needed to be done with the dangling wires in the cellar. He returned later and corrected the obvious problem; however, he could not declare the electrical problems corrected as he did not have access to a large portion of the area that was blocked by piles of Jane's and Ben's possessions.

While cleaning out a closet off the kitchen, Ken came across Jane's old chemistry set. "She could've blown up the entire place with this," Ken remarked.

Many boxes of things from the apartment filled the dumpsters quickly. The garbage company was called to empty the dumpsters several times and were asked to bring two more containers. "Sometimes when we came by she smiled at us. Other times she would cuss us out," shared the driver.

A Baptist minister stopped to inquire about Jane. He helped get word out that we were looking for help. That evening, a call was received from Ethan, whom the minister had referred. Ethan became a lifesaver and stuck it out through the last day.

Between five and six o'clock each evening, the cleaning was suspended. Covered in grime from head to toe, we headed straight to the motel to shower and change clothes before going to dinner.

On Thursday morning, Roger stopped by to see if there were any books he would like to take. "You have a very big job here!" he exclaimed as he left. He could not stay to help.

Three Hispanics appeared with a truck and trailer. They hauled off the mattresses and made several trips of large items to the dump. Monty, one of the Hispanic helpers, stayed to help.

Ken had purchased a gallon of medium gray paint and painting supplies in preparation for Thursday morning's goal to paint the entire lower area of the outside wall to cover the graffiti. While Ken saw to the wall, Julie and I filled boxes with family photos and miscellaneous items, which were salvaged from the middle room.

I directed Ethan to start cleaning out the cellar. "The city inspectors need to get in here," I expressed as we opened the door from the outside near the back steps. The dark space appeared impervious.

"This is more than a two-man job," Ethan declared.

"Just do what you can," I told him. "We will have to leave the rest."

The quest to clear the cellar lasted through Saturday during which time Ethan and Monty brought out camping gear, tools, and many other items. A dresser belonging to Ben was retrieved that contained two handguns. "They aren't loaded," announced Ethan as he removed one from its light-colored leather case. The guns were Ben's. Jane probably did not know they were there.

As more of the cellar was cleared, we were relieved to learn the cellar did not extend the length of the apartment but reverted to a two-foot crawl space.

The garbage truck was not keeping up with the need to have the dumpsters emptied. Julie arranged for the dumpsters to be replaced with a twenty-two foot roll-away container.

Ken had widened the narrow path through the middle room the previous day. The outside wall was still piled high with a mountain of clothes and a variety of objects that were encroaching on the ten-foot ceiling, barely letting in light from the window. I cleared a portion of the floor that was covered in copious miscellaneous objects that were covered in a thick layer of dust.

Julie had been going through papers from the desk and two file cabinets in search of vehicle titles and was collecting stray keys and coins until it was time to meet Ben at the police station, which was within walking distance. Because of the restraining order against him to stay away from Jane's apartment, he needed to be cleared to enter to claim his belongings.

After being gone over an hour, Julie returned with Ben. Julie was impeded by Ben, who relied on his walker and moved excruciatingly slow. He looked older than his actual years, being younger than Julie. His gums had receded badly displaying teeth with wide gaps, which were black at the roots and yellow from tobacco stains. Ben reeked with the smell of tobacco and urine. He smoked a hand-rolled cigarette as he sat on the seat part of the walker, which he had placed at the bottom of the back steps, making it difficult to get past him as the workers made trips to the dumpsters. He then migrated to various parts of the apartment and observed as others worked.

The paid workers took a lunch break, while Ken and I returned to the motel to make peanut butter and jelly sandwiches.

We had not brought enough bread to make sandwiches for everyone. From the motel's mini refrigerator, I removed the last bit of my submarine sandwich from yesterday's lunch and the piece of chicken leftover from my dinner of the first night, which served as my lunch, to allow for Ben to have my sandwich. The lunch set precedence for Ben to appear succeeding mornings before lunchtime.

After eating, Ken and I unearthed a twin bed and kitchen chair from beneath the mountain of miscellaneous articles that had overtaken the middle room. Two guitars and other items that were thought to be Ben's were stacked against the wall under the window in the kitchen. The helpers with the pickup loaded Ben's belongings to deliver them to his storage unit.

That afternoon, Frank from next door appeared. There was a discussion about possibly buying the apartment. Both he and his wife were realtors.

It had been decided to have a garage sale on Friday and Saturday, even though there were still areas that needed cleared. In preparation for the garage sale, first thing Friday morning, Monty began working in the first room, sprucing up the wood-burning stove area, which was surrounded by paint cans, ashes, and trash. I swept dirt into piles from the small porch and removed as much as possible. People would be coming through this area to inspect more garage sale items.

Small garage sale items were placed on an orange tin folding table and a dilapidated card table with wobbly legs in front of the porch. Julie brought two garage sale signs that were placed outside the apartment. Ethan had made two green neon posters the night before. At nine o'clock, he placed them strategically on the street for people to see. A stream of bargain hunters appeared in full force.

Some people were curious and asked where Jane was. A lot of them knew her and wished her well. Among the garage sale customers was a tall, older man who entered the apartment, looking to see what else was being sold. He sported a long white beard that rested on his chest. His long neatly groomed braid nearly reached his waist. "I like your braid," Julie commented.

"I was a Hell's Angel in California," he shared.

"But you look like a good guy now," Julie responded. He had sparkling blue eyes with a pleasant demeanor.

"Yes. It cost me a lot of money to get out. I'm sixty-nine and lucky to be alive."

"Did you know Jane?" Julie inquired.

"Yes. I spend a lot of time at the Bass Club. She came over frequently, causing trouble."

He came back out to pay for the items I was holding for him. "You both are Jane's sisters?" he questioned in disbelief.

"Yes, we are," I responded.

"But you two are so nice," he said in disbelief. "She was very nasty and rude. So rude," he repeated as he walked away.

Roy, a man who owned a used car lot and dealt in antique cars, came by, asking about the vehicles. Julie took him out to the vacant lot near the apartment where the blue Plymouth Belvedere was parked along with the camper trailer and the two non-drivable trucks. Upon opening a rear door of the blue car to exam what was on the seat, Julie disturbed a wasp nest. She flew away at lightning speed.

"I bet you've never seen a sixty-five-year old woman move so fast!" Julie said jokingly to Roy, who was laughing. Ken helped negotiate the sale of the vehicles. Another car dealer had previously agreed to buy the newer truck. The buyers would haul the vehicles away.

I manned the garage sale the majority of the two days. It was interesting talking to the neighbors who came by. Frank spoke to Ken and me while waiting for his wife. "When we were moving in, Jane met us in 'full battle regalia.' She had an ice cream bucket on her head with the handle under her chin and was holding a broomstick."

Norman's wife, Rita, stepped out of their apartment and joined in relating more details. "You can't move in here. I'm the manager, and this apartment is mine, Jane told us. She tried to keep us out by duct taping the doors and windows in the front and back shut. She wrote "Quarantined" on the door." They were both smiling and speaking about Jane in a jovial matter.

"I came home to find vomit in the mail slot. It smelled really bad. I wondered how she got it in there," Rita said, laughing. "She almost through a container of urine on me. I threatened to call the police."

"She appeared at our door, saying we couldn't have noisy children here. She insisted she could hear them," stated Frank. "We have two dogs that she may have heard but no children. She came to our door and slipped past me, looking for children under the bed and in the living room. We escorted her to the back door and told her to leave. She kept telling us to push her off the back steps."

"She said when we are gone, our teenage children come in and have sex, and they shouldn't be doing that. We don't have teenage children. Our children are all grown. She got in loud arguments with the guys who live near the end of these apartments. She called them jerks and got right up in their faces."

"Did it get violent?" I asked.

"No," Frank stated. "I called the police before it got that far. I've called the police many, many times."

"Before she went away, we were woken up several times in the middle of the night. It sounded like a parent was beating their child. We could hear the voice of a parent telling the child to behave, and a child was screaming, 'Don't beat me! Don't hurt me!' Jane was really good at mimicking voices. It sounded like two people over there!" Frank exclaimed. "We called the police. It sounded real."

"I used to talk to Ben a lot before he was banned from the apartment. I had conversations with Jane also about Charles Dickenson," stated Frank.

"We talked about flowers," Rita added. "I planted some for her as well as strawberries that we told her she could eat. She is a character. She was very entertaining. We are going to miss her."

While I manned the garage sale, Julie and Ken ran errands.

Julie entered the bank to close Jane's checking account. "I've known Jane for fifteen to twenty years. These last two years, she has gone down significantly," stated the lady who was assisting them. "She came in and bothered the tellers. Sometimes I had to tell her to leave, and she did. I felt sorry for her. It wasn't her fault, but at the same time, it was for not taking her meds."

Another stop to acquire duplicate vehicle titles provided the opportunity to speak with another lady who knew Jane. Julie explained she was Jane's sister, bringing her to attention. "You are Jane's sister? We wondered what happened to her."

"She is safe living in an assisted-living facility in Preston," explained Julie. "She is supervised and required to be on her medications."

An appointment had been made to meet with James King at two o'clock that afternoon. Julie and I walked to the attorney's office two blocks away. We entered the law office together with Ben, who had just arrived. James ushered us into a conference room, where the topic of Ben and Jane ending their marriage was discussed. Since both were low income, they qualified for free legal services.

Jane had begun the separation process but was confused about their marriage status. She told Julie they were divorced, but Julie had a court document stating they were still legally married. Ben declared he had no claim to the vehicles or apartment and its contents. Everything was in Jane's name.

Ben was invited to stay while conservator issues were discussed. He chose to leave. James King explained the financial reports Julie was required to submit as conservator and gave examples of items to include. The topic of selling the apartment was discussed. "It will be difficult to sell. A realtor will not make much profit," James declared.

After the business portion of the appointment, James shared some amusing incidents involving Jane.

"We attended the same church. There had been a fire, and the congregation was meeting in a temporary building. When the building was completed, we had a big service. Jane sung in the choir and was in the front row center, directly in front of the microphone. When the choir sang, Jane was the only one that could be heard." He laughed. "She was off key and hit wrong notes. After the services, it was suggested to move the microphone.

"There was another time when Jane was misbehaving. The choir director told her she was out of the choir. She appeared the next Sunday and put on the bright-blue choral robe as usual. The director told her to take off the robe and leave. She left but did not remove the robe. She walked down the street in the blue robe to the Catholic Church. Of course, my church wanted their robe back, so they called the police. In the meantime, she joined the Catholic choir. They didn't know what to do with her, so they called the police. My church got back the blue robe. She kept things interesting.

"They had a strange marriage. Ben walked behind her, following ten steps back. They did not sit together in church. She sat on one side, and he sat on the other. You would not know they were married."

After the appointment, I went back to the apartment while Julie made one more stop at the courthouse. It was raining lightly. Ken and Ethan had brought the garage sale items into the porch area, and Ethan had left. While waiting for Julie to return, Ken and I walked to the vacant lot. We watched as Roy hooked up the camper to his pickup truck. After pulling it a short distance, he realized it was too heavy to pull over the curb and tried to back it out. He decided to return for the camper the next morning.

Meanwhile, Julie returned, spotting Ken and me at the lot as she walked down the street. Renee, Jane's temporary guardian, had gone by the open apartment and joined our group on the street. "You all have done an amazing job clearing the apartment. It looks so much better from the outside too," she stated with enthusiasm.

"We still have another day for the garage sale, and there is more stuff in the cellar, but we have made a remarkable amount of progress with the help from some workers," Julie agreed.

The garage sale was back in business at eight Saturday morning. People were not coming early, but traffic picked up as more items were carried outside to sell. Ethan and Monty continued to remove items from the cellar; however, they were running out of room in the dumpster to toss unwanted items.

I was taking a break in the first room, sitting on the beat-up desk chair, when the building inspector entered the first room. The wood-burning stove was in full view. "I won't approve this for occupancy until that stove is removed," he stated sternly. "That bathroom sink is about to fall off the wall. It has to be fixed."

I nodded as he pressed on toward the kitchen. He checked the cellar where an old washer and dryer that did not work remained. He could see where the small stackable washer/ dryer unit in the kitchen was vented directly into the cellar. "The venting is not incompliance," he told Julie.

Ken suggested Julie offer to sell the apartment to Frank and Rita at a fair price. Since getting the apartment off Julie's hands could prove to be a challenge, that idea was appealing. When the offer was presented, Rita jumped at the offer. They would take the apartment as is, complete with the items that were remaining. They were fully aware of the necessary improvements the inspector required before it could be approved for occupancy.

Our group checked out of the motel on Sunday morning and met Frank and Rita at their real estate office. After the purchase agreement was discussed and completed, a copy was made for James King. It would be dropped off through the mail slot at the attorney's office, along with the set of keys. Julie included a note explaining the details. James would handle the legalities of the sale.

By the grace of God, things had fallen into place, down to the detail of Ken finding the keys to the apartment on top of the refrigerator.

The week had been a taxing ordeal both physically and mentally. We had gotten through it, and things would be better for all. "I know it will be hard for Jane to let go of this place," Julie expressed.

The sale of the apartment had yet to go through. Julie had many details to contend with, including a potential blowup from Jane. Sure enough, Jane objected formally to the sale.

"I talked to Jane yesterday," Julie told me over the phone. "She said she is happy where she is and would like to spend the rest of her life there. I asked why she objected to selling the apartment. She said, 'That's just what I do.'"

It was a no-brainer when the court ruled to allow the sale.

CHAPTER THIRTY-FIVE

A New Era

A new chapter had begun for all of us. The assisted-living facility would maintain stability and provide a safe place for Jane to stay. Julie and I would no longer have to wonder what kind of trouble she was getting into or worry about what would become of her.

"Do you think you will ever go see her?" Julie asked me.

"I am ambivalent on that. For now, she is okay. That is all I need to know. What about you, Julie?"

"I will go see her eventually. I will call her and make sure her needs are met and pay her monthly care bills and copays from her Social Security. She won't come into my personal life."

I attained the calmness I had aspired all my life. Julie would inform me how Jane was doing now and then, which was good to know from a fly-on-the-wall perspective. Julie felt reassured in her role as Jane's conservator, knowing she would never be put in a compromising situation.

Upon returning home, Julie diligently took over her conservatorship responsibilities. Working in tandem with Jane's guardian, Jane's living quarters were spiffed up with new furniture, bedding, and a desk. Since Jane had left Blackburn with only the clothes on her back, Julie spent considerable hours on the Internet buying her clothes and other items, which Jane appreciated.

Jane settled in, realizing she might not ever be released to live freely. From time to time, Julie sent books, cookies, or something to cheer her up. Julie sent Jane's general studies diploma and her poetry books to make her feel more at home.

Jane's conversations with Julie were "disconnected" with unrelated responses. Sometimes Jane's words were slurred, and other times, she spoke somewhat normally with less rambling.

* * *

As 2016 arrived, Jane was not living a fulfilling life and was not happy. She did not want to have a phone or computer, expressing they were too complicated. The medications impaired her thinking. Jane was losing weight, and she was depressed. She gradually snapped out of it as summer arrived.

Julie felt a need to check on Jane and informed me she was going to visit Jane in September. Time had paved the way for me to consider joining Julie, but I would have to wait and see how my shoulder was progressing as I had just undergone surgery in mid-August to reattach torn tendons. Julie put her trip on hold, waiting to see if I would be up to going later.

I decided to join Julie's road trip. Ken dropped me off at the Mason airport to meet Julie, and we rented a car. We spent the night and following day at our cabin in the mountains. Angelia's family and Ken joined us. The time was filled with hiking and sightseeing to observe the spectacular fall foliage. Julie and I spent Sunday, October 2, driving to Preston. We joined our friend Georgia for dinner at a Mexican food restaurant and then went on to spend the night with Julie's friend Lindy.

Monday morning at nine thirty Julie and I arrived at the assisted-living facility that had become Jane's home. It was a red brick complex that was originally built in the 1950s as an army barracks. It was not fancy, but it was well kept.

Jane had gone to an appointment to have her blood drawn and was expected back in two hours. This provided an opportune time to meet with Tony, the director of the facility, who had stopped by for a quick visit. We followed him by car to his office a few blocks away. Tony, a tall, slender man of six foot seven was very pleasant. He commented on how sweet Jane was. Monthly or bimonthly, dental cleaning appointments were suggested for Jane as she was neglecting her teeth, and they needed attention. A senior citizens' center was across from his office. He thought Jane might be interested in signing up for activities. The assisted living facility could provide transportation. Knowing we were treating Jane to lunch, in parting, he recommended going to a small café not far from there, which served good food.

Upon returning to "Jane's house," as Tony called it, we went to her room. At first glance, I was not sure it was Jane. She was thin. Her hair had grown long and was in a ponytail. But most of all, her face looked like that of an eighty-year-old woman. She was smiling and happy to see us. She babbled something that was indistinguishable.

"Would you want to go to lunch?" Julie asked.

"Let me get my coat," Jane responded.

"Do you need a new coat?" Julie asked. We had planned to take her shopping for clothes since we knew she had lost weight.

"No, this one fits fine," Jane replied while looking for her cane. She had left it at the health clinic that morning.

As we walked to the car, Jane picked up a twig that had fallen from a tree onto the lawn and was looking for more. Tony had assigned her to keep the lawn tidy since she insisted she needed a job. "You can do that later," Julie told her as she took the twig from Jane and laid it on the ground.

Jane chose to sit in the back seat. Julie had to assist her with her seat belt. As we drove off, Jane said, "I don't care much for men anymore."

"They are a lot of trouble," Julie agreed with a big smile.

"I'm very religious," Jane said next.

"What church do you attend?" Julie asked.

"You can take me to any church. It doesn't matter."

"We aren't going to church. We are taking you to lunch," stated Julie.

Our group arrived at the small crowded café Tony recommended. Julie had to unbuckle Jane and pull her out of the car. Jane moved slowly through the parking lot toward the restaurant's entrance. Once inside, we were seated in a booth; Julie sat next to Jane. The waitress smiled sweetly as if she thought we were taking our elderly mother out for lunch. It was difficult to believe we were less than two years apart in age.

While our orders were being prepared, Julie presented Jane with some gifts. Jane liked the pocket book that contained $60. Julie then gave her a silver drawstring pouch, which contained two bracelets and a turquoise cross on a silver chain.

Before exploring the contents, Jane held up the pouch and dangled it before her eyes. She then attempted to loosen the string while tilting her head. Her vision was very poor. She should have had her cataracts removed when she had the chance. She put on the bracelets and attempted to put the chain over her head, but it was too small. Julie helped her with the clasp.

After eating, Julie suggested we go shopping. Jane said she was tired and did not need anything.

"Would you like to stop by the senior citizens' center while we are out? Tony thought you might like to check out activities," I suggested.

"That costs money," Jane expounded.

"Money isn't a problem," Julie insisted.

"Before we go back, let's go to a park where we can talk," Julie suggested.

I pointed to a large park that happened to be across the street. We had already taken our places in the car. This time Jane wanted to sit in the front seat. Upon arriving at the park,

Jane began gathering pine needles from the grass. "You don't need to do that," I stated. "You are on vacation."

A cool breeze had come up, and Jane was tired. Back to Jane's house, we went. Jane was unsteady on her feet and wobbled when she walked. Julie stopped to speak with the staff about retrieving Jane's cane.

Jane headed off to her room in a hurry with me on her heals. Jane abruptly opened her door and entered quickly, slamming the door in my face. I knocked, with no response. I knocked again, only louder. Still with no response. Julie arrived just then and, without knocking, entered the room to find Jane wrapped up in a gray blanket on her bed, taking a nap.

Jane was startled and rose from her bed.

"We want to get some pictures before we leave," said Julie.

Jane removed the rubber band from her hair and located her brush. Her gray to white hair was thick and pretty when it was brushed out. She sat in a chair and started singing. After taking pictures and departing chitchat, Jane was left to rest.

Rachel, Jane's guardian, was awaiting our arrival. Along with Rachel, Irene, the owner of the agency, joined the meeting. Rachel was a brunette in her forties. Her supervisor was a lovely slightly older lady. Changing Jane's venue to the new county, where she now resided, was discussed, along with other topics pertaining to Jane's wellbeing.

There was one more stop to make. Julie needed to meet with the mortuary director where she had begun to make arrangements for Jane's passing. After completing some forms, we were back on the road headed for Lindy's house.

Julie and I took leave the next morning headed for Mason to return the rental car and to meet Ken. We mulled over our experience on the drive back. "We didn't know what to expect, but she was very amiable," Julie related.

"I am glad I went with you. I can't help but feel sorry for her," I expressed. "The Jane we just saw is not the Jane I dealt with for over sixty years. It is like she is not the same person. She appears to be a cordial, sweet, old lady who wouldn't hurt a fly. If she would have displayed the same temperament to us earlier, dealing with her would not have been so daunting. Mind you, she is now monitored to be on psychiatric medication."

"Her life has been full of turmoil," Julie expressed. "All is well now."

That night, we stayed at a motel in Mason for Julie to make a quick getaway to catch an early morning flight back home.

EPILOGUE

Julie and I had returned to our busy lives, which, for Julie, involved working part-time in an antique store, managing the accounting for her church, handling paperwork for the farm, and being the grandmother to five growing grandsons as well as keeping track of Jane's well-being. There was an endless list of tasks on her plate.

January of 2017 found me hurrying to complete a quilt project and other responsibilities prior to undertaking a total left shoulder replacement. The plan was to be mostly recovered before May to fly out to attend our granddaughter, Stacy's, college graduation.

All was well with Jane, or so we thought. On February 23, Julie received notice from Jane's guardian. Jane had gotten out on her own. She slipped out a back door of the assisted-living facility unobserved. Our information was sketchy. Her *outings* as we understood had been in the daytime and at night. She came upon a lady walking her dog and was pulling the dog's fur. She was trying to get in people's cars. Jane was picked up one night in her nightclothes by the police and taken to the behavior facility for a "tune up."

Jane phoned Julie from the behavioral facility. She had taken up where she had left off with her peculiar thinking. She claimed she had set Julie up with her first husband, Doug. Worst of all, though, Jane talked about getting her things back and returning to her apartment. She wanted Julie to return her checkbook. Jane remained true to her lifelong pattern of defying reality.

On March 8, Jane leveled off and was moved to a different assisted-living facility. It sounded like a lovely place to live on the outskirts of the city. But most importantly, it was a lockdown facility and monitored constantly. She would still be able to go out with an escort.

Julie and I were disturbed by this incident. We had assumed there would be no more concern for Jane's well-being, but she proved us wrong. For now, all is good. We trust it will remain so.

ABOUT THE AUTHORS

ELAINE TAYLOR (pen name) completed two years of college with a major in accounting. Elaine is currently retired after spending forty-one years in the work force as a bookkeeper and administrative assistant. She continues her favorite hobby of sewing and quilting and spends as much time as possible at their mountain getaway. Her husband, Ken, continues to teach college mathematics. They have three children, six grandchildren, and one great grandson.

JULIE HANES's (pen name) career began as a secretary after graduating from a business college. She gradually evolved into a computer programmer/analyst after receiving her bachelor's degree in information systems development in 1989. Julie traveled extensively throughout Europe while living in England and Germany with her husband, Doug, while he served as a fighter pilot and flight instructor. She became a widow in 2000 when Doug died of cancer. Julie married her second husband, Gerald, in 2008. She is the proud step-grandmother of five adoring grandsons.